CHILDREN OF THE LIGHT

DARKNESS RISING

By

Tracy Earle

Printed in the United States of America

Paperback ISBN: 978-1-959096-33-7
Ebook ISBN: 978-1-959096-34-4
Library of Congress Control Number: 2023934819

DartFrog Plus
A division of DartFrog Books
4697 Main Street
Manchester Center, VT 05255

This book is dedicated to my children Becky and Jamie
. . . I told you I would finish it one day!

EARTH
Beach
N
NE
NW
E
W
SE
SW
S
The Eternal Library
Virtual
Classroom
Rainbow Forest
Dama
Garda
TERHUM
VALHANDRA
Throne Room
Stone Cell

PROLOGUE

As the Darkness crept further and further into the souls of humanity, the Light turned in desperation to the Universe and begged for help.

"You have allowed your hatred of the Darkness to distract you from your true purpose," the Universe told the Light. "The second Prophecy is now coming to pass." The voice of the Universe echoed through time and space, and the Light hung its head as it finally saw the magnitude of its failure.

"The Darkness is rising," the Universe warned. "Every day it becomes stronger, and with each human soul it destroys, you will become weaker. When the light is extinguished from the last human soul on Earth, you will cease to exist. The heart of the earth will stop beating; its lands will blacken and die."

"There has to be a way to stop it," the Light pleaded.

"There is one way," the Universe explained, "but you must act quickly. However, know beyond doubt, this is the final hope. If it fails and you are defeated, an eternity of Darkness will fall on all time and space."

"Anything . . ." the Light promised, and the Universe knew the Light spoke the truth, so it granted it one final chance.

The vast expanses of time and space started to pulse and spin as the Universe began its creation. Faster and faster, it swirled into an infinite vortex of stars and planets, the entire solar system a spinning kaleidoscope of light and color. The Universe took the blueprints of the past and thrust them into the whirling mass. The very matrix of existence, the equation of life itself, spun into the maelstrom, circling furiously toward its central point, and as it disappeared without trace into the vortex, the whirling stopped as suddenly as it had started.

There was peace and calm in the stillness that followed, and the Light watched with new hope as the Universe began to create a different possibility for the future. The solar system parted, and a blinding beam of golden light appeared from the distance. Shooting forward to the ancient land of Valhandra, it fell across the fields, mountains and seas, turning them to a shimmering gold. The colors of the Rainbow Forest, which had dulled over time, brightened once more, sparkling with fresh life as a golden haze flowed through the seven Gozzit trees one by one, bestowing unto each of them the infinite power of the Universe.

"This is my gift . . . and your final chance," the Universe explained to the Light. "I have created a new Consciousness, which can turn humanity away from the Darkness. The seven colors of the human soul will become one with the infinite powers of the Universe; the Golden lands of Valhandra will be the source and center of all light and life on Earth."

"And this will destroy the Darkness?" the Light asked.

"No!" the Universe boomed. "If you destroy the Darkness, you will also destroy yourself. Both are an intrinsic part of the fabric of life; each exists only because the opposing force exists. Without both, there is nothing. You must learn to accept the existence of the Darkness, to understand it and then to navigate a path beyond it. The Darkness will never be a conscious force in time and space. That task falls to you, and to fulfill it you must find a way to live with its existence. That is what you have failed to do . . . until now."

The Light felt overwhelmed with this knowledge but knew it was the only way to save humanity, the earth, and itself.

"This is no small task," the Universe continued, "but when the new Consciousness is bestowed to every soul on Earth, the Darkness will lose its power over humankind."

The Universe told the Light to gather together all those beings on Earth still possessing all the colors of their souls. These beings would be strong enough to receive the new Consciousness, strong enough to rescue the broken human souls and to build an army to fight the Darkness.

"You are to call these beings to Valhandra," the Universe instructed the Light, "for they are to become Lightworkers. Their old souls will be merged with the new Consciousness, gifted with the powers of the Universe . . . and each of them will be taught how to use these immense gifts. The Lightworkers will bear children, a new generation of infinite beings and the most powerful souls on Earth.

"It is vital that these children are concealed from the Darkness until they are physically strong enough to have my power activated within them. This will happen on their fifteenth birthday, when each and every one of them will be called back to Valhandra, to fulfill their destiny and take their place in the Circle of Light."

At that point, the Universe spun another vortex deep into space. Out of it rose a ring of pure, clear crystal, shining with blinding white light.

"This crystal annulus is the Circle of Light," the Universe declared. As it spoke, the ring began to shudder, increasing in intensity, its vibrations reaching the furthest depths of the solar system. Suddenly, the ring of crystal exploded, bright shards of light shooting down into the vortex from which it had risen. When the explosion settled, the Light saw that the ring was now in hundreds of separate pieces, each one hovering in perfect proximity to its neighbors and pulsing with a life force of its own.

"Each and every Lightworker must receive a piece of the Circle of Light at the point their soul is transformed," the Universe continued. "They must keep it with them always, for it holds the heart of the new Consciousness, and its power should not be underestimated. The purity and power of these crystals make them vital tools for the Lightworkers when they venture into their final battle with the Darkness; they will be the key to bringing forth the New World."

"When will this final battle happen?" asked the Light.

As it spoke, a huge leather-bound book appeared in the middle of the pulsing ring of crystals, surrounded by a golden glow.

"This book will depict the past, present, and future of the world and of humanity," the Universe declared, "and there will always be many possible futures. When the time for the final battle arrives, all possible futures of the world will become blank pages in readiness for the choice-point—the crossroads to a world of light, or a world plunged into darkness."

"How must the crystals be used?" the Light asked.

"When the time comes," the Universe replied, "you will know what to do."

And so, the Light began its quest.

CHAPTER 1

Aurora flew through the rainbow mists, a tunnel of colors swirling around her like a kaleidoscope. Waves of energy flooded through her body, and a bright beam of golden light stretched out in front of her, coming from a point just between her eyes and reaching out into the distance. Her vision followed the beam of light, and she saw the large white house come into view at the end of the rainbow tunnel, the same house she saw each time this happened. Her vision focused in on its wide porch steps leading up to a wooden, double-fronted door, which was flanked on either side with a stone statue of a rearing horse. She wondered if, this time, she would reach it.

Aurora felt a calm certainty in her destination, a deep knowing that she was meant to be there. As she drew closer to the white house, her mind was filled with the same hauntingly familiar voice calling their names: "Aurora, Aaron." But something was wrong. Something was missing. Instinctively, Aurora reached for her twin brother's hand, expecting it to be there, but her hand grasped at air.

"Aaron." She heard herself call his name, though the sound didn't come from her mouth. It seemed to come from another place, a place deep inside her. Not from her mind, but somewhere else, a part of her that was familiar, yet simultaneously unknown and mysterious. But as her movement slowed, her body suspended in a kaleidoscope of color, her attention shifted back to Aaron.

Aurora turned her head away from the golden light at the end of the tunnel, toward a spot behind her far in the distance, where Aaron stood with his back to her. Looking from him to the empty hand she held out to him, Aurora felt a sense of panic rise suddenly inside her.

"Aaron." She heard that voice within her again, calling to him through the rainbow mists that swirled around her.

"Aaron, come with me, please," she begged, feeling a sudden pain deep in her chest as she pleaded with him to join her.

The distance between them increased, and as her brother drew farther away, his image began to fade. The pain in Aurora's chest intensified, the bright colors around her started to dim, and she closed her eyes as an overwhelming feeling of hopelessness washed through her. Suddenly she felt herself falling, and as she tumbled out of the rainbow mists into blackness, she heard her own voice calling out loudly once more.

"Aaron!"

Her body jolted sharply in her chair, shoving it backward. A loud screech pierced the air as the chair legs scraped across the surface of the floor. Aurora winced at the noise, opening her eyes to a silent classroom with all eyes focused on her.

Realizing with embarrassment that she had yelled her brother's name out loud, Aurora clamped her mouth tightly shut, grabbing the edge of the desk as the image of the classroom swayed in front of her eyes. As she readjusted to the surroundings, a low hum of laughter began to ripple around the other students. Aurora looked hesitantly over at her brother, who sat with elbows on the desk and hands over his eyes, shaking his head in exasperation.

The loud and irritated voice of Miss Broach, the biology teacher, shattered the laughter around her.

"Quiet!" she shrieked, and silence fell instantly across the class. "Aurora Clarke!" she continued, and Aurora winced again, the teacher's shrill voice feeling like knives through her head. Miss Broach began to walk slowly toward Aurora's desk like a predator, her head dipped and angry eyes fixed on her prey. Aurora glanced upward sheepishly as the figure of her irate teacher towered over her.

"Did . . . we . . . wake . . . you . . . Miss . . . Clarke?" The slow and purposeful words dripped with sarcasm. Without waiting for a reply to her question, Miss Broach turned and strode back to the front of the classroom, where she swept around and focused her gaze back on Aurora.

"I will ask you the same question, Miss Clarke—for the third and final time—in the hope that at some point during this lesson you will at least attempt to *listen*."

Miss Broach drew a deep breath and began to repeat the question to Aurora, the board pointer she held out in front of her shaking in her hand. Aurora stared at her enraged teacher, trying hard to focus her attention on the repeated question. But something strange was happening and Aurora's eyes were fixed on that instead. The familiar redness was rising up Miss Broach's long, thin neck, the usual sign that her temper had reached boiling point. But in the space around her, it was as if the individual molecules of air were moving, growing, like bubbles expanding nearly to bursting. Aurora stared, her eyes widening with shock as a dark shadow appeared around the tall figure of the teacher. The redness on Miss Broach's neck had now spread to her sharp cheekbones, and in the next second, fire flamed out from each side of her face. Aurora stared openmouthed at the sight, knowing she should be saying something but unable to find any words.

"*Well?*" Miss Broach shrieked, her flaming face now dangerously crimson and the dark shadow around her pulsing with a life of its own. "It is highly unlikely, Miss Clarke," the irate teacher continued, "that during your end-of-year exams the mitotic division of a cell will miraculously explain itself. *And . . .* as you obviously have *no* intention of attempting to understand it today, you will spend *one hour* after school on Friday studying it in *detention.* Class *dismissed.*"

At that moment, the end-of-school bell sounded, and Aurora's attention snapped back to the present. None of the others in the class appeared to have noticed anything strange, as they all busied themselves packing up their books.

Miss Broach hauled in a long breath before angrily slamming the board pointer down on the desk as a stream of students rushed for the door. She watched them go, shooting one final angry glare at Aurora before grabbing her paperwork and flouncing out of the classroom, slamming the door after her.

Aurora's best friend, Hazel, appeared at her side, putting her arm across Aurora's shoulders and hugging her reassuringly.

"Did you . . . do you see that?" Aurora sputtered her words out to Hazel, directing her eyes to the shadowy mist left in front of the whiteboard, which was still flaming slightly around the edges.

Hazel followed Aurora's gaze to the whiteboard, a slightly confused look on her face.

"What?" she asked. "Miss Broach? Yeah, well you know what she's like. I can hang around after school on Friday and wait for you."

"Thanks," Aurora sighed with resignation, while in the back corner of the room Aaron huffed loudly as he crammed his books into his backpack.

"*Pffff*, sis, get a grip. For all our sakes," he complained. Rolling his eyes, he stood up, swung his backpack over his shoulder, and shoved his hands in his pockets, before slouching grumpily toward the door.

"It happened again, didn't it?" whispered Hazel to Aurora as they were walking home after school. Aurora turned to check the whereabouts of her brother, who, true to form, was dragging a few yards behind them. With his headphones in and eyes focused on the ground, Aaron was totally oblivious to their conversation, his floppy dark blond fringe swinging back and forth in front of his face as he kicked a pebble with his foot along the pavement in front of him.

"It's so weird," said Aurora in a soft voice, staring into the sky as if searching for answers. "Every night it's the same. Now it's happening when I'm awake, and I've got no control over it; it just kind of happens," she sighed, a faraway look in her eyes. "It's more than just a daydream, I'm sure of it . . . and I know the voice, I know . . . I've seen him . . ."

"Him who?" asked Hazel confused.

"Never mind," Aurora said quickly, realizing she was in danger of saying too much. "I can't explain. You'll think I'm going mad. *I* think I'm going mad."

Aurora's voice tailed off, and they stopped walking as they reached the bus stop. Hazel put her arm round Aurora's shoulder and hugged her, not knowing what to say and trying hard to act like she understood. But it wasn't easy, and she was worried about her friend.

Hazel and Aurora had been best friends for ten years, since their first day at West Lea Infant school. That day, five-year-old Hazel had stood sobbing at the window as her mother drove away with her beloved new baby sister in the back. Aurora had come quietly up behind Hazel, putting one hand gently on her shoulder. Hazel vividly remembered the sudden, intense-yet-calming heat from Aurora's hand, as clearly now as the day it happened. Her tears stopped instantly and she turned to look into the clearest blue eyes she had ever seen. Hazel briefly glimpsed something else in the depths of Aurora's eyes, which mesmerized her momentarily. But a five-year-old's acceptance is unquestioning, and within seconds, a friendship formed between them that had never faltered. In later years, Aurora had filled some of the emptiness inside Hazel that the loss of her younger sister Sienna had left.

Sienna had disappeared while playing out in their garden the day before her sixth birthday. One of three mysterious kidnappings of young children in the area at around the same time, it had baffled the authorities, who worked tirelessly on the case over the months that followed. Finally, in a storm of media embarrassment, the police conceded they had no leads at all and no information as to what could have happened to Sienna, or the other two missing children. Sienna's disappearance had driven a wedge between Hazel's parents that never healed, ultimately leading to their separation and more pain for Hazel to wrap her troubled mind around.

Though the two girls were strikingly different to look at, their bond grew over the years and was more like one of sisters. Hazel's curly, dark auburn hair fell to her shoulders—wild, unruly, and later termed by the teenage Hazel as "the hair from hell," though Aurora thought it beautiful. She never understood Hazel's loathing of it, nor her friend's intense hatred of the pretty smattering of caramel-colored freckles over her nose.

"Why couldn't I have been born with hair like yours, Rory, instead of like a wire brush?" Hazel would moan to Aurora as she brushed her friend's long, straight golden-blond hair. In truth, Aurora struggled to understand anyone's negativity about their looks, genuinely believing there was nobody in the world who was not beautiful in their own way. Hazel, however, teasingly advised Aurora that this outlook came down to the fact that Aurora was "one of the lucky ones with perfectly clear skin and beautiful hair!"

Despite her occasional affectionate teasing of Aurora, Hazel loved her friend dearly, though she had always known there was something very different about Aurora, which had nothing to do with shiny hair or perfectly clear skin. Aurora was always calm, always quiet and gentle, and she never spoke a bad word about anyone; she didn't even seem to think anything bad about anyone, either. She could end arguments just by being there, even though she was never actually involved. It was amazing to watch.

Hazel recalled one particularly vicious argument between two of the most popular girls in the year (the argument stupidly being based on who was the most popular!). Aurora walked up to the girls and quite calmly put one hand on each of their shoulders, smiling, just as she had done to Hazel all those years ago. The arguing girls turned to Aurora in angry surprise, and Hazel had cringed, thinking that her best friend was about to become the new focus of their anger. Instead, the two girls stopped arguing, turned, and walked calmly away from each other as if nothing had happened.

That was one of many similar incidents, and Hazel thought that Aurora's ways probably scared people a bit, or at least made them cautious of her. Everyone liked Aurora; there was no doubt about that. There was nothing about her to dislike, and Hazel always felt that same intensely calm feeling whenever they were together. But there was something about her that people didn't understand—weird, maybe; different, yes. Hazel never tried to explain it more than that even to herself. Maybe because, despite their close friendship, there was something about Aurora's "difference" that scared her too.

CHAPTER 2

"In here," Aspen Clarke called out from the direction of the kitchen as Aaron shoved open the heavy front door of their large Victorian detached house with his foot in his normal style, sending it crashing into the wall and increasing the already existing indentation in the plaster. Aurora followed him into the house as their mother appeared from the end of the hallway to greet them, reaching Aaron first and putting her hands on his cheeks to plant her usual kiss on his forehead, which in turn received the customary "*Eurgh*, Mum!" from Aaron as he wiped the offending kiss away with his hand. Aurora smiled as she reached her mother, affectionately wiping a smudge of flour from Aspen's nose before receiving her kiss.

"Been baking, Mum?" she laughed. "What have you made today, then?"

"Cookie dough muffins," replied her mother. She pushed her shoulder-length blond hair away from her eyes with the back of one hand before smoothing her slightly creased and flour-covered apron. "And they're *hot!*" she turned to yell after Aaron, who had discarded his coat and shoes on the hall floor where he took them off and disappeared into the kitchen, to begin his normal afternoon routine of filling his stomach.

As Aurora hugged her mum, she suddenly and unexpectedly felt tears pricking her eyes. She took a deep, unsteady breath, which didn't go unnoticed by Aspen, who held her shoulders and looked at her thoughtfully. Aurora avoided making eye contact.

"Come on," her mum said gently, "let's go into the den and leave your brother to stuff his face in peace."

Aurora sighed again, suddenly tired, and followed her mum into the den. It was Aurora's favorite room in the house, aside from her own bedroom. Decorated in deep reds with heavy oak furniture and a huge, soft, red-and-gold sofa, it felt warm and safe. The late afternoon sun streamed through the bay window of the den, which was another reason Aurora loved the room so much. She sank down onto the soft cushions of the sofa, resting her head against its high back and curling her knees up under her. Closing her eyes in the sunlight, she pulled one of the huge cushions close to her in a hug.

"You look tired, sweetheart," her mum began, gently lifting the hair that had fallen across Aurora's eyes and tucking it behind her ear. "How was your day?"

"Okay, pretty normal really," Aurora lied, trying desperately to steady the shakiness in her voice as she spoke.

Aspen took a deep breath, putting her hands on Aurora's shoulders and squeezing them reassuringly.

"Look," she pressed gently. "I know you," she said, looking directly at Aurora. "I've known you your whole life. I know you're not fine . . . and that's okay . . . but can you try to talk about it? I'm always here to listen, but I don't know what's going on with you unless you tell me."

Aurora smiled back halfheartedly. "I honestly don't even know where to start, Mum," she said, looking down at the cushion she was hugging rather more tightly than she needed to.

"I had a call from school . . ." her mum began.

"Oh, okay. Sounds about right," sighed Aurora, her cheeks growing warm as she stared down at the cushion as if it would somehow give her the answers she so desperately needed.

"Sweetie, I'm not mad about it. Although perhaps you could try to avoid upsetting Miss Broach in particular; she almost deafened me in a five-minute phone call, and I'm not certain she actually drew breath once. I swear there was smoke coming out of the phone afterwards!"

Aurora giggled weakly, thinking that was entirely possible as she recalled the earlier incident in class.

Aspen gently put her hand on Aurora's arm. "These 'episodes' you've been having. It's not just the teachers who've noticed it. Nana told me you were all but asleep with your eyes open at the dinner table last weekend, and she couldn't get a word out of you. She thought you were having some sort of seizure!"

Aurora remembered Sunday dinner at Nana's and the sharp kick under the table from Aaron, which had pulled her out of the rainbow mists with such a jolt she had struggled to catch her breath.

"You know how much I love you, darling, don't you?" Aspen said hesitantly.

Aurora knew her mum was working up to telling her something because she was chewing on her bottom lip, which she always did when she was about to say something she knew wouldn't be well received by her children.

"There's a doctor I would like you to see, if that's okay. It's somebody your dad knew a long time ago. She's called Donna Marsden; I spoke with her the other day about these episodes you've been having, and she thinks she might be able to help. I'm going to make an appointment for you with her . . . just for a chat. Just to make sure everything is okay. Is that all right with you?"

Aurora felt the usual twinge of sadness at the mention of Dad. She nodded her head in agreement, and her mum hugged her, looking at her intently again for a few seconds before dashing back to the kitchen to rescue some of the muffins before Aaron devoured them all.

There had been times in the past year without Dad when Aurora had been aware of something she could only describe as a golden bubble suddenly appearing from her mum and enveloping Aurora's body, but it disappeared almost as soon as she had seen it. Aurora had tentatively told Julia, the bereavement counselor she had seen at school, about this golden bubble. Julia explained to Aurora that the mind did strange things when it was dealing with grief. This golden bubble was clearly a manifestation of the increased attachment Aurora had to her mum since her father, Dane Clarke, had disappeared. It was the early days, Julia went on to say. It was just her imagination playing tricks on her, and she shouldn't worry, as with time it would no doubt stop happening.

It hadn't stopped happening, though Aurora had not mentioned it again to Julia or anyone else. Whenever it happened, she had a feeling of intense warmth filling her body as the golden glow shone around her. She felt safe in it, protected. In truth, she didn't want it to stop happening, because it felt comforting, giving her back some of the strength and determination she had been losing lately.

Aurora pressed her palms to her temples as the tiredness took over again and felt the familiar heat from her hands soothing the pressure in her head. She knew the stress her mum had been under this past year without Dad around, and she didn't want to give her any more to worry about. But Aurora knew without doubt that everything wasn't okay, just as she also knew there was nothing this Dr. Donna Marsden could do about it . . . except maybe put her in the hospital, thinking she was losing her mind!

And do you know what, I wouldn't blame her one bit, Aurora thought closing her eyes and dropping her head back against the high sofa cushions in resignation.

With her mum back in the kitchen preparing dinner, Aurora quietly reflected on the day, which once again had not brought any of the answers she'd begged for every night since the visions and dreams started. Again, she asked herself the same question she had asked a million times in recent months: *Why me?*

Aurora had always known she was different. Not different in a bad way; it was never something she resented or even particularly questioned—at least when she was younger, anyway. The heat from her hands that eased physical pain, that calmed people and stopped them arguing or crying, was okay; the visions, the things she just kind of knew before they happened, weren't really that unusual, were they? The dreams in bright colors beyond her imagination were just lucky, especially when Hazel had such awful and confusing nightmares most nights. But lately things had happened that weren't normal, even in her world, and which she couldn't explain or begin to understand.

Aurora felt the tears rising again, and she instinctively reached for the precious piece of crystal in her cardigan pocket, holding it tightly as it began to glow. She felt the heat from it increasing, energy pulsing through her hand, up her arm, and spreading through her body. That crystal alone was proof *they* existed, proof she had been *there*. It was proof that she wasn't going insane, but that proof was her secret, and for now it had to stay that way. As Aurora held the crystal tightly in her palm, the tears subsided and her waning strength and determination began to return.

CHAPTER 3

Later that evening after dinner, Aurora overhead the phone call between her mum and Dr. Marsden arranging an appointment for the next day after school. Up in her bedroom, Aurora sat on her bed staring at the wall in front of her. She closed her eyes, remembering the start of it all three weeks ago—the twenty-first of April, her fifteenth birthday. Her mind's eye instantly transported her back to that day, and as clearly as when it had first happened, she experienced once more the moment that changed her life as she knew it . . .

That morning, bright golden rays of light had streamed through the room, disturbing Aurora's sleep. She opened her eyes and panicked momentarily, thinking that she must have slept through her alarm. But gazing sleepily over at her alarm clock, she rubbed her eyes in confusion at the display which showed 0430—the time she had been born, she thought, not really knowing why that fact had suddenly popped into her head. The light in her room seemed odd, an iridescent gold, and Aurora sat up in bed, her eyes following the beams of light to their source on the far wall of her bedroom. She heard her own sharp intake of breath as she watched the wall disappear in a swirling mist of colors stretching out further and further before her eyes—a kaleidoscopic tunnel edged by golden rays of light. Aurora heard a deep but gentle voice in her mind.

"Come to us, Aurora. Come to us." She felt herself moving through the air, drawn across her bedroom toward the tunnel.

Convinced she was dreaming, she relaxed slightly and let the rainbow mists pull her into their unknown depths. In an instant, she found herself flying through the swirling colors to a point where the rays of light seemed to center. She held out her arms in wonder at her weightlessness and stared at the sight before her, which became clearer as she moved closer to it, feeling strangely familiar, warm, and welcoming. It was a forest.

Aurora's world stopped spinning, her senses settled, and her eyes adjusted to her surroundings. She had never seen bluer skies, or greener fields all tinged with the same iridescent golden light that had filled her room. She stood on a hill at the edge of a green forest, and as she held out her arms in front of her, she gasped. Her skin was a shimmering gold color and a white haze surrounded her arms. As she looked down, she saw the same white haze surrounding her whole body. She felt light, weightless, as if she could fly if she wanted to.

Try it, she said to herself, enjoying her dream, but before she had chance to try, a voice interrupted her thoughts.

"Come to us, Aurora," the same gentle and familiar voice instructed again from within the green forest, and she felt her body move instinctively in the direction it came from, floating through the forest without effort. Aurora gazed in wonder at the light streaming through the branches of the huge canopies above her. The branches appeared to be all the colors of the rainbow, and she had thought it must be a trick of the light. She was more surprised to see smiling faces in the huge old trunks of the trees and arms that reached out and guided her way toward the center of the forest. But it was just a dream, she told herself, and she went with it.

The path in front of her ended at the base of the most enormous tree she had ever seen. She guessed the trunk must have been the size of her house, and her gaze wandered up it to a vast canopy of purple branches, which seemed to be bowing down toward her. Shielding her eyes from the golden light above her, Aurora looked up to meet the gaze of the tree as it smiled down at her warmly. Somewhere deep inside her was surprise at the sight before her; somewhere even deeper was the feeling that this was not a dream. It was certainly like no dream she had ever experienced before, but she felt no urge to run away and was comforted by the intense warmth flowing through her body. The voice in her head was clear, and she knew it came from the tree-being who stood before her, but the mouth of the tree didn't move and she felt her own eyes transfixed on the deep purple eyes before her.

"I am Namogoz, Aurora" the voice said. "It was I who called you here."

Aurora heard herself reply in her mind but felt no movement of her lips.

"Why am I here?" she questioned Namogoz.

"Your path has already been chosen, Aurora; it has been from the moment you were born," Namogoz explained.

"I know," Aurora heard her mind reply, "and I know this place. I don't know how, though, because I've never been here before." She felt suddenly confused and panicked, wondering where that sudden knowledge came from. Namogoz smiled.

"Your mind is confusing you, Aurora. Your soul knows its purpose, but your logical mind has still to let it in. Now is the time, Aurora, for you to begin your journey."

Aurora felt a sudden and strange sense of separation deep inside her, as if she were two people. One had knowledge beyond the understanding of the other, who was fighting the reality of this place and of the words she was hearing, because this was just a dream, right?

"Trust yourself," the voice of Namogoz reassured her. "You will find your way and discover your purpose on Earth. Then you must return here to the Rainbow Forest to complete your journey and take your place in the Circle of Light." Aurora stared transfixed into the eyes of Namogoz, hypnotized as the deep swirling purple drew her into them. She caught her breath as through his eyes she saw vast solar systems full of stars and planets, an unending space that seemed to stretch into infinity.

"You are looking into the whole Universe, Aurora. You too possess the gift of its power deep in your soul. Soon that power will be ignited within you, and the course of your destiny will be set."

Aurora's mind was spinning with questions, but as quickly as she thought of them, they melted away. Out of nowhere, a golden chair appeared in front of her, and she felt herself float toward it.

"Don't be scared." Namogoz said gently.

The instinctive sense of fear that had momentarily surged through her body subsided, and as she sank into the chair, she closed her eyes, the voice of Namogoz talking her through what was happening: "You will feel a gentle pressure around your head, Aurora. Don't worry, there will be no discomfort. This is the first stage of your transformation. It will clear your mind of all that human life has impelled on you, enabling the power of the Universe to be awakened in your soul."

Aurora felt an intense peace and calmness wash over her body and through her mind. Opening one eye slightly, she saw the white haze around her body glowing brighter. As she closed her eyes again, relaxing more now, a purple tunnel of light stretched out in front of her from a point just between her eyes. As she watched, it opened out, surrounding her whole body with the stars, planets, and solar systems she had seen through the eyes of Namogoz, and she floated within it.

"You are witnessing the birth of humanity, Aurora," Namogoz explained, "a journey which began long before you were born." The scene before her played through like a movie, and she watched it unfold as Namogoz narrated the story. "Before humanity was created, two ruling forces existed: the Light and the Darkness. For billions of years, they fought a fierce battle for control over the dimensions of time and space, but the strength of both was equal—good and evil were pitched head-to-head and neither reigned supreme.

"In its efforts to overcome the Darkness, the Light tirelessly roamed the far reaches of every dimension, searching for a way to triumph over its enemy. Finally, it found a unique planet within one of the star systems, a planet which had the capability to support life, and it called this planet Earth. It subsequently created humankind, a race of beings formed in the Light's own image. It sent these new beings out to inhabit the planet Earth, spreading the energy and life force of the Light across its lands. And so, the Old World was born. In doing this, the Light hoped that it would become stronger than the Darkness as humankind grew.

"Humankind did indeed grow, spreading wide across the continents of the Old World, and the Light began to overpower the Darkness, as it had hoped. But in those times, human beings could not exist independently of the Light, needing it to provide their energy and life force. As the years passed, humankind grew in numbers exponentially, beyond that which the Light had expected. As it grew, humankind began to drain the energy of the Light with its dependence on it, and weakened by this burden, the Light began to dim. As the energy of the Light diminished, it felt the power of the Darkness creeping in, infiltrating the atmosphere on Earth. Thunderous clouds rolled across the sky, casting a deep shadow over the Old World, and in desperation, the Light searched for a way to stop it.

"The Light decided humankind needed its own life force, to be able to live independently whilst continuing to spread the energy of the Light on Earth. For this task, the Light knew that every being would need all the powers the Light itself possessed, and these numbered seven: Courage, Creativity, Willpower, Love, Truth, Wisdom, and Bliss. The Light decided that every being on Earth should be bestowed a soul, and that soul was to have seven colors. Each color would hold one of the Light's own powers for humankind to build its future with; each would provide its own strengths and abilities. Only all seven together would form the full energy and life force of the Light, enabling every human being on Earth to continue its work.

"The Light created a sacred realm called Valhandra, existing as a separate dimension alongside the earth's realm and invisible to the eyes of humankind. A forest of seven ancient trees stood on a hill at the center of Valhandra, and the Light cast its energy out to this forest through an enchanted rainbow. As the rainbow fell from the skies onto the trees in the forest, it bestowed each of them with one of its seven colors, one of the seven colors of the soul. The Light breathed life into the trees through the rainbow, and as it did so, they began to shift and move, faces appearing in the vast ancient trunks as they stretched their branches toward the Valhandran sky. The Light named them the Gozzits.

"Stories of the Gozzits were passed down over the years from generation to generation. Their adventures were brought to life in bedtime stories told to children, of an ancient, enchanted forest of trees, which, with time, was believed to exist only in legend as the Gozzits of the Rainbow Forest.

"Now, Aurora, it is time for you to meet the other Gozzits."

Namogoz paused and Aurora felt herself rising up from the chair.

"The first of us," he continued, "is Mulagoz, the red color of the soul."

Aurora opened her eyes and found herself face to face with the wide, gnarled trunk of another huge tree. Her gaze traveled upward to a wide leafy canopy in deep red colors, and Mulagoz smiled kindly as he bowed down toward her.

"He gives us our Courage, our stability, peace, and calm. His roots spread deep underground, connecting us with nature and the earth's energy, giving us strength in times of weakness."

Aurora floated further through the Rainbow Forest as she proceeded to meet the remaining five Gozzit trees.

"The second Gozzit is Sacragoz," Namogoz went on, "the orange color of the soul. He give us our Creativity, our sense of fun. He helps us fill our lives with happiness, possibilities, and enjoyment.

"Next is Puragoz, the third Gozzit and the yellow color of the soul. She gives us our Willpower. She enables us to make our own choices and act on them, giving us hope and helping us accomplish our dreams.

"Now meet Hanagoz, the fourth Gozzit and the green color of the soul. Hanagoz is our heart energy, our Love. She gives us compassion, empathy, and forgiveness, helping us to love ourselves and others.

"The fifth Gozzit is Vigoz, the blue color of the soul. He gives us our Truth, our gifts of understanding and communication; He helps us to find our voice and express ourselves truthfully to others and to ourselves.

"Next is Ajnagoz, the sixth Gozzit, and the indigo color of the soul. She gives us our Wisdom, our intuition and inner knowledge. Ajnagoz helps us to see our future clearly, learn from our experiences, and use our Wisdom to create the future.

"I, Namogoz, am the seventh and final Gozzit, the violet color of the soul and the tallest tree in the Rainbow Forest. I am your Bliss, the direct connection to the Light and to the deepest parts of the soul. I am connected with the Light by a single white lotus flower which grows at the highest branch of my canopy. When the petals of my lotus flower open, a silver beam of energy joins the realm of Valhandra with the Light."

Aurora found herself back in front of Namogoz, as he continued the story of the Old World.

"The Light cast a protective golden shield around the sacred land of Valhandra, hiding it from the Darkness. It gave the Gozzits the task of bestowing a soul of all seven colors to every human being on Earth. And, casting their energy out across the world, the Gozzits began their work.

"When the colors fell on the Rainbow Forest, creating the Gozzits, the Forest became the source and center of all life on Earth, the master soul of humankind. The pure energy of the new human souls shone brightly out from Earth into the solar system, and the Light looked on with pride. In the face of its defeat, the Darkness retreated back to the fiery depths of its own world, Terhum.

"With its energy restored, the Light stepped back from humanity, pleased with its work and putting its faith in each human being to use its soul for the good of all humankind. Weary from the completion of their task, the Gozzits slept for many years."

The scene in front of Aurora faded away. She suddenly became aware of something clasped in her hand and opened her eyes and fingers to see a piece of clear crystal glowing in her palm.

"It is part of the journey, Aurora," Namogoz explained, "your piece of the Circle of Light. It will guide your way, and you must trust it."

"Why did you wake up?" Aurora asked Namogoz, intensely curious to hear more of the story.

"That is all you need to know . . . for now," explained Namogoz, smiling gently. "You are curious, Aurora, and that is a gift. It will be invaluable on your journey, but equally the journey must take its course and now you must return to Earth."

Aurora saw the light dimming around her and felt herself being pulled back through the swirling kaleidoscope of colors.

"I want to stay," she heard her mind calling to Namogoz, reaching out to him as he became smaller in the distance.

"Listen to your inner voice, Aurora," he instructed. "Follow your knowing. Open your mind to the Universe and ask it for guidance; it will provide all you need to know. You will find your way back to us in time, and all will be clear. But Aurora, you must bring Aaron with you. He too is a vital part of the Circle of Light, and he is not allowing us to reach him yet."

Great, no pressure then, was Aurora's last thought as the light dimmed to nothing and she woke in her bed to the familiar bleeping of her alarm clock.

Aurora glanced around her at her disappointingly normal-looking room, staring at the far wall in expectation, but there was no iridescent light, no swirling kaleidoscope of colors. She saw only her noticeboard and posters, and she rubbed her eyes, sighing at her own ridiculous belief in her dream because it had felt so real. Suddenly, though, a memory tugged at the back of her mind, and she became aware of something held tightly in her hand. Opening her fingers slowly, she looked down at a piece of clear crystal lying in the center of her palm.

Aurora found life in general very difficult to concentrate on after that night. The weeks that followed seemed like years, and the memory of the Rainbow Forest haunted her. The words of Namogoz replayed in her head over and over; the kaleidoscope of colors reappeared every time she closed her eyes. Then there were the visions, the spontaneous flights through the rainbow mists, but Aurora just felt lost; she hadn't found anything and, in truth, felt like she was losing her mind. What if time was running out? How much time did she actually have? During her visions and flights through the rainbow mists, she had felt a deep sense of certainty in the "journey," a sense of calm and knowing. But back in reality, this gave way to confusion and frustration, and what good was knowing when she didn't actually know what she knew!

This confusion was accompanied by a constant nagging feeling deep inside her that she needed to be somewhere else, doing something else. The destination was obviously already decided for her—Namogoz had said so—but she didn't know how to get there. What path was she supposed to take, and how would she find it? What was she supposed to do? School, homework, day-to-day life were all just inconveniences getting in the way of her finding out.

Aurora's thoughts were pulled back to the present by her mum's exasperated voice from the kitchen. "Aaron, you can have another muffin *after* you've done your homework, *not* before!"

Aurora stared deep into the crystal, remembering the instructions Namogoz had given her: "*Listen to your inner voice, Aurora. Follow your knowing . . . your piece of the Circle of Light . . . you will find your way and discover your purpose on Earth.*" She stood up, clenching her fists tightly to her sides, and breathed out hard with determination.

"I can do this," she promised herself.

Somebody somewhere could help—she was sure of it. It was just a matter of finding that person.

CHAPTER 4

Later that evening, after dinner, Aurora wandered up the stairs and stood at her brother's open bedroom door, wondering whether to interrupt him or not. She was desperate to speak with him about all this but didn't know where to begin. They had shared everything since they were old enough to communicate. Even before they learned to talk, their parents told them, they would lie on the brightly colored blanket Nana had knitted for them when they were born, holding hands and giggling at each other. Aurora found it hard to keep something like this from her brother, but it wasn't just this that had affected their bond. Dad's disappearance had not so much put a wedge between them as created a silence that neither knew how to fill.

Aurora's attention was drawn back to her brother sitting in silence at his desk. Aaron hadn't noticed her there and was busy, not doing his homework as instructed, but lost in concentration painting the rocket boosters of his newly constructed model space shuttle.

Just like Dad, thought Aurora with the same familiar twinge of sadness. It was nearly a year since Dad had gone. Left? Disappeared? Went missing? Aurora had so many unanswered questions, but every time she had tried to ask about it, her mum had frustratingly sidestepped giving an actual answer.

Aurora vividly remembered the day Dad didn't come home: the twenty-first of June the previous year. She and Aaron had been clearing away the dinner dishes, Aaron impatient to show

Dad the new model space station they had ordered, which had arrived in the post that day, excited for a weekend of building it. It was not unusual for Dad to be home late from work, but Aurora had noticed their mum to be unusually distracted and distant that day, busying herself around the house with chores since dinner, which had overcooked while she rushed from one room to the next, cleaning.

Just after seven o'clock, a slow, heavy knock at the door had interrupted the early evening routine. Their mum stopped abruptly, mid-clean of the hall sideboard, taking a long breath in and shakily letting it out as she made her way to the door, brushing her hands over the front of her jeans as she went. As she answered the door, Aurora and Aaron stood silently at the end of the long hall where it entered the kitchen, the dim evening sunlight illuminating the front of the house, casting their mother's shadow down the hallway as she pulled open the heavy wooden front door.

Two men in white suits stood at the door talking in low tones. As they spoke, their mother put one hand to her chest, the other to the hallway wall beside her, as though she needed to steady herself. Aurora strained her ears trying to hear the conversation from the other end of the hallway, watching as one of the men placed his hand on her mum's arm and only hearing him say, "Be strong, Aspen, we're here if you need us," before they both turned to leave. As the men left, Aspen closed the front door and leaned her body sideways against the wall, facing the door with one hand still resting against it. As the light that had flooded the long hallway dimmed, the twins retreated back into the kitchen, looking at each other with a heavy sense of what was to come.

Mum had sat the twins down in the den, her arms around both of them as she gently told them that Dad wouldn't be coming home, hugging them both tightly as their lives crumbled around them. Aurora recalled bits of the conversation. Dad was missing in the course of his work; he had been on a trip abroad, and there had been an incident, an explosion; they couldn't say for sure what had happened; they hadn't found a body, but he hadn't been seen since; so the company had confirmed him missing, presumed—Mum hadn't said the word. Aaron broke away in silence and went to his room. Aurora held on tightly to her mum, for how long she didn't remember, only recalling the depth of sadness and loss and the tears, which, unlike Aaron, she let flow freely for the days and weeks that followed.

Dad's work had often taken him away from home as the twins were growing up. Not for long periods, but always in a shroud of secrecy about which she remembered being intensely curious as a young girl. In her active young mind, he was a secret agent, working for the government and traveling the world. Whenever she asked her mum about Dad's work, Aspen had gently explained that it was very important but couldn't be spoken about, and Aurora knew from the finality in her mother's voice at those moments not to push it. As time went on after Dad's disappearance, Aurora had tried not to hope for the impossible, but despite the void it had left in their lives, she had an unexplained sense deep inside her that she would see him again someday. That unexplainable sense had become stronger and more insistent since her journey to the Rainbow Forest on the morning of her birthday.

Aurora knew that, although she missed her dad with all her heart, it had been harder on Aaron. They had been as close as it was possible for any father and son to be. Since Dad had gone, Aaron staunchly refused to speak about it with Mum or the school counselor, who had tried unsuccessfully for months to engage with Aaron and help him deal with his grief. As time went on, Aaron did to some extent return to his old self, though Aurora felt his pain as her own in a way that only twins do, and she knew just how far he was pushing it down, hiding from facing the truth.

From an early age, Dad's obsession with outer space had fascinated Aaron too. Dad happily encouraged this and turned the garage into their own private workshop, even having a wooden sign engraved with the words "Dad and Aaron's Space" for the door, which led from the far end of the hallway into the garage. They had proudly hung their new sign on the door together in a little family ceremony and spent hours in there between Dad's work trips, building their models of planets and space shuttles, painting them and displaying their creations by hanging them from the wooden beams in the ceiling. Walking into the garage was like walking into the solar system itself, Aurora thought, and she had always been seriously impressed with their creations, even though she had never entertained much interest in the solar system or space shuttles. Mum had even bought them a small fridge for Christmas one year so they could have a supply of their favorite canned drinks in the garage, within easy reach while they were working in there.

These days, Aurora and their mum never went into the garage. In the early days after Dad disappeared, Aaron had found Mum in there one day moving a cabinet and had exploded with rage at her.

"Never *ever* move *anything* in here; it's not yours to move, Mum! It's *not your space*! Do you get it, do you *get it*?" At hearing the shouting, Aurora had come running in from the den to see Mum rooted to the spot and Aaron red-faced and looking like he would explode, fists clenched by his side and his body rigid with anger. Aurora had never seen him like that and realized the extent to which Aaron had locked up his grief inside himself. Mum had gently tried to put her arms around Aaron, but he shrugged her off, storming off up to his room, while Aurora had retreated back to the comfort of the den, sad at the unfamiliar air of anger in the house.

She and Mum both respected Aaron's feelings and never went into the garage after that day. Aurora didn't feel like she needed to anyway, as she had her own special memories of Dad, but she loved her brother and wanted to protect his special memories too. She was sure that Mum felt the same, though they never spoke about it. Aaron didn't do his modeling in the garage anymore as he and Dad used to, and Aurora supposed it may have just been too painful for him. His workspace now was his bedroom, where he would make and paint his models, then once finished go and carefully display them in the garage. He never spoke about it or showed his work to Aurora or Mum, and neither of them asked him to, though Aurora would sometimes have a sneaky peak through the outside garage window at the amazing displays inside. She admired her brother's patience with his hobby; she had a lot of talents, but patience with fiddly details was not one of them!

Aurora's thoughts dragged her back to the present as she stood at her brother's bedroom door, watching him carefully painting his latest creation and wishing she could do something to heal his pain, the pain she always felt in her own body too., She suddenly realized that the stabbing pain she experienced herself when she thought of Aaron's struggles was always around the same place in her own body, starting in her upper chest, radiating through her shoulders and down her arms, feeling like her throat was being constricted and squeezed tightly. Was that relevant? Once again, her mind began desperately searching for answers and, finding none, filling her with a rising panic at the blankness inside it. Where were the answers she needed? Out of nowhere, she heard the voice of Namogoz in her mind.

"Let go of the need to understand, Aurora. Allow yourself to see what is."

Aurora breathed in deeply and then out again slowly and purposefully, feeling the panic and the pain dissolving and falling away from her body. As she watched Aaron, his form began to fade in front of her, the molecules of the air around him appearing to expand, as if she were looking through a magnifying glass. In a split second, it wasn't Aaron sitting there, but Dad. Aurora blinked and shook her head, looking back, and in the same space of a split second, it was Aaron again. Her vision still hazy, she again heard the voice of Namogoz in her mind replaying his words to her in the Rainbow Forest.

"Trust your knowing. Open your mind to the Universe and ask it for guidance; it will provide you with all you need to know."

Suddenly Aurora knew what to do.

"Show me how I can help Aaron?" she asked silently, and the fog in her mind instantly cleared, replaced with the peace, space, and the same intense calm she had felt in the Rainbow Forest.

Closing her eyes, Aurora saw a vision of her mum standing at their kitchen window, looking out to the sky and holding her hands to her heart. Her mind's eye focused in on her mum's hands, and Aurora suddenly realized she had never felt the same heat from her mum's hands that she had felt from her own. She wondered at that moment why she had never thought about it before. She remembered feeling that same heat from Dad's hands, which would comfort her when she fell. Aurora's cuts and bruises always seemed to have healed by the next day, when similar injuries on her friends would still be there a week later. Surprised at why this had never occurred to her as strange before, Aurora caught her breath as a new awareness was taking form somewhere in her mind, a deep inner knowledge of something, and she searched to grasp hold of it.

Leaning against the frame of Aaron's bedroom door, Aurora felt this new awareness rising like a tidal wave inside her body, tugging her memory back to her childhood, back to the heat from her father's hands and—his eyes, what was it about his eyes? Something she suddenly remembered seeing in his eyes was linking itself intrinsically in her mind to another time, another place. Her mind searched around for an answer, and she knew at that moment it was imperative that she remember it.

"Universe, show me," she asked again silently in her mind, and she felt the crystal in her pocket start to pulse with heat and energy in response to her question.

Aurora instantly felt herself propelled forward into the swirling rainbow mists. But this time, her journey stopped abruptly, and she remained suspended in time and space surrounded by the kaleidoscope of colors. Suddenly, in the vision, her dad appeared in front of her. He stood with a boy around Aaron's age and height, with thick black wavy hair and dark eyes. Aurora was confused. What was this supposed to be telling her? Something about the boy seemed strangely familiar, but before she could give it more thought, her vision focused in on her father's face, as if through a zoom lens. Staring into his clear blue eyes, she gasped, tears forming in her own as she saw within them what she remembered from her childhood but never questioned, because she hadn't known what it was until now. She saw the stars, planets, solar systems . . . the infinite space of the Universe, which she had also seen through the eyes of Namogoz in the Rainbow Forest.

"Dad," Aurora whispered to herself. "Dad is part of this." The realization washed over her like waking up from a long sleep, and she gasped out loud, pulled back from the rainbow mists with a jolt as Aaron jumped in his chair, suddenly aware of her presence.

"Jesus," he said, glaring at his sister. "Aurora, you nutter. What are you doing standing there talking to yourself? You scared the life out of me." Aaron held the model rocket up in front of him. "I've smudged it now because of you," he huffed.

"Sorry, bro," she said and walked off smiling to herself, leaving Aaron muttering grumpily behind her.

CHAPTER 5

Thursday seemed to pass Aurora by completely. She felt disconnected from everything, but it was at least a comfortable disconnection after the revelation the previous night, and a relief from the anxiety of the past few weeks. She recalled her homeroom teacher, Mr. Marsh, talking about a new boy who was starting at the school the next day and who would be in their class. As the bell went after the last lesson, she checked the notes she had made during the day in her planner—homework, a new lunchtime club, and an upcoming school trip—but had no recollection of actually writing them. Aaron was walking back to a friend's that day while Mum took Aurora to the appointment with Dr. Marsden, and Hazel had her drama class after school, so Aurora walked home on her own.

Aware of what was happening around her as she walked, Aurora had a new sense of being unaffected as the world passed her by. She was surprised yet relieved that the impatience, confusion, and frustration of the past few weeks had suddenly disappeared, replaced with a feeling of calm certainty that everything was okay, that whatever lay ahead, she was at least on the right path to it. As she arrived home, she found herself with an unexpected anticipation of her appointment that evening. Maybe, she pondered as she changed out of her school uniform into jeans and a hoodie, it was even excitement?

Their thirty-minute journey felt like hours, though Aurora felt strangely detached, watching the scenery out of the car window change as they drove through the countryside beyond the main town. She recalled a vague memory of driving out this way with her dad many years earlier but pushed that to the back of her mind as they finally pulled into a long and winding tree-lined driveway. As they made their way down it, Aurora's senses suddenly seemed to heighten and an unexpected surge of adrenaline rose in her chest, flowing down her arms and making her skin prickle. She squirmed in her seat, a strange unease overtaking her, and she fought a sudden urge to jump out of the car and run away.

After a few twists and turns in the long driveway, it finally opened out and Aurora gasped out loud at the sight which met them. The huge white house stood three stories tall, including the top windows in its eaves. Gray stone steps led up to a wide porch and a double-fronted oak door, which was flanked by two stone statues of horses. It was the house from her visions, the house at the end of the rainbow tunnel! But she had never been here. How could she have seen it? How could she have known?

As they got out of the car, the adrenaline was still buzzing uncomfortably through Aurora's body, and she closed her eyes, breathing out heavily from the intensity of it. Her mother walked round to her, putting her hands on Aurora's shoulders gently.

"How are you feeling, sweetie?"

Aurora opened her eyes, and as she did so, she saw the golden bubble from her mother enveloping her, although this time it appeared bigger than usual. She felt its warmth calm the rising anxiety inside her, and she managed to force a smile.

"Okay actually, Mum. I'm really okay. Just wondering what to expect."

Aspen hugged her daughter. Looking directly into Aurora's eyes, she hesitated before she spoke.

"You know, it might not . . . might not be what you . . . think it might be . . . here," she began.

"To be honest, Mum, I don't know what I think it might be. But it's okay. I'll be okay."

"I know you will," Aspen replied, nodding as she turned to lock the car before they walked toward the vast porch.

Aspen tugged at an old-fashioned iron bell pull to the right of the front door. A young girl, only a couple of years older than Aurora, opened the door to them and smiled widely when she saw them.

"Hi, come in. I'm Eden Marsden. Mum's with somebody, but she won't be long."

The girl gestured toward a brown leather sofa to the left of the vast open hallway they entered. Above them, a galleried landing extended across the entire expanse of the hallway, which was bigger than any hallway Aurora had ever seen. There were various oak-paneled doors around the hallway, all closed and with ornate gold handles. A staircase ran from the landing down each side of the hallway, the ivory carpeted steps widening as they ran into the hallway itself.

"Sit down. Can I get you a drink? There's water, juice, tea, or coffee."

Aspen asked for strong tea, emphasizing "one large sugar, please" as she always did. Aurora declined a drink but found herself transfixed by the eyes of Dr. Marsden's daughter: dark brown, but twinkling with a familiar depth and as she recognized it, Aurora felt a sense of peace. Eden smiled back at her before turning to go get Aspen's tea.

Aurora distractedly pulled a magazine out of the carved wooden rack by the side of the sofa and began randomly flicking through it. Just a few minutes passed before a door in the corner of the large hallway opened. A tall, elegant woman walked out, catching sight of Aurora and her mother briefly and smiling warmly before turning back to speak with the two people who followed her out of the door. Aurora saw the older of the two first, a tall man with tanned skin and thick, wavy black hair flecked with gray. As the older man turned to extend his hand to the woman with them, a younger boy around Aurora's age appeared from behind them, and Aurora gasped out loud with shock. It was the boy she had seen with Dad in her vision the night before!

"Are you okay, sweetie?" Aurora's mum asked, putting her hand on her daughter's knee. "You look like you've seen a ghost."

"I . . . no, I . . ." stammered Aurora, looking from her mother to the boy and back again.

"Thank you, Donna," the older man said to the woman with them as he shook her hand. "Cal will see you on Sunday evening."

Dr. Marsden smiled warmly at them both, putting her hand on the boy's arm briefly before they turned to leave. As they walked across the hallway toward the door and passed the sofa, the older man nodded and smiled in greeting to Aspen before he went to pull open the heavy oak door, and Aspen smiled back at him. Aurora sensed a familiarity between them, which surprised her. She knew all of her mum's friends and had never seen this man before, though she had the feeling she knew him from somewhere. The boy, Cal, followed behind the older man, similar in height and so strikingly similar in looks, now she saw them at closer quarters, that Aurora guessed they had to be father and son.

As the younger boy passed Aurora, their eyes met, and instantaneously an iridescent golden glow appeared around his body, shining out from him and expanding toward her, wrapping around her like a blanket. Momentarily hypnotized by his eyes, she felt a pulling sensation in her body toward him, making her catch her breath, and she instinctively looked to the floor in embarrassment, her cheeks burning. The golden glow remained, if anything intensifying as Aurora fought uncomfortably against the temptation to look back at Cal, instead burying her head back in the magazine on her lap until she heard the front door close. Her sigh of relief came out much louder than she had intended it to, and sensing her mother's eyes on her, she busied herself with putting the magazine back in the wooden rack, with far more attention than the task actually required.

Dr. Marsden was without doubt the most beautiful woman Aurora had ever seen. Tall and slim, with long dark hair and piercing gray eyes, she wore a mid-length emerald-green skirt that seemed to float around her as she walked, a black short-sleeved fitted shirt and black patent high-heeled shoes that shone like polished glass. She seemed to glide rather than walk—*like an elegant ballerina*, Aurora thought—as she made her way across the vast hallway toward them. Aspen stood up from the sofa as Dr. Marsden approached, and Aurora hurriedly followed. Introducing herself as Donna, Dr. Marsden took Aspen's outstretched hand with both of hers in a greeting as elegant as she was herself. Dr. Marsden turned and led the way back to the room at the far corner of the hallway, and Aspen and

Aurora followed her into the large but welcoming room. Huge leather seats surrounded a beautiful old stone fireplace, which was dwarfed by white wooden bookshelves stretching from floor to ceiling on either side of it. To the left of the room as they entered, French doors framed a beautiful view of the grounds of the house: a wonderland of trees, flowers, and winding paths that reminded Aurora of a book her mother used to read to her when she was younger.

"Wow!" Aurora gasped, her attention pulled back to the hundreds of books before her, imagining herself in heaven being left with the depths of their worlds to explore.

"Do you like my library, Aurora?" Dr. Marsden asked, smiling warmly, and Aurora marveled at how perfectly proportioned her facial features were, like a glamorous Hollywood film star.

"I *love* it," Aurora replied, sighing and settling herself into one of the big leather chairs, sinking into it and feeling at home already. Her mother looked to the ceiling in mock exasperation.

"Give her a room full of books and she'd be happy for weeks!" Aspen said, looking sideways to Aurora and winking at her.

"Curiosity is a valuable trait," Dr. Marsden replied, smiling, her words sparking a brief moment of *déjà vu* in Aurora's mind, which she quickly brushed away.

Once all three were comfortably seated, Dr. Marsden turned to Aurora, clasping her hands on her neatly crossed legs.

"So, Aurora," she began gently, "tell me what's been happening."

Aurora suddenly felt very exposed; the intensity of Dr. Marsden's gray eyes seemed to look straight into her soul. Aurora blinked and looked away into the fireplace instead, suddenly very unsure of herself and what she was about to disclose.

"Erm, well I've been having these . . . um . . . episodes . . . sort of funny turns," she said, echoing the words that Nana had used after the incident at Sunday dinner. Aurora looked blankly at Dr. Marsden, suddenly at a loss for what more to say about it, because saying more meant explaining about her flights through the rainbow mists, about Namogoz, about the crystal. How on earth would she begin to explain all that? Her gaze fell to the floor and Aspen took over the conversation, though the words were entirely not what Aurora expected to hear.

"I haven't questioned it too much, Donna," Aspen said, her voice breaking slightly, "but it's happening exactly as Dane said it would."

Aurora looked up in surprise to see her mum brushing away a tear and taking a deep breath before she continued.

"As far as I know, it's just Aurora and hasn't happened with Aaron yet. He is, well, not communicative and still very much taken up with grief over Dane leaving. But Aurora has been acting differently for a while. From what I have heard and seen, I've realized it must be starting, and I thought it best to phone you."

"You did the right thing, Aspen." Donna Marsden reached forward and put one hand over Aspen's hands, which were clasped tightly in her lap. "I understand it's hard for you."

Aurora felt confusion overtake her, then a brief flash of something else—perhaps anger?

"Mum, what's starting, what's happening to me?" she whispered, her own voice breaking now, the new calm and peace she had felt previously shattering and panic rising as her mum looked to the floor, avoiding Aurora's eyes.

"Aspen, will you let me have some time with Aurora?" Dr. Marsden asked gently.

Aspen nodded silently and the doctor led her to the door, hugging her and whispering something to her before she left the room. Dr. Marsden closed the door and walked back toward Aurora, who felt like the world was crashing around her. Maybe she was mad, maybe ill, maybe worse, maybe . . .

"What's the matter with me?" Aurora begged, unable to control the feeling of panic rising through her. "I don't understand, am I ill? Am I dying? What's going to happen to me?"

Dr. Marsden leaned forward, putting her hands on Aurora's knees and sending a familiar warmth flooding through her. It was the same warmth Aurora felt from her own hands, which she used to feel from her dad's hands, and it instantly calmed her rising panic. The tears stopped and Aurora looked up to meet Dr. Marsden's eyes.

"You're not ill, Aurora. You are unique . . . and you have been destined for this since the day you were born."

Dr. Marsden picked up Aurora's hands and held them in her own. "Trust me, Aurora. Let me show you."

As Dr. Marsden held Aurora's hands, the warm energy flooded through them, up her arms and through her body, increasing in intensity. The form of the room around her began to change, swimming, swirling, and transforming as she blinked her eyes and tried to refocus on the chaos that was unfolding in front of them. Her breathing became rapid, her heartbeat pounding in her ears, making her panic and want to scream . . . or run. The molecules of the air seemed to be expanding, like they had the day before when she had looked at Aaron in his room, like she was looking at the world through a magnifying glass.

Dr. Marsden maintained her hold on Aurora's hands and looked directly into her eyes.

"Aurora, let go of the fear, take a deep breath, and look at what's in front of you. Allow yourself to see it and to trust it. I promise you are safe."

Aurora closed her eyes and took a deep breath as instructed, letting the intense energy flow through her body as she heard the familiar words of Namogoz in her mind: "Let go of your need to understand, Aurora. Trust yourself."

Aurora sensed the warm pulsing of the crystal in her jeans pocket and felt her body relax, the fear slowly melting away back to a feeling of calm and peace inside her. She slowly opened her eyes to be faced with a new reality. As she refocused on the world around her, she gasped in wonder. She could see the molecules of the air, of life, of energy and being, the molecules of even the furniture in the room, which no longer appeared solid, its edges wavering and moving, the forms almost translucent and ghost-like. At that moment, she realized she had moved beyond reality as she had known it, and as she looked toward the previously solid stone fireplace, it faded away to the houses beyond, which faded away to the trees and fields beyond that. Her vision rushed on to the sea, the sky, past the clouds and through the stars into the vast expanses of the Universe itself, its planets and solar systems— and the Universe welcomed her home.

"This is your destiny, Aurora. Reach out to it." Aurora felt Dr. Marsden's hands leave hers, and for a moment she panicked. The vision surrounding her dimmed slightly, becoming blurred and unfocused again, and she heard Dr. Marsden's voice in the distance.

"Keep the connection, Aurora, stay with it, ask the Universe to help you."

"Show me what to do," Aurora heard her mind instinctively command, and instantly she felt the gentle buzz of energy through her body increase, lifting her up further into the Cosmos, and she watched as the stars, planets, and solar systems surrounded her and began to move, swirling together in front of her and forming a channel which focused in toward the center of her body. Aurora closed her eyes, feeling her arms extend widely out to the sides of her, her body arching involuntarily forward toward the swirling mass until . . .

She felt only a deep warmth as the swirling vortex entered her body through a point at the center of her torso, the center of her soul. The warm energy spread through her body, filling her with an intense peace. Her whole body felt as if it were expanding, becoming as vast and expansive as the Universe itself. Aurora opened her eyes and looked down at her body, which glowed with iridescent light as if it were made entirely of gold. She willed her body to turn, and as she willed it, it did. She looked beyond the stars and planets and saw the earth spinning into her view. Her vision shot forward like a zoom lens toward it, past the clouds, the plants and trees and down into the ground, moving through the layers of the earth to its molten core where her journey stopped. As her senses adjusted to their surroundings, she became aware of the sound of deep, distressed moans, which slowly increased in intensity. She felt a heavy pain in her chest, immense sadness and grief rising inside her.

"The earth is in pain," Dr. Marsden's voice rang through Aurora's mind. "She is suffering because of what humanity is doing to her. She can provide us with everything we need to sustain life, but we are killing her, suffocating her, and ignoring her cries for help. There isn't much time left for humanity on Earth." Aurora's vision backed up out of the center of the earth, and she watched history play through like a movie trailer in front of her eyes. The beginning of time, the fierce fight between the Light and the Darkness, which she learnt about on her visit to the Rainbow Forest, the gifting of the souls by the Gozzits. But this time, the story continued, and Aurora watched as a new and horrifying chapter played out in front of her.

CHAPTER 6

After the victory of the Light, the Darkness remained in hiding while humankind began to use the power of their new souls. But over time, that power created its own problems, for power through greatness can quickly turn to the need for power over others . . . and any "need" becomes a weakness of the mind and soul. This is what began to happen to humankind, and it was in these moments of weakness, in the need for power over others, that the Darkness was able to creep in, stealing energy from the weaker beings and leaving them without one or more of the colors of their souls.

Many thousands of years passed by, and the weaknesses of humankind created great problems across the world. The Light watched with sadness as humankind became greedy for power, and in its greed began to destroy itself. Business and industry grew at an exponential rate, creating a cloud of smog over the cities of the earth, polluting the land, skies, and oceans—killing the life forms within them. The search for wisdom became a fierce battle for power instead of the peaceful journey the Light had intended it to be. Human beings competed against each other, always searching for the next great discovery, their intense need to win destroying the lives of others because each wanted to be the best. Dictators ruled over the most powerful countries on Earth. Species were genetically mixed, creating monsters that could not be controlled. Bacteria was developed in the name of science, which then mutated out of control in the atmosphere and spread diseases that required the subsequent creation of vaccines to repel them. The very air that sustained life became the conduit for viruses with the capacity to end it.

The weaker beings became more fearful; the strong became more powerful, waging wars against those who stood in their way. The battle for success created a path to destruction. Humanity, distracted from its purpose, turned away from the Light, and the Light turned away from humanity in shame. The Light saw that humankind was tired, frightened, and angry, unable to control the powerful tools the Gozzits had bestowed on it, and as the colors of the human soul dimmed across the world, the Darkness grew stronger.

When the last light in a human soul went out, in that minute space between life and death, the Darkness would creep in and steal the bodies, dragging them through a burning portal of fire into its own world, Terhum, where they underwent a terrifying transformation into the demonic creatures of the Dark Army.

Once again, the Light felt the power of the Darkness creeping into the world, depleting and destroying more and more souls and growing its Dark Army. Frustration and anger took hold of the Light, as it could see that the souls of humankind no longer served their purpose, no longer functioned in the world the way the Light had intended them to. The human souls were too easily manipulated and divided. Love, trust, honor, kindness, and peace too easily turned into anger, jealousy, hate, violence, greed. Humanity was losing its way, and it was losing its life force to the Darkness as a result. A heaviness was falling across the earth, and the Light felt this heaviness as a black hole growing inside of it. At that moment, the Light realized it had let its fierce hatred of the Darkness take over, and in doing so, the Light was slowly dying.

In time and space, the only force greater than both the Light and the Darkness was the Universe. The Universe is all-seeing, all-knowing, and its infinite power can be gifted to any being willing to receive it. But the Universe can only bestow its power if and when it is asked for. All this time, the Universe had waited for the Light to wake up to what it had become . . . and finally, in desperation, the Light had turned to the Universe and asked for help.

The vision playing out in front of Aurora faded, a kaleidoscope of colors swirled in front of her and the face of Namogoz appeared through the rainbow mists.

"It is here where your story begins, Aurora, here that your destiny and your purpose in the world was decided," Namogoz explained. "When the Light finally woke up to what it had become, the Universe gave it one last chance; a new Consciousness was born that could set humanity free from its limited existence, turn it away from its path to destruction. The seven colors of the human soul would be merged with the infinite power of the Universe. Stronger as one force, the new soul would be powerful enough to fight the Darkness."

Aurora was pulled into the depths of the eyes of Namogoz as a new chapter in the story began to play out. She watched and listened as it unfolded before her, the voice of Namogoz echoing through her mind.

"There were certain beings on Earth who still possessed all the colors of their souls and were strong enough to receive the new Consciousness, to rescue the broken human souls and to fight the Darkness. The Light called those beings to the Rainbow Forest, in the ancient land of Valhandra . . . for they were to become Lightworkers and their quest to be changing the future for humankind.

"The Light channeled the infinite power of the Universe to each and every being it had called to Valhandra, and as the power of the Universe entered the souls of the Lightworkers, they began to change and evolve. As their old souls merged with the new Consciousness and they became one with the Universe, their beings took on a new form, beyond reality as we know it. They became able to see things beyond solid matter, they received knowledge surpassing the logical mind, they transformed into infinite beings, with gifts far beyond anything within the physical realm.

"The Lightworkers returned to Earth and spread wide across all continents and countries. They went on to bear children, a new generation of Lightworkers. Born with the pure power of the Universe in their souls, these children possessed capacities and abilities greater than any beings on Earth, even the Lightworkers, and as such, it was vital they were kept hidden from the Darkness as they grew up. The Universe decreed that at the age of fifteen, the Gozzits would call each and every child of the Lightworkers to Valhandra. For at this point in their human development, their physical bodies are on the brink of adulthood, and it becomes more difficult for the Protectors to shield them. At that point, though, they are also strong enough to withstand the change when the power of the Universe is fully activated, the power that had lain hidden in their souls since the day they were born.

"During the year leading up to their fifteenth birthday, the Lightworkers were called back to Valhandra, to prepare for the arrival of the new generation. The Lightworkers left under the guise of human "death"; too many questions would have been asked otherwise. When they left, the remaining parent of each child became their Protector, bestowed with the power of the golden shield the Light had placed around Valhandra, so that in the absence of the Lightworkers they could continue to conceal the children from the Darkness, until the day came for their calling.

"And so it was that the Lightworkers and Protectors began to prepare the world, and the world beyond, for the day when the Light's army would be ready to face the Darkness, raising the new generation to fulfill their destiny as Children of the Light."

The vision cleared, and a mass of figures appeared far in front of Aurora, bathed in light, its beams emanating toward her. Aurora heard Dr. Marsden's voice again.

"They are the Lightworkers, Aurora. Those beings who still possessed all the colors of their souls, who were strong enough to stand against the Darkness, those who were called to the Golden Planet of Valhandra sixteen years ago to receive the power of the Universe into their souls . . . and on the twenty-first of June last year they were called to return." Dr. Marsden's words sparked an instant awareness in Aurora's mind.

"Wait!" she gasped, her heart pounding in her ears. "The twenty-first of June?"

At that moment the mass of figures parted, and one lone figure came forward from the middle of the group, moving slowly toward her. Aurora felt a pull toward the figure and a beam of light became visible between them, as if connecting them together. As the figure moved closer and closer, the face came into focus and Aurora gasped as she recognized him.

"Dad," she breathed out, tears of amazement, relief, and love rising in her eyes. As quickly as the urge to run toward him entered her mind, she was there in front of him, holding out her arms as he took her in his and hugged her tightly, the golden aura of light around him merging with her own. At that moment, back in her father's arms, Aurora understood where she had needed to be over the past few weeks.

"I missed you, Dad," she whispered and he hugged her tighter to him.

"My darling Aurora," her father said as he held her, "you've been so brave. But there is more you need to know; you must be fully prepared for what is to come."

CHAPTER 7

Later that night, Aurora sat curled up in the den, her dad's words playing through her mind as she reeled from the new world she had entered, which now seemed more real than the one she was leaving behind.

"There is an ancient manuscript," Dane had explained to his daughter as Aurora learned more of the Old World.

"Many say that the manuscript was written by the Gods. But in truth, "the Gods" are just souls, beings just like us. But they were beings who were gifted with the highest powers of awareness and psychic vision so that they could channel information, guidance, and insights from the non-physical to the physical realms, intended for those who would use it to create the future which the Light originally intended for humankind.

"The original manuscript was written in two parts. The first part is a compendium of all life; every soul ever to have existed, every thought, word, and intent ever to have occurred is documented there. The second part was written in later years. It chronicles the past, present, and future of the physical and spiritual worlds."

Dane paused thoughtfully before he went on. "The future chronicles contained two prophecies, two possible futures for humankind. One foretells the triumph of the Light, the second the downfall of humankind and the world to the Darkness. When the Light first discovered the existence of the prophecies, it rejected the validity of the manuscript and refused to acknowledge it. You see, the Light at that time was blind to the weaknesses of the human souls it had created; it was unable to see past its fierce need to triumph over the Darkness.

"But, when the Light turned to the Universe for help and the new Consciousness was created, the Universe forced the Light to acknowledge the truth of the manuscript, and in doing so, the Light finally acknowledged the truth within its prophecies. The manuscript was kept safe, hidden by Namogoz in the Rainbow Forest for many years, its message made known only to the Lightworkers when they were called to Valhandra to begin their quest. But the Darkness discovered the prophecies of the second part of the manuscript when they were disclosed to it by one being who betrayed the Light.

"The Light protected the original manuscript by encoding it within a non-physical plane of existence—in essence creating it as an Eternal Library. Only certain beings can enter the Eternal Library, and only they are able to access and read the records within it.

"Unless we stop it, the Dark Prophecy will come to pass. Humanity is becoming weaker by the day. Its greed, jealousy, and hate will be its ultimate downfall, and as more and more human souls are destroyed, the Darkness becomes more powerful. The Prophecy warns that if the Darkness wins power, all Light on Earth will be extinguished—fish will die in the streams, birds will fall from the sky, the waters and lands will blacken, and all of nature will perish. Life and humankind as we know it will cease to exist; the earth will solidify, overtaken by the Darkness."

Aurora asked what it would take to fight the Dark Prophecy, and her father continued.

"It was foreseen in the manuscript that keepers of the infinite power of the Universe would have the ability to save humanity and life on Earth. They would be the soldiers of the Light and the key to the survival of humankind. It spoke of the day of awakening when the soldiers of the Light will be called to battle against the Darkness and its Dark Army, to form a New World of peace and freedom with the energy of the Universe at its core. The soldiers of the Light will show all of humankind how to live within the energy of the Universe, will teach them to be guardians and protectors of the earth. It spoke of a rainbow bridge connecting the earthly realm to the Golden Planet, bringing unity, love, and harmony to every corner of the New World. Freed of its greed, jealousy, and hate, humanity would become one with the Universe."

"And how does the second Prophecy end?" Aurora had questioned.

"The end of the world," came her father's reply.

Aurora felt a shiver run through her as she recalled the next part of the story.

"When the new Consciousness was born, the Darkness knew that something had changed, that its very existence was threatened. Since that time, it has been building its army, preparing to fight . . . and it is ruthless in its recruitment of that army."

Dane swirled his arm to his side, opening a portal to a dark and ominous scene.

"The being I spoke of who betrayed the Light was named Micah," her father shook his head sadly as he spoke.

"He too was called to Valhandra with the Lightworkers and gifted the power of the Universe. Micah was the most powerful of all the Lightworkers, and the Light had great hopes for him to lead the Light's army into battle with the Darkness. But Micah began to crave more and more power over the other Lightworkers. We all tried to help him, but he resisted, believing we were trying to diminish his power and his potential. You see, Aurora, when we try to use our power over others instead of for creation of the future, it becomes a weakness. Micah's resistance created a space between power and weakness and caused his soul to split. In that second, he had a choice between Light and Darkness . . . and he chose Darkness. As the Darkness took hold of him, it poured itself into his being, and Micah's soul underwent a terrifying transformation. It solidified, turning him into a freak mutation of the Darkness and an even greater evil in the world. He left the Lightworkers and Valhandra, taking the secrets of the two prophecies with him. It was—"

Dane broke off from his story, and Aurora noticed an unfamiliar look in her father's face, a tension she had never seen before, as if it were becoming painful for him to recall the details. As soon as she noticed this change in her father, the white light emanating from the Lightworkers behind them glowed brighter, extending and flowing out in a stream toward Dane, enveloping him. He took a deep breath, breathing in the light flowing toward him, the pain that had flashed through his face releasing as he continued with his story.

"For a time, Micah remained on Earth in hiding. He created a following, a cult called the Children of Darkness, recruiting followers whose souls had been so depleted by Darkness that they had no free will of their own. They were desperate for a leader, a purpose. Micah fed them with Dark energy like starving animals, promising them riches beyond their wildest dreams but giving only enough for them to always need more, remaining dependent on him for their life force. The cult followers lived with Micah in a deserted mansion in the middle of a deep forest, hidden from life . . . hidden from the living. Unspeakable acts were impelled on his followers in that house, but the most terrifying part of all was Micah's recruitment process for his Children of Darkness.

"Nobody ventured into the forest of their own free will, but several people in the nearby town disappeared under mysterious circumstances. It would happen that a member of the community would suddenly fall ill, a sickness of the mind, signaled at first by a deep depression setting in and dark suicidal thoughts. The victim would start forgetting their past, their family members, their own names and identities. Their ability to communicate would start to degenerate; their senses and mobility would begin to fail them.

"Once immobile, the second stage of the illness brought horrific nightmares which would plague both their waking and sleeping hours. In its final stage, this terrifyingly swift and cruel dementia left its victims lying silent and unmoving in their bed. Their skin would turn pale and their eyes would darken, stripped of their humanity by the horrors which were attacking their minds. All outward signs of life would be gone, except the slow rise and fall of their chest, to signal death had not yet spared them from their inner hell.

"It was said to be some kind of plague. But there was more, witnessed by some though never spoken of from fear that it was just their imagination playing tricks on them. When the final stage of the illness had set in, a dark fog was seen to blow through the town, winding its way along the streets until it reached the house of the latest victim. Nobody ever admitted to seeing more. Maybe that was chance . . . or maybe choice, but the bodies of the victims disappeared, seeming to have disintegrated as all that was left was black dust where the victim had lain.

"One day an elderly member of the town disclosed he had seen two dark figures, one with head bowed appearing to be led by the other from the outskirts of the town toward the woods. It was a matter of hours from his disclosure before that elderly witness could no longer recall what he had seen and began to sink into a deep and unfathomable depression.

"Micah intended these followers to form an army for the Darkness to one day overcome the Light once and for all, but that did not work out how he had planned. These beings were too dependent on Micah for energy and incapable of functioning independently. Realizing they were useless to his purpose, one day Micah disappeared, leaving his followers alone and lost without their leader. Cursed with an insatiable hunger for the Dark energy they no longer had access to since Micah's disappearance, their anger at his desertion of them festered and grew into demonic levels of fury. Desperate for their fix of Dark energy, they broke out of the building one night and disappeared. A cloud of black smoke hung over the deserted mansion from that night, unmoving, and it remains there even to this day."

"What happened to them?" Aurora asked her father.

"They disappeared, never to be seen or heard from again. Their souls were incapable of anything but Darkness, and they had no memory of their human origin. It is believed that they were subsequently captured by the Darkness and imprisoned within the depths of Terhum. But . . . if they were ever to be released into the world, it would be catastrophic; they are evil, depraved mutations with an insatiable hunger for Dark energy. We can only hope that they remain hidden."

"So what happened to Micah?" Aurora asked. "Where did he go?"

"He returned to the Darkness to rule by its side. We have seen this through the eyes of the Universe. He still resides there, his hatred of humankind matched only by the hatred the Darkness itself holds for the Light.

"Micah is still recruiting the Army of Darkness. He hunts the lost and broken souls of those whose humanity is failing, weakened by the frailties of earthly existence, the vulnerabilities created in mind and body by human feelings and emotions. When humanity finally fails and the soul dies, the Darkness is waiting. It takes possession of the soul, and that soul is lost forever, recruited into the Dark Army, to an eternity of suffering and enslavement. Those beings could never be released from their fate, even if the Darkness is ultimately overcome by the Light. The power of the Universe may still be able to save even the most damaged human souls, but the soul itself must still be alive for the power of the Universe to enter and change it. When the last spark of light in the last color of the soul is extinguished, the soul dies and nothing can reignite it. The Rainbow Forest is the master soul of all humankind. But as more and more beings are lost from Earth and more souls are born again into the Darkness, its power becomes weaker. The Darkness is rising. Time is running out on Earth, and we must act fast."

Aurora breathed out heavily, shaking her head in disbelief, struggling to comprehend the magnitude of what her father was telling her.

"There is more," Dane went on, "and as difficult as it might be, you need to hear it. For many years now, children have been disappearing from Earth in strange circumstances, spirited away without trace."

"What?" Aurora gasped, his words instantly triggering the thought of Hazel's sister Sienna, but her attention was pulled back to the story as her father continued.

"Micah's greatest wrath was at the High Council's plans for the children of the Lightworkers, for them—you—to lead us into battle against the Darkness. He thought the idea ridiculous. He was not willing to accept that anybody, especially children, could be more powerful, more valuable to the future of the world than him. We saw the potential in the pure energy of children; unaffected by the negativity, fear, and doubt that the struggles of human life impel on a being once it matures to adulthood. Micah could not see this, and as a result, he developed an intense hatred for children, which only became more intense after he turned to the Darkness.

"There is no doubt that Micah and the Darkness are hunting the children of the Lightworkers. But they are unaware of the shield the Gozzits gifted to the parents who remained on Earth after the Lightworkers returned to Valhandra. Up to now, the shield of the Protectors has been effective enough to hide you all, as it is formed of the pure light of the Universe, which the Darkness is unable to perceive."

"So have any children of Lightworkers been taken?" asked Aurora.

"Not yet," replied Dane. "But—" he paused, a look of concern and worry on his face as if anticipating his daughter's reaction "—we have been able to trace every missing child to some close connection with a Child of the Light. That connection is what the Darkness is perceiving and mistaking for that child being a child of the Light's army."

Aurora went instantly icy cold. "Oh God—Sienna," she whispered feeling dizzy and physically sick as his words hit her like a punch to the stomach. Her memory reeled back to the day before Sienna's disappearance. That morning, she and Hazel had been playing in the park with the little girl . . . Aurora and Hazel were eleven at the time and Sienna, just five years old, was climbing excitedly up the steps of her favorite slide, a yellow curly tube slide. Hazel was watching Sienna as she climbed up, and Aurora waited at the bottom of the slide for her. Aurora loved the little girl, feeling as protective over her as if she were her own sister. In fact, she was so close to Sienna that Hazel joked Sienna would one day run away to live with Aurora, instead of with Hazel and their mother.

Aurora's mind went back to the awful day it had happened. It was the day before Sienna's sixth birthday, in the middle of a beautiful warm summer, and Aurora remembered being intensely happy—excited about Sienna's birthday party that coming weekend, loving the sensation of the sun on her back and feeling like she could rise up and fly if she wanted to. She recalled looking down at her arms at the time and noticing an unusual golden glow around them, though at the time she had passed it off in her mind as just a reflection of the sunlight. Crouching down at the end of the slide, Aurora held out her arms as she always did, waiting to catch Sienna as she hurtled out of the slide squealing with laughter. She remembered her confusion as Sienna's descent down the slide seemed unusually slow and she didn't appear out of the bottom of the tube as quickly as Aurora was expecting her to. When the little girl did finally slide out of the bottom of the tube, she looked petrified. Crying and visibly shaking, she rolled over and dropped off the end of the slide, ran to Hazel and flung her arms tightly around her older sister's waist.

Clinging to Hazel, Sienna refused to let go, sobbing, "I wanna go home," over and over. Hazel and Aurora looked at each other, baffled by the bizarre change in the usually lively and happy little girl.

After trying and failing to encourage her sister onto the swings, Hazel finally conceded.

"Okay, let's go," she said, and with the still sobbing Sienna clinging tightly to her, she turned to leave. Aurora had bent down to pick up the backpack lying by her feet, which held their drinks and snacks, and as she did so, her attention had been drawn to something halfway up inside the tube slide: wisps of black mist snaking around the inner edges of the tube disappeared almost as soon as she saw it. Blinking her eyes, Aurora thought at the time she must have been imagining it, though now it was becoming terrifyingly clear it had been no trick of her mind, and the Darkness had been stalking Sienna.

The next day, on her sixth birthday, Sienna disappeared. Gone missing while playing out in her garden with their new puppy Duke, it was as if she had vanished into thin air. Nobody could understand what had happened, and the police were as baffled as the distraught family as to what had happened to her. The search was exhaustive, going on for weeks and months afterward, before the authorities finally admitted they had not a single lead or clue as to what had happened to Sienna. Heartbreakingly, they closed the file.

It had been an awful time for everyone, and Hazel and her family had never been the same since. Though they all tried their best to go on with their lives, Aurora could feel the heaviness and pain in the family every time she went in the house, and her heart had ached for her best friend and for her own feelings of loss. Aurora recalled her own father at the time sitting with her as she cried for Sienna, his arms tightly around her, the intense warmth from his hands coursing through her body, comforting her. Eventually, over the weeks that followed, it soothed the pain of loss to a calm acceptance, though she never forgot the little girl.

Aurora stood staring at the ground between her and her father, fear and grief rising simultaneously in the pit of her stomach.

"It was because she knew me. It was my . . . my . . . faul—"

Dane put one hand on her shoulder gently but firmly, lifting her chin with the other and looking directly into her eyes. Once again, she felt the familiar warm energy from his hands flowing into her body, as it had done all those years ago.

"Sweetheart, it wasn't your fault," he told her, shaking his head.

"How could it not be?" Aurora asked softly but insistently. "It wouldn't have happened if I hadn't been around her."

"This is so much bigger than 'fault' on anybody's part, my darling. But this you also must know: the missing children are alive. We are sure of it. The Light has seen them through the eyes of the Universe, though it is not yet clear where exactly they are being held."

With a glimmer of hope, Aurora's fear and panic calmed slightly, and she looked up at her father, taking a deep breath to steady her racing mind.

Aurora felt her crystal pulsing strongly in her pocket. The warmth from it seemed to emanate deep into her body, and along with the energy from her father, her strength began to return.

"If she is still alive, I'll find her," she said with firm determination.

"Yes," Dane replied, pulling his daughter into a hug. "We will find them all . . . and bring them home."

CHAPTER 8

Deep in thought, Aurora was unaware of her mother coming in and sitting on the sofa next to her, but Aspen's hand on her knee brought her back briefly from the horror of the second Prophecy to the safety of the cozy, warm den.

"Sweetie, it's late. You need to sleep," Aspen said softly.

"I know," Aurora replied, sighing. "I'm tired, but there's so much that's different now, Mum."

Aspen looked at her daughter intently. "You saw Dad?"

Aurora saw a flash of sadness in her mother's eyes as she asked and instinctively hugged her, with a new awareness of being able to send the heat and energy from her hands directly into her mum's soul.

"Yes," she said as she pulled back from Aspen. "It was . . . strange. But good, really, *really* good to see him again," Aurora sighed, as her mum took both her daughter's hands, smiling but still with the same sadness in her eyes.

"I know how much you miss him, Mum" Aurora said quietly. Aspen's eyes momentarily filled with tears, but she breathed them away as Aurora had seen her do a hundred times before.

"Yes, sweetie, I do, very much. But I knew for a long time that this was coming in our lives. And I know he is always with me, just in a different way than he was. You understand . . . why I couldn't tell you before?"

"Yes," Aurora replied. "You did what you had to do, there was no other choice."

Aspen moved sideways on the sofa, putting her hands on Aurora's shoulders, and looked intently into her daughter's eyes.

"Aaron . . . he isn't there yet, Aurora . . . and I'm worried about him. Dad said he needed to be, that he has to be ready to go with you on Sunday. He mustn't know the truth about Dad before that, though; he has to find his own way first. That's the way Dad said it has to happen . . . or it could jeopardize it all. I've done everything I can, but I can't get through to Aaron, and there's not much time." Her mother shook her head, sighing and biting anxiously on her bottom lip. "Don't go to bed too late, sweetie," her mum pleaded as she got up to leave the den. "Love you."

"I love you too," Aurora smiled. "Oh, and Mum," Aurora interjected before Aspen walked out the room, "don't worry. It'll all be fine, I promise." As her mum blew her a kiss before pulling the door shut after her, Aurora couldn't help wishing she believed her own words.

Grateful to be left alone, Aurora recalled the final part of her conversation with her father, the part that was lodged in her world like a sharp splinter, and as she faced the inevitability of pulling that splinter out, she wondered how she would find the inner strength to do it.

"Aaron is in danger," Dane had explained to Aurora. "We believe there is a grave risk to his safety from the Darkness."

Aurora had panicked at his words. In an instant, that along with her father's disclosure about Sienna's disappearance overwhelmed her. Fear took hold of her mind, and adrenaline surged swiftly through her body. Suddenly her father's image had begun to waver in front of her, flickering back and forth with the image of the study at Dr. Marsden's house, like a TV program breaking up from an unstable connection.

"Stay with me, Aurora. You need this information," Dane had instructed, his voice breaking through the fog that was growing around her and blurring his image. "Any negative emotions will take you back. Concentrate and keep the connection."

He took her hands, and she became aware of bright white light flowing from his body into her, traveling up her arms and calming the rising panic at the thought of her brother being in danger.

Once the space around Aurora had stabilized again, Dane continued. "Aaron was never as strong-minded as you, right from when you were both babies." Putting his hand to Aurora's cheek affectionately, her father smiled down at her with intense love in his eyes.

"You were such an independent little one and always led the way for the two of you. Running before you could walk, you were ahead of yourself and the rest of us in everything you did . . . and you never wanted or needed anyone's help to do any of it. You did everything for Aaron too, which he was happy to let you do!"

Aurora giggled at his description of her.

"I love you both equally. Don't ever doubt that, Aurora," her dad explained. "But I felt like Aaron needed me more . . . and I became too protective over him. I allowed my connection with him to become too intense, and as a result he became dependent on me, instead of developing his own strength. I thought that loving and protecting him would be enough, and I tried to be everything to him, thinking that could protect him from any danger. I didn't see how much that had affected him. I was too close that I couldn't see it . . . until I had to leave and the distance from him gave me the clarity I had been avoiding."

Dane looked intently at Aurora. "Aaron hasn't yet accepted me leaving. That lack of acceptance, him blocking his grief, is creating a barrier in his human soul and weakening it. Only a human soul with all its colors intact and no barriers can be transformed with the new Consciousness. Until the barrier inside him releases, the Gozzits are unable to call him to Valhandra to complete the transformation . . . and he *must* be here. He is part of the Circle of Light, and each and every one of you, the Children of the Light, must be brought to Valhandra to complete the circle. If it is incomplete, we have lost the battle before it has begun."

Her father took a deep breath, taking Aurora's hands in his as the tone of his voice became more serious.

"There's more, Aurora," he continued. "When barriers are created in a soul, the soul becomes susceptible to the Darkness. The High Council of Valhandra have reason to believe this has alerted Micah to Aaron's existence. Micah is aware there is something very different about him, though as yet he has not discovered what that is. If he does, it could put the entire future of the Lightworkers at risk . . . and the future of the world as we know it. It's the first time this has happened with a Child of the Light. We thought the Protectors would be enough to hide you all from Micah and the Darkness until the Gozzits completed the soul transformation. This barrier in Aaron must be broken; until it is, he cannot be reached by the Gozzits. The Darkness is stalking his human soul, and there is not much time for us to act once it begins a soul hunt. And . . . Aurora, please know—this is the *most* important part—Aaron must *not* know about me until his soul has been transformed."

"How is that possible?" Aurora pleaded with her father. "How can he get past this when he still thinks you're—"

"There is always a way," Dane replied, interrupting her, "and it will show up. Trust in that."

He took her hands and squeezed them with his.

"Aaron must release the grief, and then he will be forced to make a choice between the Light and the Darkness. But . . . that choice is Aaron's to make and his alone. None of us can influence it. You've begun your journey, Aurora, and this is his. It will happen . . . and when it does, you cannot help him and you cannot affect his choice. If you go to him while it's happening, if you intervene, if you try to help him through it, you will lock the grief back inside him and it will all be in vain."

Aurora winced as she felt the familiar sharp pain in her chest, which she always picked up on from Aaron's grief, and her eyes filled with tears at the thought of not being able to help her brother.

"What if I can't do it?" she whispered, her voice breaking as she choked back tears.

"You must," Dane insisted, pulling her hands tight to his chest. "You have to be strong with this, Aurora. I know it will be the hardest thing you ever have to do, to stand back and watch it happen. But this is beyond human emotion and there is more at stake . . . *so* much more. All we can hope now is that he makes the right choice."

"I need you there with me, Dad," Aurora pleaded with him.

"I can't be, my darling," Dane replied, shaking his head with tears in his own eyes, "but I have sent somebody to help you both, to be with you when it happens. It's because of me, I know that . . . and I'm so sorry to be putting you through this . . . but—" he hesitated before continuing and a shadow fell across his face "—because of my history with Micah, I cannot be involved with fixing it. Because above all else, Micah must not know that Aaron is *my* son."

Aurora took a deep breath, and as she pushed her tears back down her strength returned; she was determined to help her brother no matter what that took.

"What happened between you and Micah?" she asked.

Dane dropped his head in resignation of the story he knew he had to tell. "Micah and I were close friends from childhood, best friends," he explained, and Aurora detected a nostalgia in her father's voice.

"We were inseparable from an early age. We went to school together, to all the same clubs in and out of school. We did everything together, had that special connection between two friends that you can never quite put words to."

Aurora thought about her own friendship with Hazel and knew exactly the special connection he was talking about.

"He was . . . extraordinary," Dane continued. "There was something about Micah which hinted he was destined for greatness. His physical strength was phenomenal, he was always top of the class with grades, he fought to be the best in all that he did . . . and he was. He was there for me through everything; we were there for each other, and he was like the brother I never had. He was also a born leader, and he brought a lot of his qualities out in me too. I'll always be grateful to him for that, or at least to the memory I have of him, as he was then." Dane put his arm around Aurora's shoulders as he guided her back toward the other Lightworkers standing behind them.

"As it turned out, there was more to our connection than either of us ever imagined," Dane continued, "which we discovered when we were both called to Valhandra to become Lightworkers."

Dane stopped in front of the sea of bright silhouettes before continuing his story. "Micah was immediately noticed by the High Council of Valhandra as the most powerful of all the Lightworkers. They began to prepare him to be our leader, to eventually lead the Light's army into the battle for the New World."

Dane raised his hand toward the space above them. A portal spun open like a kaleidoscope, and Aurora's vision immediately zoomed in to the scene playing out within it.

She saw her father as a young man, standing on a hillside, looking out at the most beautiful scenery she had ever seen. Green hills, fields and trees, brightly colored flowers, and a high waterfall cascading into clear blue waters at its base surrounded him, and he appeared to be looking toward a large white building in the distance. The building seemed to rise not from the ground but from a golden mist that hovered just above the level of the furthest reaches of the visible landscape. It stood at least four stories high, the huge double door at the center flanked with tall pillars on either side of it. Aurora instantly felt a strong connection with the building, as if she had been there before though she had no physical recollection of it.

Her attention now, though, was drawn back to her father. Dressed in white linen robes, his hair was longer than it was now, and as he turned sideways, she could put his age at about the time he and her mother had married. Dane reached out his arm in the vision toward another young man who came into view from the left, walking up to her father and taking his hand before the two embraced in a firm hug, appearing relieved to see each other.

The second man stood slightly taller than her father, broader in the shoulders and with a physical strength that was clear through his robes, identical to those her father was dressed in. His black hair fell in short waves to a square jawline and as he pulled slowly away from Dane's embrace, Aurora caught a defiance set in his face that made her feel slightly uneasy. She saw a look of concern in her father's eyes as the second man put one hand on Dane's shoulder. The two were speaking, inaudibly to her at first, then their voices became louder in her mind as if somebody were turning up the volume on a television.

"Is this really a good idea?" Dane appealed in the familiar calm tone Aurora had always known her father to use, even in the face of conflict. "Why not just go with it, at least for now? Listen to what they are proposing?" Dane clasped the taller man's hand, which was still on his shoulder, earnestly gripping it as if trying to put across some piece of vital information. "It could work, Micah," he insisted. "Maybe we should give it a chance."

Aurora gasped as she heard her father speak the name of the second man, and a shiver ran through her body. As she watched the scene more intently, her vision focused in on the hands of the two men, Dane's right hand clasping Micah's on his own shoulder. Aurora noticed bracelets on the wrists of both men, identical gray metal chain bracelets attached on either side of one singular charm: a side-on figure eight. Aurora recognized it as the bracelet her father had given to Aaron on his thirteenth birthday, which Aaron now wore on his own wrist and never took off. The infinity symbol, Aurora recalled Dad telling Aaron when he gave it to him. It symbolized a connection to everything to remind him that "the future has no limits and anything is possible."

Aurora's attention was pulled back to the scene before her, as Micah's tone changed drastically at Dane's previous words.

"Yanus doesn't know what he's talking about," Micah responded angrily, shaking his hand away. "Are you turning against me now too?"

"No," insisted Dane, looking directly at Micah. "I'm here for you, always. You know that."

"Do I?" accused Micah, and Aurora saw his fist clench at his side as he narrowed his eyes in challenge to her father. "Yanus thinks that he can defeat the Darkness with an army of children! He's deluded, and I intend to prove to all of them that he isn't fit to lead us." As Micah shook his head with a short, derisive laugh, a wisp of dark mist appeared, wrapping around his torso before it swiftly disappeared again.

Dane took a step away from his friend. "Micah, the anger, can't you see what's happening?"

"What's happening is I am finally waking up to their control over *all* of us," Micah reproached, his face clenched with suppressed rage as he shot an accusatory look at Dane. "Isn't it time you did too?"

Micah turned his head toward the white building on the horizon, a look of ominous determination in his dark eyes.

"Come with me, Dane," he said, turning back to her father and speaking with a tone of insistence. "We can do this together. We can finish Yanus and his followers, lead the Lightworkers . . . side by side, just like we've always done. Together, we are stronger than all of them."

Dane dropped his head forward as if in defeat as Micah continued, a threatening edge in his voice that sent a chill deep into Aurora's soul.

"The Lightworkers will all realize who their true leader is destined to be," Micah said. "Once that happens, Yanus will easily be taken down . . . and I will lead the Light Army into battle. A real army built of men, not weak, pathetic children. Soldiers strong enough to go to war . . . and to win."

The scene in front of Aurora faded out, replaced by the surroundings of a large white hall. Marble pillars lined the edges of the hall and a gallery stretched around the upper half of it.

Hundreds of figures lined the edges of the hall and the upper gallery, though all appeared as bright silhouettes, their faces unclear. To the front of the room stretched a wide staircase. Halfway up it stood a tall figure wearing golden robes, three more figures in similar robes standing behind him. The facial features of the robed figures were obscured by bright light, though Aurora could instinctively tell the deep voice which cut through the silence in the room came from the tallest of them at the front.

"The decision of the High Council of Valhandra has been unanimous," the tallest robed figure announced, sweeping his arms out in front of him as a sense of foreboding fell across the room. In the middle of the hall a more sinister vision began to materialize, the identity of this one clear and menacing—it was Micah. Unshaven, with his black hair longer and disheveled, he knelt on the floor, hands and feet bound with glowing golden rope from which he was struggling to pull free. His eyes were filled with hatred, and a dark and sinister energy surrounded him, in stark contrast to the bright white surroundings of the vast hall and the other figures within it.

"You're a fool, Yanus," Micah taunted the golden-robed figure on the stairs, before swinging his gaze around the figures standing at the edges of the hall. "You're all fools to think you can beat the Darkness with an army of *children*."

"Your betrayal has put the quest and future of the Lightworkers at risk," Yanus announced, his voice echoing around the vast hall. "The decision of the High Council is final. You are to be banished to the farthest reaches of the solar system, eternally bound to your fate and never to return."

"You think you have that power, Yanus?" Micah sneered. "I am more powerful than you will ever know or be." His words filled with hatred and fury, a thin wisp of dark smoke suddenly appeared from underneath him and began to swirl around his lower body. "I will defeat you; I will reach every child on Earth before you. I will make sure you never build your pathetic army of babies."

At that moment a figure broke away from the crowd of shining silhouettes at the side of the great hall and Dane rushed forward toward his friend.

"No, Micah! You have a choice, there's still time . . . you can still choose the Light," Dane begged, but a feeling of hopelessness washed over him, as if he knew the choice had already been made.

Micah looked at Dane through narrowed eyes. "We could have done this together; together, we could have been the leaders of the New World."

Something in Micah's words pulled at Dane, dragging him back to a distant memory. The young Dane and Micah sat on a beach, skimming stones over the water and planning the future, as they often did.

"We'll change the world one day," Micah had said with unwavering certainty, "you and me together. We will, I know it."

Dane had chuckled at the time, glancing sideways with admiration at his friend's vision and determination. With another sudden rush, his mind flew back once more to the vast white hall—to Micah kneeling on the floor in front of him, his jaw clenched so rigidly that the veins pulsed menacingly in his neck. Straining against the golden ropes around him, the darkness in Micah's eyes seemed to bore into Dane's soul.

Despite the rising pain in his chest, Dane dropped his head and took a slow step back.

"This is where I belong, Micah," he whispered in a pained voice. "This is the life I choose."

"Then you've made your choice, Dane," Micah replied, his voice thick with hatred, "and I've made mine."

At the front of the room, Yanus raised his hands, and a golden cage began to descend from the ceiling of the hall. As the golden cage descended toward Micah, the onlookers gasped as the thin wisp of dark smoke rising from below him became thicker, darker, swifter. Micah looked to the cage above him, then down in confusion to the dark smoke curling around his lower body.

"What's happening?" he shouted, terror rising in his voice as the dark smoke rose thicker and faster around him. "Dane, help me!" he yelled suddenly in desperation.

Dane moved to run toward Micah, but two other figures broke away from the crowds at the side of the room, grabbing him and holding him back from reaching the twisting, contorted figure of Micah in the middle of the room. As the cage descended from above and the darkness from below, Micah's terror increased. He began to roar in pain, the blood vessels in his neck swelling and pulsing as he threw back his head, his body rigid inside the dark mist curling tighter and tighter around him.

Yanus held his arms out to his sides, creating a shield to protect the Lightworkers standing around him and looked on in horror at the scene unfolding in front of him.

"No," Dane pleaded, still pulling at the figures who held him back as he looked away, unable to bear the sight of his friend writhing in agony. In that instant, the cage suspended above them exploded in the air, the force of the explosion throwing Yanus and the others behind him backward onto the stairs. Thousands of fragments of light dissolved in the air as a stream of dark, flaming lava fell from where the cage had been suspended, cascading over Micah as his screams faded and he disappeared into the darkness.

Aurora turned in stunned silence to her father, whose face held a deep sadness she had never seen in him before, as the portal closed and faded away behind them.

Dane shook his head and sighed deeply at the memory. "In that moment, Micah was lost to the Darkness," Dane explained. "His being survived but changed into a totally different and terrifying form. The Micah I knew died that day."

"But you said earlier that he chose the Darkness," Aurora expressed to her father, confused by what she had seen. "It didn't look like he wanted to go."

"Not every choice is a conscious one," Dane replied.

Finally, Dr. Marsden had guided Aurora gently back from the Lightworkers to the once again solid surroundings of the study. It had taken her a while to readjust, and as warned by Dr. Marsden, she had been unsteady on her feet when she first got up from the chair.

"The changes your soul is experiencing right now are very intense for your physical body to handle," Dr. Marsden advised, taking Aurora's arm gently to steady her as she swayed on her feet, feeling a little like the floor in the room was a trampoline. "Give it time and it will adjust."

As Dr. Marsden led her back out into the hallway to meet her mother, Aurora caught sight of the large clock on the wall by the front door. To her surprise, only five minutes had passed while she was in the study with Dr. Marsden. How could that be? It had felt like hours since she and her mother had arrived at the house.

Shifting her weight on the sofa in the den, Aurora pressed her palms once more to her temples, realizing suddenly how tired she was and how heavy and uncomfortable her body felt. Bed did actually sound like a very good place to be.

She and her father had agreed that Mum need not know the full extent of what Aaron would have to face and the choice he would be forced to make—not yet, anyway. But the reality of it was weighing heavily on Aurora, and it was testing every bit of strength she had not to buckle under it.

"Don't worry, Mum. It will all be fine, I promise." Aurora's own words to her mum earlier played over in her mind as she climbed the stairs for bed, wishing she believed them herself. In that moment, just as Aurora found herself falling back into doubt that she was as strong as her father seemed to believe she was, she suddenly felt the warmth of the crystal in her pocket pulsing as if in silent reassurance that she was.

CHAPTER 9

The next morning at school, Aurora sat in her tutor group feeling a mix of excitement, fear, and restless impatience. School was the last place on earth she wanted to be at that moment. Her impatience for more information was pushing her tolerance for the tediousness of day-to-day life to non-existent. She slumped over her desk, sighing and tapping her pen impatiently on the pile of books in front of her.

She recalled the conversation between her mother and Dr. Marsden before they had left the night before. There was a class or something that Aurora would attend on Sunday evening, and Aspen had arranged to drop Aurora back at Dr. Marsden's for it. Hearing this, Aurora had also recalled the words of the boy Cal's father as they had left Dr. Marsden's: "Cal will see you on Sunday." Unexpectedly, the connection she had felt to Cal also came flooding back to her, and she just as quickly pushed it away, embarrassed by the strength of her feelings.

At that moment, the classroom door opened and Cal walked in, escorted by the Headteacher Mr. Thomas. Aurora's homeroom teacher, Mr. Marsh, looked over to them smiling warmly as Aurora's heart rate became annoyingly fast again.

"Good morning, Joe." Mr. Thomas nodded to Mr. Marsh. "It's Cal's first day with us."

"Cal, welcome. Come on in," encouraged Mr. Marsh.

Cal scanned the room as he walked in, his eyes meeting Aurora's, and she instantly felt the same intense pull and connection she had experienced when she first saw him in the hallway at Dr. Marsden's. He was tall, Aurora concluded, and surprisingly strong-looking for a boy of their age. Cal grinned at her, and his thick, dark, "curtains" style hair fell forward over his eyes, making her suddenly aware that she was staring open-mouthed like a goldfish at him. Clamping her mouth shut and feeling her cheeks burning, she immersed herself in opening the first book she could lay her hands on in an effort to appear busy.

"Take a seat over there, Cal," Aurora heard Mr. Marsh directing, and she held her breath with her heart still pounding, knowing that the only spare seat was the one between herself and Aaron. As Cal sat down, Aurora buried her head in the pages of the book she was holding a little too tightly, and though she was aware of Cal's eyes on her and the pull she felt toward him, she took a deep breath and kept hers firmly on the book in front of her.

Mr. Marsh had spoken with Aurora that morning about the incident with Miss Broach the previous day. Calling her outside the tutor room almost the minute she sat down, he told her he had discussed her detention with Miss Broach and that it had been "postponed for now" pending "behavior review."

Aurora had always liked Mr. Marsh. His casual dress and short black dreadlocks gave him an approachable and gentle air that ensured his popularity with the students, and he was more like a friendly therapist to many of them than a teacher. There was a slight tinge of silver winding through his coarse, perfectly manicured beard, and the sheen of his ebony skin made it difficult to place his age, though Aurora surmised that he might be older than he actually seemed. He had a way of saying things without saying them, Aurora had often noticed, and from this and the smile that tugged only very slightly at the corners of his mouth, she guessed that there would be no behavior review—nor detention.

"How are you . . . after your appointment?" Mr. Marsh asked her, and something in the tone of his voice caught Aurora's attention. It was a note of concern, though when she looked directly at him she noticed a tinge of gold sparkling in the deep brown of his eyes as he spoke.

"I'm okay," Aurora replied hesitantly. Knocked off guard by his apparent knowledge of her "appointment," she struggled to find anything else to add, her mind suddenly preoccupied with wondering exactly how much he might know.

"Thanks," Aurora said eventually, shifting uncomfortably and looking at her feet. "You know . . . for sorting out the detention."

"You're welcome, Aurora," Mr. Marsh replied. And as he turned and put his hand on the handle of the classroom door he added, "You know, very often things—people, situations—are rarely what they may seem to be."

Sitting in the classroom twenty minutes later, Aurora was still wondering about Mr. Marsh's words and exactly what he knew about her, when her eyes were drawn instinctively to the small square window in the upper part of the classroom door. Miss Broach stood outside the door staring in, looking first at Mr. Marsh and then slowly over toward Aaron in the corner of the room. The look on her face was strange, blank and expressionless, but it made Aurora instantly uneasy. She looked at her brother and then back at Mr. Marsh, who it appeared had also seen Miss Broach at the window and seemed to straighten up almost as a soldier to attention. He turned and caught Aurora's eyes, and as he did so a golden beam of light emanated from him reaching out to her, Cal, and Aaron all sitting alongside each other at their desks and wrapping around the three of them like a blanket.

Mr. Marsh was a Protector! Aurora realized it with a sharp intake of breath. Time seemed to stand still and silent around them, and she glanced sideways at Cal, who was also looking wide-eyed at Mr. Marsh, letting Aurora know that he had seen it too.

Aaron, on the other hand, seemed completely oblivious to it all, busy trying to balance his pen upright on the back of his hand. Aurora took a deeper, steadier breath and relaxed into the warmth of the golden blanket enveloping her, smiling back first at Mr. Marsh and then sideways at Cal, whose wide grin and deep brown eyes met hers in a silent acknowledgement that they shared a secret. Looking back toward the classroom door Aurora saw Miss Broach had gone, though she swore she saw a dark shadow remaining for a second outside the glass window before it dissipated in the air.

Blinking hard, Aurora's senses drifted back to reality, and the low hum of chatter rose up again in the classroom around her. She scanned her eyes quickly around the other students in the class. Had any of them also seen the golden light? It appeared not; some were absorbed in arranging books and stationery, while most were engaged in their phones or chatting. Aurora's attention rested on Hazel, sitting on the other side of her, who was rubbing her eyes and yawning.

"Late night, Hazel?" Mr. Marsh asked as he passed by her, delivering the school newsletters around the class.

"Yeah, sir, something like that," replied Hazel, looking to the floor and sighing.

Sat in the canteen at lunchtime, Aurora picked unenthusiastically at her sandwich, only half listening to Hazel who chattered away beside her. Something about the tone of her friend's voice was niggling at Aurora, though, and she pushed her lunch away, forcing her concentration back to Hazel and what she was saying.

". . . if I could sleep, I'm sure it would get better," Hazel was saying, "but as soon as I go to sleep the dreams start. They're getting worse, and I don't even want to go to sleep any more. I'm so tired."

Aurora looked at Hazel, suddenly realizing how drained and worried she looked.

"Worse in what way?" Aurora asked gently.

"Mainly about Sienna," Hazel sighed, "but they're darker now, more frightening. It's like I'm trying to get to her, but she's being pulled away from me by this black shadowlike figure, and I can't reach her. Other times I see bits of my own body disappearing, leaving holes where they used to be. It's awful, and it feels so real." Hazel dropped her head onto her arms, which were folded on the table in front of her.

Aurora fought the instant urge to tell Hazel what she knew about Sienna. Thinking more on it, she doubted Hazel would believe her; she would probably think she was totally nuts, and anyway, she decided, it was likely just to upset Hazel more in that moment. Instead, Aurora gently put her hand on Hazel's arm, unable to find words that would help but aware of just how deeply she cared about her best friend.

"Whoa!" Hazel exclaimed as a sudden rush of sensation shot up her arm from where Aurora rested her hand, surging through her whole body. Hazel's tiredness suddenly disappeared, replaced by an intense alertness, a buzzing throughout her body like she'd been plugged into an electric socket or downed an energy drink in one gulp. Hazel stared at Aurora and pulled her arm away abruptly, a look of uncertainty, bordering on fear, in her face.

"What did you do? What the hell was that?" Hazel asked accusingly, pulling farther away, her chair scraping across the floor as she did so, in an apparent panic to put some distance between the two of them.

"I . . . I'm not sure," muttered Aurora, and shocked at the intensity of the energy that had rushed from her into Hazel's arm, she clamped her hands together, shoving them between her knees. Seeing Cal and Aaron heading over to their table with their lunch trays, Aurora got up hurriedly and rushed out of the canteen.

Sitting on the low brick wall at the far end of the cloisters, Aurora stared up into the sky, watching the clouds skate by and envying them their weightless freedom, as right now her whole body felt like lead. She felt trapped here in a reality from which she couldn't escape, with time that wasn't moving fast enough and with the sense now more than ever before that she was too different, too weird, and didn't belong here in this world. Even her best friend was scared of her, and there was nobody she could talk to about what was happening to her. Tears pricked at her eyes, and as one fell down her cheek she brushed it away, frustrated at feeling so weak and lost. Hearing footsteps coming up behind her, she turned her head to see Cal walking toward her.

Cal sat down on the brick wall beside Aurora, swinging his legs over and leaning forward to rest his elbows on his knees. Aurora noticed how strong his arms were. He bowed his head and looked sideways at her, blinking at the sun in his eyes, his black, wavy hair falling forward over his forehead. Aware she was holding her breath and not wanting him to know how he was affecting her, Aurora breathed out a little too quickly, making it sound like she was cross at the intrusion, and Cal looked at the ground.

"Sorry," he said. "I wanted to check you were okay, but I can go."

Aurora could see his cheeks flushing slightly, an uncertain look on his face, and she shook her head. "No, don't go. Thanks for checking on me," she responded quickly and looked at her feet, unsure what was happening in the pit of her stomach from the way he had looked at her.

"Things are moving pretty fast, aren't they?" Cal asked, looking intently at his own feet.

"I don't know what to think," Aurora replied, her voice breaking slightly, "about any of it. I'm not sure I know what's real and what's not anymore."

"Yeah, I know what you mean. Did you meet them?" Cal asked, hesitating slightly. "You know, in the Forest?"

"Yes," Aurora responded, relieved at the prospect of talking with somebody about it but still doubting her sanity; it all sounded too crazy even to try to talk about it.

Cal turned his body slightly so he was facing her. "The appointment with Donna Marsden, what happened when you were there?"

Aurora sighed. "God, I'm not even sure I can put it into words." She looked up into the sky, her hands clasped tightly in her lap. "She took my hands—" Aurora put out her own hands and then re-clasped them in her lap "—and then I was . . . somewhere else. I can't even describe it . . ." She paused, recalling the Lightworkers and seeing her father again. "There was more," she continued, "more than, you know, in the Forest. I saw my . . ." her voice trailed off, breaking as she remembered being back in her dad's arms.

"Aaron was telling me about your dad just now," Cal said and hesitated, biting his lower lip as if uncertain whether to continue. Aurora sensed he hadn't finished, and so remained silent.

"Last year . . . the twenty-first of June," Cal went on, staring straight ahead of him, "my mum left. No warning. One day she was there and the next, gone." Aurora felt a shiver run through her body, and she turned to Cal, listening more intently now as he continued.

"Two men came to the house and told Dad she was missing. It was weird, I know I should have been upset, but I wasn't. I didn't believe she was dead right from the start. Not that they actually said that; they just implied it. She was always a bit, well, different to other mums. She worked . . . a lot. She was away a lot too. Abroad and helping people, Dad said, though he would never say any more than that. I gave up asking in the end."

Cal paused, looking down at the ground now with sadness in his eyes. "I missed her. I wasn't used to her being around as much as the other kids' mums, but it was still tough. My dad, he's always been great, and when Mum was home it was like being a normal family. But I never felt normal, and that wasn't just because Mum wasn't around much. It was this weird sense of something else, like I was waiting for something, like we were all waiting for something, kind of in limbo." Cal took a deep breath before he went on.

"When she left it was like time stood still for a while. And I knew there was something Dad wasn't telling me. When I was at Donna's, the place I went to, wherever it was . . . she was there, Mum was there. Is that what . . . did that happen with . . ."

"Yes." Aurora breathed the word out with relief. "My dad was there." Tears welled up in her eyes, more from happiness now because Cal knew and he understood. In that second, Aurora had a sudden, intense urge to turn and hug him, though she pushed the thought away quickly, embarrassed and slightly worried that the connection they seemed to share meant he might actually be able to read her mind too.

"Thank you for telling me." Aurora smiled at Cal, and he grinned back at her. Trying to ignore the flip her stomach did when he looked at her, she went on talking. "It's just a relief, I guess, that somebody else knows. So we aren't . . . you know . . . going mad?"

Cal laughed out loud. "Well, we might be! Can you imagine trying to explain this to the others in class?"

Aurora giggled and looked up to the sky, shaking her head. "They would think we were going insane, wouldn't they!" She sighed, her mind going back to Hazel's reaction to her in the canteen earlier. "Even my best friend is scared of me." She dropped her head. "I don't want to lose her."

"You won't," Cal said reassuringly, "and you've got me now too." He smiled at Aurora and she smiled back, feeling more at ease with him now despite the acrobatics her stomach did at his smile.

"So, what about Aaron?" he asked. "It seems weird he wasn't there at Dr. Marsden's. Like, especially with you guys being twins. I didn't say anything to him, by the way," he went on quickly. "Just in case, you know . . ."

"Mmmm, Aaron," Aurora said hesitantly. "He—well, he should be going on Sunday too. But there's a problem. He's blocking receiving the call from the Gozzits. He's still too caught up in grief about Dad." She sighed heavily. "I'm not sure I understand totally."

"Can't you just tell him you saw your dad?" Cal questioned, and Aurora shook her head in resignation.

"I wish it was that easy, but he needs to release the grief first. Dad said it has to happen that way; he has to receive the calling from the Gozzits before he finds out Dad is still alive. His soul has to have been changed first, and that can't happen until he releases the grief. If it happens the other way round and his soul is still human, then it could expose him to the Darkness. Once his soul has been changed, they can't access his thoughts anymore." Aurora paused, frowning. "I think that's it, anyway."

"Wow, that's pretty intense." Cal sighed. "So how did he deal with your dad leaving?"

"He didn't. He wouldn't ever talk about it," Aurora answered sadly. "When Mum told us, Aaron got up and just walked away. He never cried—not that Mum or I know, anyway. He just buried himself in his model building, which is what he used to do with Dad. It's almost like nothing happened. But, you know, the twin thing. I can feel him suffering, Cal." Aurora pushed her fist into her chest. "Right here. It's like a pain twisting through my chest, in my throat, down my arms, and now . . ." Aurora paused, remembering her father's words. "Well, what if he can't release the grief, can't be changed in time for Sunday? I don't know what to do."

"You know," Cal said, looking thoughtful, "I think I'm meant to help with Aaron."

"Really?" Aurora asked, her eyes widening with a sudden feeling of hope.

"I've got a really strong feeling about it," Cal went on. "I'm just not sure yet what I have to do."

Aurora stared at him as everything began to slot into place in her mind. She remembered the vision she had had of Cal with her father two nights previously. She heard again in her mind her father's words as he told her what Aaron would have to go through: *I have sent somebody to help you both, to be with you when it happens.*

"Yes," Aurora said, smiling at Cal, "I think you're right," and instantly she felt the piece of crystal in her blazer pocket begin to pulse. Reaching instinctively into the pocket, she pulled the crystal out in her hand, opening her palm as she held it sideways toward Cal. He smiled and reached into his own pocket, bringing out an identical piece of crystal and holding it out toward Aurora's open palm. As they held the crystals down in the space between them, the gemstones began to glow, the light from them stretching out and connecting with the other as they began to shudder and shake.

"Can I try something with them?" Cal asked, holding his other hand out toward Aurora, and she nodded.

Cal took her crystal and held the two of them close to each other. Instantly they flew toward each other. Snapping together like magnets, they glowed brighter, hovering in the air just in front of them. Aurora gasped. They were a perfect fit, as if they had been one crystal cut into two. As the bright glow from the crystals enveloped the two of them, Aurora felt a connection to Cal she had never experienced before and couldn't even begin to put into words, even to herself.

"There must be others, Cal. It isn't just us, is it?" Aurora could hear her mind communicating with Cal instinctively now, though her mouth wasn't moving and no sound came from it.

"My dad said more will be there on Sunday," Cal answered her, and as she looked sideways at him, she could see by his unmoving mouth that answer came from his mind too.

"Are you nervous?" Aurora asked.

"A bit," Cal responded. "I don't know whether I feel like a freak or a superhero right now."

Aurora giggled, and as they sat together communicating telepathically, the rest of the world seemed suddenly irrelevant to the unknown adventure that lay ahead of them.

They were also unaware of Joe Marsh, who stood nearby with his hands raised in their direction, a golden bubble shining out from his palms and surrounding them. In a direct line of sight behind Joe was the science lab, where Miss Broach stood at the window, staring out toward the cloisters where Cal and Aurora were sitting.

As the school bell for the end of lunch rang, interrupting the peace around them, Aurora and Cal grabbed their crystals out of the air, the white light dimming as quickly as it had appeared as they shoved them back in their blazer pockets.

Cal jumped up and held his phone out to Aurora.

"Let's swap numbers. Then . . . well, you know. If you want to talk over the weekend . . . about Aaron, or anything really—"

"Yes, okay." Aurora nodded with a smile as they quickly exchanged numbers.

As she and Cal started back toward the science block, Joe Marsh stepped out from behind one of the pillars.

"Oh!" said Aurora in surprise. "I didn't see you there, sir."

"Just having a lunchtime walk," he replied with a smile.

Aaron sauntered out of the canteen, fist-bumping Cal as he joined them. Walking on to their first afternoon class, Aurora felt ready to face whatever was to come with refreshed strength and determination.

At the science lab window, Miss Broach stood unmoving, still staring out as Aurora, Aaron, and Cal entered the science block talking and laughing together. Eyes blank in her expressionless face, a dark mist appeared from below her feet, curling around her body as she watched them. The ominous dark mist swirled up and around to the front of her body, and a black hole opened in her chest. As the swirling darkness flowed into her body, her eyes flamed briefly before the hole in her chest spiraled shut and her body returned to its normal state. As it did, the classroom door behind her swung open and in flowed a stream of chattering students—including Aurora, Aaron, and Cal—for the afternoon biology lesson.

CHAPTER 10

Aurora settled into her seat in the science lab, Cal to her right and Aaron on the other side of Cal. Noticing that there was an empty seat to her left where Hazel would normally sit, Aurora glanced around the classroom looking for her. She noticed with a pang of sadness that Hazel had sat on the other side of the room next to Jess, one of the other girls in the class, clearly refusing to look up when Aurora tried to catch her eye as the class began. Cal nudged Aurora, smiling sympathetically, and she shrugged, busying herself by digging books out of her backpack.

"Right, books open and ready to copy!" shrieked Miss Broach from the front of the classroom, grabbing her whiteboard pen. Aurora winced, wondering if it was her sense of hearing becoming more acute or Miss Broach becoming more shrill. Looking closely at the teacher, Aurora determined there was something different about her today but couldn't quite make out what it was. She seemed agitated, more so than usual, and distracted. Pushing it to the back of her mind as an insignificant detail, Aurora opened her workbook and began to copy out the processes and formulas as instructed, which Miss Broach was frantically scribbling across the board at the front of the classroom.

A low hum of whispering voices began around the room, at the same time as Aurora realized that, having copied down half a whiteboard full of formulas, Miss Broach had begun to repeat the same formulas again that she had started with at the top of the board. Completely engrossed in what she was doing, Miss Broach had not looked up or back at the class once since she had started writing. As Aurora looked more closely it appeared that the teacher's pen was moving faster and faster, flying across the board at a bizarrely unnatural pace. Aurora looked around the class to see if anyone else had noticed. Tom, who was sat just in front of Miss Broach, spoke up.

"Er, excuse me, Miss, but you've already written those ones," he pointed out tentatively.

Miss Broach stopped abruptly, turning slowly round to face Tom, and as she did so, Aurora took a sharp breath in, putting her hand out to nudge Cal next to her as a swirl of black smoke snaked around the teacher's body. Tom appeared not to have noticed anything unusual, but as silence fell across the classroom, the other students in the class all stopped writing to watch the exchange. A familiar redness began to rise on Miss Broach's scrawny neck, and she hauled in a long deep breath leaning over the desk toward Tom. He moved slightly backward with a look of trepidation, his chair legs scraping along the floor as he did so.

"What . . . did . . . you . . . say?" Miss Broach said slowly and purposefully, as sudden and intense anger rose in her face. Unexpectedly, it was a deep, almost male-sounding voice that emanated from her mouth, so different from her usual shrill tone that Aurora gasped out loud, and the events that followed seemed to progress as if in slow motion.

The classroom door suddenly swung open, and Mr. Marsh rushed in, slamming the door shut behind him. Sweeping his right arm out from one side of the room to the other, the bright golden light from his hands enveloped the students.

Each one froze in their position like somebody had pressed a pause button, with the exception of Aurora and Cal, who both jumped out of their seats and backed up to the far wall of the classroom.

Miss Broach instantly straightened up, turning swiftly toward Mr. Marsh. Her face contorted with fury, and a black mist appeared from below her, circling swiftly up and around her body.

Aurora and Cal instinctively reached in their blazer pockets for their crystals which had begun to pulse and vibrate.

"No!" shouted Mr. Marsh telepathically to them, and he flung his left arm out toward them, sweeping the golden light round in a semi-circle over their arms and torsos and pinning them against the wall at the back of the classroom, their arms frozen in their pockets before they could pull out their crystals. Miss Broach turned her head sharply toward Aurora and Cal with narrowed eyes, but quickly her attention moved across to Aaron who was frozen along with the rest of the class. Her eyes glowed fire red as she focused in on him, reaching out her skinny arm in Aaron's direction. The dark mist snaked along her arm, around her forefinger pointed toward Aaron, and out through the air, moving rapidly toward him. Aurora tried to cry out but no sound would come from her mouth. Mr. Marsh thrust out his right arm toward Miss Broach and the bright beam of golden light followed its direction, whipping against her chest and knocking her backward against the wall between the classroom windows.

Miss Broach hit the wall with a sickening thud before falling to the floor. Aurora and Cal looked on in horror as her body slowly rose up again and stopped in midair, suspended as if it were a puppet on strings.

"You'll regret that." The deep voice emanated from Miss Broach's mouth. "They know what they've stolen from me, and you will all pay for it." Mr. Marsh stood firm, his eyes fixed on her as her body began to twist from side to side as if possessed.

"You don't have to choose this, Marta," Mr. Marsh said to her, shaking his head, and Aurora was surprised to hear his voice breaking slightly with emotion. "There is another way."

"It's too late." The ominous voice came again from the body of Miss Broach. "The choice is made."

Her body contorted gruesomely in the air, and dark smoke appeared out of the floor beneath it, flowing up thick and fast as it curled and twisted around her body, a black hole spinning open in her chest as she threw back her head screaming in pain. Mr. Marsh moved closer to her one step at a time, the golden beam of light from his hands now expanding like a wide shield between him and the class and her body writhing in the air in front of them.

As Mr. Marsh edged closer to her and the golden shield grew wider, the ceiling above her dissolved. A stream of thick black liquid lava poured from it like a waterfall over Miss Broach's body . . . and she disappeared from view into the darkness.

As the black mist slowly began to clear, Mr. Marsh dropped his hands, letting out a heavy breath as he looked back at Aurora and Cal, still pinned against the back wall of the classroom, eyes wide with shock at the scene they had just witnessed.

"Are you okay?" Mr. Marsh asked, as their arms released and they found themselves once again able to move their bodies freely.

"I'm sorry for doing that to you," he said apologetically as he walked quickly over to them, putting one hand on Cal's shoulder and the other on Aurora's arm. "I know you were trying to help.

But I couldn't risk her seeing the crystals; there's too much at stake for your identities to be discovered yet."

"Is she . . ." Cal began, still in shock as he stared back at the space where Miss Broach had disappeared.

"Taken, by the Darkness," Mr. Marsh replied. "I have seen this coming for some time now; I've been watching her closely, and it became more and more apparent her humanity was failing fast."

"There's been an incident," he continued. "When I spoke with her about your detention, Aurora, she—" Mr. Marsh stopped suddenly mid-sentence and shook his head he looked toward Aaron, still frozen at his desk along with the rest of the class. "Never mind that now. She was homing in on Aaron because the Darkness growing inside her picked up on the grief in his soul. That is how the Darkness will attach to another being."

Mr. Marsh put his other hand on Aurora's arm, looking directly into her eyes, and her heart sank with his next words: "The Darkness is hunting him, Aurora—time is short."

CHAPTER 11

A heavy sense of anticipation hung in the dimness of the vast circular chamber. Black stone columns edged the room, stretching up into tall arches and joined at their highest point in a terrifying mass of demonic faces carved into the ceiling. Flames emanated from a deep pit in the center of the room, the black smoke from them curling upward in the shape of demonic hands, clawing and grasping at the air as if in starving desperation. Sinister figures stood in the shadows around the edges of the chamber, giving it the appearance of a dark and menacing arena. At one end of the chamber was a tall throne-like structure; black and ornately carved, it stretched upward disappearing into a dark mist that hung ominously above it.

It was unclear to the physical eye what it was that occupied this throne. A form rather than a being, it appeared as if it were a black hole, a portal of dark emptiness but with a presence that held the occupants of the room to it as subjects, bound to their leader by invisible chains. By the side of the throne stood a figure wearing dark hooded robes—human in form and standing with its head bowed, hands clasped to its front.

As the sinister audience watched and waited in the darkness, the deathly silence in the room was infiltrated by the distant sound of blood-curdling screams, growing louder and seemingly closer. The demonic hands stretching from the central fire pit began clawing faster and harder at the air above them, and as they reached a frenzy of activity, the swirling smoke above them began to part. Human faces, warped and contorted with pain, appeared one by one in the darkness. As if pulled from the flames by some invisible force, their broken bodies levitated forward from the seething pit of hands, before dropping from the air one by one onto the cold stone floor around it. A thin dark steam of mist flowed out from beneath the throne at the head of the chamber, ominously snaking its way toward them and wrapping around their bodies as they began to change.

Stretching and morphing into tall, thin, shadowy figures, their facial features melted away to blackness as they stood before their leader, unearthly hybrid forms somewhere between human and demon. Evil yellow eyes were just visible beneath the hoods of their long black robes.

The cloaked figure to the side of the Darkness slowly lifted its head, and the black menacing eyes of Micah surveyed the newest recruits of the Dark Army. As Micah moved forward to greet the demon forms congregated before him, the shadowy figure of the Darkness on the throne behind him slowly melted away into the ground and disappeared.

In another room near to the chamber, a cloud of dark smoke rose up from the floor as the Darkness emerged, and standing silently in the shadows, it waited, a sense of anticipation filling the room as the molecules in the air began to swirl and pulse. As they spun faster and faster, a hole began to open, a whirling black tunnel beyond it spiraling out to another time and place. A sudden explosion emanated from the spinning vortex as a solid form was expelled from its depths out into the room, falling to the floor in a mass of black smoke with a nauseating thud.

The smoke cleared to reveal a body lying on the floor, appearing at first broken and lifeless. The dark figure in the room held out one long thin limb toward the being on the floor, sending black mist snaking out from it, winding its way swiftly through the air toward the being collapsed on the ground. As the black mist entered the body, its torso arched, slowly at first, then lurching upward as it heaved in a rasping breath, as if suddenly coming to life.

Rising slowly to its knees, the muscles in its arms and shoulders pulsated, sallow gray skin stretching around them as the body began to take on a tall and thin human form. As the being reached a standing position, it slowly raised its head. Empty black eyes met the two sinister yellow ones that had appeared within the shadowy figure before it, and the Darkness spoke in a low, menacing tone.

"Welcome, Marta Broach," it drawled. "I have been waiting for your arrival."

CHAPTER 12

As Aurora walked home from school with Aaron, she reflected on the day: Hazel's reaction to her at lunch, her talk with Cal in the Cloisters, Miss Broach's disappearance . . . but most of all the dark warning Mr. Marsh had delivered about her brother. Hazel had avoided Aurora for the rest of the day, continuing to sit next to Jess in all of the afternoon lessons, and had rushed out ahead of Aurora when the end of school bell rang.

It was the first time Aurora had felt any distance between her and her best friend. Even on the few occasions they had come anywhere close to arguing over the years, it had always ended in them collapsing into fits of giggles; such close friends, they were unable even to argue seriously with each other. It made Aurora sad, but she knew there was nothing more she could do with the situation right now. More pressing things were on her mind—mainly Aaron, the second visit to Dr. Marsden's on Sunday, and exactly how she and Cal were going to get Aaron there too. Aurora sighed, trusting (because she had to) that her friendship with Hazel was strong enough to withstand this separation . . . for now.

"You okay, sis?" Aaron commented as they turned the corner into their road, and Aurora realized she had been silently miles away in thought for their entire journey home.

Aaron, like the rest of the class, had no recollection of the incident with Miss Broach in the biology lab earlier. Upon returning the students to normal, Mr. Marsh had continued the lesson, explaining that Miss Broach had a migraine and had gone home to rest.

"Yeah, just got some stuff on my mind, I guess," Aurora replied, smiling at her brother. "Aaron?" she asked thoughtfully, wanting to test the water with her brother following Mr. Marsh's warning. "Do you ever wonder, well, think that maybe there's something else to life? You know, more than we can actually see around us?"

"Jeez, sis, that's a bit deep for Friday afternoon, isn't it?" Aaron mocked, but as Aurora turned to him, raising her eyebrows and about to elbow him in the ribs, she caught a strange look on his face as he stared straight ahead chewing at his bottom lip—one of the few traits he shared with their mum and which he only did when he was deep in thought about something.

Aurora's heart tightened, a lump catching in her throat as she felt an intense urge to grab her brother's arm and tell him Dad was alive, that she had seen him, spoken to him, that Aaron could too if he could only open himself up past his grief. But she knew that she couldn't tell him yet, and she sighed deeply, wondering how on earth (or beyond it) that was going to change.

Since they were very young, Aaron's laid-back attitude to life had both frustrated Aurora and made her laugh. Nothing ever seemed to faze him or concern him much. He sauntered through his days, usually with his headphones in, shirt hanging out, and hands stuffed in his pockets. He never seemed to take anything seriously, except his model building, and he had always been able to make people laugh easier than anybody else Aurora knew—though this would often get him into trouble, especially with certain teachers at school. He was annoyingly clever too, with an amazing memory for facts and figures, and his ability of recall was beyond anyone else in the class, without his ever having to put much effort in.

The change in Aaron since Dad left had been noticeable to everyone, though more so to Aurora because of how close they were. Despite his inappropriate humor and relaxed attitude on the outside, she knew better than anyone else how kind, caring, and thoughtful her brother was. Since Dad had gone, underneath that seemingly chilled-out exterior, she could feel his pain as intensely as if it were her own.

Aaron reached the front door of their house first, and fiddling with his key in the lock, he stopped unexpectedly before opening it, turning to Aurora with the same look on his face she had seen as they were walking.

"Those weird turns you've been having, sis," he began, before pausing and looking awkwardly at the ground. "Is that doctor you saw helping with it?"

"Yes." Aurora hesitated before continuing, working out in her mind what to say. "She's . . . helping me to understand why it's happening. Why do you ask?"

"No reason," Aaron replied, shrugging as he turned, shoved open the front door, and wandered in, though giving Aurora the sense there was more behind his question than he was prepared to say.

"In here," Aspen called out from the kitchen as the twins clattered into the house, dropping their backpacks on the hallway floor.

Aaron yelled his usual greeting, "What is there to eat, Mum? I'm starving," promptly disappearing into the kitchen in search of food.

Aurora was left standing aimlessly in the hallway, still wondering what exactly had been going through her brother's mind for him to ask her about Dr. Marsden. Had he seen anything? Did he know anything? What would it take for him to find his way . . . and more importantly, what did Aurora need to do about it? As she headed to her room to change out of her school uniform, she wondered for the hundredth time how that was going to be achieved before Sunday. Dropping her phone on her bed, she opened her wardrobe, finally deciding that she would message Cal about the "Aaron situation" later, as he had suggested.

Aaron was even quieter than normal at dinner that evening, as if he were zoning out, and Aurora sensed his distraction. She was worried. He felt distant to her, like the invisible thread that existed between them as twins was stretching. At one point, while they were clearing away the dinner dishes, she asked if he was okay, only to be met with his usual grunt of "yeah" before he turned away and busied himself with loading the dishwasher, in obvious dismissal of her attempt to engage him in conversation. Aspen had gone for a walk after dinner, saying she needed some fresh air. Aaron disappeared up to his room with his monthly model-building magazine which had arrived that day, while Aurora retreated to the den with her phone.

She sat indecisively typing, deleting and retyping messages to Cal for half an hour. Unsure of what she wanted to say, and equally unsure of what she needed to do, she eventually threw the phone down on the sofa beside her and put her head in her hands, groaning out loud in frustration.

"Help!" she called out in her mind, to whom she wasn't sure. A few moments later her phone began buzzing beside her, and the caller notification flashed up on the screen: "Cal."

"Hey," Aurora said as she answered the phone. "I was just thinking about you," she blurted out before she could stop herself, instantly cringing for not thinking before she opened her mouth. Cal laughed on the other end of the call.

"Yeah, erm, well . . . me too," he said slightly awkwardly and paused before he went on. "Though I can't get that stuff with Miss Broach earlier out of my head." Aurora put aside her embarrassment at the spontaneous admission and agreed.

"I know," she sighed. "I mean, I didn't like her, but I can't help thinking she didn't deserve that."

"Mmmm, it looked pretty rough, didn't it?" Cal responded. "Look, I was talking to Dad about Aaron. He asked if you both wanted to come over to our stables tomorrow and meet the horses. Have you ridden before?"

"Yes, but not for a couple of years," Aurora said, remembering previous summers when Dad had taken her and Aaron to the local stables. They had gone out riding through the forest, and she recalled how much she had enjoyed it. "Sounds great," she continued hesitantly, "but . . . shouldn't we be focusing on helping Aaron?"

"Well," Cal responded, "I find I can think better when I'm out riding. Plus, horses are good therapy, and maybe if we spend some time with Aaron together, we might get some idea on how to deal with it? Dad will ride out with us, but he said he'll stay back and not get in our way."

"Okay then," Aurora agreed, thinking anything was worth a shot at that point, and it wasn't like she had any better ideas. "I'll talk to Mum when she gets back and let you know."

CHAPTER 13

urora watched Cal's dad, Mack, as he saddled up the four horses at their stables the next day. A tall, stocky man with wide, obviously strong shoulders and the same dark, wavy hair as Cal, he wore a blue checked shirt, jeans, and black riding boots that looked well-worn. He was very different in looks from their dad, whose slim, athletic figure had hidden the strength of which the twins knew he was capable, having witnessed it on a few occasions in their life. Cal helped his dad, laughing and joking together as they worked, and Aurora caught Aaron watching the two of them with a distant look in his eyes, one hand resting upon his horse's muzzle. She felt a pang of sadness for him, for the bond she knew he missed so much with their own dad. Aaron turned back to stare into the eyes of his horse, Spirit, a serenely elegant-looking gelding with a shining gold coat, white mane and tail; Palomino, as Mack had explained to them, and with the calmest temperament he had ever known in a horse. He was great with less experienced riders.

Mack checked the girth on Aurora's horse, a gray Andalusian mare named Pepper. Helping Aurora up on the mounting block, he guided her foot into the stirrup before she jumped up with a small spring, swinging her right leg over the back of the horse and lowering herself gently down onto the saddle with ease.

"Just like a pro," Mack commented with a wide grin, and Aurora smiled back, quietly pleased with herself as she slipped her right boot into the second stirrup and adjusted herself comfortably in the saddle.

Enjoying her vantage point and excited to get going on their ride, Aurora watched Mack as he helped Aaron up onto Spirit, with a little more awkward fumbling than her own smooth mount. As Aaron finally settled himself, he turned to Aurora, sticking his tongue out at his sister as she raised her chin and grinned smugly at him. Cal trotted up beside Aurora on his horse, Autumn, a gorgeous, deep-brown-colored chestnut gelding with mesmerizing eyes and a wide white blaze on its face.

"Ready?" he asked her, and she turned to look at him, feeling her heart beating a little bit faster suddenly, though knowing it was less to do with the excitement of getting out on the horses and more to do with Cal's knee resting gently against hers as he had pulled up beside her on Autumn.

As her eyes met Cal's, she saw an intense bright white flash. Suddenly the stables around her disappeared and the two of them were in a pale-colored room. The surroundings were blurred, but it was definitely Cal's face in front of her, though he looked a few years older. There was a different energy between them, a different feeling from the surroundings and the situation, and Aurora couldn't make out what it was . . . or where they were. Before she could gain any more perspective of the vision, there was another bright white flash and they were back in the stables again, with Cal sitting to the side of her on Autumn, a concerned look in his eyes.

"Are you okay?" he asked. "You looked like you were going to pass out for a minute."

Aurora shook her head in an attempt to stabilize her vision, closing her eyes briefly. "Yes . . . I'm okay . . . fine," she said, frantically searching for an excuse. "Maybe I just got up on Pepper too quick."

"Okay," Cal said gently. "Well, take it easy, and let me know if you need to stop."

Aurora smiled at him, still wondering what the heck had just happened, but took a deep breath and looked ahead to the bright sunshine outside the stables.

Mack quickly checked the girth on his own horse—a strong and majestic Palomino stallion named Dante with unusual markings on his face—before mounting it swiftly and expertly. Aurora imagined Dante's markings as a torch with a separate flame above it, but Mack had proudly explained it was termed a "star and strip," unusual and only called so when the "star" was a lot wider than the separate "strip" below it.

As instructed by Mack, Aurora lightly squeezed Pepper's wide body with both of her legs to ask her to step forward. As they set off with Mack and Cal leading the way out toward the heathland, Aurora relaxed, letting her body sway comfortably along with the rocking movement of Pepper's rib cage, her arms moving in a natural rhythm with the mare's head as it bobbed up and down. She felt instantly as one with this amazing animal and reached one hand forward to stroke the soft mane, smiling as Pepper gave a gentle snort in response.

Rising up and down easily with the motion of the trot, Aurora breathed in the cool late morning air as they reached the open heathland. Putting the strange vision she'd had inside the stables to the back of her mind, she felt the stress of the past couple of days melting away as they rode. *This was a really good idea*, she thought, and she watched impressed as Cal cantered off in front of them, after a distance turning Autumn swiftly to trot back toward them with the effortless grace of a horse and rider totally in communion with each other. Aurora thought again, as she had before, how much older than them Cal seemed . . . and stronger. She shook her head, feeling embarrassed by her thoughts and brushed them out of her mind quickly before she lost her concentration to them.

The weather was set to be clear that day; Mack said he had checked again just before they arrived. Mum had dropped them both off and was going for a coffee with a couple of friends, agreeing with Mack that he would drop the twins home later in the day when they were done. Aurora had noticed a slight hesitation in their mum as she said goodbye to Aaron on the path leading from Cal's house to the stables. She had also noticed the golden bubble of protection connecting her to Aaron for longer than usual and stretching between them even as she walked away with Mack, back toward her car. Aurora had heard Mack reassuring her mum that they would be fine, before their voices became low and inaudible, and Aurora had wondered if they were discussing the situation with Aaron between them. Putting all that to the back of her mind, Aurora brought her concentration back to the moment and Mack, who was guiding them through bringing their horses to a rising trot.

As they picked up the pace of the ride, Aurora relaxed into it, her hair whipping behind her in the wind and feeling totally at peace and connected to everything around her. Out of nowhere she heard her father's voice.

"Aurora, remember what I told you, remember what you must do for Aaron."

She instantly felt her throat tighten, and anxiety rose in her chest.

"Stay calm. Focus on your breathing," Dane's voice went on.

Aurora followed her father's instructions and took a deep breath. The brightness of the sun in the sky seemed suddenly to intensify and as her attention was drawn upward toward its source, a rainbow appeared in the clear blue sky. Cal and Aaron, trotting on ahead of her seemed not to have noticed it, and Aurora could hear the easy chatter between them continue as they rode.

Warmth emanated from the rainbow as if from the sun itself, and Aurora felt an intense peace wash through her body, instinctively closing her eyes for a second to bathe in the warm light. Suddenly she heard her father's voice again, echoing through the air and breaking the calm peace around her.

"No, wait . . . pull it back," she heard him say, an uncharacteristic hint of panic in his voice and other voices in the background talking frantically.

Aurora opened her eyes abruptly to see that the rainbow had disappeared. She tried to make out what the voices were saying, but the sounds crackled as if on a failing phone connection before silence fell through the air around her.

"Aurora, be aware," whispered the voice of Namogoz echoing through the now heavy silence. There was an unfamiliar urgency in his words, and Aurora felt a sudden chill on the surface of her skin.

Staring around at the bank of hedges they were passing on their left and the horizon of the heathland stretching out ahead of them, nothing looked unusual in that moment, but as Aaron trotted on ahead, Cal had stopped. Drawing himself up to attention in his saddle, Cal turned to look back at Aurora with a concerned look on his face that told her that he had heard the voice too. Aurora felt a surge of adrenaline through her body, and her senses heightened. Time slowed down as the molecules in the air around her began to pulse and expand as they had done in the room around her at Dr. Marsden's, like bubbles swelling to the point of bursting. She sensed Pepper slow down and tense under her as a dark shadow began to move across them. Looking up, she saw a mass of ominous, black clouds appearing in the previously cloudless sky, expanding like a dark carpet rolling out above them, obscuring the sun as the gentle summer breeze began to pick up quickly, swirling the long grass below them and whistling through the air as if a low volume warning siren.

Aaron's and Cal's horses stopped in their tracks, and the events of the following minutes seemed to spin the world in on itself. As time both stopped and raced around Aurora, she watched as a terrifying scene unfolded. The ground in front of Aaron and Spirit began to shudder and move, splitting and rising first as a mound of earth and then, as the earth fell away, a twisting, whirling mass of dark mists rose out of the middle. Pieces of earth fell from it as it swirled higher and higher, reaching up toward the black clouds gathering in the sky above it.

Both Autumn and Spirit reared up, terror in their eyes as they turned their heads sharply away from the scene in front of them. Cal instinctively braced himself against Autumn as he reared. Reaching toward Spirit's cheek piece, he tried to grab at it but missed as Spirit strained his head and shoulders sideways away from him, forelegs frantically pawing at the dark mists rising and swirling in front of him.

"Christ, Aaron!" Aurora heard Mack shout behind her, twisting round sharply to see him tug hard on Dante's reins, galloping forward past Aurora toward Aaron, who was trying desperately to hang on to Spirit's reins as he was flung backward, then forward against the horse's neck. Aurora screamed out as Spirit bucked a second time and Aaron's body was thrown clear off and down to the side of the horse. Still hanging onto the reins, Aaron hit the ground with a sickening thud and was dragged backward as Spirit began to back away from the dark swirling mass, which was stretching from the ground to the sky now and disappearing into the menacing clouds above it. Mack jumped down off Dante and ran toward Spirit, reaching him just as Aaron let go of the reins and tumbled sideways into the long grass.

By this time Cal had backed Autumn up to Aurora, jumped down, and grabbed hold of both Autumn's and Pepper's reins. Aurora swung her leg over Pepper's back, dropping down off the horse and running frantically toward Mack, who was crouched down where Aaron lay in the grass at the side of the track. Dante stood firm and strong against the wind, eyes on Mack as he was trying to get a reaction from Aaron. Spirit was backing nervously away from the scene, and as Cal let go of Autumn's and Pepper's reins to follow Aurora to his dad and Aaron, the three younger horses turned and galloped quickly away from the scene in front of them.

"Aurora, stay back!" Mack yelled, holding his hand out toward her as his voice was being carried away in the wind, still rising in intensity around them. Bright golden light appeared from Mack's hand, stretching back toward Aurora and Cal and wrapping around them both.

"No!" screamed Aurora as she reached Mack and dropped down on the ground beside him, still surrounded by the golden light, tears streaming down her face and panic spiraling through her at the sight of a trickle of blood running down the side of her brother's head as he lay motionless in the grass.

In that moment, the tall spiral of dark smoke began to part vertically, as if a door were opening in it, and a figure began to materialize in front of it. A tall, hooded figure in black robes appeared with its head bowed, but as its appearance became clearer it slowly raised its head, black eyes staring out from a menacing gray face.

Micah surveyed the scene before him, his gaze moving quickly past Mack, Cal, and Aurora as if he didn't even see them, before resting on Aaron's body lying still on the ground. Mack pulled back as Micah's eyes narrowed on Aaron and the open space in the dark swirling mists closed behind him.

Mack turned to Aurora and, grabbing both her arms at the sides, stood up, lifting her up to standing too as he did. "You need to get back, Aurora," Mack insisted.

"I'm not leaving him!" yelled Aurora, her voice being lost in the wind as she struggled against Mack's hold on her, but he turned and pushed her away from him toward Cal.

"Get her away, Cal!" yelled Mack, and Aurora felt Cal's arms tighten around her middle from behind her, pinning her own arms against her side and dragging her backward as she screamed and fought to pull away from him.

"Aurora, you have to stay back," Cal pleaded with her, holding her even more tightly around her arms as she continued to struggle against him.

Mack stood up and backed slowly away from Aaron's body on the ground, still holding his arms out to either side of him and moving back toward Aurora and Cal, away from the dark figure of Micah who was focused intently on Aaron. Tears still streaming down her face, Aurora's gaze was drawn away from her brother, and she saw the face of Namogoz appear in the air in front of her. His gentle voice flooded her mind, and she stopped struggling.

"The Darkness cannot perceive Mack or either of you with the shield around you. You are safe, Aurora," Namogoz said, "and we are here with you."

As he spoke, the faces of the other six Gozzits appeared on either side of him, smiling gently down at her as her father's voice took over, replaying his words in her mind.

"The Darkness is stalking his human soul. Aaron's choice is being forced now and we cannot stop it. But that choice is his alone to make, Aurora. If you go to him while it's happening, if you intervene, if you try to help him through it, you will lock the grief back inside him, and it will all be in vain. We must trust in him that he is strong enough to choose the Light."

Aurora collapsed exhausted back against Cal as she gave up the struggle, dropping her head in surrender to what she knew she had to do.

Micah stepped closer to Aaron's body, his dark robes flowing behind him as he held his hand out and pointed down toward Aaron.

"Up," Micah commanded in a slow menacing voice, raising his hand slightly, and as he did so Aaron began to rise up from the ground. Aurora gasped as she saw her brother's almost translucent form standing in front of Micah, risen up from the feet of his body, which still lay motionless in the long grass.

"Micah is calling his soul from his body," Namogoz explained from behind the golden shield, which Mack held firm around Aurora and Cal. It felt as if they were in an invisible viewing gallery.

Aurora stared at her brother's soul standing as clear as day in front of her, and as she stared, she saw there was a hole through his upper chest, exactly as she had seen in Miss Broach.

"Is he . . ." Aurora said, choking back tears with the words she was telepathically communicating to Namogoz.

"He's not dead," Namogoz said, hearing her thoughts and looking back toward Aaron. "Look, his body and soul are still attached. He is at the choice-point though, Aurora. That hole you can see in his chest, it is where his soul has been weakened by the grief of losing your father, grief which he has not dealt with. The decision he makes now will determine whether he accepts the Light . . . or crosses over to the Darkness."

Aurora's breath caught in her throat as a sob at his words as she watched the scene before her helplessly.

"Who are you?" Micah asked Aaron, questioning but with a suspicious undertone to his voice.

"Aaron," Aaron's soul replied simply, holding out his arms and staring at them, confused as he then looked back at his body lying on the ground. "What's happening?"

"Well, you have an opportunity . . . Aaron," Micah continued, smiling slyly at Aaron's soul. "You see, you're dead," Micah told him, staring directly into Aaron's eyes and speaking in a coldly calm voice as he took another step toward him.

"No!" Aurora yelled, pulling forward toward her brother again as Cal tightened his grip around her. "Cal, he's lying. Aaron's not dead," she cried.

"Stop, Aurora, please stop," Cal begged her. "You can't interfere."

"Oh, okay," Aaron's soul replied calmly. "So what shall I do?"

"Well, that's really your choice, Aaron," Micah replied with feigned innocence. "You see, you are being hunted by . . . shall we say power-hungry leaders, who are intent on making you fight as part of an army for all eternity. So . . ." Micah paused as he rubbed his chin with his hand. "You could go with them." He gestured his hand dramatically out to the side of his face. "Or you could come with me for an . . . easier life."

"Well fighting in an army doesn't sound like much fun," Aaron's soul replied as if in a trance, and Micah shook his head in a fake show of sympathy, which was obviously false to the unseen onlookers.

Aaron paused before shrugging in his usual laid-back manner and continuing. "Maybe I'll come with you then, if that's easier."

Micah nodded and pointed toward Aaron. As he did so, a thin sliver of dark smoke appeared from the end of his forefinger. Snaking its way slowly through the air toward Aaron's soul, it started to wrap around him like a sinister rope.

"That sounds like the . . . right choice for you, Aaron," Micah drawled with satisfaction, and as the head of Aaron's soul dropped back, his eyes slowly shutting, a swirling black mass began to form above his soul, exactly as it had done with Miss Broach in the biology class.

"Aaron, no!" screamed Aurora, sobbing as she turned to bury her head in Cal's chest, unable to watch her brother being taken by the Darkness in the same horrific way as their teacher.

As the swirling black mass above Aaron's soul began to part, his body unexpectedly stirred in the grass behind him. Sensing the movement, his soul opened its eyes, looking back toward its body before his gaze shot upward in shock toward the swirling darkness above him. Instinctively, Aaron's soul threw his arms up above his head, his long sleeve moving down over his wrist as he did so. Micah took a sharp intake of breath and dropped his arm suddenly, causing the black swirling mass above Aaron and the dark rope around him to disappear instantly. For Micah had spotted something on Aaron's wrist as he raised his arms: a gray metal chain bracelet with a single charm in the shape of the infinity sign.

As the black clouds above him dissipated and disappeared, Aaron's soul looked back toward Micah now with a look of fear, dropping his arms down by his side. Micah stared at Aaron intently with a confused look on his face, as if he were remembering something long forgotten. His shoulders dropped as he let out his sharp intake of breath suddenly, as if in shock.

"Dane?" Micah almost breathed the word, as his black eyes continued to stare from Aaron's now lowered arm to his face.

It was the turn of Aaron's soul to look confused at the figure standing in front of him.

"Dane is . . . my dad's name . . . was, I mean."

"Was?" Micah echoed, suddenly seeming a much smaller and less imposing figure now and looking into Aaron's eyes with an intense, unwavering stare.

"Dad is . . ." Aaron and Micah stared at each other for what seemed like an eternity before Aaron went on, ". . . dead."

Aaron's soul began to repeat the words "Dad is dead" over and over as his face began to strain with a new realization, his head dropped back as he looked upward, and tears started to roll down the sides of his face, his shoulders heaving as the tears fell faster. Aurora turned back from where she had buried her face in Cal's chest toward her brother, her eyes wide. As they watched and as Aaron sobbed, releasing more and more of the grief locked up inside his soul, the black hole in his chest began to change, pulsing with bright light and swirling, the hole gradually becoming smaller. As the hole shut and disappeared, Aaron's soul suddenly snapped back down into his body, which heaved up in an arch with a sudden deep breath as he sat bolt upright on the ground in front of them.

Aurora's attention was dragged from Aaron back to Micah, who still stood rooted in the same spot, now staring at the ground in front of him. In that instant, a deafening roar echoed through the air around them like thunder. A black hole appeared in the sky above Micah, and as the inside of it opened and surged down toward him, it enveloped him, dragging him back up into it before it swirled closed and disappeared from view as quickly as it had appeared, leaving once more clear blue skies in its place.

Once Cal and Mack had rounded up all four horses again, between them they lifted Aaron up onto Dante and settled him into the saddle. Mack sat up behind Aaron, one hand on the cantle and the other held loosely around Aaron, supporting him as he leaned back into Mack's strong, broad chest. In the absence of the mounting block, Aurora was trying unsuccessfully to lift her foot up high enough to Pepper's stirrup. Seeing her struggling, Cal came over to help, offering his hands gripped together for her to use as a step. Aurora accepted his help gratefully and as she hopped up, swinging her right leg over Pepper's back, she wobbled sideways toward Cal. He grabbed hold of her arm to steady her, and Aurora felt a bolt of energy shoot up through her arm where he held it, making her catch her breath. Pushing herself back up hastily and readjusting her position in the saddle, her eyes met Cal's briefly, and she was momentarily lost to the intense pull she felt toward him each time it happened. Feeling her cheeks burning, Aurora looked away, embarrassed, but not before she noticed Cal's face flushing with embarrassment too, and not least as she had also seen Mack watching them both with raised eyebrows and an amused grin on his face.

Cal rode ahead on Autumn, leading Spirit alongside them and with Aurora and Mack following closely behind on Pepper and Dante. Aaron was quiet all the way back, his eyes closed as he lay against Mack's broad chest, though Aurora had the feeling that he wasn't sleeping. As they rode, she looked over and saw a tear fall from her brother's closed eye. She felt her heart ache for him, but at the same time something was definitely different in Aaron, a freedom and lightness she had not sensed in him since before Dad left. Thinking back to her first journey to the Rainbow Forest, Aurora wondered whether she needed to do anything else now for Aaron. Was it okay? Could he be called there now? Did she need to go with him, or to take him herself?

In answer to her silent questions, she heard the voice of Namogoz in her mind: "Patience, Aurora. All will become clear."

With a deep sigh, Aurora relaxed into the rhythmic motion of Pepper's graceful trot, content for now that the future, though just as unknown and uncertain, suddenly felt like it held new hope. Looking from Aaron to Mack, she caught the older man's eyes as he smiled warmly at her. She perceived the familiar golden bubble of protection emanating out from Mack, wrapping around Aaron and stretching out toward her and Cal. Smiling back at Mack, Aurora turned her face to the sun, knowing without doubt now that whatever path lay ahead of them and whatever the future held . . . she, Aaron, and Cal would face it together.

Back at the stables, Aurora held Pepper's reins after she dismounted, gazing into the eyes of the beautiful, gentle mare she had quickly become so attached to.

"Come on then, mate," Mack said to Aaron as he helped him down from Dante's saddle. "Let's get you inside the house to lie down. You had quite a fall back there; you were out for a couple of minutes."

"I had the weirdest dream, though," Aaron said, shaking his head incredulously and wincing as his head injury reminded him of its presence by pounding at his brain.

Cal looked over at Aurora as he stroked Autumn's cheek affectionately, raising his eyebrows to her at Aaron's words. Aurora raised her own eyebrows in response, blowing her cheeks out as she exhaled heavily and nodding with her eyes wide as Cal stifled a laugh.

CHAPTER 14

Mack placed a tray with three mugs of hot chocolate down on the table by the side of the sofa where Aaron was lying, with Aurora sitting on the floor next to him and Cal leaning casually over the back of the sofa above him.

The lounge of the single-level converted barn had a high, vaulted ceiling with solid oak beams and huge windows overlooking the fields at the back and sides of the property and the stables. The large brown leather sofa sat on perfectly conditioned floorboards, which were partly covered with oriental pattern rugs of varying colors that gave the room a warm, homey feel. Mack built the house himself, Cal had proudly explained to them as Mack cleaned up Aaron's wound when they got back.

"Yeah, well, I was pretty much brought up on building sites," Mack explained to the twins, laughing and winking at Aurora. "So it's less of an achievement than he makes it sound!"

Even so, Aurora was heavily impressed as she gazed around at the craftsmanship of the house, the early afternoon light casting a warm glow around the large open-plan room.

"How's the head?" Mack asked Aaron with concern in his voice.

"Bit sore," Aaron winced, touching his hand to the cut on his forehead, which Mack had carefully cleaned and was now starting to swell into a visible lump.

At the sound of a car pulling up on the gravel drive outside, Mack turned his head to the lounge window as Aspen jumped out, slamming the car door shut and running to the front of the house. Greeting Mack hurriedly as he opened the door for her, she rushed over to Aaron, shuffling Aurora out of the way and sitting down on the sofa beside him, her mascara smudged where she had obviously been crying. She grabbed his hand.

"Here we go," Aaron groaned.

"Muuuuum, I'm fine," he protested, rolling his eyes as Aspen leaned over him, pressing her hands to either side of his face to examine the lump on his forehead with a frantic look on her face.

"I was so worried when Mack phoned me," she said, sounding out of breath. "How are you feeling? Does it hurt? Can you see okay? Are you dizzy or is your eyesight blurry?" She chattered at top speed as she stared into his eyes, still holding on to his face.

"*Mum!*" Aaron said, dragging her hands away from his face. "I'm *okay*. It's just a bump." He lifted his head slightly. "Ow . . . and a headache," he added, wincing, laying his head back down on the cushion again and closing his eyes as he put his own hand to the offending bump.

"It won't do any harm to get him checked out at the surgery. He was out cold for a while," Mack interjected, nodding to Aaron and raising his eyebrows as Aaron opened his mouth to protest. "Just to be on the safe side."

"Of course," Aspen agreed, squeezing Aaron's hands.

Aaron sighed in resignation, backing down for the sake of not having to talk, as it was making his head hurt. Aurora and Cal giggled behind him.

Aspen dropped Aurora home before taking Aaron to the minor injury unit at the hospital to get him checked out. Suddenly realizing how drained she was, Aurora retreated to the den. Feeling the warm afternoon sun streaming through the window on her, she dropped down on the huge comfy sofa. Resting her head back on its high cushions, she closed her eyes and fell asleep in seconds.

CHAPTER 15

Aurora looked down at herself sleeping on the sofa in the den. Holding her arm out in front of her, she noticed the translucent glow around her as she floated up away from her body. Before she could wonder too much about what was happening, she was pulled suddenly and swiftly into the familiar swirling tunnel of rainbow mists. The fleeting annoyance she felt at being dragged away from her peaceful sleep disappeared, and assuming that she was on her way to Namogoz and the other Gozzits, she closed her eyes and held out her arms as she soared weightlessly through space.

As her flight came to an unusually abrupt halt, she became aware of a silence around her that was strangely oppressive. Feeling a chill on the surface of her skin, she opened her eyes to darkness and realized with a sense of unease this was not the Rainbow Forest as she had expected.

The stifling heaviness of the room around Aurora hung in the air like lead. As her eyes accustomed themselves to the darkness, she could feel it pressing down on her, suffocating her soul and squeezing the life out of every molecule of her being. As she looked around, some part of her knew she was in no danger, but her body clung to each breath she took like she was drowning, desperate to return to the surface yet with a strong awareness to stay, that there was something here which she needed to see.

Black stone arches stretched from floor to ceiling of the vast room around her. Terrifying demonic faces were carved into the ceiling, an eternity of suffering encapsulated in their contorted features. In the spaces between the arches, the air began to swirl in dark masses of smoke. Hundreds of shadowy figures began to appear out of the black mists around the edges of the room, which looked like some form of arena, its menacing audience looking expectantly toward a round pit in the center of the room where Aurora's vision now rested. Formed of dark gray stone and carved around its edges into the shape of flames, the outer edges of the pit curved inward slightly, giving it the look of a giant bowl.

Though aware she was dreaming, Aurora also had a strong sense of purpose for being in this place, bearing witness to the scene playing out before her. She watched carefully, feeling all her physical senses heightened, intensifying to the point of discomfort. Her vision sharpened as if she were looking through a magnifying glass, and she realized she could pick out the minute grains of sand in the stone of the pit at the center of the room. The sound of a low hum penetrated her awareness, at first in the far distance, but it quickly became louder and more intense, echoing deep in her ears and her body and seeming to vibrate through the air around her. Catching movement from the edges of the room, her eyes were drawn toward the shadowy spaces between the huge stone pillars.

The blackness was illuminated as if she had night vision, revealing menacing silhouettes of the dark entities also present as they moved forward out of the shadows. Aurora's breath caught in her throat as their forms became clearer: tall and thin demon-like bodies wearing black hooded robes that reached to the floor. Black, ghostly, elongated hands were visible out of the sleeves of the inky black robes, bony fingers clawing menacingly at their owners' sides. As the gruesome audience moved closer, Aurora heard their slow rasping breaths and could sense their anticipation as they stared intently toward the activity within the pit. As they inched forward, some of the figures raised their heads enough for Aurora to catch a glimpse of evil yellow eyes peering out from underneath the hoods of their robes.

Aurora's attention was pulled back to the dark center of the pit as it began to pulse and move, rising, and falling in increasingly rapid succession from the murky depths. She could perceive the molecules of the air above the pit swirl and expand like bubbles as the activity from its center increased to a frenzy. Flames burst suddenly from the seething mass, rising rapidly upward and casting an ominous glow over the dark figures congregated around the room. The figures pulled quickly back into the shadows, though not before Aurora caught a glimpse of their terrifyingly lifeless faces. Illuminated by the flames, blackened skin stretched over hollow cheekbones and dark mist filtered from their mouths with each hideous, rasping breath. The fire from the pit intensified, and as it did, something else began to appear within the flames. Aurora watched as a figure began to take shape, a human form wearing black hooded robes hung in the air limply with its head dropped forward, torso hunched over. The figure moved forward through the air, out of the flames as if on an invisible pulley, coming to a stop just outside the edge of the flaming pit.

Aurora's eyes were drawn to the far end of the room beyond it, where a tall, black, throne-type structure had appeared from nowhere, gravitating slowly forward toward the middle of the dark arena, where the figure still hung motionless in the air. Aurora squinted, trying to make out who or what occupied the throne.

Whatever it was had no physical form to speak of, and though its presence in the room was tangible, it appeared no more solid than the air around it, a black hole that seemed to swirl into a deep, endless chasm of darkness. As the throne moved farther forward, the shadowy figures around the outer edges of the room dropped to their knees with heads bowed, pathetically subservient to the presence that had entered the room. The throne came to a halt in front of the suspended figure, which suddenly fell out of the air as if cut from invisible ties. Dropping to the ground with a heavy thud, it lay unmoving where it fell.

The dark mist in the chair began to swirl fiercely, taking on a more solid form. Though it had no distinguishable features, a thin black head appeared from the swirling black hole, which now appeared as if it were a torso, multiple limb-like shapes extending from either side of the terrifying being that was taking shape.

"Get up, Micah," a deep, ominous voice echoed.

Without doubt, Aurora knew the voice came from the dark being on the throne, though it seemed to infiltrate every molecule in the vast chamber, the vibrations of terror in the words hanging in the air as the audience around the room looked on from the shadows.

Aurora gasped as the identity of the figure lying at the foot of the throne became clear, and at that moment the figure began to stir, rising slowly and pushing itself up to kneeling, its head still bowed forward, black hood covering its face.

"Face me," challenged the being on the throne in a low, intimidating tone as its demonic form rose up before Micah. "Face me," the Darkness repeated, "and face your failure."

Aurora's breath caught in her throat, her heart beating wildly against her chest with the realization of who, or rather what, sat on the throne. The presence of the Darkness was all consuming, existing as everything and yet nothing, sucking the life out of everything around it. A pair of yellow eyes appeared within the form of the Darkness as it moved closer to Micah, flames burning in their depths.

"The child has power over you," the voice of the Darkness echoed around the room. "Look at what you have become—weak, like them."

"Never," growled Micah, and renewed energy flowed through his body at the mocking words . Micah drew himself up from his kneeling position, his strength returning with each breath as he raised his black eyes to the Darkness, his face rigid with defiance.

"Good," observed the Darkness with amusement. "Use the hatred. It will make you stronger."

As Aurora's attention remained locked on the menacing form of the Darkness on its throne, she felt an intense curiosity as to how such evil existed in the world. In that instant of curiosity, she felt a physical tug toward the Darkness, a sharp jolt shot through her solar plexus, and in the blink of an eye, her view of the scene before her changed, like camera angles switching in a TV program. She was now positioned directly in front of Micah, so close she drew a sharp breath in, fear consuming her and a rush of adrenaline surging quickly and uncomfortably through her body.

In that second of fear, Micah's image began to waver and fade before her. Almost instantly, Aurora heard the voice of Namogoz echo through her mind, his image appearing before her.

"Trust your awareness, Aurora. Use your power."

Aurora took a deep breath, focusing her energy, and the adrenaline began to retreat.

"Good," Namogoz encouraged. "Hold the connection."

Aurora's awareness of her new position sharpened and she began to notice new senses, thoughts, and feelings not her own. Her breath felt slow and labored, her body like lead beneath her. An unfathomable sense of dark and deep hatred filled her mind and body, coursing through her and infiltrating every cell, every molecule of her being. Confusion, fear, and panic swept through her mind as she felt herself simultaneously fighting against the invasion and drowning in it, knowing it was separate from her but, at the same time, afraid it would consume her.

"Namogoz, help me!" she cried out in her mind as she felt herself pushing against the darkness that was seeping into her mind and taking over her body. "What's happening?" she asked, panicked.

"Aurora."

The voice of Namogoz rang through her consciousness, and she swam toward it through the murky blackness engulfing her, clinging frantically to its familiarity.

"Aurora . . . relax and focus on my voice. You are still you. You are still Aurora. Stop fighting it—release your struggle and let go of the fear. The more you fear something, the more you fight and the more intensely that which you are fighting will cling to you, will become part of you. It cannot affect you unless you allow it to. You are space. You exist between the molecules of this reality, not trapped within them. Let go of your attachment to everything physical and be space. Then the Darkness will pass through you and cannot affect you."

With time appearing to stand still around her, Aurora did as Namogoz instructed. As she consciously let go of her fear, she saw herself as pure space, floating matter, wisps of energy in the vast matrix of all existence. She breathed out slowly and felt the release as the Darkness passed through her. Regaining control of herself, her awareness settled and her perception shifted. She was Aurora again, the blackness now appearing separate from her body, forming an outer layer around her like a costume and no longer consuming her.

With calm restored, she took a deep breath as Namogoz continued.

"You have achieved soul transference, Aurora; you have stepped into the form of the Darkness itself. Your powers are developing rapidly, and this is one of them. Soul transference is one of the greatest of all the Lightworkers' powers, and few are able to achieve it as early as you have. Your potential is immense, Aurora, and you are being shown this for a vital reason."

Aurora's surroundings came back into focus, and she watched as Micah raised his eyes to stare directly at the Darkness. Finding herself staring directly into Micah's eyes, her world began to blur once more, and she felt another tug toward his body, as if she were being impelled into his soul.

"No!" she screamed inwardly with instant panic.

"You are being called to go further," Namogoz encouraged her. "You can do it, Aurora, but only if you choose to."

"No more, not yet," she pleaded.

"All right," Namogoz replied, "remain focused where you are and you will not be pulled further."

Aurora did as he instructed, and her surroundings stabilized once more as she retreated from Micah's body.

"These children present a threat to the future of the Dark Army," she could hear the Darkness continue, its voice echoing out into the room. "I have trusted you to apprehend them, but this one," he questioned menacingly, ". . . it seems clear this one affects you in some way?"

As the words emanated from the being in which Aurora resided, she realized she could perceive the intent of her host, its words cloaked in an accusatory tone the Darkness knew would incite hatred in Micah. Micah's face contorted with anger, and the Darkness laughed—quietly at first, but the low mocking sound became louder and louder, echoing around the cold stone arches that edged the chamber as Micah's rage grew to a frenzy.

"Enough!" yelled Micah, his voice booming out above the mocking laughter of the Darkness. Swinging round with his black cape flying out behind him, Micah stormed out of the chamber via a huge wooden door to the far side, his strength powered by his anger to such an extent that the force with which he flung the door open against the wall behind it reverberated around the entire room. Micah stormed furiously into a room visible at the end of the stone corridor that led from the chamber, slamming the door behind him.

Aurora saw one of the thin limbs of the Darkness stretch out in front of her as if it were part of her own body. Reaching out in the direction of the door by which Micah had just left, she watched as a heavy gray metal chain appeared in the air in front of the Darkness. It began to move slowly through the air in the direction of the door.

"You will not fail me again, Micah—ever," the voice of the Darkness echoed ominously as the chain increased its speed through the air, clanging as it snaked its way through the doorway, out of the chamber, and down the corridor. As the chain reached the room Micah had entered, it embedded itself swiftly into the stone wall to the left of the heavy door, as easily as if the stone were putty. Possessing a life of its own, the chain grew, extending out and slamming into the stone wall to the other side of the door, barricading it shut. The movement of the chain became fast and frantic as it reproduced over and over; embedding itself into the wall left and right, top and bottom of the door. Within seconds the door was completely obscured by the heavy gray chains, and a huge metal padlock appeared with a large black key in it. Linking swiftly through the middle of the chains, the shackle of the padlock slammed shut, and the black key turned as the lock inside clicked. The key disappeared, and a short silence followed before a thundering yell was heard from inside.

The menacing laugh of the Darkness echoed around the chamber once more at the sound of Micah's fury. Reaching out again, this time in the direction of one of the stone arches, the Darkness appeared to beckon someone or something forward. The demon-like figures cowering between the stone arches retreated further and parted as a lone figure emerged. Cloaked and hooded, it moved silently toward the front of the room, stopping in front of the Darkness. A sudden and inexplicable sense of foreboding rose in Aurora as she watched the scene before her.

"It's time for you to prove your loyalty to your master," the Darkness commanded in a menacing tone. "The child . . . bring it to me."

"Yes, master," came the flat, monotone reply from the hooded figure standing before the Darkness.

The figure slowly raised its head, as it reached up with thin bony hands to remove the hood covering its face. Even with a cold, gray pallor and empty black eyes, the sharp features were unmistakable.

"Miss Broach!" gasped Aurora, as the scene around her faded away and she found herself back in the warm safety of the den at home.

CHAPTER 16

Aaron sat quietly at dinner, pushing the food around his plate with a disinterest uncharacteristic for him toward food. Aspen looked from him to Aurora, raising her eyebrows at her daughter before staring out of the kitchen window in contemplation.

"Hey, Mum," Aaron announced out of the blue as he put his fork down on the plate and pushed his dinner forward away from him, "if you want to come see the new planets I've put up in the garage after dinner, that'll be okay." He looked sideways at their mother as she tried unsuccessfully to conceal her look of surprise, but then placed her hand on his arm and smiled.

"I'd love to, sweetie," she said simply as she got up and started to clear away the dinner plates.

"You too, sis, if you like," Aaron offered as he went on with feigned innocence. "Not that you know a moon from a mothball . . . but whatever."

Aurora mouthed a silent and sarcastic laugh to her brother in response, before grabbing some plates to help clear the table. His invitation for them to go into the garage was a huge change, Aurora knew, remembering his heart-wrenching outburst all those months earlier. It was clear something big had shifted in Aaron, though inside Aurora was alternating between relief that her brother seemed happier and the worry weighing heavy on her shoulders about his calling to the Rainbow Forest. When would it be? It had to be soon, surely . . . very soon. She had received no awareness, signs, or communications at all from her father or the Gozzits since her visions of Micah, which were now hours ago, and it was all creating an uncomfortable restlessness in her body. The Darkness and its ominous words to the demonic mutation of Miss Broach played over and over in her head as anxiety mixed with impatience spiraled through her whole being with frustrating insistence.

With dinner cleared away, Aurora half-heartedly followed Aspen and Aaron as they headed to the garage. Lagging behind them, she noticed the bubble of protection shine out from her mum toward Aaron, wrapping around him. Contemplating that it still seemed brighter than she had seen it before, Aurora went to step up through the internal hallway door into the garage but stopped instinctively at a noise behind her, which sounded like a whispered voice whose words she didn't quite catch. Looking down the hallway, she saw a bright light shining out from underneath the door of the den.

"Aurora . . . come," she heard the whisper again from the direction of the den, clearer this time.

Aaron and their mum were already deep in conversation, so Aurora quietly shut the garage door behind them and headed instead farther down the hall in the direction of the den. As she reached the old oak door to her left, the handle clicked and turned on its own and as the door swung open very slightly, sharp golden beams of light shone out into the dimness of the hallway. Aurora cautiously pushed at the den door, wondering what she was going to find behind it. As she did so, the heavy oak moved away from her hand, swinging open on its own. Shielding her eyes with the back of her hand at the sudden blinding brightness beyond it, Aurora walked forward through the doorway, hearing the door click shut behind her.

As she tried to accustom her eyes to the surroundings, a warm breeze brushed across her face, the fresh smell of the outdoors telling her she was definitely not in her beloved den at home anymore. The brightness around her dimmed, and she looked down to see that the oak floorboards had disappeared, replaced by green grass. She turned to shut the door behind her, but it was gone, replaced by green fields, trees, and mountains as far as she could see. As her eyes scanned the beautiful, serene views around her, they rested on a huge white building to the front of her, towering toward the sky. A huge double door in the center of the building sat between tall pillars on either side of it. The building seemed to rise from a golden mist over the ground below it, and Aurora recognized it immediately as the building she had seen her father and Micah in front of as younger men.

Aurora's body began to move toward the building without physical effort; levitating through the air, she was suddenly in front of the high doors. As the den door had done, they began to swing open without her touching them. As Aurora went to walk physically into the building beyond them, she instead felt herself floating forward in automation into the vast hall inside the doors. Her journey progressed with no effort on her part, up a marble staircase, and then down endless white corridors, her speed increasing so much that the surroundings blurred around her. In what seemed like seconds, she found herself in a large empty room, white from floor to ceiling, though the outer edges and walls of the room were strangely translucent—appearing there, but at the same time not there.

Aurora shook her head, blinking hard, and as she reopened her eyes, she saw images coming into focus in front of her. Instantly recognizing the figure of her father to the right, she instinctively went to rush toward him, stopping herself, though, as something else began to appear beside him. The space next to Dane was opening up, stretching out like it was made of rubber and expanding as another room began to take shape. Aurora stared hard and could make out a long table with figures sat all around it, bright silhouettes without distinguishable features, appearing as if they were a digital image on a projector.

"Who are they, and where are we?" she asked her father.

"We are in a vibrational portal, Aurora," Dane replied. "They are all members of the High Council of Valhandra, as am I."

Aurora looked in awe at the long table, which she could now make out was set in the middle of a vast and grand-looking room. White walls were set with panels edged in gold; the white marble table sparkled from the light of a huge crystal-and-gold chandelier hanging from the ceiling above. As Aurora gazed more closely at the beautiful chandelier, she noticed it did not appear to be physically attached to the ceiling, but rather hovering in the space and with a glow to its light that seemed very different—brighter, warmer, and more luminous than any light Aurora had ever seen on Earth.

"What's a vibrational portal?" Aurora asked her father.

"It is a space between two realities," Dane explained. "It connects them and allows us to move from one to the other. Those realities can be close to each other in time and space or eons apart, but the portal is able to merge the energetic vibrations of the two realities within it to allow them to exist at the same frequency without affecting the stability of either."

Dane paused, looking intently at Aurora.

"There are great risks to moving between realities, Aurora. If the vibrations of two separate realities were to intersect, it would change the course of all time and space irreversibly, causing a glitch in the Universe which could destabilize the future, to the point where life could not exist in it. When the Lightworkers left Earth for Valhandra, we took the chance we may never be able to return, that we would lose contact with our families and loved ones forever. But in our willingness to let go of our Earth-bound lives and souls, the Universe saw our commitment to creating a greater future. That in itself allowed the new Consciousness to become even more powerful. Through our willingness to evolve, the Universe has now been able to gift us the power to move between realities. But this ability is new and intensely powerful; we are still learning to use it, and in the wrong hands this knowledge would be catastrophic."

"Wow!" gasped Aurora, her eyes wide. "I have *so* much to learn."

"And you will, my darling," Dane assured her, smiling warmly at his daughter's curiosity. "But," he continued, as Aurora caught the look of concern in his face, "first we have to get Aaron to the Rainbow Forest, and that has become more complicated since his meeting with Micah."

The meeting with Micah seemed like a lifetime ago now to Aurora, though it had happened earlier that same day, a day that, Aurora reflected, seemed to have gone on for years so far!

"I have to tell you what happened," she began, eager to reveal what she had experienced when she transmuted into the Darkness.

"I know, Aurora," Dane interrupted her before she could go on, "and I assure you we didn't foresee it happening in this way. The situation with Aaron and Micah meeting—it achieved the aim of eliciting a choice-point in Aaron, but at the same time it . . ." he paused.

"What is a choice-point?" Aurora interjected. "Namogoz mentioned that too."

"In the face of Micah's attempts to control him, Aaron had a choice," Dane continued. "To surrender or to come back to himself and look at what he was blocking in his life. The choice-point is inevitable for a broken soul. If it is made in favor of the Light, then the soul can heal—though in truth that rarely happens, because once a soul loses one or more of its colors, the Darkness is too easily able to latch on to it. When Aaron chose to release his pain, his soul was able to heal; he chose the Light over the Darkness. But—" Dane shook his head "—it has created instability in time and space. We believe this has happened because the meeting with Micah has alerted the Darkness to Aaron's gifts. The Darkness will suspect there are more like him, will be searching for more like him. It was not planned to occur like that," her father finished.

Aurora hesitated, remembering Micah's reaction to her father's bracelet on Aaron's wrist, and her mind filled with uncertainty. Had Aaron consciously chosen . . . or had Micah's sighting of the bracelet broken the hold enough so that the Light was the only way that Aaron could go?

"But Dad . . ." Aurora began, as she tried to formulate words to express the doubts she knew she had but couldn't quite grasp enough to verbalize, that Aaron's choice-point may not be what they thought it was. But as her awareness spun away from her and her mind fought to keep up, a more insistent and nagging thought broke through the turmoil in her head.

"Wait . . . 'not *planned* to occur like that'?"

As Aurora repeated her father's words, her attention began shifting sharply. A sudden surge of panic rushed through her body as a very different and unwelcome possibility began to materialize in her mind.

"How was it planned to occur, Dad?"

"Aurora, I know this might be hard for you to understand, but there is a far bigger purpose here."

Taking Aurora's hand, Dane looked over toward the High Council. Aurora followed his eyes to the brightly glowing figure sitting at the head of the long table in the vast room beside them and saw it slowly nod. She looked back toward her father who dropped his head, closing his eyes briefly. Dane took a deep breath, and as he raised his eyes to meet Aurora's, she knew deep inside her she wasn't going to like what was coming.

"The High Council had planned to initiate a Vex for Aaron," Dane explained.

"A Vex?" questioned Aurora.

"A visionary experience. Basically, a simulation of a situation which would elicit a choice from him, a choice to follow the Light . . . or not. That was the rainbow you saw appearing in front of you on your ride earlier today. That was when it was meant to happen, but Micah got there first. We didn't know, so we couldn't have warned you or intervened. Somehow the Darkness had known Aaron's whereabouts . . ."

"Wait," Aurora interrupted her father abruptly, "so you set up this Vex thing?"

"We did, yes," her father replied, gesturing to the High Council before them.

Aurora went quiet. She suddenly felt dizzy, adrenaline surging through her body and her mind spinning toward awareness she knew on some deep level she didn't want to have, like a car out of control and speeding toward a precipice, aware of what lay ahead yet unable to stop it.

"If Micah hadn't turned up . . . if the Vex had worked . . ." Aurora paused as she looked at her father. "What if Aaron hadn't chosen to follow the Light?"

Dane paused before he continued, and a shadow passed across his deep blue eyes. It did not go unnoticed by Aurora, who felt a sudden stab of anxiety in her chest. She held her breath, her heart pounding in her ears as her father continued.

"The Vex was created such that if Aaron hadn't chosen the Light, he could not have chosen the Darkness. I promise you, sweetheart, he wouldn't have known—it would have been just like going to sleep. We couldn't take the chance that a Child of the Light turned to the Darkness, like Micah had done," Dane explained softly. "It would be catastrophic to the future of the world."

As he reached for Aurora's hand and held it gently between his, she felt the familiar wave of energy flowing up her arm and into her body. This time, though, there was a resistance in her body, a force that pushed involuntarily against the warm, comforting energy, refusing to let it in. The same energy that had always been such a comfort to her suddenly felt like an invasion, an uncomfortable and unwelcome threat of which she was struggling to make sense.

"You have to understand, Aurora, there was no choice," Dane continued, sensing her resistance. "This is bigger, so much bigger than you know yet. We are still learning too, but above all else we must let go of our attachment to the emotions of humankind. They distract us from the true purpose of the Universe; they stop us being able to create the future. Mack and Cal were there to ensure you didn't intervene in the process, because I knew you wouldn't be able to stand by and let Aaron make his own choice. But Micah and the Darkness got there first. We don't know yet how they were aware of Aaron . . ."

Aurora wasn't listening, her mind reeling with the volume of information.

"If Aaron had gone to sleep—" She hesitated, her breath catching in her throat as she stumbled on the next words. "Would you ever have woken him up?" she asked slowly.

Dane looked at her solemnly and sighed, dropping his head. "Once he had made his choice . . . *if* he had made that choice, and Aurora, I truly believe he would have chosen the Light . . . but if he had not, there is usually no going back."

Aurora let out a shaky breath as the horror of the truth hit her in the chest like a bolt of lightning. "That's not sleep, Dad," Aurora whispered, stunned. "That's not sleep."

Dane put his hands on Aurora's shoulders gently, looking intently into her eyes.

"Aurora, the Darkness is irrational, unpredictable, and unfathomable. Its power is increasing as it builds its Dark Army, and it is becoming more and more difficult for us to anticipate its actions. The level of its hatred for humankind is so intense that it is creating a black hole in time and space, which is growing and beginning to infiltrate the earth's atmosphere, poisoning it. Both prophecies talk of a being who alerts the Darkness to the existence of the children of the Lightworkers. The High Council of Valhandra believes this being is Aaron, in which case a shift has already begun. From this point, the course of the future is unknown, fluid, unstable. The balance of power could tip either way at any moment. Aurora, please understand the magnitude of this. We are talking about the end of the world . . . and we don't have much time."

The image of Miss Broach appeared suddenly in Aurora's mind, and she heard the familiar voice of Namogoz: "Aurora, trust your knowing."

Momentarily, she hovered on that image, trying in vain to grasp its relevance. Knowing she should be doing something or saying something, but too lost in the magnitude of what her father had done, she felt that brief awareness slip away, as she was quickly being engulfed by the raw and painful emotions of what could have happened to her brother.

"He could have died. Aaron—he could have died. If he hadn't chosen the Light, he *would* have died," Aurora whispered. Her heart pounded in her ears as tears pricked the corners of her eyes, and she felt her heart constricting, as if an imaginary hand were squeezing it.

Dane gently rocked her shoulders back and forth with his hands. "Aurora, please listen to me and try to understand. Human emotions are not real; they make us weak. You have the power to move past them now, to let go. But you can still get lost in them if you allow them to take over you. Try to control the feelings which are coming up and release them. You are a Child of the Light, and we need you. We need you all, and we need you to be strong." Dane squeezed Aurora's shoulders, dipping his head to look into her eyes, with deep concern in his. "Aurora, can you hear me? Do you understand what I'm saying?"

"He could have died," Aurora repeated, looking at her father in confusion, her eyes glazed over, her head heavy with the painful weight of imagined grief.

"He's my son, Aurora, and I love him," Dane went on. "I love you both, you have to know that. I had to trust that he would make the right choice, but I had to be willing to allow him to make that choice for himself. I *did* trust it, Aurora . . . and I was right to trust it."

"You were right? You were *right*?" Aurora repeated incredulously, her mind and body stunned, and in an instant something deep inside her snapped.

"The choice-point is an inevitable—" Dane began insistently.

"No!" she yelled, pushing her father away from her with a strength she didn't know she had. "No!" she yelled again as her father took a step back toward her, thrusting her hand out in a "stop" gesture between them.

"That's not choice, Dad! *None* of this is choice, not for us. And you weren't right—you weren't *right*. You were willing to let Aaron *die*; nothing in the world makes that right. I've had *enough*, Dad."

Tears poured freely down Aurora's cheeks, her fists clenched at her side, her body shaking as—for the first time in her life—anger, rage, and hate filled her uncontrollably from her toes to the top of her head, and in that instant she lost herself within it.

"You want me to be strong to make you feel better that you left, that you left for *this,* and you let us think you had *died*. He's my brother; he's your *son*. He could have died and—and you would have let him. You didn't care. You *don't* care. And you tried to stop me helping him." She choked the words out, sobbing as both hatred and despair rose inside her. "You sent people I don't even know to make sure I didn't stop you trying to kill my brother." Her face contorted as tears rolled down her cheeks. "How could you do it—any of it?" Thrusting her hand into the pocket of her hoodie, Aurora grasped the piece of crystal within it.

"Aurora, that's not how it was . . ." Dane began. "It's the hardest thing I—"

"Shut up!" Aurora screamed. "I don't want to hear how hard this was for you. Have you got any idea what you did to us, to Mum and Aaron? What it was like to try to go on without you there? Aaron was devastated."

"With time, you will understand; there was no choice," Dane pleaded, reaching his hand out to Aurora, but she pulled angrily away from him.

"There was a choice . . . but it was *your* choice, not *ours*. Time *out*, Dad. I'm sick of hearing about choice. I'm done!" she yelled at him. "Done with *you*, with *this*, with *them*!" She threw her arm out sideways toward the sea of bright figures, which were starting to blur into the distance, their images flickering like an unstable digital projection. Aurora blinked hard, shaking her head as her anger grew and the surroundings swam in front of her eyes.

"You *left*, Dad!" she carried on shouting. "You left us for *them*, for *this*—and I *hate* you for it. We would have been okay without you; we don't need you in our lives." For a second, Aurora paused, seeing the intense pain that flashed through her father's eyes at her words. Feeling her resistance weaken momentarily, she took a deep breath and held it in, fighting a sudden urge to run to her father and throw her arms around him, to tell him she loved him and that she didn't mean it. But it was too late for that. The need to punish him was stronger in that moment, taking over her mind and body, and she could do nothing but surrender to its overpowering pull.

"This obviously means more to you than we do. You do what you want to do, Dad. I never asked for this," Aurora said, shaking her head, tears running down her face. "I just want a normal life. For once I just want to be normal, and I don't want it. I don't want any of it."

Taking her hand out of her pocket, she held it out in front of her, uncurling her fingers to reveal the piece of crystal lying in the palm of her hand.

"And I don't want this."

In that moment, a numbness began to take over Aurora's body. Looking up from the piece of crystal in her hand, her father's image began to flicker in front of her, gradually fading along with the room around them. Looking down, she saw her own body begin to disappear, as if it were dissolving in the air.

"Aurora, no," Dane begged her. "Don't let it take over. You're strong. Hold the connection Aurora . . . please."

A wave of intense tiredness washed over Aurora and she fought to keep her eyes open. She felt a rushing sensation in her ears like she was going to pass out. Letting out a heavy breath, her shoulders dropped, and all the strength she had left in her drained away. Empty and defeated, she raised her eyes to her father as her body continued to fade away.

"You should have stayed away, Dad. I wish you had just left us alone," she whispered, and blackness descended around her.

As Aurora's image disappeared completely, the crystal fell from the palm of her hand. Clinking as it hit the floor, it rolled toward Dane and came to a halt by his feet.

Drained and exhausted, Dane dropped slowly to his knees, picking up the piece of clear white crystal and holding it out in front of him. As its bright light faded, he turned to Yanus, who had risen from the head of the table and now stood at Dane's side.

"Have we lost her?" Dane asked quietly, grasping his daughter's piece of the Circle of Light in his hand and holding it tightly to his chest. "Her soul will be weak, Yanus, and we can't reach her without the crystal."

Yanus put his hand on Dane's shoulder with an air of authority, counterbalanced with the ease and kindness of a long and true friendship.

"Time will tell," he replied and gestured toward Dane's clenched hand. Taking Aurora's piece of crystal, Yanus held it high in front of him, gazing deeply into it.

"There is still a spark of light," Yanus announced. "Aurora is strong and does not yet know the true extent of her own power. But as you know, human emotions will encompass and suffocate the new Consciousness—if we allow them to."

As Dane rose and turned to meet the eyes of his friend and leader, Yanus took his hand in both of his, flowing his immense energy deep into Dane's soul. In a short time, Dane's own energy began to return. The white glow around him, which had dimmed in the face of Aurora's anger and hatred, expanded once more, glowing brightly, and his body seemed taller, stronger again. Smiling with gratitude, Dane took a deep breath, taking his daughter's crystal back from Yanus and putting it safely in the pocket of his robe.

"You must maintain your own energy too, my friend," Yanus continued. "All we can do now is trust . . . that the Universe will help Aurora to find her way back."

CHAPTER 17

In the gloom of the cold and dank chamber, the molecules of the air seemed suspended in time and space, as empty and lifeless as the gaunt, gray face of Marta Broach as she stood before the dark throne that dominated the room, her vacant eyes fixed to the stone floor in front of her. The ornate carvings that covered each side of the imposing throne depicted thick, twisted thorns, crawling upward into the black mists above it where they disappeared from view. If one were to look closely, one would see something else deep within these carved, gnarled branches, something far more sinister, which could be mistaken for leaves from a distance, but close up one would realize they were not leaves, and it would be impossible to ignore the horrors trapped within the thorns. Even the demonic followers of the Darkness would look to the ground rather than focus their gaze between the branches on the dark throne, for to look closely would be to witness their alternate fate. Even demons have their demons—a nightmare that exists beyond that which they are already living.

A rumbling sound rose up from somewhere deep below the ground, and from the base of the throne an ominous thread of black smoke emerged. Snaking its way slowly around, it flowed up and into the seat of the structure. More and more of the dark mist appeared, flowing faster now and beginning to swirl fiercely like a cyclone, pulsing and expanding. Marta's bony frame moved back slightly, dropping down to her knees.

Her black robes flowed in the swirling winds as she bowed subserviently to the hideous form of the Darkness beginning to take shape out of the mist.

As the seething mass of blackness settled, the being on the throne seemed to straighten, pushing the top half of its terrifying form forward toward Marta, who held out one gray bony hand toward it as she remained bowed low to the ground.

The voice of the Darkness echoed through the air, emanating from every corner of the chamber, reverberating through the structure of its very walls as it commanded the figure at its feet in a deep, sinister tone. "Come closer. Show me what you know."

Marta Broach slowly rose, her long, thin fingers pulling back the hood of her heavy black robes as she lifted her head toward the Darkness.

The Darkness reached out one long, limb-like shape, black mist snaking around it as it slowly extended toward her head. At the point it made contact with her forehead, a wisp of smoke appeared and her torso lurched forward as the wisp was pulled further from her mind. Expanding to a bubble of swirling silver between them, it began spinning faster and faster until an image appeared within it, a projected memory from deep in her unconscious, solidified brain. As the image sharpened, its brightness illuminated the gloom of the chamber. Marta visibly grimaced with pain as she closed her eyes to the light emanating from the memory. The Darkness laughed at her discomfort as it moved its shadowy head closer to the memory portal. The scene within the portal sharpened: the cloisters, a clear blue sky, two figures sitting on a low brick wall chatting and laughing, oblivious to all around them. The scene zoomed in to Aurora and Cal, and also to Joe Marsh, who stood nearby holding his hands out toward them where they sat.

The memory played on as Marta Broach had watched them from the science room window, and the Darkness moved closer still, watching intently as Aurora and Cal held out their hands. Something was missing, however, from the original scene; the crystals had been shielded by Joe Marsh and therefore were not visible to the still human eyes of Marta Broach. The scene in the portal suddenly shifted to the biology classroom, the final memory before Miss Broach was taken by the Darkness. The class was frozen in time, with Joe Marsh holding out his arms toward the class, Aurora and Cal stood at the back wall of the room. But the golden shield was not visible to the Darkness, neither could it detect anything different in the souls of Aurora and Cal behind the protection of the shield thrown around them by Joe.

"Hmmmm," mused the deep, echoing voice of the Darkness. "Find him," it sneered, pointing its shadowy finger toward Aaron. "He is clearly a link to the Light's army of babies. Bring him to me."

As it pulled away, the memory portal disappeared and Miss Broach fell to her knees, drained, at the foot of the dark throne. Imminently, the air around the throne began to move, as the menacing figure of the Darkness dissolved to black mist. Spinning and whirling swiftly into a cyclone, it rose up first in the air, and then like a rocket it shot down through the middle of the throne, disappearing once more back into the fiery depths of Terhum.

In another chamber within the temple of Darkness, chains barricading the outside of the door, sat Micah. A lone figure in the room, which had no windows, he sat in silence. A large, hideously disfigured black rat scuttled back and forth in the shadows at the far end of the cold and dank room.

Leaning forward, Micah sat unmoving in the small chamber on a bed-like structure against one wall. Made of cold gray stone, it was the sole structure within the room. His head, covered with the heavy hood of his robe, was bowed almost to his knees, where his hands were clasped tightly together. The only visible movement was the slow rise and fall of his shoulders.

A second enormous black rat scuttled out of a hole in the stone wall, and the first rat emitted a high-pitched shriek of territorial warning. Micah's head turned swiftly to the commotion in the shadows, and as the two squabbling rats scurried past his feet, he abruptly and angrily swung one arm at them, catching one of the gruesome mutations and slamming it squealing against the stone wall to his side. As he did so, his robe sleeve fell back slightly and Micah's attention was drawn immediately to his exposed left forearm. Flexing his hand into a fist, he raised it in the air slightly in front of him, his black eyes fixed intently on something around his wrist—a gray metal chain bracelet attached either side of one singular charm, a side-on figure eight.

Micah sat motionless, staring at the bracelet as if in a trance. Since his imprisonment, his anger toward the Darkness had intensified by the day. However, unknown to Micah, as that anger and resentment grew, another entirely unexpected change was occurring deep in the darkness of his soul. Something was shifting very slightly, imperceptibly. In the deepest parts of the solidified mass that had been his humanity, a small green flame flared, and a long-forgotten memory stirred, from a past the Darkness had sought to eradicate from Micah's mind when it poured into his soul. In that moment, as Micah stared at the bracelet, a minute flicker of light appeared in the inky blackness of his eyes. His body arched sharply with a sudden intake of breath, and he instinctively closed his eyes as his head fell backward. When he opened his eyes, the darkness in them slowly cleared like clouds in the sky. He looked back down at the bracelet hanging around his wrist and touched one finger to the figure eight charm.

"Dane," he breathed.

The Darkness felt the change in Micah instantly. Rising up through the seat of its throne, its demonic limbs appeared, reaching out, clawing in all directions as the Dark Army cowered before it. The Darkness let out a hideous roar that echoed throughout all of Terhum, causing the oceans of the world to swell as earthquakes shuddered entire continents.

When the Darkness had entered Micah's being many years before, it was at the pinnacle of Micah's anger and hatred toward Yanus and the High Council for their decision to banish him. The Darkness had been watching Micah for some time and had seen his strength and potential. It had watched as Micah's frustration grew to fury and waited for the perfect time to enter his soul. The level of Micah's hatred and his refusal to conform compromised the stability of his soul to such an extent that it had split; the good in him had begun to give way to the inevitable evil and immorality that comes with such intensity of anger, negative feelings, and emotions. The Darkness saw potential in Micah's physical strength and defiance, and it knew that Micah could lead its army into battle against the Light's army. And so, in the very second Micah's soul split, the Darkness took its chance and poured into him, taking over his body and mind, solidifying his human soul and transporting him into the dark world.

Micah was different from the demon-like creatures of the Dark Army, whose souls had been depleted before being reborn into the Darkness at the point of death. These beings were slaves, created by the Darkness and inextricably bound to it for all eternity. Micah's soul had been claimed by the Darkness before its human light was extinguished, and so he retained his human form, though it became cold and gray, possessed by Darkness and devoid of life force. After Micah was turned, the Darkness had groomed him, training him to use his anger and hatred of the Lightworkers to increase his already immense strength to superhuman levels.

With the solidification of his soul, all memories of the human life Micah had lived ceased to exist, his eyes reflecting the empty black void inside him. From then on, Micah became the leader of the Dark Army. Hiding in the shadows of the world, he hunted the lost and broken humans on Earth, stalking them and slowly dripping Dark energy into them to feed their anger, hate, depression, fear, jealousy—all the negative emotions that were contributing to the slow demise of their humanity. And he waited, waited until the last spark of light in their souls went out. Then, at the point of death, he moved in, intercepting the souls and compelling them into the world of the Darkness, where they underwent a terrifying transformation to the black, demonic creatures of the Dark Army.

Since Micah, no other living being had been turned by the Darkness in the same way . . . until Marta Broach.

CHAPTER 18

Aspen emerged from the garage, smiling to herself contentedly as she looked back to Aaron, who was now rearranging the display of planets about which he had just spent the last half an hour happily chatting to her. Aspen's relief at the unexpected change in her son was swiftly interrupted, though, as she closed the garage door. Stepping into the hallway, her skin instantly prickled with an awareness she had come to recognize as a warning, and a familiar voice echoed through her mind.

"Aspen, she needs you. It's Aurora . . . go to her *now*!" came the sound of Dane's voice. The golden shield flowed out from Aspen's body in the direction of the den, and ignoring the stab of pain in her heart at the sound of her husband's voice, she rushed down the hallway, pushing the den door open.

"Oh God, Aurora!" Aspen cried out, falling to her knees by the side of her daughter, who was collapsed face down on the wooden floor of the den.

"Aaron, help, come quickly!" she yelled, and rushing footsteps were followed by the sound of the garage door opening and slamming shut as Aaron ran into the den to join her by Aurora's side.

"What the hell happened?" Aaron said in a panicked voice, and as Aspen gently rolled Aurora over, his sister's arm fell limply to the floor where she lay, her eyes closed. Aaron grabbed a cushion from the sofa, putting it on the floor as Aspen lowered Aurora's head onto it.

At the sight of his sister's deathly pale face, Aaron hauled his phone out of his jeans pocket. "I'll call for an ambulance," he said and began dialing.

"No, no ambulance," Aspen heard Dane's voice say insistently, and she grabbed Aaron's arm to stop him.

"No, Aaron, wait. No ambulance," Aspen told him, shaking her head frantically as Aaron stared at her, confused.

"Mum, what are you talking about? She needs to go to hospital," he argued anxiously, trying to pull his arm away from Aspen's hold.

"Her soul is in a coma without her crystal. You must call Mack," Dane continued in Aspen's mind, and she breathed out heavily, repeating his words to Aaron.

"Mack!" Aaron raised his voice with frustration. "What the hell is Mack going to do? She needs an ambulance."

"Please, sweetheart," Aspen begged, "call Mack. I'm so sorry; I will explain, there are things you need to know . . ."

"What do I need to know? For God's sake, Mum, look at her. Aurora needs medical help."

"Wait," Dane's voice interjected her thoughts. "He cannot know yet, Aspen. It's imperative he doesn't."

Aspen dropped her head, and closing her eyes briefly, she breathed out heavily, steadying her mind and trying to pull her thoughts away from the panic building in the room.

"Aaron," she said, managing to exude a calmness she didn't feel, "you have to trust me. Please trust me. *Please* call Mack," she said looking directly in his eyes.

Looking from his mum to the phone in his hand, Aaron sighed in resignation, tapping delete on the emergency number before scrolling to Cal's contact details and hitting the call button.

As Cal answered the phone, Aaron stood up, putting his free hand to his forehead as he spoke. "Hey, mate, look I'm sorry to dump this on you, but Aurora's ill. She's collapsed. I don't know what's wrong. I think she needs an ambulance, but Mum's insisting your dad comes for some reason."

"Christ, okay," Cal responded and immediately called out to his dad. Aaron waited as a brief and muffled conversation went on between them before Cal came back on the line.

"We're just leaving, ten minutes tops, bud," Cal said, and Aaron could hear car doors slamming on that end of the phone as he spoke.

"Okay," Aaron sighed as Cal ended the call, "but I wish somebody would tell me what the bloody hell's going on."

Less than ten minutes later, Mack and Cal's dark blue jeep pulled up outside, and the two of them rushed up the front path of the house, where Aaron was waiting to let them in. Mack immediately joined Aspen at Aurora's side, and Aaron strained his ears to hear the hushed conversation between them, watching as Mack took Aurora's pulse and held his hand to her forehead to check her temperature.

"How did it happen?" Cal asked Aaron.

"I don't know," Aaron replied. "Me and Mum were in the garage. Mum went back into the house, and then I heard her yelling. I ran out and Aurora was like this on the floor." He shook his head, shrugging his shoulders helplessly. "She was fine earlier at dinner, totally fine. I don't understand it."

Mack and Aspen moved away slightly from Aurora, who was still unconscious and deathly pale.

"She'll be safer at mine," Mack said, putting his hand on Aspen's shoulder supportively. "You all will be; there's plenty of room." He turned to Aaron, who was sitting on the arm of the sofa looking lost and confused.

"I know it's a lot to take in, Aaron," Mack said, "but despite how it looks, it's not a hospital Aurora needs right now. Your mum's right, there are things you need to know, but it has to be at the right time . . . and right now the priority is getting your sister somewhere safe, where we can look after her. You and your mum go and pack up what you need, quickly—just what you need." He gestured toward Cal. "Cal will get Aurora into the jeep, and we'll see you out there in a minute."

Cal knelt down by Aurora and lifted her with effortless ease, settling her in his arms as he slowly stood up, her head resting against his shoulder. Mack grabbed a blanket from the basket by the side of the sofa and laid it over Aurora before he and Cal headed out to the car. Pushing away the mass of questions in his mind, Aaron followed his mum upstairs to pack.

Flinging the holdall and suitcase into the open back of the jeep, Aaron pushed it shut and jumped into the back seat next to Cal, who was holding Aurora. Aspen got in the front next to Mack; he was talking on his phone, a somber tone in his voice.

"Okay, my friend, see you soon," Mack finished before ending the call. Starting the engine, he turned to Aspen. "Joe's meeting us there, so we can set things in motion as quickly as possible. Donna is on her way too."

As they pulled away from the Clarkes' house, a cluster of dark clouds were gathering in the sky above them. Aaron stared out of the window of the jeep at the sinister formation, and in the ten minutes it took to get back to Mack and Cal's house, the weather changed dramatically. The dark black clouds grew in density, rolling across the blue skies of earlier in the day. Obscuring the sun and casting ominous shadows over the ground, they seemed to be chasing the jeep as it made its way to Mack's estate. As they turned into the long drive that led to the house, the vehicle dipped and swayed as the suspension negotiated the camber of the unmade road. Gusts of wind picked up around it. Mack slowed the jeep to allow his stable hand, Jed, who was leading a visibly anxious Spirit from the reins back toward the safety of the stables, to cross in front of them.

As they pulled up outside the house, Mack got out and rushed to the door to let them in. Aspen and Cal followed closely behind him with Aurora still in Cal's arms. Aaron jumped out and opened the back of the jeep, pulling out the bags. Throwing his large sports holdall over one shoulder, he pulled up the handle of Aspen's wheeled suitcase and headed after the others up to the front door of the house, dragging the suitcase behind him over the gravel. As he walked away from the jeep, his attention was momentarily drawn to the long grass in the field behind the house, watching it roll in hypnotic, rhythmic waves with the force of the wind. He stopped, captivated by the movement. Rooted to the spot as if in a trance, Aaron didn't notice the wisp of dark smoke that had emerged out of the front edge of the field and was winding its way around the side of the house toward him.

The black mist edged out onto the wide driveway of the house, and as it snaked closer to Aaron's feet, the wind picking up and swirling around him, Mack appeared at the front door. Instantly registering what was happening, he ran toward Aaron.

"No! Aaron!" Mack yelled, reaching him just ahead of the wisp of dark smoke. Throwing out his arm in the direction of the swiftly encroaching Darkness, a beam of light shot out from the palm of his hand, expanding to create a wide golden shield.

The black mist hit the shield and veered off at a sharp angle, colliding with a bush. The impact caused an explosion of flames and smoke, thrusting the snaking mist backward before it shot up in the air and then careered downward, smashing through the surface of the soil as it drove into the ground and disappeared.

Mack grabbed Aaron's upper arm and shook him. "Aaron, *focus!*" he yelled as the wind blew more violently around them and the branches of the trees to the side of the house whipped punishingly against it. "Get inside!"

Mack headed back toward the front door, pulling Aaron by his arm and fighting against the force of the wind as it competed with his own strength to push them farther from the house. The suitcase rolled and flipped from side to side as Aaron hauled it behind him over the gravel surface of the drive.

"Keep going!" Mack shouted against the wind as he dragged Aaron forward into the house slamming the door behind them, falling back against it and breathing heavily.

Dazed with shock and from the spell of the Darkness, Aaron leaned back against one of the thick oak pillars supporting the beamed ceiling of the lounge. He opened and shut his mouth, struggling to speak, but was interrupted from even trying to by the sound of cars pulling up at the front of the house, just as large heavy drops of rain had begun to hammer insistently against the windows.

"They're here," Mack said to Aspen. "Quick, help me get them inside." Looking out of the large window by the front door, Aaron saw a black SUV outside, with a bull bar on the front. A sleek red sports car was pulling up just behind it. He watched as a broad male figure wearing a green windbreaker with the hood up got out of the SUV and rushed to the red car behind. He helped the driver—a slim silhouette with long dark hair blowing out of the raised hood of a black belted coat—out of the low-slung sports car. Hurrying toward the house, they fought against the wind. As they reached the door, Mack opened it, hanging tightly to it as the force of the wind nearly took it out of his grasp. The new arrivals stumbled into the house amid that distinctive smell of cold and wet wind that catches in your nose and throat as it wraps you in its blast, mixed with the smell of freshly damp material from the heavy jackets, which their occupants began to take off.

As the large broad figure removed the heavy green windbreaker and turned slightly toward the center of the room, Aaron took a sharp breath in, recognizing the occupant.

"Mr. Marsh!" he gasped in shock.

"Hello, Aaron," Joe Marsh said, slightly out of breath and with a half-smile that quickly faded as his gaze then moved over to the sight of the still unconscious Aurora on the sofa.

Mack greeted Donna Marsden as she removed her coat and Aspen took it from her. Donna's long dark hair fell around her shoulders as she took his hand in both of hers and smiled with the warm affection of an old friend.

Aspen walked over to Aaron, concern in her eyes for the vast influx of information her son was trying to digest. Taking him in her arms, she hugged him, which did nothing to ease the rigid tension in his body. Knowing the conversations that had to follow, Aspen put her hand up to the back of Aaron's head affectionately, and as she gently pulled it toward her own, the bright shield of protection emanated out from her body, wrapping them both in its golden light.

Mack moved over behind Aspen, putting his hand on her shoulder. "The Darkness is moving in fast; we have to get the shield in place around the house."

As Aspen turned to face Mack, a shadow began to move ominously across the lounge, and the gusting wind whipped a tree branch against the side of the house with a heavy thud.

"Now." Mack nodded, and Aspen put her hands on Aaron's shoulders, looking intently into his eyes.

"I know all this is really strange and confusing," she said softly, "and it will be more so, just for a short while. But then we will explain it all to you. You just have to go with it right now, as we have things to do." She turned him toward the sofa where Aurora lay, Cal sitting on the floor next to her. "Go and sit with the others," she urged Aaron and gave him a nudge forward.

Walking slowly toward the armchair by the sofa, Aaron's face was expressionless as he sat down. He and Cal watched in silence as the four adults gathered together, Donna talking in low tones and gesturing around the house in an instructional manner, with the others nodding along as she spoke.

After less than a minute of intense discussion, the adults moved apart to stand one at each of the four corners of the large open-plan lounge as the growing gloom outside began to infiltrate the house. Seeping through the edges of the windows and doors, the dark mist crawled its way through the air like demonic fingers. Aspen, Mack, and Joe all raised their arms outstretched to their sides, palms forward, looking toward Donna. She nodded, raising her own arms and thrusting her hands forward in the air as bright golden beams of light shot from her palms, illuminating the darkness.

The beams of golden light connected through the hands of Aspen and Joe, who stood on each side of Donna, growing brighter as the final connection was made from their hands to Mack's, who stood at the opposite side of the room from Donna.

The beams of light expanded upward and downward behind them, creating a shield around the occupants of the room. As the wisps of black smoke collided with the outside of the shield, they veered away. Collecting in clouds of darkness behind it, they began to rush at the shield like live battering rams, trying to break through it.

"Hold strong!" Mack yelled to the others, his voice strained. "Keep going!"

The shield continued to expand, the sides of it spreading rapidly across the ceiling and floor. The dark mists emitted a low, ominous hissing sound, frantically chasing the progress of the shield as it cocooned the entire room in its golden light. As the final edges of the shield met, an instant silence fell within its center, the brightness settling to a warm golden glow that gently pulsed as if it were alive.

The four adults slowly dropped their arms, letting out heavy breaths of relief in unison. Joe moved toward Mack, putting one hand on his friend's shoulder and nodding.

"We did it, Mack. They're safe now."

Aspen and Donna embraced each other before heading over to join Mack and Joe. A short, hushed conversation followed between them all, and then they turned to Aaron, Cal, and Aurora.

"Nice one, guys." Cal grinned widely. "Pretty impressive, to be fair."

"Thanks, son," Mack chuckled.

The swirling black mists collecting behind the shield had slowed. Just visible from inside the golden bubble, they seemed to be watching the occupants inside, piercing yellow eyes appearing from time to time within the ominous silhouettes crawling over the surface of the shield.

Seeing Cal and Aaron looking upward, Donna reassured them. "They can't perceive us anymore through the shield, though we can see them."

"They?" Cal questioned.

"Dark demons," Donna replied, looking toward the black clouds above them. "Slaves to the Darkness, sent to hunt Aaron, to prevent him being turned to the Light."

All eyes turned to Aaron, who sat rigid in the chair with tightly crossed arms, wide eyes, and clenched jaw, looking tentatively around him. Aspen moved over and knelt down in front of her son, resting her hands on his knees.

"This wasn't how you were meant to find out about all this, sweetheart," she said gently, the emotion breaking her voice as she met the confusion and uncertainty in his eyes.

A minute of silence followed as Aaron dropped his head, chewing thoughtfully on his lower lip.

Finally, he took a deep breath and lifted his eyes to look from his mother to his still unconscious twin sister on the sofa beside him.

"Aurora," he whispered, his voice breaking slightly, "is she— is she going to be okay?"

"She's weak," Aspen said gently, "but she's with us, just sleeping right now." Tears rose in her eyes, and she breathed them away before continuing. "The things you need to hear, Aaron, the things you need to do . . . we believe they will help Aurora to find her way back to us."

Taking in her words, Aaron nodded along slowly, his eyes still fixed on Aurora. Pulling in a deep breath, he held it for a few seconds before letting it out with a heavy sigh and uncrossing his arms.

"Okay. Well . . . I'm not sure you can say much which will surprise me after all this, so go for it," he said with resignation. "I'm ready."

Taking Aaron's hands in hers and squeezing them, Aspen turned to Donna Marsden expectantly, rising up from her kneeling position as Donna walked forward and Mack moved one of the high-backed oak dining chairs in front of Aaron for her to sit down.

Cal's gaze rested on Aurora, lying by his side. Momentarily overwhelmed by the intense feelings that flooded through him at the sight of her, he looked away again, a telltale redness rising on his cheeks as his eyes met his father's and he caught the knowing glint in Mack's eyes. The connection to Aurora was something he had never experienced before. He'd had crushes on girls like all the lads at school, and they on him, but this was different. It was a level of connection he didn't understand, but he felt in the deepest parts of his soul from the first moment he had seen her at Donna Marsden's that he knew her, had known her for lifetimes. That instant awareness had thrown his mind into further turmoil, having just been spun on itself multiple times while in the meeting with Donna, experiencing the intensity of the journey through time and space, meeting the Lightworkers, seeing his mum again.

Quietly reflecting on the past weeks since his own calling to the Rainbow Forest, Cal felt his crystal pulsing in his shirt pocket. His mind drifted between the insanity of the whole situation and the normalness it had now taken on in his world. It felt like a weight of intense responsibility now lay on his shoulders, which prior to these revelations were concerned primarily with horse care, ground maintenance at their estate, and school studies, while trying to deal with the constant ache his mum's disappearance had left in his life. In that moment, he also realized the extent of the part Aurora now played in that responsibility and in a yet unknown and largely incomprehensible future. Unable to convince his mind to go there yet, he instead allowed his attention to be drawn back to the room and the sound of Donna's voice as she explained the same fate that had changed his own life and future to a stunned Aaron sat on the chair beside him.

"So what now?" Aaron asked in a surprisingly matter-of-fact tone, as Donna paused to let him assimilate the history of the Battle between the Light and the Darkness. She had stopped at the point of the Gozzits calling the children to Valhandra, and Cal noticed she had left out any mention of the identity of the Lightworkers so far.

"Now," Donna continued, "you must journey to the Rainbow Forest to receive the new Consciousness into your soul, just as Cal and Aurora have already done. You are the final link, Aaron. It has been a much tougher journey for you than it was planned to be, but with you the Circle of Light will be complete."

"Does it hurt?" Aaron asked hesitantly, looking toward Cal, who shook his head, smiling reassuringly at his friend.

"Not at all," Donna also reassured him. "It will feel like coming home."

Aaron glanced at Aurora. "How do I get there?" he asked with determination in his voice.

"They are already waiting for you, darling," Aspen interjected, smiling.

Donna held out her arm beside her, and the molecules of the air began to move, swirling and turning faster and faster in a kaleidoscope of emerging colors. Aaron stood up and took a few steps toward the whirling rainbow mass. Its movement slowed, and as its central point began to part, a bright light beyond it shone through. It illuminated Aaron's body, and he briefly looked away, shielding his eyes with one forearm. The portal entrance widened still further, expanding to reveal the serene beauty of the Rainbow Forest as Aaron looked up, catching his breath at the sight before him.

"Aaron, come to us," the voice of Namogoz filled the air around them. "We have been waiting for you."

Aaron looked toward Aspen, and she nodded to him, smiling. With a final glance back at Aurora, Aaron took a deep breath, clenched his fists to his sides, and strode forward through the rainbow portal, which spun shut behind him and disappeared.

CHAPTER 19

Aurora floated above the scene in front of her. She immediately noticed a numbness in her body from the neck down; could she move? She tried to wiggle her fingers but felt nothing—her toes, nothing. She tried to impel her legs to move, straining for the message to transfer from her brain to her body, but still nothing happened. Feeling like she was encased in stone, she closed her eyes as a tiredness she had never experienced before washed through her, infiltrating every cell, every molecule of her being.

What's happening to me? she wondered, suddenly panicked. Feeling like she was drifting in and out of consciousness, her mind a fog of confusion, she put all her energy and concentration into the effort of simply opening her eyes to look around her, which in itself seemed to take every ounce of energy she had.

Distant thoughts pricked at her awareness, and she wondered what she had forgotten. Was she supposed to be somewhere? Do something?

No matter, she thought as the fog cleared somewhat and she was able to focus on the scene in front of her, which appeared to be an old-fashioned drawing room.

Her eyes drifted over the decor of the room. The muted blues and sage greens of paneled walls were dotted with paintings of animals, landscapes, and the trite smiles of posed family groups all set within thick gilt frames, befitting the elegance of the surroundings.

As her eyes wandered to the central area of the drawing room, more of the scene began to take shape. She became aware of movement within the room, and figures began to appear out of the fog, distant muffled voices drifting through her consciousness. As the moving shapes before her sharpened in clarity, a large sofa came into view. Its smooth, silver velvet upholstery was edged with pale gray painted wood, with a high back and ornately curved arms that flowed into its molded feet. The sofa stood on a patterned rug in brighter tones of blue and green that covered the majority of the floor but revealed seasoned wood floorboarding beyond it, around the edges of the room.

"I don't understand, Will. Why? She's lying—it's all lies."

Aurora heard a desperate but strangely familiar female voice pleading as two figures came into view on the sofa. She squinted in an attempt to focus her eyesight, and she could see that one was male and one female. The male's face was still blurred, and Aurora's vision rested first on the female, who was sitting to the side of him, her head and upper body turned toward him and her hands clasped around his. The muted rose tones of the woman's long, plaid skirt fell elegantly over the edge of the sofa to the floor. With it she wore a white blouse with a black ribbon tied in a bow at its high neck, long white sleeves, and a black corset-style waist belt. Her blond hair was held up in beautifully styled curls to the back of her head by an antique jeweled barrette.

A male voice spoke in a soft, low tone, full of caring but with immovable determination.

"There is no choice, Rebecca. You know that," he said, removing one hand from hers and putting it up to her cheek affectionately.

"Family honor is paramount. I cannot—I will not—sacrifice my family name. For lies, for anything. You must understand, my darling, this is simply how it must be."

His broad shoulders and slim build seemed familiar to Aurora, but with her mind and body still feeling like she was swimming through mud, she struggled to recall the memories it was sparking in her consciousness.

He was smartly dressed in dark gray tailored trousers, a pale gray shirt, and dark blue waistcoat, the gold chain of a pocket watch hanging from the front of it. As Aurora's gaze traveled upward, the features of his face began to come into focus, and she gasped with shock as she recognized the square-set jaw, dark eyes, and thick black hair.

"Cal!"

Reeling with shock at his identity, Aurora's vision moved around as if it were a movie camera circling the scene. Another bolt of surprise hit her as the female's face came into view and she found herself staring into her own eyes. She was older, maybe by ten years, as was Cal, and from her memories of history lessons at school she guessed it to be Victorian times, but unmistakably it was the two of them.

Her shock gave way to curiosity as distant and deeply hidden memories began to bubble up uncontrollably to the surface of her conscious mind. She recognized the house—it felt like home—and her mind's eye was suddenly flooded with images of the rest of the house outside of the drawing room: the large, opulent hallway with a grand staircase rising up onto a wide galleried landing. She recalled the vast grounds—ornately shaped shrubs and fully stocked borders in all the colors of the rainbow. She remembered the stables, horses; she saw herself riding over green fields, through open countryside, with Cal riding alongside her, laughing and talking together as they rode.

Her attention was drawn back to the conversation between the two people on the sofa, and she listened to her own voice as it pleaded with him, tears welling in her eyes.

"But a duel, Will. It's crazy, unnecessary. Not to mention illegal! What if you . . . you . . ."

She watched herself grasping more tightly at Cal's hands as she stared into his eyes, her body shaking as the tears were now spilling down her face.

"I will win," Cal said with firmness, putting his hands on her shoulders and looking intently into her eyes. "I won't leave you . . . ever. I promise you that."

Like a TV channel switching, the scene faded and changed. Now it was a ballroom, full of people dancing and milling about. Beautiful ball gowns swirled and spun as their wearers moved elegantly with the music, the men grasping the hands of their partners as they led them around the dance floor. The buzz of chatter was muffled and incoherent in the background, but through it, Aurora became aware of insistent and angry voices. Her vision zoomed in to the far end of the room, where a small group of four stood by the tall French bay windows, which were open to the dark night sky.

She saw herself standing with Cal. Dressed in an ivory and gold ball gown, she held one of her gloved hands against his chest as he held out his arms in an open gesture of question to the second couple standing in front of them. He was shaking his head with confusion on his face, and her breath caught in her throat momentarily at how handsome he was, though some deep sense of foreboding rose up from deep in the pit of her stomach.

Her attention moved to the couple with them, also a man and a woman. Aurora had never seen the tall, fair-haired man before and was taken aback at the rage in his face in that moment as he gestured angrily with clenched fist toward Cal. There was something vaguely familiar about the woman, though Aurora couldn't place where she knew her from. Petite, with olive-toned skin, her thick black hair was arranged in a high bun and edged with a sparkling tiara. Huge emerald-green eyes dominated a stunningly pretty face, and she wore a deep emerald-green dress, covered with gems that matched the color of her eyes. It clung to the soft curves of her body, which was in stark contrast to Aurora's slim, elegant frame, and Aurora felt a sudden and unexplained bolt of intense jealousy, bordering on hatred and cutting deep into her chest. The feeling was so alien to Aurora it caused her physical discomfort, and she breathed out heavily, trying to force it from her body as she watched the scene play out in front of her.

"The accusation is insane . . . and absolutely untrue," Cal told the fair-haired man, looking him directly in the eyes with unwavering certainty in his voice. "Rebecca is my only love—always has been and always will be."

"Prove it," threatened the fair-haired man, aggressively gesturing to his dark-haired companion beside him. "She says you are in love with her—not Rebecca—and she with you. That you plan to run away together. Why would she say that if it were not true?"

"That I cannot answer," Cal responded, and Aurora watched as he turned to the dark-haired girl, raising his eyebrows at her in question. The girl swiftly turned her gaze downward, and Aurora knew without doubt that it had been a lie.

As Cal turned back, the fair-haired male squared up in front of him, speaking in a threatening voice.

"I will have no option but to make this information public," the second man said. "Your family name will be ruined."

"For what?" Cal asked, looking him straight in the eyes. "Because she doesn't love you, or because she's willing to lie to get out of marrying you?"

"I challenge you to a duel," the fair-haired man declared in a low, hostile tone. "Pistols at dawn, two mornings from now."

"No!" Aurora heard herself cry out as the scene faded to blackness.

An overwhelming tiredness overtook her once more. She closed her eyes and floated in numbness, confusion consuming her as she tried to make sense of where she was and what it was she needed to do. An awareness was trying to get through somewhere in the depths of her mind, and as she struggled to take hold of it, she felt like she was trying to grasp at air.

"Aurora," a voice called out from far in the distance.

She closed her eyes, not caring, blackness falling around her once more.

"Aurora," the voice said again, clearer, more insistently.

She forced her eyes open and found herself floating no longer in blackness but in swirling rainbow mists.

A face appeared in front of her, wide eyes set in the trunk of a huge tree. Aurora stared transfixed into them as stars, planets, and unending time and space opened up in their depths. There was a familiarity about it and about the rainbow mists swirling around her, a peace and a safety, like coming home. She knew these eyes, had looked into them before, but couldn't recall in that moment when.

"Aurora, can you hear me?" the familiar voice questioned gently.

"Mmmm," Aurora heard herself make the sound, though she wondered why her mouth didn't seem to move.

"You are lost, Aurora," it said. "We are trying to reach you."

Aurora instantly felt a resistance to the words deep in her soul. An irrational anger rose suddenly in her awareness, and she felt herself jolt backward out of the rainbow mists and back into darkness.

"I'm fine," she heard herself shout toward the voice, though again her mouth didn't move with the words. "I'm not lost. I'm fine. I have to go back to Cal . . . to Will . . . home . . . to . . ." She paused, not sure what she was saying or why.

"Aurora," the voice repeated, more distant now, "you *are* home. You've always been home. Home is you the Being; whatever its surroundings are—or have ever been—*you* are home."

The words vibrated through her mind, forcing her to listen.

Her brain was suddenly reeling with information she couldn't grasp, as memories began to surface randomly from somewhere deep in her subconscious. Like a pressure valve had suddenly released, she saw herself, Cal, her parents, Aaron, all in different times, different places, and cultures. They appeared in her mind's eye, expanding as if they would engulf her and then fading to nothing. The visions continued exploding in the air, like a pack of cards in front of her; she saw herself in lifetime after lifetime, body after body. Information overloaded her mind, and she felt like screaming.

"Please stop!" she heard herself cry out. "Please, please stop! I can't take it anymore!"

"Aurora, still your mind; listen to me and listen to only me," the familiar voice continued calmly.

Pulling in a deep breath, Aurora followed the instructions of the voice, instinctively slowing her thoughts while not really knowing how or why she was doing so.

"So," she said, as some space opened up inside her mind, "what now?"

"Aurora," the voice declared with a certainty that told her she needed to listen, "there is nothing you haven't done, nowhere you haven't been. In nearly a billion years of life on Earth, you have been, lived, and experienced everything from the smallest molecule of existence to the kings and queens of continents. There are some who will have been constants in your time on Earth; they are there to show you the way, and you for them, to facilitate each other's journeys in all your lifetimes. The future is created only from and with the choices you make on that journey, Aurora—together and separately. The destination can never be a given factor; it is fluid, uncertain, and infinitely changeable across an unlimited number of realities that exist simultaneously through time and space.

"So what is destiny, then, if it's so uncertain?" Aurora heard herself question the voice.

"Choice," came the reply. "Yours . . . for the future you wish to create. Whether you are willing and brave enough to receive all the Universe holds in store for you in your current lifetime."

She sensed a deep awareness rising, as if it came from deepest parts of her soul, a long-awaited awareness and the release of some profound knowledge she welcomed but still had yet to understand. As the pressure continued to release in her chest, her previously panicked breathing stilled, and a space began to open where before there was only blackness.

"Embrace it or deny it . . ." the voice continued. "The difference lies only in your choice. Take notice of the past, learn lessons from it. But do not live from what has been, rather what can be. Everything can be overcome, and anything is possible. Ultimately, all that is required to create a greater future . . . is a different choice."

Aurora's mind responded before she had the chance to.

"But what if I've been wrong?" it asked, and she listened to it as if it were a second person, existing simultaneously alongside her and yet within her.

"Your mind is speaking from your experiential self," the voice said in answer to her unspoken awareness that she was in fact two people.

"That is the part of you which doubts, which fears, which suffers with human emotions, thoughts, and perceived failures. None of it is wrong. All is simply a part of the journey."

"You also have a higher self," the voice continued, "which holds your true power. It is the 'you' which exists at a higher frequency throughout all time and space. It will help and guide you, if you are willing to listen to it."

The information washed through her in waves, filling her soul, as if she had waited an eternity to hear it, as if every question she ever had was being answered in that second.

"How will I know which is which?" Aurora asked.

"When you received the new Consciousness into your soul in the Rainbow Forest, your experiential self merged with your higher self. It created a new light in your soul, a light which is held in the crystal you were given. You already have the power, Aurora, but when you allowed your anger toward your father to overtake it, you dropped your crystal and you separated from the light."

"Can I have it back?" she asked, her voice breaking with emotion and the memories resurfacing.

"Of course," the voice responded gently.

At those words, something shifted inside of her, a subtle but perceptible change, and as a sense of peace moved through her mind and body, Aurora's attention returned to a different time and place.

"So how did it end—the duel?" she asked hesitantly.

A scene emerged from the blackness in front of her, expanding out to show a field, surrounded by trees and bathed in early morning light.

Cal and the second man from the ballroom appeared in the center of the picture, back to back. With heads held high, they stared forward determinedly. As they walked slowly away from each other, a voice in the distance counted their paces. As the voice reached the count of twenty, the two men stopped, and time itself seemed also to stop as they slowly turned to face each other.

Two shots rang out, the air reverberating with the sound, and the scene in front of her ran in slow motion. Aurora watched helplessly as Cal's body was flung backward with the force of the bullet that entered it at the middle of his chest. As he landed on the ground, she heard her own screams, watching as Rebecca ran to Will, falling to the ground at his side and sobbing with grief as she cradled his head in her arms. The scene zoomed in as if Aurora were there, and she found herself looking directly into the eyes she recognized as Cal's.

"I won't leave you . . . ever," he whispered.

The scene faded, and blackness descended once more.

CHAPTER 20

Aspen and Mack paced the room simultaneously while the golden shield held strong, gently pulsing against the dark silhouettes still gathered ominously on the outside of it. The demonic forms floated among them, their evil yellow eyes staring into the middle of the golden bubble within the house. The darkness outside cast a deep gloom over the occupants inside the lounge, and though in reality it was minutes, it seemed like hours since Aaron had entered the portal to the Rainbow Forest. Aspen stopped by the sofa, crouching down at Aurora's side and resting one hand on her daughter's arm. As she did so, Aurora unexpectedly stirred, taking a sudden deeper breath that startled Aspen and brought Donna also rushing to Aurora's side. Mack and Joe followed and all stood watching her, waiting expectantly for any further sign of consciousness, but none came. After a minute of no further movement, Aspen sighed, dropping her head, and as she slowly stood up, Donna put one arm around her shoulder supportively.

In the second that they turned away from Aurora, a change began to occur within the room. The dark demons gathering outside the golden shield suddenly and without warning began to disappear, suddenly turning and floating away like wisps of smoke. The dark mists moved away from the golden bubble, retreating back up into the sky, though they remained hovering in the air, and although the intense gloom lifted slightly, the shadow of the clouds above the house remained.

Mack and Aspen looked at each other with expectant anticipation in their eyes, both knowing instinctively what this meant. If the Dark demons could no longer detect Aaron, that meant the change had occurred. Aaron's soul had received the new Consciousness; he was safe, protected from the Darkness. Aspen clasped both hands to her chest, holding her breath with renewed hope.

"Listen," Cal said eagerly, "can you hear that?"

A low hum was audible in the distance, and the molecules of the air where the portal had previously opened began to change. Like bubbles, they swelled bigger and bigger, then one by one began to burst. The space they had occupied became a swirling mass of color, spinning from its central point as a beam of bright light appeared and the vortex finally began to reopen.

The light initially was blinding as the portal spun wider and up past the height of the beams in the lounge. As it reached the full height of the room, the brightness began to settle, the vortex slowly clearing to reveal a misty path, winding back into the distance. Around the edges of the path, the intense colors of the Rainbow Forest began to materialize, framed by the magnificent backdrop of Valhandra. A figure became visible, slowly walking forward along the path toward them, a silhouette at first. Then, as it moved closer, its form began to sharpen into focus. Finally, Aspen let out her breath with a gasp of emotional relief as Aaron stepped back out of the portal.

Aspen rushed forward toward her son, throwing her arms around him in a tight hug, which he lovingly returned. As they drew apart, she held him by his arms with tears of joy, as she looked into the depths of the Universe through his eyes.

"You're the image of your dad, darling," she said with emotion breaking in her voice.

"Thanks, Mum," Aaron replied softly, a new maturity in his demeanor, and as he pulled his shoulders back he seemed taller to her somehow—a man emerging from the boy she had known. The tears flowed freely down Aspen's face, a mix of intense pride along with the knowledge that she had brought him as far as she was always meant to . . . and now had to let him go on.

"I'm happy, sweetie . . . honestly!" she told him as Mack joined them behind Aspen, putting his hands on her shoulders in silent understanding.

"Well done, Aaron," Mack said with pride in his voice. "You killed it, buddy."

Aaron nodded to Mack before looking over to Aurora. Holding out both his hands, he opened them slowly to reveal a perfect piece of clear crystal lying in each palm.

"I have Aurora's too, Mum," he said. "Namogoz said she's ready to have it back."

White light glowed around Aaron's body as he walked over to his sister, pushing his own crystal in his jeans pocket as he knelt down beside her. Taking her left hand in his, he placed Aurora's crystal in the palm. Closing her fingers over it, he clasped her fist in both his hands as the rest of the room looked on, waiting anxiously.

Slowly, the white light around Aaron's body began to permeate into Aurora's. As it flowed up her arm, the color began to return to her skin, and the depth of her breathing gradually began to increase. Cal's eyes never left her, his hand resting gently on her shoulder over the arm of the sofa. As the energy of the crystal made its way through Aurora's body, Aaron felt his sister's hand begin to flex and clasp the crystal on its own. Releasing her hand, he looked up at Cal and smiled, their eyes meeting in an unspoken acknowledgement of a new reality and of new hope.

Aurora opened her eyes and looked first at her brother.

"Hey," she said, smiling weakly. "Well, at least you got there eventually."

"Shut up, sis," he laughed, shaking his head as Aspen smiled, clasping her hands to her mouth in a prayer motion.

Aaron helped Aurora to sit up on the sofa, pushing the cushions around her, while she weakly and unconvincingly protested that she was fine and didn't need help. Once propped up, Aurora turned instinctively to her left toward Cal. As their eyes met, they both sensed a deeper and unspoken connection between them, a sure but not yet fully understood awareness that the bond between them was not just of this lifetime. They stared at each other in silence, overwhelmed but at ease in the knowledge that the time would come for them in this life, but that time was not yet.

Tearing her eyes away from Cal, Aurora looked back at Aaron. She felt a deep relief mixed with amazement as she looked into the Universe and the depths of the solar system through her brother's eyes. A thousand questions tumbled around in her head, though none would come out of her mouth. Instead, she heard her soul speaking to him telepathically, just as it had done with Cal in the cloisters.

"You look so . . . different," she communicated to him, and he laughed.

"Well, yeah, I guess I am, aren't I!" he sent back. "I mean . . . talking trees . . . you could have warned me, sis!"

It was Aurora's turn to laugh now, though she fought back tears at the same time, for all she had been forced to keep from him and all she knew he had been through.

"There was never a really good time," she joked and held her brother's hand as he offered it out to her.

"Did you see . . ." Aurora began.

"Dad?" Aaron finished for her. "Yes." He nodded, squeezing her hand affectionately with tears in his own eyes.

"It's okay, sis," he continued. "I know . . . I understand it all now, and I also know you did what you had to do." Aaron paused, looking around the others in the room and smiling. "Everyone did."

Aurora opened her hand and looked down at her crystal, which was pulsing with warm light in her palm.

"I just wanted to hurt him," she said sadly. "I don't know what came over me. I felt so much hate."

"He knows, and he understands," Aaron reassured her. "He gave it to me to bring back for you."

"I wish I could see him and say sorry," Aurora said sadly.

Donna moved forward toward them, and the attention of everyone in the room was drawn to her as she spoke.

"There is more to be done . . . and it is time now," she announced, raising her hands toward the portal as, once again, it began to spin and change.

All eyes in the room turned to the swirling vortex of light as the view of the Rainbow Forest within it spun away into the distance and a different scene began to materialize. From the depths of the vortex, a vast white room appeared, reaching back to a golden staircase. As the scene slowly settled, a figure became visible walking down the staircase toward them, fuzzy and distorted at first, but as it walked closer they could see it was a male. Golden beams of light projected from Donna's outstretched hands into the swirling vortex and toward the figure, who held out his own hands as he reached the entrance of the portal. The golden light emanating from Donna's hands connected to each of his, and as she helped him cross over into the reality he had left nearly a year before, Dane stepped out into the room.

With a choked gasp, Aspen rushed forward, throwing her arms around him as they wordlessly hugged each other. Eventually pulling apart, they both turned simultaneously toward the sofa, and with Dane's arm around Aspen's shoulders, they walked over to their children. As they reached the sofa, Aaron stood and embraced his father before standing back together with Aspen. Dane turned his attention on Aurora and crouched down beside her.

Aurora opened her mouth to speak, but no words came out. Tears began to stream down her face as she closed her eyes, dropping her head.

"I'm so sorr—" she began, but Dane put his hand to her cheek, shaking his head to silence her words.

"You have nothing to be sorry about, my darling," he said gently, his voice breaking slightly. "You did nothing wrong. Everything is as it should be."

Taking a deep breath, Aurora opened her eyes and looked up at him as he took both her hands in his. Bright white light appeared around him and began to flow swiftly into Aurora, through her hands as he held them, up her arms and through her body, flowing the energy she needed back into her soul. The white light grew around both of them, emanating out into the room, and as it did so, Aurora's life force began to increase. Within a minute she stood up from the sofa of her own accord, seeming to stand even taller and more radiant than she had ever been, her long golden hair shining in the light that surrounded her. Aspen and Aaron moved forward as Dane and Aurora turned toward them. Mother, father, son, and daughter embraced, finally together again. The other occupants of the room looked on, unable to hide their emotion at the reunion.

CHAPTER 21

Aaron, Aurora, and Cal sat listening in stunned silence as Dane and Donna spoke in turn, revealing the extent of what had happened since Miss Broach had disappeared.

"The High Council of Valhandra have been carefully monitoring the possible courses of the future since Marta Broach crossed over to the Darkness," Dane explained in a somber tone.

"You will learn more of this once your transfer to Valhandra has been completed. Right now, it is enough to say that there has been unprecedented change in the temporal forecasts. The stability of the world is fragile . . . to an extent we have not seen for many, many years. The balance of power in the Universe is shifting dramatically toward the Darkness, and the Light is beginning to lose its life force. A black cloud is descending over Earth. The Darkness is impelling fear in humanity, and it is spreading uncontrollably, causing a deep, viral depression to infiltrate the hearts and minds of every being on Earth. It is imperative that we get you all to Valhandra as soon as possible."

At this, Dane swept his arm out to the side, and a vision appeared before them like a TV screen. The evening news was playing, and the usually cheery anchor looked tired, his face expressionless and his eyes blank as he somberly read from the teleprompter in a monotone voice.

"The black smog which has descended over large areas of the country during the past twenty-four hours shows no signs of dissipating," he droned on. "Many world leaders report similar phenomena, and a meeting of international heads of state has been called tonight by the prime minister as a matter of urgency. Officials believe that the viral symptoms exhibited by many are a direct result of the atmospheric changes. Hospitals have been overrun in just the last few hours with admissions of the as yet unidentified virus."

The newsreader paused and sighed deeply, while the screen behind him in the newsroom played live footage of people lining up outside a hospital. The crowds wore face coverings and coughed uncontrollably from the black mist hanging in the air around them, parents carrying their young children in their arms while struggling to stand themselves. Bodies lay motionless on the sidewalks and streets, where they had fallen after breathing in the lethal smog, being stepped over by those panicking to get into the safety of their houses or the hospitals.

"At this time, everyone is being urged to remain inside until further notice," the newsreader continued somberly. "Any developments in the situation will be brought to you as they come in."

"What the hell?" Cal breathed, in shock.

"That's insane," Aaron added, shaking his head. "So what happens now?"

As the vision faded away, Donna continued.

"It is imperative that we move quickly. But it is also important that you understand the significance Marta Broach plays in this," she said with a gravity in her soft voice they had not heard before. "Because that is not as straightforward as it might first appear."

Donna pulled up a chair in front of the sofa, and Aurora, Cal, and Aaron waited in silence as she sat down.

"Marta Broach came into this life with a powerful soul," Donna began. "She was destined to be called to Valhandra with the first wave of Lightworkers. But her deepest longing was to have a baby, and she was not willing to wait. The Gozzits tried to intervene through her dreams, to delay her choice. But the young Marta was very strong-willed and would not listen. She became pregnant before the Lightworkers received their calling, and in doing so, she renounced the future she was destined for. The soul who came to her as her baby was also destined for Valhandra in the future, as a Child of the Light, like yourselves. But it was all too soon. It caused significant ripples in the quantum entanglements of time and space . . . and devastating consequences to those involved. The situation had to be resolved, and this is something you all must be aware of too. Once a predetermined future has been tampered with, there is usually no control over the way the natural course of events will right itself once more.

"The baby's father, Marta's husband, was killed in a freak plane crash. With the extent of emotional trauma Marta experienced, their baby died in the womb, and its soul returned to the spirit plane to await its calling at the right time. Marta never recovered from her grief, and a major part of her soul died with the loss of her baby. Her grief began to eat away at her, destroying more and more of her soul as the years went by."

"So that's why the Darkness took her?" Aurora asked, an empathetic lump in her throat as she assimilated the sad story. "Because her soul was too damaged?"

"Yes," Donna confirmed, nodding and pausing briefly before she continued. "The soul of the baby was born again into the world as a Child of the Light, to a Lightworker mother and Protector father, some years later. The High Council, however, did not anticipate the repercussions the history would have on the future situation. They did not foresee the strength of Marta's attachment to her baby's soul."

A heavy feeling of foreboding filled the air as the story unfolded, and a sense of unease began to surge through Aurora's body, making her squirm with discomfort. Cal appeared to be feeling it too, though Aaron sat silently, listening intently to the story.

"Marta tracked the child down, and because of the danger to her safety, it became necessary to remove her to a secret location until the time arrived for her calling to the Rainbow Forest. Even though Jasmine's soul has now been transformed, there is still great risk with the situation, more so since Marta was recruited by the Darkness."

The name Jasmine triggered a vague connection in Aurora's mind, increasing her feeling of unease, but Donna continued her story before she could think further on it.

"Initially, we thought that the one who alerted the Darkness to Aaron was Micah, but we now know that is not the case. It was Marta who released this information to the Darkness, and it would appear from what we have seen through the eyes of the Universe that she now stands beside the Darkness. The joint force of both her and Micah will provide the Darkness with much greater power against the Light and the Light's army."

Dane moved closer behind Donna, putting his hand on her shoulder as he continued the story. "There is more you will need to know in time. But for now, the priority is to get you all safely to Valhandra so the development of your powers can continue."

"When?" Cal asked.

"You will all sleep here tonight, within the shield, where we know you will be safe," Dane continued. "At dawn, you will be taken from here to Donna's house, where you will meet with other Children of the Light to be transported to Valhandra. Mack, Aspen, and Joe will remain with you here and will escort you in the morning. Donna and I must leave, in order to prepare for your arrival in Valhandra. But I will be waiting for you all when you get there."

Dane hugged both of his children before moving from Cal to Joe and then to Mack, clasping their hands with both of his in affectionate farewell gestures. Moving toward Aspen, he took her in his arms, assuring her gently that all would be okay as they said an emotional goodbye. Immediately after he and Donna stepped back into the Vortex, the rainbow mists began to rise within it, then it swiftly spiraled shut behind them and disappeared.

CHAPTER 22

Aspen stared out of the window of the jeep, distant and preoccupied, as Mack drove down the gravel track the next morning. Aurora, Aaron, and Cal sat in the back, the hazy yellow-bronze of the dawn light dimmed by the eerie black mists that floated through the air around them. Joe followed closely behind them all the way, as the adults had agreed between them.

The occupants of the vehicle were silent as they drove, each deep in their own thoughts of what lay ahead of them. As they drew closer to Donna's house, a mass of vehicles were converging on the roads leading up to it. Mack turned in to the long gravel drive, amid a stream of other vehicles on their way in and out of the property, while Joe drove past. He pulled his vehicle over on the far side of the entrance rather than interrupt the traffic flow on the main route to and from the house. At the end of the long driveway, Mack reversed the jeep in one swift maneuver into a free space near to the front of the house, and they all got out.

The hovering black mists cast deep shadows over the pure white beauty of Donna's house, giving it a sinister look. Aurora shivered from the chill in the early morning air, pulling her coat tighter around her as they headed quickly toward the door, with Mack and Aspen leading the way. The two parents were talking in low voices as they headed toward the imposing wooden front door of house. Hearing the mention of her father's name, Aurora increased her pace, straining to hear, but she couldn't make out any more of the conversation. As they reached the house, Eden was already standing at the open door, smiling warmly at them as she stood back, ushering them quickly inside, along with other groups arriving at the same time.

Once inside the vast hallway, Aurora looked around, trying unsuccessfully to count the other children. All looked around the same age as she, Aaron, and Cal. All were arriving with one parent, some with their mums, some their dads. All were engaging in hurried and emotional goodbyes before the parents turned to leave, with Eden in permanent post at the huge oak front door of the house.

Aurora and Aaron stood either side of Cal, and Aurora continued scanning all of the faces around the hallway. She didn't recognize any of the other children from their school but instantly felt comfortable in their presence. As she met the eyes of a couple of the others, she felt their energy converging with her own, like a deeply shared force pulling them all together as one.

At that moment, the wide double doors at the far end of the hallway opened and Donna appeared, pulling both the doors inward into the room and fully open before she walked out toward the group. The room beyond the door was situated in the center of the house, below the galleried landing that extended from one side to the other of the massive hallway. As Donna walked elegantly toward the group, Aurora caught sight of the room behind her—a huge lounge, brightly lit by an ornate crystal chandelier, which hung from the center of the ceiling. Donna wore a mid-length black pencil dress, perfectly tailored to her tall, slim figure, with a wide red shiny belt and matching red patent high-heeled shoes. Aurora wondered if she ever looked anything less than perfect.

"Welcome to all of you," Donna announced to the group, "and thank you all for getting here so quickly in the more urgent circumstances."

The remaining parents, including Aspen and Mack, made their way back to the front door. Aurora turned to look at her mother, and Aspen smiled lovingly at her before she turned to leave the house. Aurora watched her mother walk back toward the jeep with Mack, disappearing into the gray smog that hung in the air outside. As the door closed, she felt a sharp twinge in her heart. It was a strange new emotion to her—love for her mum, but mixed with a strange sense of moving on toward a new future, and she wasn't yet sure what part her mother would play in that future. Tears rose suddenly in her eyes, and she blinked hard to clear them as a rush of intense energy flowed through her mind, making her momentarily dizzy.

As the last of the parents left, Eden finally closed the huge oak door, and they all looked back toward Donna, who turned and gestured to the room behind her.

"Follow me, everyone," she said as she made her way back into the room. Walking to the far end of it, she stopped in front of the large French windows. Turning, she held her arms out to her left toward two rows of chairs in a semi-circle laid out to one side of the room. Aurora gazed around her, taking in the beautiful lounge as she followed behind Cal and Aaron and sitting down in the chair next to Cal and nearest to Dr. Marsden at the far end of the semi-circle. The chairs were situated in front of a huge marble fireplace, framed by clean white shelves. Built into the walls either side of the fireplace, the shelves displayed a variety of unusual artifacts, ornaments, and crystals.

As Aurora settled into her seat, one item in particular caught her eye. Positioned centrally on the marble fire surround was a large ring of clear crystal, standing upright on an antique gold plinth. As Aurora looked closely, she realized the ring consisted of individual pieces of crystal fitting perfectly together to form the ring. It appeared as if they comprised a whole that had been split apart and put back together. Aurora stared transfixed as the light from the chandelier caught the facets of the crystals, sending shards of light glistening through the air around them. The individual pieces appeared to move and waver slightly in front of her eyes, as if each one hovered in the air, independent of, though precisely positioned next to, the pieces around it. Aurora shook her head and blinked her eyes hard, staring again at the pieces of crystal, which continued to waver very slightly. Now she began to see particles of light traveling back and forth through the middle of the crystal ring, and she felt strangely drawn to the center space of its structure. The form of the room around it started to blur and fade away as she felt herself pulled in further and further, feeling like she might lose herself in its beauty.

Donna's hand on Aurora's shoulder brought her abruptly back from her thoughts.

"A replica of the Circle of Light, Aurora," Donna commented, smiling, as Aurora jumped slightly in her chair, "a magic annulus of crystals."

"It's beautiful," Aurora answered, still unable to take her eyes off it.

"And powerful," Donna added with a slight squeeze of Aurora's shoulder before she let go, walking gracefully to the front of the semi-circle of chairs and standing directly in front of the fireplace as she turned to the group. She held out her arms to either side of her and, with palms facing down, lowered them slowly as if to command a large crowd. Instantly, a hushed silence replaced the hum of chatter among the group in the room, and Aurora stifled a giggle, imagining the likelihood of one of the teachers at school having the same instant effect on a class.

"Welcome . . . Children of the Light," Donna announced, an air of authority in her soft, calming voice as her eyes scanned slowly around the group. "The past weeks have been an immense journey for each of you. For some, they have been more intense than others." She smiled warmly toward Aaron, Cal, and Aurora. However you got here, you have reached this point, this day, and that journey has only just begun.

"You are the future leaders of the Light's army. The first born with the purity of the new Consciousness within you, the power of the Universe, which has lain dormant since the day you were born, waiting for this point in your human lives to arrive. Now is the time to reach out to your destiny. The world needs you; it needs all of us—now more than ever."

Aurora realized she was holding her breath and let it out a little quicker than she had intended to. Cal turned to her and raised his eyebrows as he mouthed, "You okay?"

Aurora smiled up at him and nodded, noticing how much more settled she was with the connection between the two of them now. Cal smiled back at her, and as he did so, Aurora's eyes were drawn past him to a girl sitting on the far side of the semi-circle from them.

It wasn't the girl herself who caught Aurora's attention, but more the stream of energy that had suddenly emanated out from her toward Cal, as his eyes had met Aurora's. The glowing white threads of energy appeared to be pulling at Cal, connecting with his body and turning to flow back toward the girl. Cal didn't seem to notice it, casually turning his attention back to

Donna, who had begun calling out names to confirm everyone had arrived. Aurora's attention remained on the girl because a distant and deeply buried memory was stirring somewhere in her awareness, and she struggled to grasp it.

The girl was staring intently at Cal, which Aurora found strangely disturbing and uncomfortable. She was exotically beautiful, with caramel-toned skin and long dark hair, falling in thick waves around her shoulders. A sense of recognition was nagging at Aurora, and as she was trying to place her, the girl suddenly turned her attention away from Cal. As her emerald-green eyes met Aurora's, the recognition hit. Aurora was transported in her mind's eye back to the vision of her and Cal in the ballroom, the night before the duel. An icy chill surged through Aurora's veins as she realized it was her. It was the girl who had loved Cal, whose lies had brought about the duel that killed him. Her skin tone was different now, but the eyes were unmistakable. Aurora stared open-mouthed, shocked by the revelation and the girl's presence here.

"Jasmine?" Donna called out, and the girl turned quickly away from Aurora.

"Yes, here," she called out softly in response, looking sideways again briefly toward Aurora before focusing back on Donna and the proceedings in the room.

Aurora's mind was full of questions, instantly spinning with the shocking realization of the girl's identity. She looked back at the girl again with unmasked curiosity. Was this the same Jasmine Donna had spoken about the day before while they were within the golden shield? Was she not only Aurora's past-life nemesis but also the soul of Miss Broach's lost baby? Hearing her own name called out, Aurora forced her mind back to the present, focusing her attention on Donna's words as she finished calling out names and went on to explain what was going to be happening.

"As you know," Donna announced in a somber tone, "events are progressing quickly as the Darkness is spreading across the planet. At this moment, Children of the Light all around the world are coming together, as we are. Very soon, the portal to Valhandra will be opened, and we will travel together through it, to your new home."

Silence fell across the room as Donna paused briefly.

"You will find Valhandra very different from Earth," she went on. "Time does not exist there in the same way as it does here."

"What do you mean?" asked a tall red-haired boy from the front of the room.

"Time is not real, Jack. It is merely an invention, created by humankind," Donna explained. "On Valhandra, there is no day and night, no changing of the seasons. Reality as you know it will become fluid, malleable; time is basically immaterial."

Aurora's eyes were drawn suddenly to the Circle of Light on the mantelpiece behind Donna, which had begun pulsing and glowing with light. She felt her own crystal pulsing in response from the pocket of her coat, and she dug her hand into the pocket, clasping the crystal and feeling its warm energy flowing up her arm and throughout her body.

Donna was silent at the front of the room, looking around her.

"It's time," she announced, "Please, everyone stand up, take your crystals, and hold them out toward me."

The group in the room did as she instructed, and Aurora watched as the light from the crystal annulus expanded, creating a bright halo around Donna, who swept her hands elegantly out to either side of her as if conducting an orchestra.

Aurora stared open-mouthed as the light from the annulus shot out of it, amid gasps from others in the room. The stream of light connected one by one through each crystal held out toward it, the bright glow expanding farther and farther around the room. The entire wall behind Donna began to dissolve and Aurora glimpsed a view of the most beautiful scenery she had ever seen: green hills, lush trees, and blue sky. Waterfalls ran into clear streams, and flowers in the brightest colors, as if in a painting, were all edged with gold and sparkling in the sunlight. Aurora felt a sensation of complete calm and peace wash through her, and as she felt herself being propelled forward into the rainbow mists, she let go to the weightless flight.

CHAPTER 23

As the rainbow mists cleared around her, Aurora's eyes readjusted to her surroundings and came back into focus. Standing in a huge hall with the group she had been with at Donna's house, she became aware of many, many others around her. Group after group appeared out of nowhere through portals of bright white light, which faded to reveal the hall filled with young people of her own age coming in from all over the world.

"There's so many," Aurora heard her mind whisper to Cal, who stood next to her, staring at him with wide eyes.

"Look," Cal replied, catching Aurora's arm and nodding upward. She followed his gaze to the top half of the vast hall. Formed entirely of marble, the outer edge was flanked with tall ornate pillars, above which a balcony extended from a wide staircase in front of them, stretching around the entire hall. As Aurora looked more carefully, she saw rows of figures slowly coming into view, hazy silhouettes of light lining the gallery above them and looking down at the developing crowd below.

Suddenly, Aurora felt Cal's hand tense its hold on her arm.

"Mum," Cal breathed out, and Aurora followed his gaze up to the balcony to their right. One of the bright silhouettes came slowly into focus: a tall slim woman with shoulder-length dark hair. As her facial features sharpened, Aurora looked up into stunningly beautiful eyes identical to Cal's. Resting her other hand on his arm too, Aurora felt his relief and joy to see his mother as deeply if it were her own.

Aurora looked around her in awe of what was happening. *I wonder what they're all thinking,* she mused. In an instant, her head filled with the noise of chatter all around her, becoming louder and louder through her mind; it was almost deafening in its volume. Words and conversations in her head, as if a hundred radio stations were playing at once. She looked around her, feeling as if time were running in slow motion. The molecules in the air around her expanded, pressing uncomfortably against her body before bursting like bubbles with yet another intensity of noise that vibrated endlessly in her brain.

The thoughts of every person in the room grew to form an unbearable pressure in her head, becoming even more intense as the noise increased in volume. She noticed that wherever her attention went to in the room, her vision instantly shot forward as if on a zoom lens, making her dizzy from the speed. With the roar of noise in her mind, Aurora suddenly felt like she was going to pass out. Pressing her hands frantically to the sides of her head, she yelled in her mind, *Stop!* and immediately the noise ceased. As calm resumed within her, she breathed out hard with relief, looking around her and trying to make sense of what had just happened.

"Aurora." She heard a familiar voice in her mind, coming from somewhere nearby. She instinctively looked up at the gallery surrounding the top part of the huge hall, scanning along the rows of shining silhouettes until her gaze reached the staircase in front of her and rested on one figure coming into focus, one of two figures in the center of the staircase—her father.

Dane smiled down at his daughter. She smiled back, relieved to see him there, and immediately the energetic connection flowed between them.

"Try to stop thinking, Aurora," Dane communicated telepathically to her. "Here in Valhandra, the reality around you is shaped by your thoughts. Whatever you think will instantly become the reality surrounding you. This is your new way of being, and there's nothing to be scared of. You are powerful beyond all you can yet imagine. Now that you are here, you will be taught to use those powers."

Aurora smiled at him as his words wrapped around her like he was hugging her soul. She was nervous, yet excited, and filled with an intense anticipation of the journey she was about to begin, the journey they were all about to begin.

As her father's image became clearer, so too did the image of the second figure standing to his side in the center of the staircase. Aurora's vision zoomed in from where she stood, and she saw them both as clearly as if they were standing directly in front of her. As the second figure began to come into focus, Aurora saw it was a man, surrounded by warm golden light and standing a good few inches taller than Dane, who was enveloped by the white light of all the Lightworkers she had met before. Both were dressed completely in white, her father in a linen suit and the taller man in white robes. The taller man was older than Dane, with white hair, a short white beard, and the most piercing blue eyes Aurora had ever seen. There was something familiar about him that tugged at a memory in Aurora, but she couldn't quite place it. His skin, hair, and even his eyes appeared to have a golden sheen in the light, and as he held his arms out in a welcoming gesture toward the children in front of him, silence fell across the vast hall.

"Welcome, Children of the Light. I am Yanus, Head of the High Council of Valhandra." His deep voice commanded the entire room as he smiled gently, his gaze sweeping across from one side of the hall to the other. As he spoke, Aurora's mind went back to the visions her father had shown her of Micah's banishment from Valhandra by Yanus, and she realized where she recognized him from.

"We have awaited and prepared for your arrival for many years. Now the time has come for each of you to master the powers of your new soul and take your place in the Circle of Light."

Yanus looked out at the sea of children in the hall. As her vision zoomed in to his eyes, Aurora saw in them the planets and stars swirling in the depths of the solar system, familiar but still mesmerizing her. Raising his right arm out in front of him, Yanus swirled his hand elegantly in a circle just above his head. The molecules of the air expanded and danced with the movement of his hand, and a large, glowing white crystal appeared, hovering in the space above him. Aurora felt her own crystal pulsing with heat in her pocket in response.

"You will discover your soul's true purpose here in Valhandra," Yanus went on. "You will learn to use the powers gifted to you by the Universe itself."

Yanus pointed his finger to the space above the floating crystal. An image of the earth appeared, spinning in space, but a dark and ominous fog was moving over its surface.

"Humanity is on a path to destruction. As each second passes, and as the Darkness takes hold, it moves further along that path. If humanity dies, the earth dies too. Valhandra, the Rainbow Forest, all life as we know it will cease to exist, and the Darkness will reign as the supreme force in all time and space. You, the Children of the Light, are the last chance to rescue humanity and the earth from the clutches of the Dark Prophecy. Together we can change the course of the future for humankind, bring the first Prophecy to bear, and lead us all into the New World."

Yanus swept his arms out to either side of him, and Aurora sensed movement above her. As she looked up, she saw each Lightworker along the top gallery of the room holding out pieces of crystal identical to her own. The vision of the earth above Yanus melted away, the crystal suspended in the air in front of him rising up level with the top gallery around the hall. Yanus flicked his hands forward and the light from the crystal shot out either side of it, joining to and through each of the Lightworkers' crystals. As the Circle of Light formed above them all, it illuminated the entire room in its golden glow, feeling as if they had landed in the center of the sun.

"Whoa," Cal breathed out beside Aurora, and she looked sideways at him and at Aaron beside him. She was amazed that the intense brightness of the room didn't hurt her eyes. Cal and Aaron were surrounded by the same white light of the Lightworkers standing above them, extending a couple of inches outside of their bodies with the golden glow emanating beyond it. As Aurora held out her own arm and looked around her, she saw that she and everyone else in the room were also cloaked in the shimmering white light. She closed her eyes and, breathing in deeply, she felt the intense warmth and comforting protection of the light filling her body, mind, and soul.

CHAPTER 24

As the bright light began to settle in the vast hall, Aurora could feel the energy in the room pulsing in the air around them. Looking up, she saw that the Lightworkers around the top gallery of the vast hall had disappeared, leaving only Yanus and her father at the front of the huge hall.

Yanus introduced Dane as second to himself on the High Council of Valhandra. He explained that Dane would be overseeing the training of the students through seven levels of consciousness, during which their new souls would be further developed and they would be taught to use the powers and abilities they had received from the Universe. Their training, Yanus explained, would be delivered by the Gozzits, each one imparting the knowledge and capacities of their specific colors of the old soul. It was, Yanus explained, imperative for the future of the world that the new souls were merged with the capabilities of the old. Once all seven levels had been completed, the initial development of their new souls would be complete.

Aurora felt slightly overwhelmed as she wondered how long all this training was going to take. But her mind instantly went back to Donna's words just before they had left for Valhandra: "Time is not real. It is merely an invention, created by humankind. On Valhandra there is no day and night, no changing of the seasons. Reality as you know it will become fluid, malleable; time is basically immaterial."

Yanus smiled toward Aurora as if reading her thoughts.

"I know this will all seem overwhelming right now," Yanus said kindly. "I assure you that all will become clearer in time. But time, as you know, is not the same here as it is on Earth, and it does not pass at the same rate. Go now and learn to use your new powers. Discover your new world and explore the wonders which Valhandra holds."

Yanus smiled as the air around him began to shift and turn, its momentum picking up rapidly.

"You will return to Earth when the time is right," he declared as his image began to fade. Turning, he stepped into the swirling mists and disappeared as the portal spun shut behind him.

Dane took the students through more information on how their training would progress. The building in which they stood was named Dama-Garda. Before each lesson, they were to gather in the main hall of the building. They would then be transported via a portal to a virtual classroom, where the Gozzits would deliver their training in each soul level. Some classes would involve visiting other areas of Valhandra, and there would be time between classes for the students to relax and spend time assimilating their learning.

The students were informed they would be given robes to wear during their training. At Dane's command, they found themselves instantly in their own individual changing room, with instructions to change into their choice of the two styles of robes provided, leaving their own clothes within the room. Looking around at the small space, Aurora's sight rested on a row of clothes hanging in front of her. There appeared to be no door out of the small room she was in, so she focused her attention on the outfits hanging before her.

Aurora chose the plain tunic-style robes with a tie-belt and changed swiftly. Hanging her own clothes up, she looked at herself in the changing room mirror, surprised that the plain white tunic and trousers fit her perfectly. Tying the belt of the tunic around her middle, she pulled her long blond hair out the back of it. As it cascaded down over her shoulders, she turned one way then the next, deciding with a smile that she quite liked the reflection looking back at her.

The instant she was ready, the room dissolved around her and she was back in the main hall, as the other students also reappeared one by one once they had finished changing. Cal and Aaron appeared within seconds of each other, and Aurora tried not to stare at the striking contrast of Cal's dark hair to the white of his robes. Both Cal and Aaron had chosen the tops that buttoned down the front in a shirt style, and Aurora felt the usual flutter in her stomach as she looked at Cal. Noticing his eyes on her for longer than usual, she automatically held her shoulders back slightly. Standing a little taller, she also failed to hide a slightly self-satisfied smile, even though her cheeks felt like they were on fire.

Once changed, it was time to eat. The students were directed to the edges of the main hall while Dane stood on the wide marble staircase at the far end of the room. As he raised his arms out in front of him, the floor began to open up like a whirlpool. Tables and benches appeared, lining the whole hall in rows of white marble, and the students looked on, amazed as huge bowls and platters of food began to appear along the center of the tables. As the air in the hall filled with the amazing aromas of the food, Aurora realized how hungry she was, noticing as she sat down how different the food was from that they were used to on Earth. The colors were brighter and more vibrant, the taste more intense. Dane wandered around the room as the students ate, stopping by Aaron and Aurora as he reached their table.

"Food okay?" he asked, putting a hand on each of their shoulders, and Aaron mumbled an incoherent response through a mouthful of food.

"Never seen him so quiet," Cal observed humorously, and Dane laughed before moving on around the room.

CHAPTER 25

The students filed into the main hall for their first lesson, a hum of excited chatter among them. After eating, they had all been sent out to explore the outside grounds of Dama-Garda, many of them still reeling from the beauty that adorned the various areas surrounding the immense building. Exploring the Sunken Garden, the Enchanted Glass House, walled walkways, and tunnels of trees, they had discovered lush green plants growing in abundance. Exotically beautiful flowers in all the colors of the rainbow sparkled in the sunlight as if coated with crushed diamonds.

Once all the students had entered the building, the doors to the hall had swung shut. A portal immediately swirled opened on the wide staircase in the front of the room, and Dane stepped through. Aurora still found it a strange mix of feelings seeing her father in the position he held here, caught between awe at his seniority and the familiarity of him to her as just "Dad." Catching his eyes briefly, she smiled at him, intense pride overtaking all of it as he raised his arms in a gesture to quieten the chattering crowd of students.

"You are about to commence your first lesson in the levels of consciousness," Dane announced, looking around the room as he spoke. "You will be traveling with Mulagoz for this lesson, to the farthest reaches of Valhandra. What you will see there will be . . . spectacular, though it may also prove quite overwhelming."

"Come on," Aaron whispered to Aurora, "what tops talking trees!"

"*Shhhh*," hissed Aurora, rolling her eyes at him.

"Be open in your minds to what you are about to experience," Dane continued. "An open mind will be one of your greatest tools throughout your training, to enable your souls to develop their new capacities and powers to their greatest potential."

Dane turned as another portal spun open behind him and the image of Mulagoz appeared before them, smiling gently, his wide eyes windows to the swirling depths of the solar system. Stepping aside, Dane bowed his head slightly to Mulagoz before he walked back through the portal and disappeared.

"Welcome to your lesson in the first level of consciousness," Mulagoz began. His deep voice threw an echo around the vast hall, the vivid red color of his canopy casting a warm glow across the room.

"I am Mulagoz. I represent strength and courage, and I provide the grounding capacities of the human soul. I facilitate its connection with the earth, together with the spirits of nature, the Elementals. Our strength lies in our willingness to open our hearts and minds to the great powers around us, to allow them to contribute to us, to work with us, and to nurture our souls and bodies with their own strength and energy."

An image of the earth appeared in the air at the front of the hall, and a heavy sense of sadness instantly fell across the room. As the earth spun slowly before them, a dark mist hung over its lands and seas. Like an ominous blanket enveloping the planet, the dark mist inched forward, coating more and more of the earth's surface. Aurora felt tears rise at the back of her eyes, her chest tightened painfully, and her body began to feel like lead. Looking around at the other students, she saw many of them squirming and grimacing with the same pain and discomfort she felt.

"The pain you are experiencing is that of the earth," Mulagoz explained, "and the damage humankind is inflicting on it through its weakness to the Darkness. As Children of the Light, you are as inherently connected with the earth as you are with the Universe. It is part of you, part of your body and soul. If it dies, then your powers die with it; you will become slaves to the Darkness along with the rest of humanity. The Light cannot survive without the energy of the earth and all its inhabitants, and we—the Gozzits, Lightworkers, Children of the Light— are its Guardians. For the first fifteen years of your lives, you had your own Protectors on Earth. Now you yourselves have become Protectors, and along with the Lightworkers, your job is to save the earth from the grip of the Darkness.

"You will feel the pain of the earth more intensely since receiving the new Consciousness. Your souls exist at a higher vibration now, and you are very much more empathic than other humans," Mulagoz continued as the image of the earth faded away, and many of the students breathed out heavily with relief as their discomfort subsided.

"This will happen for you now with any living form, when you put your attention on its energy. It is one of your primary powers and will enable you to pick up on whatever another person is thinking, feeling, or experiencing emotionally in any given moment. *But . . .*" Mulagoz paused, a note of warning in his voice. "You *must* maintain the control over it and not allow the emotions of others to overwhelm you and drain your energy. You will be shown how to do this during your training. Human thoughts, feelings, and emotions can be tremendously intense, which is why they have such a grip on humanity as a whole. If you do not learn to control them within your own body, mind, and soul, they will take hold and begin to control you."

"That makes it sound like emotions are dark magic or something!" a girl's voice said from the middle of the room, and as Aurora looked across she saw it was Jasmine who spoke.

"In some ways they are," Mulagoz answered. "Look at it this way: what is the definition of magic to humans?"

"Making things appear, or disappear, or change?" Jasmine suggested.

"Exactly," Mulagoz replied. "Feelings and emotions are not real; they are perceived. They are created entirely by invention of the person themselves based on their own mindset. If emotions are simply experienced and then released, they will blow away like a feather in the wind. They will evaporate. But instead, most humans hold on to them; they make them solid, as real as they themselves are. They allow themselves to drown in pain, in fear, in happiness, in love. In essence, they become slaves to their emotions, and in doing so, they unconsciously destroy their bodies and minds. They cannot see or understand the damage the emotion is doing when they hold on to it. A solid and stale emotion will manifest into physical pain, illness, even cancers. Humans cannot see that they are, in fact, capable of their own definition of magic: the creation of something real and solid from nothing.

"Nor do they understand that they have the power to reverse the creation. Over the years, suffering has become more valuable to humanity than joy, and the collective mindset on Earth has become a toxic perpetuation of that pain and suffering. They do not want to see, know, or acknowledge their own capacities and powers, preferring to believe they are largely victims, weak and powerless.

"Subsequently, the colors of the human soul have been weakened, depleted. Little by little, humanity is destroying itself, and as it does so, the life force of the Light and of the planet Earth is also becoming weaker. A plague of Darkness is sweeping through civilization, systematically dimming the Light and life on Earth."

The edges of the room began to spin slowly as a transportation vortex started up around the students.

"You are about to be transported to the far reaches of our realm," Mulagoz explained, "the vortex between the worlds. There we will continue the lesson . . ." His voice faded away as the rainbow mists swirled around them, propelling them on to their destination.

As the mists settled and cleared, the students found themselves standing on a beach. The sea in front of them sparkled a pale gray blue. Tinged with gold in the bright Valhandran sunlight, it stretched into the distance, where it disappeared into ethereal mists, seamlessly integrating the sky with the water. High cliffs either side of them were formed of rock in deep red, brown, and gold tones, their surfaces shining in the sunlight and casting shards of colored light into the sky around them. The ground beneath them looked like white sand glittering with diamonds, but underfoot it felt like they were walking on clouds rather than the grainy, malleable sands of the beaches back on Earth. Mulagoz appeared before them once more, and he explained that they stood at the farthest point of Valhandra, where beyond the mists the realm disappeared into a vortex of time and space. No Lightworker could venture into the vortex, he continued, but it provided a channel between the realms of Earth and Valhandra so the Elementals could travel between the worlds.

"When the Light created the earth," Mulagoz began, "it sourced the elements of nature from the far reaches of the solar system. Giving life to the matter from four different worlds, it created intelligent, conscious entities, each the spirit and essence of their home plane. The Light took them all and swirled them into the mix to create planet Earth, its lands, atmosphere and eco-structure for life—a home for humankind to reside."

The image of Mulagoz moved around to position itself behind the students so that they faced out to the horizon where the sea met the sky.

"You are about to meet the Elementals," Mulagoz announced.

The mists out on the skyline suddenly began to drift and separate. The central part of the sea started to swell, gently at first and then building in intensity, turning in on itself like a whirlpool. Swirling back into the vortex beyond, it was sucked in before it swelled up once more, this time exploding high into the air. Out of the depths of the vortex soared four colossal forms. The collective gasps of the students whipped away in the winds as the arrivals hovered above the waves, which were now beginning to settle below them. Aurora strained her eyes, trying unsuccessfully to make out more clearly the four hazy silhouettes in the distant sky.

"First, the Fire Fury," declared Mulagoz, and a flaming sphere shot forward from the horizon like a cannonball through the sky. Slowing and coming to a stop in the air above the students, it started to change shape, and out of the burning fireball a more defined form began to appear. First legs, then arms and a head emerged from the flames. Eyes opened in the face and looked down toward the students, flames erupting from the top of its head like a crown. To the surprise of the students who were backing up slightly in the shadow of the flaming Elemental, a mouth appeared and widened into a smile before the Fire Fury lowered its head toward them, bowing in silent greeting.

Next came the bright white wispy form that had risen from the vortex into the otherwise cloudless sky. Drifting closer and closer to the beach, it zigzagged elegantly through the air. As its huge form drew nearer to the students, its movement slowed, and hovering in the air above them, it began to part from the center. Huge white-feathered wings appeared and unfolded, opening out either side of a body that looked human in its form with torso, arms, and legs but was covered with pure white feathers. In its face sat shining bronze eyes either side of an elongated golden beak.

"The Wings of the Wind," Mulagoz announced, and the form before them wrapped one of its vast wings around its front, bowing deeply to the open-mouthed students on the beach.

"The Earth Angel," Mulagoz announced next, as the hazy brown form on the horizon began to move toward them. It became a swirling sandstorm, twisting and turning through the air and leaving ornate spiral patterns across the sky that dissolved behind it like the wake of an airplane. Coming to a halt before them, the grains of sand began to collect together, and a beautiful female form appeared out of the dust. She wore a long, flowing dress that looked as if it were made of glittering golden sand, its particles seeming to chase each other through the air as it moved and swayed elegantly around her.

"Greetings," she said as she curtsied to the students. Her long hair floated around her as her voice tinkled and echoed like music, its notes vibrating in the air.

The Serpent of the Sea arrived last, likewise announced by Mulagoz. A giant snake-type form with the face of a mythical dragon, it moved forward from the horizon, dipping in and out of the sea in explosions of circular wave formations, which rippled outward toward the surrounding cliffs. Soaring up into the air, it held its face to the warm Valhandran sun, its long tail sweeping behind it, before turning and diving swiftly back down through the glittering surface of the water. Repeating this dance, it soon reached the edge of the beach, where it lay elegantly across the sand, silver-green scales shining in the sunlight.

The group of students looked on, stunned at the sight of the Elementals before them.

"This place is off the charts!" exclaimed one of the students breathlessly, and Mulagoz chuckled behind them.

"Before you are the spirit beings of all natural life on Earth," he declared. "Unseen to human eyes but always present, they are the vital organs and fundamental energies of the planet, keeping the heart of Earth beating and existing within the solar system. As Children of the Light, you have an intrinsic connection with all the Elementals. However, each of you will have a stronger affinity to one in particular."

Mulagoz instructed all the students to stand in a semi-circle near to the water's edge and to raise their right hands out in front of them toward the Elementals. Above their palms would appear the symbol of their strongest nature connection, Mulagoz explained, and Aurora watched as a tiny wave appeared above hers. Looking up, she met the gaze of the Sea Serpent and was captivated by its sparkling emerald eyes. Glancing around her, she saw from the miniature whirlwind of dust hovering above Cal's hand that his connection was earth; the small white wings hovering above Aaron's palm revealing his was air.

Aurora found her gaze settling on Jasmine. The flames of the Fire Fury danced above the palm of Jasmine's hand, and as if sensing she was being watched, she raised her eyes to meet Aurora's. Without warning the beach around them faded away, the voices of the others reduced to muffled background noise as Aurora's vision zoomed in. The light of the Universe in Jasmine's eyes darkened and flames burst within their depths. In that instant, the image of Marta Broach appeared standing behind Jasmine and the intense, unwavering stares of both were fixed on Aurora. Taking a sharp breath in, Aurora closed her eyes tightly and shook her head. Upon opening them the image of Marta Broach had disappeared, the flames in Jasmine's eyes replaced once more with the familiar depths of the Universe. As the surroundings of the beach around Aurora gradually stabilized again, Jasmine casually looked away. Nobody else appeared to have noticed anything untoward, though Aurora's heart continued pounding in her chest afterward, a feeling of unease nagging somewhere deep inside her.

The lesson went on with the students learning how to increase their own energy fields by harnessing their connection to nature and the power of the Elementals. Holding hands in their semi-circle and under the instruction of Mulagoz, they collectively joined their energy to the Elementals, and the white light surrounding each of them grew to three times its previous size. Aurora's body felt as light as a feather, and she watched amazed as the bright glow from the group lit up the sky above them.

CHAPTER 26

At the end of the lesson, Mulagoz had announced the departure of the Elementals before they turned and made their way back toward the skyline, vanishing into the vortex beyond as the mists separated in readiness for their descent back to Earth.

Announcing that the lesson would be continued by Sacragoz, the Orange Gozzit and second color of the soul, Mulagoz too disappeared, and the deep red glow of his canopy was replaced by the lighter tone of Sacragoz as he appeared before the students.

"Greetings," Sacragoz said happily, smiling widely to the group, his energy noticeably lighter than the steadfast, down-to-earth presence of Mulagoz.

"I am Sacragoz. I am the creative color of the soul, your sense of fun, joy, and possibilities."

Aurora found herself giggling spontaneously along with some of the others as the eyes of Sacragoz sparkled mischievously.

"Mulagoz spoke to you about human emotion and the damage it can cause to the soul, physical health, and personal evolution. In the early days of the human soul, there was so much joy in the world," he explained, a sudden shadow passing across his face as he looked across the water in front of him and shook his head sadly.

"Now I am the most depleted color of the soul on Earth. Humanity has lost its sense of fun, the joy of living. It has become greedy for material wealth, status, and superiority. When the orange light of the soul is extinguished, in its place is bred sadness, fear, jealousy, and hate."

Looking back toward the students, Sacragoz smiled warmly, the gnarled branches of his arms visible as he put his hands in a prayer gesture in front of his face.

"But finally, you all are here, with new hope for the world," he said, his eyes sparkling once more.

"I am going to teach you how to release emotions when they come up, how to raise your vibration, how throw energy bolts, and how to maintain your energy when it is threatened."

"I think I preferred maths," whispered Aaron dryly to Cal, who laughed and raised his eyes to Aurora over the top of Aaron's head as she suppressed a giggle in response.

There on the sparkling sands, they learnt from Sacragoz how to make themselves infinite in order to release the grip of human emotion. In putting their attention on the space between the cells of their bodies, they were able to manipulate temporarily the solidity of their own forms, taking on a translucence which allowed all of the emotion being held in their physical bodies to dissipate and release like mist into the air. Aurora was spellbound, not only in holding out her arms and watching the release from her own body but also in seeing the other students as they first began to glow, then becoming transparent as any locked up emotions flowed out into the space around them and melted away to nothing.

Sacragoz also explained that this technique would allow any threatening energy from outside to flow through them and not harm them or affect their souls.

"But remember," he warned, "it is a conscious choice that you have to make to release emotions . . . and it will not always be an easy one because some you will want to hang on to. Sometimes that is because there is something or someone you don't want to lose, or because you want to be right about something. It may be because you wish to punish somebody for something they have done. All of these are judgments and eventually will eat into your soul. Releasing emotion will always lead to greater possibilities for the future; hanging on to it will limit possibilities and ultimately destroy the future."

The next process they were taught was raising their own energy, and that of someone else, when their energy became too depleted. Aurora was paired with Jack for the exercise and Aaron with Cal, which she was quietly pleased about as she noticed that Jasmine had been sidling closer to Cal during the class, and Aurora had the feeling she was angling to be paired with him for this part of the lesson.

Throughout the lesson Aurora had felt weird, and it had something to do with Jasmine. She wasn't sure exactly what the feeling was, or what was niggling her about it all. She didn't like thinking that it was jealousy because that was unfamiliar territory to Aurora. Jealousy was something she had often been aware of in others, but she had never experienced it herself and, in truth, didn't want to, either. This was different—she was quite sure of that—but there was certainly a strong discomfort when Jasmine was around, and definitely when she was close to Cal.

Despite the painful memory of their previous lives, this felt separate from that. It was as if something was nagging at her, some message or awareness pushing at the forefront of her mind, but she couldn't quite reach it.

Aurora decided the best thing in that moment was to release the feeling as they had just been taught to, which to her relief eased the discomfort and helped her concentrate on the task in hand. Aurora put her hands on top of Jack's forearms as Sacragoz had instructed, and he did the same with her. Putting her attention on the white light surrounding her body, she concentrated on it and visualized it flowing through her arms into Jack's body. Sacragoz had explained that in putting their attention on something and willing it to do something, it would happen automatically—and she smiled with satisfaction as she saw her own energy flowing freely up through Jack's arms immediately after she willed it to. As she continued to flow energy into Jack, she watched as the white haze around his body expanded wider and wider.

"Well done," Sacragoz praised, once all the students had achieved that part of the exercise. They were then shown how to use their increased energy to make a shield around themselves and to throw bolts of energy out from the palms of their hands as defense against attack. Surrounding themselves with golden shields, the sky filled with bursts of light, and the water shimmered in response as they all practiced throwing energy bolts out above the clear silver-blue sea.

At the end of the lesson, they were then given some time to relax on the beach, chatting with each other, soaking in the warm rays of the sun and watching as it glistened on the calm ripples of the water before they were transported back for their next lesson.

CHAPTER 27

The transportation vortex cleared around the students and they found themselves back in the vast hall of Dama-Garda, its bright white walls and ceiling a stark contrast to the warm reds and browns of the cliffs surrounding the beach from which they had just journeyed.

Dane stood waiting for them at the top of the wide marble staircase at the front of the hall, and as the last of the swirling mists disappeared, he raised one hand to silence the group.

"Your next lessons will be in the fifth and sixth levels of consciousness," Dane explained, "the blue and indigo colors of the soul. "It is necessary that your teaching in these areas comes now, as it will increase your awareness and understanding of the lessons which will follow."

The students were transported on to a virtual classroom where Dane explained some of their lessons would be taking place: a huge white room filled with individual desks and chairs that faced a huge spinning portal at the front of it. Looking around the edges of the room, Aurora noticed that its walls seemed undefined, almost fluid, as if she could have walked right through them. The desks and chairs seemed to hover rather than rest solidly on the floor. As she scanned the room, she caught sight of Jasmine, who was staring back at her. In that second, Aurora saw a white flash, the classroom around her disappeared, and another scene began to flicker into focus in front of her eyes, initially. She saw what looked like a hospital room, a bed with a figure lying in it, encased in a shimmering golden bubble. Another white flash and now she was closer to the bed, looking down at the figure: a woman with long dark hair, seemingly unconscious, and as Aurora stared at the woman's face she saw an unmistakable likeness to Jasmine in her features. As she looked away from the sleeping figure to the outside of the room, Aurora realized the bed was inside a cage with thick golden bars. A heaviness filled her chest, bringing a memory with it. She had seen a cage like this before. She had sensed that same heaviness but in that moment could not recall where she had seen it. Another white flash and Aurora was back in the virtual classroom. Feeling suddenly lightheaded, she claimed the desk nearest to her and, steadying herself against it, sank down onto the supportive safety of the chair.

The portal at the front of the classroom began to spin open from its center, first to the view of a dense forest and then to the face of the blue Gozzit tree, Vigoz.

"Greetings, Children of the Light," Vigoz announced in a soothing voice, as the vivid blue from his canopy illuminated the classroom in its glow. Aurora's dizziness immediately began to recede, replaced with a warmth that flowed up through her arms and into her throat and upper chest, calming the anxiety that had started to rise in her body from the visions, and she took a deep breath as she felt the discomfort release.

"I am Vigoz, the Gozzit of truth. I give the soul its capacity to understand and to communicate. I help you express yourselves truthfully, not only to others but also to yourself, because the greatest lies we tell are those we tell ourselves. One of the great failings of humanity is their lack of insight into their own souls, their refusal to acknowledge that they have a greater purpose in the world, and their unwillingness to listen to their own awareness. They have lost the ability to live by their own truth. When you lie to yourself and others, you destroy your ability to create the future because you refuse to see what is true. Only when you are willing to live truthfully with yourself and everyone around you will you be able to receive the guidance and wisdom of the Universe.

"Your powers of telepathy originate from me, and I will help you to develop them further," Vigoz continued. "Since arriving here in Valhandra, your senses may have experienced moments of overwhelm, picking up on multiple telepathic frequencies all at once."

Aurora knew that overwhelm, recalling when she had first arrived in Valhandra and feeling like she was drowning in the thoughts of everyone around her.

The lesson went on with Vigoz showing them how to direct their thoughts and communication telepathically in the same way they did with their physical voices. It required a good deal more concentration than physical talking, Aurora found, but by the end of the lesson the students were all holding conversations with each other telepathically as normally as they would using their voices.

Aurora's mind kept going back to the visions she had experienced earlier and the woman in the hospital bed who looked like Jasmine, though she still couldn't recall where she had seen that cage before. It was bugging her, and as the lesson from Vigoz finished she rested her elbows on the table, putting her head in her hands and searching her memory unsuccessfully, frustrated by the missing information. The lesson from Vigoz led straight on to an input from Ajnagoz, who appeared within the portal, changing the glow across the classroom from a deep blue to indigo and interrupting Aurora's thoughts.

"I am Ajnagoz, the indigo Gozzit. I am your wisdom, intuition, and inner knowledge; on Earth I am often referred to as your psychic ability. Many humans are scared of me in the modern day; they cling to the solidity of life and resist the thought that there may be a world beyond their physical existence. Their belief systems are failing. They scorn the idea of a higher power, believing that if it existed it would not allow horrors in the world to occur. They cannot see that they collectively have created their own demise with their behavior, that if they were willing to open their hearts and minds to the Universe, they would receive everything they require, all that they desire. Their resistance has allowed the Darkness to creep into their souls, instilling fear in their hearts and minds, and as the fear grows, the separation in the world also grows, and the connection between humanity and the Light becomes weaker."

Aurora knew the fear of which Ajnagoz spoke, recalling how Hazel had backed away from her in the canteen, from the strength of her energy flow, and how scared she had looked.

"Intuition, inner knowledge," Ajnagoz continued, "is a whisper, a feather touch on your cheek, possibly even a vision, which gives you awareness, guidance to go in a certain direction, to take a particular action. If you listen to it, it will lead you wherever you wish to go; whatever you desire to create for your future will be possible with the help and guidance of the Universe. But there has to be peace in the heart, mind, and soul to hear the whispers of consciousness, and that peace has been waning in humanity for many years. Life on Earth is constantly stressful, chaotic, and intense."

"True story," Aaron interjected in a cynical tone, which drew laughter from around the classroom as Ajnagoz continued.

"That in itself creates a noise in the mind which drowns out the whispers of the Universe. The pressure and anxiety of day-to-day living has created its own noise, which also drowns out the whispers of the Universe. Humans are now ridden with angst, anger, frustration, and fear. They do not learn from their experiences, as I taught them to, and they function from lies which distract them from their truth and authenticity. All of this is feeding the Darkness, and the indigo color of the soul grows weaker by the day."

Ajnagoz invited questions from the class, and Aurora, who had been intently listening, put her hand up instantly.

"If the whispers are visions, like bits and pieces of information, how do we know what to do and what's required from us?"

"Trust in the Universe," Ajnagoz replied. "Ask it if something is required to be done now or later. It will always respond when you ask."

Aurora remembered being back at home and asking for guidance with Aaron—incredibly just days ago now, though it seemed like forever.

"Okay," she began hesitantly, "but—" Before she could ask another question, Ajnagoz continued.

"And Aurora, also trust yourself. Think of it as a puzzle from the Universe. Each piece will be provided to you at a certain time, the right time in the journey. With any puzzle, the full picture only becomes totally clear when *all* the pieces are fitted together. Be patient. The pieces will come at the right time, but if you act too soon you may miss something vital. When all the pieces combine, then you will know what to do. You will know what action to take."

"Thanks," Aurora said, and with a contented smile she closed her eyes and took a deep breath, putting the visions to the back of her mind for now.

Ajnagoz cast her gaze over the rest of the class and continued. "Remember this one thing, all of you. You have the wisdom and power of the Universe in your souls. Even if you do not yet understand your full potential . . . at the right time, you will *know*; you will *always* know."

CHAPTER 28

"How long have we actually been here, Dad?" Aaron asked as he, Aurora, and Dane walked together toward the peak of the hill adjacent to Dama-Garda. The huge white mansion was the hub for the Lightworkers and the center of education for the Children of the Light. The High Council of Valhandra were based on the top floor of the high building, and Aurora and Aaron had debated many times so far how many floors the building had, though each time they counted it seemed to change.

"As Yanus explained, time on Valhandra is very different to time on Earth," Dane said, keeping his eyes firmly ahead of him as they walked. "Time here does not exist as such, but in basic terms, it passes quicker on Earth than it does here."

"Kind of like human years to dog years, then," Aaron said, grinning at Aurora, who shot him a withering look in mock boredom.

"You could say that," laughed Dane, before continuing. "Or in other words, time as you know it ceases to exist here; it is no longer significant and we do not live as slaves to it like humans do."

"Wait," Aaron said, grabbing his father's arm as a sudden realization entered his mind. "If time doesn't exist here, will we ever age?" he asked.

"Well . . ." Dane hesitated and stopped walking. Taking a deep breath, he turned to the twins. "To an extent. As Children of the Light, your physical bodies will continue to age until you reach your optimum strength and physical condition, which in Earth years would be the equivalent of around the age of twenty-one. Then the aging process will stop. Your soul will continue to develop and evolve. But your physical body will not change past that point, nor will it degenerate further through age because it will be one with your soul, and it too is infinite."

The reality of what they were hearing hit the twins like a bolt of lightning as they realized what their father was saying.

"So . . ." Aaron said slowly, taking a deep and slightly shaky breath himself as he and Aurora exchanged shocked glances, ". . . basically you're saying . . . that we're going to live forever?"

"That has always been the case," Dane explained gently, putting one hand on each of his children's shoulders. "You just didn't cognitively know it before. Souls exist forever; they are infinite and have always been so. They inhabit different physical bodies over many lifetimes, and upon each consecutive lifetime the memory of the previous one is erased from the physical mind because the human mind as it is could not cope with that level of knowledge. When the soul is freed from the bounds of physical reality and returns to the spiritual plane, it remembers its purpose and the entirety of its existence. The minute it is reborn to the physical world, it forgets once more."

"So, on Earth," Aurora interjected, "are things getting a lot worse since we left?"

"The situation on Earth is becoming more serious and is being closely monitored by the High Council," Dane said reassuringly to Aurora. "Hence, we are progressing your training as quickly as we can. When it is completed, we will all be translocating to Earth, though don't worry about that right now; you need to concentrate on your training."

"Okay," mused Aaron. "So . . . translocation . . ." He closed his eyes briefly, pointing one finger in front of him and bobbing it back and forth as he recalled the lesson. "Moving from one realm to another, migrating across time and space, using three spatial coordinates and one time coordinate together to specify the destination within a specific reality."

"Excellent recall!" Dane praised, looking sideways and smiling at Aurora's fake yawn as she raised her eyes to the sky.

"Ah, yes," Aaron sighed dramatically as they reached the peak of the hill, and flopping down on the grass, he lay back, closing his eyes. "Brilliance is exhausting."

"Pfffft," Aurora scoffed, crossing her arms and glaring down at the still smirking Aaron. Her earlier feelings of inadequacy returned as she remembered her overwhelm in their previous lesson on soul-level recall, especially with the scientific definitions that seemed to roll off Aaron's tongue with ease.

Within the seven levels of consciousness the Children of the Light had to master for the full development of their new souls, soul-level recall was a major part of the sixth level, taught by Ajnagoz, the Gozzit of Wisdom and inner knowledge. Aurora recalled Ajnagoz explaining the concept to them in the lesson: SLR involved accessing the deepest subconscious level of learning, which recalls every detail of what it hears, sees, and experiences, like an eternal recording device. Most humans on Earth use only a minute amount of their inherent capacity for SLR, Ajnagoz had told them. Some have access to more than others, and those are the humans labeled "genius" in the physical reality. Only those human souls with all their colors intact would have the capacity to learn these skills, but even then, many still limit themselves because of the desire to avoid the judgment of others. It is not sought after nor widely celebrated to "stand out" as special or unique from the rest on Earth, and that constant repression only serves to perpetuate the cycle of fear within humanity, the energy on which the Darkness feeds.

Aurora reflected on how different it all was from "Earth School," the term they all now used to refer to their schooling experiences before Valhandra. Each lesson on Valhandra began with all the students congregating in the vast main hall. The whole room would begin to spin around them, transporting them in an instant to a virtual classroom—a huge room with pure white ceilings, walls, and floors, within which they all sat in rows and rows of individual desks of pure white marble with ornate golden chairs. The Gozzit teaching the class would appear at the front of the room as if on a projector screen, its specific soul color casting an ethereal glow across the room so that in each lesson the whole class would be bathed in a different colored light.

"Soul-level recall is one of the most difficult skills to learn, darling," Dane said to Aurora reassuringly, bringing her mind back to the present as he put his arm around her shoulders. "Those who had more advanced academic skills on Earth generally find it a lot easier to grasp."

"That figures," Aurora observed, raising her eyes with frustration. "Aaron never even had to try to remember stuff, he just did—no revision required!"

"True story," interjected Aaron smugly from the ground.

"Shut up!" Aurora shot at him in an annoyed voice.

"You both have different capacities and gifts," Dane went on calmly, ignoring their bickering, "different strengths which will translate in some way from your human life on Earth to life as it is for you now in your new world. Each soul has specific purposes, and its differences are essential to your roles

here . . . and to the future you all are destined to create together."
Giving Aurora's shoulder a squeeze, Dane let go and took a step
in front of them as they reached the pinnacle of the hill.

"Micah was always the more academic one of the two of
us on Earth," he mused with a nostalgic sigh. "Actually, his
academic capacities surpassed those of all of the Lightworkers.
I remember him helping me with soul-level recall when
we arrived here." Turning briefly back to Aurora, he smiled
reassuringly. "Like you, I found it the most challenging skill to
learn."

Dane looked out across the green valley that lay before
them, a deep sadness in his eyes as he finished. "He always had
my back with everything in those days."

Aurora joined her father, and taking his hand, she smiled
up at him, flowing her own energy into him. Dane placed his
other hand over hers in appreciation of his daughter's caring.

"You still miss him?" she asked softly.

"Yes, in a sense. I miss who he was. I don't know the Micah
he became. Sometimes I wonder, though . . ." Pausing mid-
sentence, Dane sighed and dropped his head.

"What do you wonder?" Aurora asked.

Squeezing her hand, which was still in his, he took a deep
breath and continued. "There have been times I've still felt . . . a
connection to him, especially just recently since the incident
with Aaron back on Earth. Maybe it's wishful thinking. Until I
met your mum, Micah was more like family to me than my own
ever were."

Aurora recalled her mum telling her about Dad's upbringing
during one of his longer trips away from home. An only child
with parents who were more interested in their own lives than
raising him, he had learned to look after himself at an early age.

Left on his own for much of the time while they pursued their social lives, holidays and parties were frequent, though never with him, their son. He never wanted for anything financially; there was always more than enough money for whatever he needed. But money could never buy the love and time they couldn't find it in themselves to give him. For many people, that would have hardened their own hearts, her mum had explained, but not with Dane; he had more capacity for caring and giving love to others than anyone she had ever met.

"He saw everything so differently from anyone else," Aspen had recalled fondly. "When others would have seen something as negative, he would see the positive in it—literally in everything!" She recalled her mum laughing as she went on. "It's exasperating sometimes, no lie! But it has prepared me . . ."

Aspen had suddenly broken off mid-sentence at the time, as if she had said too much.

"Prepared you for what?" Aurora had asked curiously.

"Oh . . . life," Aspen had commented casually, getting up and busying herself with housework to signal an end to the conversation. Aurora felt a sudden pang of sadness for her mum, knowing now what she had needed to prepare herself for, along with a new and intense admiration for how she had coped with it all.

"I wonder whether I could have done more to help him," Dane continued, breaking Aurora's thoughts and bringing her attention back to the conversation about Micah. "I was completely taken up with the work we were doing here, the plans we had to make before we returned to Earth—to raise you, the Children of the Light. I thought Micah was too. I didn't—I chose not to see how much he was starting to resist those plans."

"Why was he so resistant?" Aurora asked.

"It went back to his childhood," Dane began. "In some ways, his story was similar to mine. His parents were career driven, highly respected, and incredibly wealthy. His father was a brilliant scientist and his mother a top psychologist, which is where Micah's own academic abilities came from. Children were not on their agenda, and Micah came along by accident." Dane chuckled. "Well, of course there are no 'accidents' with the Universe, but in their human world his arrival was . . . inconvenient. Micah was brought up by his grandparents from the time he was a baby; his parents were never around, and so he never really missed them. He was very close to his grandparents, and they were more like parents to me too, once he and I became friends. There did come a point when his parents cut all contact with him and the grandparents. Nobody knew why or where they had gone. But as Micah got older, he became determined to find them, more to know who he was, I think, as he saw his grandparents as his true family. By the time he was in his late twenties, he had a high-paying job himself, so he hired a private investigator, who tracked his parents down." Dane shook his head sadly. "It was discovered that they had two young children—a whole new life and family, without Micah."

"Did he see them?" asked Aurora, shocked at the story. "Did he find out why they did it?"

"He chose not to," Dane replied. "Micah had a strength of character I had never encountered before . . . and have never encountered since, either. But much more than that, it was the bond he and I shared, of friendship, of brotherhood, which got us both through. That bond enabled us to maintain the integrity of our souls, to move past the rejection from our parents, to be family for each other in place of them. But . . ." Dane paused thoughtfully. "Micah's discovery happened just days before we received the first calling from the Light. I didn't realize, neither did Yanus until later, the effect that discovery had on Micah. He had always wanted to be a father." Dane smiled, lost in his own memories. "When we were younger, we used to sit for hours talking about the things we would do when we had families of our own: coaching the boys at football . . ."

Aurora looked sideways at him, raising her eyes in a mock challenge, and Dane stifled a laugh.

"Well, it was twenty years ago," he said defensively. "What did I know? Turned out you're better at football than your brother!"

"I *can* hear you," Aaron retorted from the ground, lifting his head slightly and glaring at them both as Aurora giggled.

"But not at model building, mate," Dane added swiftly, looking down at his son with amusement.

"True, of course," Aaron said and settled his head back down on the grass with a sigh.

As Dane continued the story, Aurora smiled. Feeling the strength of the closeness they all shared, she was suddenly filled with a huge sense of gratitude that, throughout everything, she had never doubted the love of her parents in the way Micah and her father had done with theirs.

"After we received the new Consciousness into our souls, everything was fine for a while. But when the High Council announced the new plans for us to raise the Children of the Light, I saw a change in Micah. The idea for an army of children triggered something, which began to fester and grow. He resisted the whole idea to Yanus and the High Council, told them it was foolish, that they were foolish to consider it. He absolutely refused to raise children and said he would never have them. I had the awareness then that his resistance came from his parents' rejection of him."

"How could his soul have been changed, then?" Aurora questioned. "Aaron had to let go of his grief before his soul could receive the new Consciousness."

"Micah found out about his parents only days before we received it," Dane replied. "It was too soon for the rejection to have embedded itself in his human soul. You're right, he couldn't have received the new Consciousness if it had. But every weakness of the soul begins as a human emotion experienced in the physical body; it takes time for it to begin to eat away at the soul. In Micah's case, the rejection had lain there imprinted in his body. He hadn't even had a chance to assimilate it consciously, to understand it, but it created a weakness in him which the Darkness was subsequently able to prey on. I should have taken more notice then of my awareness."

"Do you think it would have made a difference?" Aurora asked.

"Maybe, maybe not," Dane replied, shrugging his shoulders. "But either way, no matter how much I miss him, I have to let go of the regrets. This . . ." He held out his arms and looked around them. "Us, the future . . . is more important than anything in the past right now."

Aurora followed her father's gaze across the vast open fields that led to the Rainbow Forest. Standing like a magnificent halo of color on top of its hill in the distance, the bright colors of the Gozzits both combined and reflected off each other, creating a kaleidoscope in the sky above it, which sparkled in the Valhandran sunlight.

"Wow," Aurora breathed, in awe at the sight of it. "We're going there for our lesson with Namogoz."

"Yes," Dane replied. "The Eternal Library."

"They didn't really explain what it is," Aaron complained, looking up briefly from his position on the grass and shielding his eyes from the Light with his forearm. "Just said it was where the ancient manuscript was hidden. What is it then, just a big old book sat in the middle of the forest?"

"That," Dane responded with a sideways wink at Aurora, "is for you to find out when you go, Aaron! I'm not going to spoil the surprise."

Dane and Aurora sat down on the grass next to Aaron, facing the iridescent light from the Rainbow Forest, which cast a faint glow on their bodies. Aurora pulled her knees up, resting her arms on them and staring out at the wide canopies of the Gozzits as they illuminated the sky with their bright colors.

"I wish we could just stay here like this forever," Aurora sighed wistfully. "With Mum here too, of course."

"I know," Dane agreed, putting his arm around her, and as he hugged her to him she rested her head on his shoulder.

At the sound of movement behind them, Aurora and Dane looked around to see Cal and his mum, Eva, walking up the hill toward them. Dane and Aurora got up and turned to them as they arrived, Dane greeting Eva by taking her hand with both of his, smiling warmly at them both. Cal went and stood over Aaron, who was still lying on the ground, casting a shadow over him.

"Oi!" protested Aaron, opening one eye and grimacing at Cal.

"You comfortable?" Cal said sarcastically, with a grin.

"Yup," replied Aaron, stretching his arms up behind his head and closing his eyes again as Cal shook his head and walked over toward Aurora with the smile that warmed her heart but also gave her butterflies in her stomach whenever she saw him.

Dane, Eva, Cal, and Aurora stood facing out to the Rainbow Forest, while Aaron lay in the grass beside them. All were deep in thought for a few moments before Dane broke the silence.

"There are many challenges to come," he said in a serious tone. "Change is coming, huge change. The existence of everything held within the Light, Valhandra, humanity, and the planet Earth . . . is in danger if we do not win this battle we are facing. The future of the world and the survival of the Light rests with us."

CHAPTER 29

Gathered in the main hall of Dama-Garda awaiting their next lesson with Namogoz, Aurora's attention was drawn to Jasmine, who was standing at the edge of the hall to her right with a small group of students. She noticed a couple of times that Jasmine looked over toward where she, Cal, and Aaron were standing chatting casually with a few others around them. Aurora couldn't work out whether Jasmine was looking at her or Cal, but whichever of them she was watching, Aurora had an uneasy feeling in her stomach about it that nagged at her insistently. As she automatically began doubting her awareness, Aurora found herself recalling another sixth level lesson with Ajnagoz, on intuition.

"You will *know*," Ajnagoz had said to them all with an unquestionable certainty in her soft, calming voice. "You will *always* know . . . when you are willing to allow yourself to see what is true. On Earth, you had this drained out of you, along with every other child. It was not acceptable to 'know' more than others around you, especially when you were children and they the adults, more especially when your sense of knowing went beyond the reality they could see, hear, or feel."

Hearing her words, Aurora had remembered how many times she had pushed down her visions and awareness of things as a young girl. Things that she knew were going to happen before they did, people whom she knew were thinking certain things before they said it. Aurora remembered the first and only time she had spoken about one of her visions to a teacher at infant school. She had got up from her desk in the middle of a lesson to tell the teacher there was going to be a fire in the kitchen and that they all needed to get out of the school. She remembered with absolute clarity how worried she had been that they all needed to leave and recalled her insistence to the teacher about what was going to happen. The teacher had laughed, telling the young Aurora not to be silly, that there was no fire drill that day, that everything was fine and they didn't need to leave the school, that she should stop making up stories and just do her work. When Aurora had repeated her vision, the teacher had become angry, shouting at her to sit down and get on with her work, as she was going to scare the other children. Tearful and with her head down, the young Aurora had returned to her seat. When the fire bell had sounded five minutes later, due to an unexpected electrical fault in the school kitchen, the teacher immediately began frantically to usher the children out of the classroom . . . but not before Aurora caught the look on the teacher's face as she stared at her with fear and uncertainty in her eyes. That look of fear remained with Aurora for many years afterward, and she never again spoke about her visions.

Aurora was brought back from her memory to the present, and any further thoughts of Jasmine were forgotten in that moment as the staircase at the front of the main hall began to mist over and the vision of Namogoz appeared from within the emerging portal.

"Welcome, all of you," Namogoz announced. The lotus flower at the very top of his canopy was in full bloom, a column of silver light stretching upward from its center.

"Today you will journey with me to the Eternal Library, the sacred etheric plane hidden deep within the Rainbow Forest. It contains the secrets of the Universe, the life and story of every soul ever to have existed, and the past, present, and possible futures of the world." A few gasps could be heard around the room as Namogoz spoke, and he paused, looking around at the sea of students in the room. "Once the vortex has transported you there, please wait for further instructions."

The image of Namogoz disappeared, and the outer edges of the room began to spin, rainbow mists swirling around the students as the hall around them melted away, slowly replaced by green grass and clear blue skies. As the mists cleared, they all found themselves standing at the base of an enormous hill.

Aurora looked upward, toward the top of the huge hill, shielding her eyes from the bright sunlight above her. She could see the edges of the colored canopies of some of the Gozzits, rustling in the slight breeze as more and more of the students appeared around her. Once their surroundings settled and everyone had arrived, they waited as instructed and very soon heard the voice of Namogoz ringing through the air around them.

"Please stand back from the edge of the hill so the Beings of Light can reveal the entrance to the Eternal Library," he declared. As soon as he had spoken, bright flashes of light began to appear in the area between the group and the grassy rise of the hill. Ghostly-looking wisps of sparkling white floated through the air, circling the side of the hill, and the group edged away from them into a semi-circle to allow them room as they began to lift the grass away from the rise of the hill as if pulling open theater curtains at the start of a show.

As the grass curtains parted, a huge double door was revealed, so large it extended halfway up the hill and was at least three times the height of the tallest students in the group.

Made of heavy gnarled wood, the door was covered with ornate carvings that appeared as the root system of trees. Taken aback by the intricate beauty of the carved wood, many of the students stood open-mouthed and even more stunned once the doors slowly began to move from the center, swinging open outward. Aurora was standing in the middle of the group and strained her neck to see past the students in front of her, squinting her eyes in an attempt to see what was beyond the doors, though at that point it was too dark to make out anything inside.

"Please walk slowly into the Library," Namogoz announced, his voice emanating from somewhere above and around them. "No rushing. Take your time, please, and enter in turn. There is plenty of room for all, and only once you have entered fully through the doors will the Library reveal itself to you."

As Aurora entered through the huge doorway, with Aaron and Cal either side of her, the bright sunlight outside gave way first to darkness and then to the illuminating glow of what appeared to be lanterns around the top edges of the room they stood in. As the light slowly increased in intensity, she began to make out a gallery around the top of the Library, following the placement of the lanterns around the vast circular room.

More of the surroundings within the Library gradually began to materialize bit by bit. Below the circular structure of the high ceiling, flanked by the gallery, the ground level of the Library appeared to stretch out farther than it was possible for the eye to see, and certainly farther than the far edge of the hill under the Rainbow Forest would logically be. Endless aisles of wooden bookcases reached almost to the high ceiling, their shelves filled with huge leather books, which, upon closer inspection, seemed to pulse with a life force of their own.

Once the whole group had entered and the huge door in the hillside shut behind them, another light began to emanate from the top of the Library, casting a kaleidoscope of colors down into the room, and as Aurora looked up, she caught her breath at the beauty of the sight above them. The Library had a clear glass ceiling, through which she could see the root systems of the Gozzit trees shining in all their dazzling rainbow colors. Intertwining with each other, the roots, like the books on the shelves, pulsed with a life force all their own, slowly curling and coiling together. Among the mass of movement, stars twinkled as if a solar system were caught within the confines of the root system, catching the light of the colors and reflecting them around the Library below like rainbow sparkles. Aurora gazed up at the living, breathing life force of the master soul of humanity, closing her eyes to the intense and uplifting energy that flowed through her body from the light shining down on them all.

Not a word came from any of the students as they all gazed around the Library, stunned at what they saw. The face of Namogoz appeared once more above the group to continue the lesson, and they all listened in silence as he explained more about the history of the Eternal Library.

"You have all heard of the ancient manuscript of the Old World," Namogoz began, his voice echoing slightly around the vast space.

"When Micah was taken from Valhandra, he disclosed the future prophecies from the manuscript to the Darkness. Knowing the existence of two possible futures gave the Darkness more power. This is true for any one of us—when something is uncertain in our world, we are weaker with respect to that thing. If we become more certain that thing is possible, we push much more powerfully to create it; we put more strength and determination behind it. With your thoughts and your perception, you can and will create your reality. All humans have the capacity to do this, but few ever learn to do it or even try to do it, because they live too entrenched in human emotions, doubt, and fear of failure. When they do create something through positive thoughts, they call it luck or coincidence. They do not realize . . . nothing is luck. Nothing happens by coincidence. Everything is an energetic creation."

Reflecting on what Namogoz was saying, Aurora once more thought back to her vision of the kitchen fire at school. After it happened, she had allowed fear and doubt to stop her from ever disclosing her visions again. She wondered what would have happened if she hadn't done that, if she had continued to trust them, continued to tell people about them. Would it have changed anything at any time? Were there things she could have stopped from happening if she had not given in to the fear? With these thoughts, she suddenly felt down, anxious, and agitated. She noticed that the white light around her body, which was constantly present now, dimmed slightly with her thoughts. Recognizing that she was once again doubting herself, she pushed the thought away, and holding out her arms in front of her, she concentrated positive thoughts on the white light, which responded instantly, expanding further and brighter once more. Aurora jumped suddenly at a jab in her ribs from Aaron standing next to her, who nodded his head toward the image of Namogoz, and she forced her concentration back to the story of the Library's creation.

"It became necessary to protect the manuscript from ever falling into the wrong hands," he continued. "To ensure that didn't happen, the contents of it were encoded here in the

Eternal Library, an etheric plane of data in the form of what you see before and around you, and which only certain beings are able to access."

"Does the book itself still exist?" a girl's voice asked near the front of the group. Looking around, Aurora realized it was Jasmine.

"Not as such," Namogoz answered. "In the main, the book *is* now this place, this virtual plane of existence."

He looked to each side of him as he spoke. "It no longer is a solid item, but all it contained and more can be accessed in here. The Eternal Library has given us the ability to create the Universal records as much greater than could ever have been achieved in a physical book."

"But how can a solid object like a book . . . be turned in to this?" Jasmine continued, looking around her.

"Even inanimate objects have an energy field, a life force of a type," Namogoz explained. "Everything has a molecular structure which can be manipulated, intercepted, and transformed. It is the power of transanimation, which you will learn about during your lessons in the third level of consciousness with Puragoz."

Namogoz proceeded to explain the areas within the Eternal Library. The endless rows of high bookshelves were named the Hall of Records. Each book in the Hall of Records was a complete record of an individual soul's journey through time. Every thought, word, and intent ever to have occurred for that soul in all its lifetimes would be documented within its pages, including many possible futures for that soul. He went on to say that at this point in their training, the students were not permitted to access or read their soul records. Their new souls were not yet sufficiently developed for them to deal with some of the information they would find within the record. Once they had progressed through all seven levels of consciousness, only then would they be permitted access to the soul records. They would each then be allocated a Lightworker mentor to help them deal with what may be discovered from their past lives. But, he continued, they were only permitted to access their own soul record; it was strictly forbidden for a Lightworker to access the soul record of another person. Only the Gozzits and the Head of the High Council were permitted to know the journey of another soul.

"When the Lightworkers' souls were transformed, their soul books changed, and the possible futures they may have had on Earth were wiped out," Namogoz explained. "That has now happened with your soul books too. Your future now lies within time and space. Your souls are part of the Universe itself. There is no way back to your Earthly existence. When you look around at the books, those you see which are glowing golden are the soul books of Lightworkers."

Namogoz went on to show the students two doors, one on either side of the Hall of Records. He explained that these were the doors to the Chamber of Light and the Chamber of Darkness. Within each of the chambers was a Vex, a virtual simulation that would take them into the world of each, for the user to live for a specified time the full experience of the Light or the Darkness and to travel anywhere within those worlds. The chambers were not to be used without the express authority of Yanus and were, in fact, experimental areas. Namogoz's voice took on a more somber tone as he finished by saying they had not yet been entirely stable in the testing so far. He did not go into more detail, and despite the many hands raised for questions, he swiftly and unwaveringly moved on to the next area of the Library.

The third and final area about which Namogoz spoke was the gallery around the top level of the Library, just below the glass ceiling. This, he explained, was the Temporal Gallery, an area containing compendiums that documented the deepest secrets of the Universe. As the students looked up, they could see a wooden podium in the center of the gallery, and on it the largest book in the Library. It was leather-bound like the others, though its cover was pure gold and it was easily three times the size of the individual soul books. It seemed to pulse with a life force of its own. This, Namogoz explained, was the Great Book. Within its pages lay the past, present, and future of the world, detailing all universal events that have passed and all the possible futures that have yet to happen, along with the effects of current world events on those possible futures.

The colors from the roots of the Rainbow Forest reflected across the ancient wooden shelving, casting an ethereal glow over the huge leather-bound books within them. A few hands in the group were raised with questions, but Namogoz continued without pausing. The Temporal Gallery was, he explained simply, only accessible to members of the High Council of Valhandra; its contents were highly sensitive and extremely dangerous in the wrong hands. Looking closer, Aurora could see the golden tint of a shield in place around the outer edges of the gallery. Protection, Namogoz went on to explain, because never again could the secrets of the Universe be put at risk, as they were when Micah crossed to the Darkness.

CHAPTER 30

"It's strange," Aurora said thoughtfully as the whole group wandered slowly back toward Dama-Garda after their visit to the Eternal Library, she and Cal straggling behind the rest of the students. "I keep getting the sense that we're losing time while we are going through all this learning. But actually, time isn't passing at all on Earth, is it?"

"No," Cal said distractedly and stopped suddenly, turning to Aurora slightly but staring somewhere past her into the distance with an uncertain look on his face she had never seen before.

As she stopped too, she saw Aaron turn toward them from the back of the main group, where he had been walking and chatting with Jack since they had left the Library. Narrowing his eyes slightly, he cocked his head in question, and she smiled back, nodding toward him to carry on, which, after raising his eyes with a sly grin, he did.

"The soul books . . . the past lives stuff," Cal said slowly, running his fingers through his hair as he spoke, which set off the butterflies in Aurora's stomach again.

"Mmmm," she replied, trying desperately to sound calm and focus on what he was saying rather than his black hair, which had flopped back down over his eyes after he pushed it back.

"Do you . . . remember anything, any of it?" he asked, still looking past her, the top of his cheeks flushing slightly, which did nothing to ease the butterflies playing havoc with Aurora's stomach.

"I . . ." she began and paused, looking to the ground as she tried to quickly formulate the best way to reply.

"Some," she ended up saying softly. "How about you?"

"I get flashes of . . . feelings, I guess," Cal explained. "Kind of like a sense of déjà vu, do you know what I mean?"

"Yes," she replied, wanting to say something more but not finding the words, though Cal continued for her.

"Mum said it's unusual to properly remember any past lives until we've progressed through all the levels. But sometimes it's . . . well . . . it's been more than just a feeling. It's like real memories," he said taking a deep breath.

"Rora …" he began, using the nickname he had called her since her coma and their time within the shield at Mack's house.

"These memories . . . most of them . . . well, you're there. . . We're there, together . . ." he paused and sighed, as if searching for words.

As Aurora looked up at him and their eyes met, suddenly the butterflies in her stomach were gone, replaced by a calm knowing, a deep connection they both felt but neither of them fully understood yet in this lifetime. Cal took both her hands gently in his, and as he did so, a bright flash of white light transported Aurora instantly to another time and place. She stood in a long, Victorian-style white dress. The older version of Cal, whom she recognized as Will from her previous vision, stood before her in a pale gray suit, a high-neck shirt, and cravat. Holding hands before a large congregation to one side of them, on the other side of them stood a priest in official robes, holding a large book in front of him. Sunlight shone through stained glass windows high above them. Aurora looked up into Cal's eyes in the vision, intense love flooding through her as he smiled down at her, nodding, and said, "I will . . . always."

Looking from Cal out over the congregation, Aurora's vision zoomed in to one face at the very back: Jasmine's—or the girl who Jasmine had been then. The hatred from the girl's eyes boring into Aurora felt like a knife in her soul. As she took a sharp breath in, the white flash of light instantly transported her back once again to the field in Valhandra. Still with her hands in Cal's, Aurora found herself looking over to the rest of the group, where Jasmine was standing slightly apart from the others and staring up the hill toward Cal and Aurora. Looking back at Cal, she realized he had been looking over at Jasmine too, a look of deep concern in his eyes as he looked back at Aurora while still holding her hands in his.

Aurora felt her energy levels drop immediately, as the sudden knowledge hit her that Cal recognized Jasmine too, that he also remembered what had happened in their previous life. As the white light around Aurora began to dim, Cal squeezed her hands.

"Hey," he said, and she looked up to meet his eyes, tears of overwhelm building in hers.

"Rora, it's past . . . it's not now, not this life." He began to flow his own energy into her hands from his, and she closed her eyes, receiving the flow of white light that traveled up her arms and deep into her soul. It was the way they had been taught by Sacragoz on the beach to raise each other's energy when required, but this felt so much different than when Aurora had practiced with the other students in class. This was Cal . . . this felt like coming home to him after a lifetime apart.

Cal and Aurora were silent as they walked back toward the others, waiting for their next lesson in the third level of consciousness. As they reached the group, Aaron wasn't the only one who noticed that Cal's and Aurora's energy fields appeared joined and as one; Jasmine's attention remained fixed on them too.

"All right there, you two?" Aaron asked with a smirk, as if he were sharing a joke with himself.

"Yeah, bud. Fine," Cal said with slightly raised eyebrows and a finality in his tone that successfully dissuaded Aaron, as he had intended, from verbalizing any of the comments that were swimming around his head in that moment.

As the huge double doors to Dama-Garda began to swing open, however, all other conversation stopped instantly, and the group entered the main hall to wait for the transportation portal to the next lesson.

CHAPTER 31

As they all settled into their seats in the virtual classroom, the face of Puragoz appeared at the front, in a haze of vivid yellow light that shone out over the students. Puragoz began by talking about the third level of consciousness.

"The third level," she explained, "relates to the very central point of the soul. It is where your old human soul controlled all emotional impulses from, where your confidence and self-esteem were developed, and where your willpower resided." Puragoz had an ethereal, melodic voice, which felt as if it were vibrating right through the center of Aurora's body, and she instinctively put her hand over her solar plexus as the beautiful, golden yellow Gozzit spoke. Looking around, she was surprised to see other students doing exactly the same thing, and the reason for this became apparent as Puragoz continued to speak.

"Remember when you would get butterflies in your stomach about something? That was my energy center reacting to the situation you were in at the time."

Aurora immediately thought of Cal and the effect he had on her. She looked around instinctively toward him, and at the same time he looked over at her, smiling as he caught her eye.

"*Yep*," Aurora thought ironically, smiling back and dropping her eyes shyly. "*I know those butterflies!*"

"I am the yellow color of the soul, and I reside in the soul center," Puragoz continued, "the solar plexus. This was, and still is for humans, often the most sensitive and reactive of all the energy centers. Human emotions are very strong in the physical reality, very intense. And sadly, the medical community on Earth has largely failed to recognize or acknowledge that every illness, physical pain, and ailment of the human body begins as and originates from a human emotion. Let me assure you now, though, you have not been numbed to emotions with the changes to your soul, and you are not immune to them by far. Rather, you have a dynamically enhanced capacity to recognize them and to manifest their power and potency for you rather than against you. This is a power which humans in general do not have, and that is what I am here to help you develop."

Aurora rested her elbows on the table in front of her, her chin on her palms, captivated by Puragoz and the subject about which she spoke. She was oblivious, for the time being, to Jasmine, whose eyes never left Aurora, and therefore also oblivious to the very faint dark mist that briefly appeared around Jasmine's solar plexus as she had watched Aurora's and Cal's eyes meet—a sight that certainly was not overlooked by Puragoz herself.

"Although the colors of your soul are now as one in the energy of the new combined consciousness," Puragoz explained, "you may still feel and experience the vibrations of the old colors in the points where they used to reside. So, for example, in your solar plexus you may still feel those butterflies sometimes, but when you recognize them, they can and will now give way to a greater sense of peace and possibilities for your soul, which is now combined as one and no longer has separate parts."

Aurora remembered the sense of peace she had felt when Cal took her hands earlier, the wholeness and the feeling of coming home.

"Your body will still hold the imprint of your old soul, however," Puragoz continued, "and this should never be ignored, but rather embraced and treasured as one would a beautiful piece of artwork or an important historical artifact. It is your heritage; use it wisely to create your future."

Puragoz went on to speak in the lesson about transanimation. It related to, she explained, activating the consciousness and life force of inanimate objects, triggering the imprints of human qualities and characteristics that were intrinsically held within their molecules so that the object itself would literally take on a life of its own.

"Valhandra is a high energy and high vibrational environment, so it creates the perfect conditions for transanimation to take place," Puragoz told the students, "though it still requires the will of the person in possession of the object in order for transanimation to be activated within it. You heard Namogoz speaking earlier in the Eternal Library about the transanimation of the ancient manuscript, in order to encode it and transform it to the realm in which it now exists. This was one of the greatest feats of transanimation ever to have been accomplished in history, and only the joint powers of the Gozzits together with the Universe itself were sufficient to undertake such an enormous task."

Puragoz went on to guide the students through attempting transanimation of an object of their choice. Most chose an item of jewelry, or if they didn't have anything on them, Puragoz made a pen or pencil appear on the desk in front of them with which to practice. Aurora used her hair barrette and was entranced as she managed to make it stand up on its end in the palm of her hand, per the instructions Puragoz was giving them.

Aaron was practicing with the gray metal bracelet that Dane had given him. Holding it by each end, he focused intently on it, directing his energy to it and through it as Puragoz had explained, which would activate the object's own consciousness.

After a short time, Aaron felt the metal of the bracelet buzzing between his fingers, and the figure eight charm in the middle of the chain began to rise up, so that instead of the bracelet hanging down limply, it was hovering in a rainbow-shaped arch of its own accord between his fingers, which only gently held both sides of the clasp.

"Very good, Aaron," Puragoz commented. "Perfectly done. Now see if you can maintain the connection to it whilst letting go of it."

Many of the other students had turned to watch Aaron's efforts as he increased his concentration on the bracelet, slowly letting go of one side then the other and very gradually moving his fingers sideways away from it. The bracelet remained hovering in the air as Aaron let go of it, his eyes remaining intensely focused on it and the rest of the class now watching fascinated.

Unexpectedly, the bracelet started to quiver in the air, a humming sound emanating from it as it vibrated faster and faster. Confused, Aaron pulled his hands away, pushing his chair backward in shock as he drew back from the bracelet, which had begun flipping up and down rapidly in the air like a skipping rope.

Suddenly, something seemed to explode out of the bracelet, and as the intense movement settled, the class could see that hovering in the air above it was a second, identical bracelet.

"Is that supposed to happen?" asked Jack from the front of the class and, turning to Puragoz, added, "Can things multiply too with this transanimation?"

"Not usually," Puragoz replied, her eyes narrowed and fixed on the two bracelets, which now were lying parallel to each other, suspended in the air in front of a bemused Aaron.

Without warning, the duplicate bracelet suddenly started to move independently of Aaron's, jumping, twisting, and turning above it as Aaron's bracelet lay still in the air below it. Its rapid movements left a bright imprint in the air, which the stunned onlookers realized were letters and words. After a few seconds, the second bracelet stopped twisting and turning and returned to its original position parallel to Aaron's, both still suspended in the air. The words it had written in the air read, "AARON HELP ME," bringing gasps from the other students before the second bracelet swiftly dissolved in the air as suddenly as it had appeared. Aaron's own bracelet fell down onto his desk with a clatter, but the residue of black mist remained drifting in the air where the mysterious duplicate bracelet had disappeared.

A portal at the edge of the classroom next to Puragoz spun open in a whirl of bright light and Dane hurriedly stepped through into the classroom. He turned first to Puragoz and she nodded over toward Aaron, where the words were still hanging in the air in front of him. Dane walked swiftly over to his son, picking up Aaron's bracelet from the surface of the desk and placing it in the palm of his hand, examining it closely. He whispered something to Aaron, who got up from his desk and followed his father back through the portal, which spun shut behind them and disappeared, leaving a stunned classroom of students behind it.

CHAPTER 32

Yanus studied the bracelet, deep in thought, as Dane and Aaron waited in silence for him to speak.

"The dark mist remained after the hologram disappeared," Yanus began, "which means that the message originated from the Dark world." He held the bracelet up in the light of the large crystal, which hovered, suspended in the air in the middle of the High Council's chamber, as he examined it.

"Aaron's bracelet does not hold Darkness within it, and its molecular structure has not been affected or changed," he said. "Therefore, whatever force entered it did not enter with Dark intent, or it would have left an imprint within the molecules." Yanus stroked his beard as he stared at the bracelet. "It is imperative that we discover who sent the message, and why and how it manifested through Aaron's bracelet."

"Yanus, there is something you should know," Dane said with a hesitancy in his voice, looking at the bracelet glinting in the light of the crystal and taking a deep breath before he continued. "There are two of these bracelets in existence."

Yanus looked at Dane, and after a few seconds nodded slowly as he realized what Dane was telling him.

"Micah has the other bracelet," Yanus stated, and Dane nodded, dropping his gaze to the floor.

"I should have told you," Dane replied sighing. "I didn't think it would ever be significant . . . and," he continued, "I admit there was part of me that didn't want to lose that connection to him."

Yanus turned from his examination of the bracelet, and taking a step forward, he put one hand on Dane's shoulder.

"There is nothing to regret, my friend," Yanus said, shaking his head reassuringly and smiling. "Everything is as it should be." He turned to the crystal suspended in the air, pulsing with a life force of its own as its facets reflected golden shards of light around the room.

"So," Yanus continued, "it seems likely the second bracelet was a hologram, a separate entity projected here from Terhum using its energetic connection with this one. We know it was not a psychic attack on this one, as its molecular structure is unchanged. We must find out what this means. Is it Micah making contact, or has his bracelet fallen into the hands of someone—or something—else? Either way, it is imperative we first ensure the energetic infiltration has not created a risk to the security of Valhandra. I will convene with the High Council and Namogoz immediately," Yanus said, turning to Aaron and holding the bracelet out to him, "Aaron, we may need your help."

As Aaron went to take it, he looked uncertainly over to Dane, who nodded as a go-ahead for him to take the bracelet.

"I won't put Aaron in danger when he has not yet fully completed his training, Yanus," Dane stated firmly, stepping forward and putting one arm around his son's shoulder. "Even for Micah. Not after the Vex failure."

"I know, my friend," Yanus assured him, nodding as he looked Dane directly in the eyes. "And neither will we. I promise you both that."

CHAPTER 33

As many of the students were sat in the Antreum later, Aaron and Cal chatted quietly about what had happened with the bracelet while Aurora sat at the other end of their bench, lost in thought and staring up at one of the tall trees that reached up into the sky above them.

"That's pretty intense," Cal said, his eyes wide as Aaron told him about the meeting with Yanus. "Why would Micah be making contact here? Do they think he really does need help, or is he just trying to turn you to the Darkness again, like he did out in the field at home?"

"I don't think they know," Aaron replied, shrugging his shoulders. "Dad said he would tell me when anything had been decided, but they went off to meet with the High Council and Namogoz. That's the last I heard from them."

The Antreum was where the students would spend time between lessons. In the middle of Dama-Garda, it was a large open courtyard-type area, edged by tall glass doors that led to the inner areas of the main building. The Antreum had no roof and was open to the blue and gold haze of the Valhandran sky, which cast a warm glow down over the white marble benches dotted around on the ground below. Beautiful green trees grew within it, reaching taller heights than any tree on Earth and growing hundreds of tiny white flowers on their long branches, which fluttered in the air even though there was no breeze. Glowing with the same iridescent energy that all the plants and trees on Valhandra possessed, they cast mottled areas of shade below them, giving the whole place an ethereal feel. At the ground level of the Antreum were more plants, growing around the bases of the trees with huge heart-shaped leaves, their surfaces shining like polished glass in the light from above.

Noticing Aurora's silence, Aaron turned to her, looking puzzled.

"You okay, sis?" he asked, reaching over and nudging her arm, making her jump as it broke through her thoughts.

"Yeah, miles away," Aurora said as she put her hands over her face, briefly rubbing her eyes before smiling back at him.

"Nothing new there, then," Aaron grinned at her, subsequently dodging the swipe she aimed at his shoulder. "What's next, then, guys?" he said, looking over as the other students were beginning to head back into the main building.

"Fourth level with Hanagoz," Cal answered him as they got up and headed off after the others, "the heart center. She covers soul transference in the lesson too."

"Ah, the heart center . . . luuurrrve," Aaron sighed dramatically as he sidled in-between Cal and Aurora, draping his arms over each of their shoulders. "Now, you two," he continued in an authoritative tone, "as the protective brother and best friend, I think it might be best if I sit between you both in this lesson. You know, just to keep an eye on things."

"Pack it in, Aaron," Cal said, raising his eyes but unable to hold in his laughter at his friend's words.

"Moron," muttered Aurora, her cheeks burning as she put her hand to Aaron's head and pushed him away before striding on ahead of them both.

As Hanagoz explained the history of the heart center of the soul and the role it played within the new Consciousness,

Aurora felt strangely agitated. The soft green glow around the room, which seemed to be so calming to others in the class, was only serving to irritate her, and she shifted restlessly in her seat, unable to settle and feeling like something was pushing at her subconscious mind, poking at it as if she had forgotten something vitally important. Hanagoz paused slightly and looked over toward Aurora questioningly, to which Aurora half smiled apologetically, shoving her hands down into her lap in an attempt to concentrate. Hanagoz smiled back at Aurora and continued.

"One of the gifts of the heart center is soul transference," she explained. "It is one of the greatest powers of the Lightworkers, and few are able to achieve it early in their development."

Aurora's concentration instantly sharpened as the words ignited a distant memory. She heard another voice within the narrative of the memory saying the same words, felt a recognition in them as she tried desperately to recall more of what was nagging at her mind.

"It occurs when your soul enters another being, and as such you are able to perceive everything which that being is experiencing during the time you are within it," the voice of Hanagoz continued, now fading into the distance.

In that second, Aurora was transported back in time as the memory suddenly released. Previously pushed down by the trauma of her coma, it flooded out from the depths of her soul. The surroundings of the virtual classroom faded, and she felt a heaviness pressing on her, her body feeling like lead. She found herself staring into Micah's eyes, as she had done when she had achieved soul transference into the body of the Darkness. She was back in Terhum.

She heard once more the words of Namogoz as she relived the memory. "Aurora, you are being called to go further. You can do it, Aurora, but only if you choose to."

"No more . . ." she heard herself plead with him, but then she stopped. "Wait . . ." she said interrupting her own narrative, her current consciousness taking hold of the memory. She took a deep breath. "I choose to go further," she said and felt herself instantly propelled forward out of the form of the Darkness, through the eyes of Micah and deep into his being as the memory became a lucid reality of what she would have experienced had she chosen it at the time.

Aurora found herself immersed in darkness, cold stone walls swept up either side of her, meeting above her in an arch, which made her feel like she was inside a tunnel. In front of her, the tunnel split in two directions, and she stood still, looking right and left.

Which way do I go? she heard her mind asking, the words echoing through the dank blackness.

"Trust your instinct," the voice of Namogoz rang through the air around her. "It will show you the way. Use your powers, Aurora, and develop your own awareness."

Immediately, Aurora was drawn to the right-hand tunnel. As she made her choice, she instantly began to float forward, deeper into the solidified mass that many years before had been Micah's human soul. The heavy air around her felt stifling, as if it were suffocating her, and just as a sense of panic began to rise inside her, a faint green light appeared in the distance.

"I can do this," she told herself, taking a deep breath and letting go of the panic. Willing herself forward, she continued further along the tunnel as the light became clearer, illuminating a row of objects in front of her.

She came to a stop in front of seven stone plinths, each one carved up into the shape of a torch. Within the torch of the central plinth flickered a small green flame. As she watched, it suddenly flared brighter, and she gasped, instinctively taking a step back as she realized what she was looking at; in the remnants of Micah's humanity, these were the torches which held the flames of the seven colors of the soul . . . and Micah's heart center was still alight!

As Aurora was pulled back out of the depths of Micah's blackened soul, her eyes remained transfixed on the green flame, becoming smaller and smaller as she moved further away. With a sharp jolt, she was pulled out of Micah's body, and she found herself now looking down into a chamber formed entirely of cold and damp-looking gray stone. The only furniture within it was a bed-type structure made of the same stone, positioned against the far wall of the room. She felt an uncomfortable chill on her skin, and as her eyes accustomed themselves to their new surroundings, a lone figure came into view, sitting in silence on the stone bed. Clothed in long black robes, the hood covered the face of the figure sat on the bed, but his identity was unmistakable to Aurora, looking on. Holding his left forearm up in front of him, his fist was flexed in front of his face, his eyes fixed intently on something around his wrist—a gray metal chain bracelet attached either side of one singular charm: a side-on figure eight.

Aurora took a sharp breath in and, in a flash of white light, was back in the virtual classroom with the rest of the class and Hanagoz, all looking round at her questioningly.

"Aurora, are you okay?" Hanagoz asked.

"No," Aurora said, her voice louder and more panicked than she had intended it to come out. "I have to see Dad . . . now. He's still alive." She stood up quickly, looking down at Aaron beside her.

"Who's still alive?" Aaron asked, confused.

"You have to come too," Aurora told her brother insistently and looked pleadingly back at Hanagoz, who nodded, though Aurora was already halfway to the front of the classroom and pulling a baffled Aaron by the hand behind her. A portal appeared beside Hanagoz, spinning open to reveal the High Council's chamber where Dane, Yanus, and the other occupants sitting around the large white marble table looked up in surprise as Aurora and Aaron rushed through into the room and the portal swirled shut behind them.

CHAPTER 34

"What's going on?" Dane asked, immediately getting up from the table and walking to Aaron and Aurora.

"Micah's soul is alive. It's still alight," Aurora said quickly, out of breath and flustered. Dane looked to Aaron beside her, who shrugged his shoulders.

"First I knew," he said.

Taking Aurora's hands in his, Dane began to flow energy into her. "Okay," he said calmly, "take a deep breath and tell us what's happened."

Feeling instantly calmer from the energy flow, Aurora began to relay what she had remembered, as Dane and the High Council listened in silence.

Yanus was the first to speak when she finished.

"It explains the changes in energy from the Dark chamber recently," he said, pushing himself up from the table with his arms and heading toward Dane and the twins, "and the fact that the eyes of the Universe no longer perceive Micah at the side of the Darkness, only Marta Broach. So, it appears that the Darkness has imprisoned Micah for his failure to recruit Aaron. Interesting that it is making no apparent attempt to revert him back . . . yet."

Dane looked at Yanus, stunned, and Yanus nodded to him with compassion in his eyes.

"It's a great deal for you to take in, my friend," he said to Dane before turning to the High Council.

"We must proceed very carefully with this knowledge," Yanus said, stroking his white beard thoughtfully as he spoke. "Let us first consult with Namogoz on the matter."

Yanus held his arm out to the large crystal chandelier suspended in the air above the table of the High Council. He waved his hand in a circle toward it, and the chandelier dissolved in the air as a white portal swirled open and the face of Namogoz appeared before them.

"Namogoz," Yanus said, pressing his hands together in front of him and bowing slightly in a respectful welcome.

Namogoz nodded, looking around the room before his eyes rested on Aurora.

"Aurora, you have done well," he said gently. "And," he continued with a smile, "I think you can congratulate yourself on fully achieving the skill of soul-level recall now."

Aurora looked from Namogoz to Yanus, confused. Yanus chuckled and went on to explain.

"Aurora, my dear, the trauma which caused your coma also caused you to lock away this memory in the deepest part of your soul." He walked up to her, and putting his hands on her shoulders, he looked into her eyes, nodding slowly as he spoke. "Not only have you achieved soul transference, twice now in your early training, but in accessing this memory today, along with your bravery in choosing to recall it *and* go further with it, you have also unlocked your full capacity for SLR."

Aurora looked toward Namogoz and smiled gratefully, knowing the role he had played in guiding her through it.

"Way to go, sis," Aaron whispered next to her, nudging her arm and winking at her as she looked sideways at him.

"Thanks," she whispered back, though in that second she didn't know whether to smile or cry.

"Right now," Yanus announced, holding his arms out toward Aaron and Aurora, "you both must return to your lesson. I will send you back to the second you left, so you will not have missed anything."

"So what happens now?" Aaron asked.

"In truth, Aaron," Yanus replied, looking him directly in the eyes, "I don't know yet."

Aurora looked at Dane and saw a level of uncertainty mixed with pain in his face that she had only ever seen in him once before: when the anger had overtaken her before the coma. Dane met her concerned look and smiled, though she noticed it didn't quite reach his eyes.

"Your father will be okay," Yanus reassured them, guiding them back toward the portal, which was reopening as he spoke.

"It is a shock for all of us. But right now, it is imperative you both proceed as planned with your training. Rest assured, we will let you know once any decision is reached on how we will move forward with this information."

"I did the right thing . . . telling you?" Aurora questioned anxiously.

"Most definitely," Yanus replied, nodding his head slowly as he spoke. "There was no other choice."

As the twins walked through the portal back into the classroom, Aurora turned and briefly caught sight of her father looking to the floor and shaking his head, one hand over his eyes and Yanus with his hand on Dane's shoulder, before the portal spun shut behind them.

CHAPTER 35

66 **I**t's one thing knowing he's there in that place and functioning from Darkness himself, Yanus." Dane's voice was strained as he continued. "But if he is reawakening, becoming conscious there in Terhum, who knows what effect that will have on his mind. I can't bear the thought of it."

"I know, Dane," Yanus said, "but you must maintain your energy. You have to let go of the attachment . . . you know this. You cannot help Micah if you allow the Light in your own soul to dim." Yanus put both hands on Dane's shoulders and flowed immense amounts of energy into him.

"Thank you," Dane breathed out with relief as his strength swiftly began to return.

Yanus nodded in acknowledgment before turning to the portal in the center of the room as Dane took his place at the table.

"We must move quickly with this. What is your awareness, Namogoz?" he asked.

All eyes turned to Namogoz as he spoke. "I knew Aurora was being called to witness something vitally important when she achieved soul transference to the Darkness. I was able to intervene in her consciousness and try to guide her, but she chose not to see it at the time, and as you know, I cannot force that choice." His voice took on a more serious tone as he continued.

"Now that she has recalled and progressed the experience fully, I will be able to facilitate a portal from within the Dark Chamber to any of the areas in Terhum she has visited during the period her soul transferred. But it is very risky . . . and you *must* be fully aware of the possible consequences."

"Yes," Yanus agreed. "I understand."

Turning away from Namogoz, Yanus addressed the members of the High Council.

"Friends, we have a challenging and vital decision to make today. How we deal with this revelation could affect the future in many ways, and I ask for your highest consciousness and deepest awareness in coming to a decision.

"Micah was one of us. If his soul is still alight and he is asking for our help, he should be considered as being of equal value to any other soul. No matter his past choices, we do not seek to judge, separate, nor condemn. Our action must be for the highest good of all involved and in the true energy of the Light."

Turning back to the portal in the center of the room, Yanus addressed Namogoz.

"Namogoz, for the benefit of the High Council in making their decision, let us discuss our choices and the possible consequences."

Namogoz nodded and began to speak, his voice echoing through the silence of the vast chamber.

"A connection between our world and the Dark world exists, via the energetic link between the two bracelets, and that must be resolved. It cannot be left, as it will create a risk to the safety of Valhandra. The only way to resolve it is for us to make contact with Micah. He has been able to use that connection to make contact with Aaron once; therefore, he will be able to use it again."

"What do you know of the state of Micah's soul?" Yanus asked.

"Thanks to Aurora, Hanagoz can now sense that Micah's heart center is indeed still alight," replied Namogoz, "though it will be at its weakest while he remains within Terhum. Past that, we don't yet know how repairable his soul will be . . . or whether he would be able to adapt back to this reality. This is now wholly unchartered territory."

"What are the options for our making contact with Micah?" Yanus questioned, hesitating before adding, "The safest options."

Namogoz dropped his eyes and let out a heavy breath, shaking his head.

"All the options present their risks, Yanus, and none of those risks are small."

Looking up at Yanus again, Namogoz continued.

"In the opinion of the Gozzits, the best option would be to send Aaron in via the Dark Chamber, directly to the area within Aurora's memory where Micah was being held. Aaron has the best chance of connecting quickly, as Micah knows him and has reached out to him. Micah's mind and memory will still be primarily in Darkness. It is too risky to send somebody he doesn't recognize; it may stir an adverse reaction in him."

"Which would mean, if it is Aurora who has accessed the area . . ." Yanus began.

"Yes." Namogoz finished his sentence for him. "It is within her soul's experience. Aurora would have to go too. And remember what I said earlier, even if the mission is successful, there is no guarantee that Micah's soul could be reformed or, indeed, whether he would choose for it to be."

"What are the risks if we do this?" Yanus continued, stroking his beard and deep in thought.

"Primarily that the Darkness will sense the intrusion in Terhum. If that happens, we will need to get them out immediately. But, as you know, the Dark Chamber has—" Namogoz paused before he went on "—instabilities we have yet to fully resolve. The Vex simulations of this type of situation have not yet proved totally successful."

"No," Dane interjected, pushing his forearms down onto the table in front of him and shaking his head as he lowered it to stare at the white marble surface. "I will not put them both in that danger. I will go myself."

"Dane, Micah believes that you are dead," Namogoz explained, "and it is best he continues to believe that for now. Your presence in Terhum would create too much energetic interference because of your bond with Micah. It would be too obvious for the Darkness to pick up on, and an even higher risk to the safety of Valhandra."

Yanus looked around the room at the other members of the High Council.

"What are the views on sending Aaron and Aurora?" he asked, and silence fell across the room as one by one every member around the table slowly began to raise their hands in agreement.

Dane pushed his chair back forcefully and stood up, his hands still flat on the surface of the table as he looked around at the members of the High Council, and all eyes turned to him.

"I will not choose to sacrifice my children," he said firmly and with unwavering finality. "For this decision to be made by the High Council, it has to be unanimous. I will not agree and give you the power to decide their fate." As Yanus opened his mouth to speak, Dane raised his hand toward him to request his silence. Dropping his head, Dane paused before continuing, his voice cracking with emotion. "I will, however, allow Aaron and Aurora their choice in the matter."

Dane raised his eyes, looking directly at Yanus.

"We cannot and should not use our position as High Council to force the fate of other Lightworkers. That was done to Micah, Yanus, all those years ago, and now we find ourselves here. This," Dane gestured across the room, "is not the way for us to move forward anymore. Change is required, and we have brought these children into the world to help facilitate that change. But *we* also have to be willing to look at different possibilities. Otherwise, how can we even hope to help humanity change?"

Dane took a deep breath before he went on. "It is choice that will create change, Yanus, so let us allow them to choose their fate and their future . . . and let us trust their choice."

Yanus looked at Dane and nodded slowly, a glimmer of pride and admiration in his eyes. Casting his gaze first around the table of the High Council and then to Namogoz, who smiled, his violet light shining even more intensely around the room, Yanus finally spoke.

"So be it," he announced. "The students should complete their final lesson with Namogoz, then Aurora and Aaron will be brought to me . . . and they shall make their choice."

CHAPTER 36

Dane entered the Antreum, and all eyes of the other students turned to watch him as he walked toward the bench where Cal, Aurora, and Aaron sat chatting quietly in the golden glow of the Valhandran sun. As Aurora looked up and spotted him, she caught her breath in anticipation there may be news from the High Council about Micah.

Speaking in a low voice as he reached them, Dane asked the twins to follow him out of the Antreum. Turning back to Cal as Aurora and Aaron got up and made their way to the glass doors, he added, "Cal, I would like you to come too, please. This will also involve you."

"Sure," Cal replied and duly stood to follow them all out. Once in the corridor away from the other students, Dane turned and addressed all three in a serious tone.

"I know you've been anxious to hear . . . and there is news. However, I need you to complete your final lesson before you are told more. When the lesson is finished, the three of you should wait in the classroom with Namogoz for further instructions. Is that clear?"

All three nodded in silence, and Dane smiled, putting one hand on each of the boys' shoulders in a reassuring gesture before resting his hand briefly on Aurora's cheek.

"In the meantime, concentrate on the lesson. Everything will be okay," he said encouragingly before he turned and walked swiftly back up the corridor, disappearing through a swirling portal at the far end of it.

"Well, that's easier said than done," sighed Aurora, and as the other students began to file through the doors from the Antreum and off in the direction of the main hall, she, Aaron, and Cal followed after them.

All three were silent, taken up in their own thoughts as they joined the mass of students congregating in the main hall. The hall began to fade as the vortex picked up momentum around them, then retreated to reveal the familiar surroundings of the virtual classroom tinged with the violet light of Namogoz from the front of the room. The usual few seconds of commotion as the students settled into their seats was swiftly silenced as Namogoz began to speak.

"Welcome, all of you, to your final lesson in the seventh level of soul consciousness," he announced, casting his eyes across the occupants of the classroom.

Aurora forced all thoughts of what was coming next to the back of her mind, putting her attention on Namogoz, and she soon was lost in his voice as he explained the planes of existence.

"All of life exists on seven energetic planes, or realms of matter," Namogoz began.

"The Universe is the ultimate power, and all other planes of matter exist within it. Humanity has gone some way to looking at the presence and workings of the Universe, but this has only served to cause division and arguments as to its purpose. The Universe has no judgment of Light and Dark, right or wrong, good or evil. It holds possibilities for creation of everything . . . but it gives only what we ask for. It does not filter our requests according to whether they are good or bad, whether they will create or destroy the future, for us or the world."

"But nobody would actually ask for bad things to happen to them, would they?" asked a student sat at the front of the room.

"Humanity is responsible for its own destiny," Namogoz replied, "and for the creation of its own future. Requests can be made in many ways, some consciously and some unconsciously. Many do not understand that with their very thoughts, actions, and behaviors, they are making requests to the Universe; they are, in effect, telling it what they are willing to receive in life . . . and they will only get what they are willing to receive."

"Like what, though?" the same student asked.

"Everything . . . every person, every situation, even every thought, feeling, and emotion we have has a resonant frequency. Think of frequencies as if they were hundreds of highways running parallel to each other. You can choose to switch to another highway, or you can convince yourself that this is the only way for you and you don't have the power to change it. Your thoughts will become your reality, and you will indeed have no power to change it. A negative frequency will attract other negative people, situations, and circumstances to it along its route, so in essence, a person existing at a negative frequency will likely always be in the 'wrong place at the wrong time.' Unlucky things will keep happening to them because that is what they expect to happen; they are resonating at that frequency. Consequently, those negative or unlucky happenings then tend to perpetuate the person's opinion that they are, by nature, unlucky. It becomes a self-fulfilling prophecy. Their negative mindset becomes their request. It is the frequency which they send out into the Universe, and that is what they will pull toward them energetically in the future."

Wow! Aurora thought, incredulously. *What would the world be like if everyone knew that!*

"Exactly, Aurora," Namogoz agreed and Aurora blushed, not realizing she had projected her thoughts out to the whole class.

"We can teach them," Jack suggested, and many other students nodded in agreement.

"In the future, Jack, that is what the Light is hoping will happen," Namogoz replied, smiling, "but in the meantime, there is other work to be done."

Namogoz went on to explain the other planes of existence to the class.

"The Light and the Darkness exist in the next, the Cosmic Plane, and it is here where all life is created. Alongside the Light exists the realm of Valhandra, where the Gozzits, the Eternal Library, and the Lightworkers reside—and now also you, the Children of the Light. The Darkness also has its own realm of Terhum, and it is within that Dark World, where the broken and stolen souls are imprisoned and where the Darkness is building its army."

"So, is that heaven and hell?" Aaron asked.

"In a sense," Namogoz replied. "Heaven and hell are concepts created by humankind. They are based on the existence of the Light and the Darkness, though the idea of other planes of existence is largely misunderstood by humanity and has become widely entrenched in myths and religion, rather than being acknowledged as the Universal structure of life.

"Then there is the Physical world, where humanity resides and where you experienced your life on Earth up until your calling to Valhandra. Finally, between the Physical world and the higher planes exists the Spirit World, where souls—human and animal—reside before and after their time in the Physical world. Also within the Spirit World are those souls referred to on Earth as 'Angels' and 'Ascended Masters.' These are highly enlightened souls, sent to Earth by the Light in human form to impart specific knowledge, wisdom, and insights. When they passed from their time in the Physical world, the Light decided they would remain on the Spiritual plane, rather than reincarnating back on Earth. Their task was to guide and protect humanity, but again much of humanity decried their existence and refused to receive their guidance and wisdom. The Elementals you learnt about during your first and second levels are also part of the Spiritual plane, being the souls and master beings of the natural world and invisible to the human eye."

"So heaven and hell don't actually exist?" Aaron concluded.

"Not in the way they are believed to on Earth," replied Namogoz. "The true 'heaven' and 'hell' would in fact be Valhandra and Terhum, not the standard progression from human life they are thought to be. When souls pass on from their physical life through a natural death, they will be returned to the Spiritual plane, not to the higher planes. On the Spiritual plane, souls exist as pure energy, freed from all which has been impelled on them during their time on Earth and are prepared for reincarnation."

A second portal opened by the side of Namogoz, to an image of the Hall of Records within the Eternal Library.

"After this lesson, you will have completed all seven levels required for the initial development of your new souls, but there is still much for you to learn and discover. You will now be granted access to the Hall of Records; you will be able to read about your past lives and fully understand the progression your soul has gone through leading to this one." Namogoz paused as he looked around the room.

"But be aware, this is not always an easy experience," he warned. "You will all have a Mentor to support you with your discoveries, a Lightworker, though it will not be your parent Lightworker. There will be challenges for you within your soul record, and what you find out will bring up memories often involving extreme human emotions, which your Mentor will assist you to clear."

At the mention of previous lives, Aurora looked over at Cal, who was focused intently on Namogoz, leaning forward with his elbows resting on the table in front of him. Almost instantly, she felt a rush of emotions through her whole body—a warmth that felt comforting and exciting all at once, but at the same time that intense ache in her chest that felt like her heart was going to burst. Tears rose at the back of her eyes from the intensity of it, and feeling instantly exhausted, she put her hand up to ask a question.

"Yes, Aurora?" Namogoz asked, smiling down at her.

"I know that emotions will come up from previous lives," she began, pausing to search for what she wanted to say, "but will the new Consciousness stop us from feeling emotions now? I mean, once our souls are fully developed?"

"The powers of the new Consciousness are immense," Namogoz explained, "but . . . although you have a highly advanced soul, you still inhabit a physical body. Even though it has taken on the powers of your soul—for example, it will transmigrate with you from place to place—you will not leave your physical body behind anymore, as you did in the early stages of your soul's transformation. The new Consciousness does not provide immunity as such to human emotions, but rather the power to transmute them instantly to something far greater. That does not mean you will never feel emotions—they are part of the human experience and can be a wonderful thing for you too. But you still have to make the choice to use your power; it is not automatic. You must constantly and consciously choose the way of the Light to maintain the powers of your soul. You must remain aware at all times of your purpose and what is expected of you as Children of the Light. If at any point you fail to choose to follow the new Consciousness, the power of your soul will begin to diminish. Do not allow yourselves to be drawn in inextricably to human emotions; acknowledge them, learn from them, feel them, by all means . . . but then choose to let them go."

"How do we know if we are choosing that, though?" Aurora asked, confused.

"Be aware that what you are experiencing is purely emotion. Know that it is not real," explained Namogoz. "As soon as you acknowledge that, you will instantly free yourself from it. Beware, though, because emotions are extremely powerful and it will often be tempting to hold on to them. Withheld emotion will eat away at the soul, manifest as pain in the physical body, and ultimately will destroy it.

"The Light intended emotions to be a gift of awareness, instant and intense reactions to a thing or situation which would act as signposts, to guide each human being on its path through life. Emotions were not designed to last or to be held on to. But over the years, humans have become addicted to feelings and emotion. They crave the rush emotions give them.

"Humans hold on to sadness because they believe it proves their attachment to a thing or a person. They hold on to joy because they believe it validates their successes. But no emotion will remain as it first feels for long, and however desperately it is held on to, the initial intensity will fade. Beyond that initial intensity, there is a space of possibility, and in that space the wisdom and guidance of the Universe can be received. For humans, that space is the key to creating the life of their dreams, but that can only happen if they are willing to move past the emotion and let it go. If not, the space becomes accessible for the Darkness to creep in, instilling fear, doubt, and need.

"Humans have lost their intuition. They are unable to find validation of their worth within, so have to search for it outside themselves. They are missing vital signs and guidance from the Universe, and as time goes by they become more and more detached from the Light.

"Your task as Children of the Light," Namogoz continued, "is, in time, to teach humanity a better way, to show them how to live in the true energy and life force of the Light, and to trust in the wisdom of the Universe."

"No pressure, then," Aaron whispered to Aurora, and as she stifled a giggle, Namogoz raised his eyes in amusement.

Namogoz went on to explain other aspects of the Light's work during the early years of humanity, which over time had become indoctrinated with greed and fear, self-gain for the minority at the expense of the majority. The class listened, captivated, as he explained that when the principle of religion was born into the world by the Light, the ultimate aim was the selfless service of humanity. The Light intended it to develop the hearts and minds of humanity, allowing them to believe they were supported, cared for, and nurtured by a power greater than themselves. As with many failings of the human race, it was misused and exploited, ultimately creating instead a vast chasm of separation within humanity. Power-hungry leaders created false gods in the image of the Light, steeped in myth and legend, but with the ultimate aim to foster fear, submission, and servitude in the people.

He went on to speak about government and majority rule. Aurora knew that in Earth School, she would have struggled to follow any of what he spoke about; in fact, she mused, quietly smiling to herself, she may even have struggled to stay awake! But now, comfortable in the knowledge that she could recall any of this at any time should she need to, she relaxed in the violet glow of the classroom, letting the information soak into her as if it were food for her soul, and on a very different level than she had ever known before . . . she understood all of it.

CHAPTER 37

As the final lesson concluded, Dane and Yanus appeared at the front of the classroom on either side of Namogoz. Yanus swept his arms out widely as a gesture to everyone in the room.

"Congratulations on completing all seven levels," he announced with a wide smile. "You have done well, and now there will be some hard-earned respite for you, before you are gathered and prepared for the next stage." Lowering his arms, his expression became suddenly more solemn.

"It is no small task, this calling which has been bestowed on you," Yanus declared. "You can be sure of that. But you all have been chosen, your souls prepared over many years for this mission. Now is the time for you to take your place in the Circle of Light."

Silence fell across the class, the students deep in their own thoughts about what their future held. At the front of the room, Dane stepped forward to address the group.

"The transportation vortex will take you back to the main hall for food. After that, you will be free to spend time with your parent Lightworker in the grounds of Dama-Garda or in the Antreum, wherever you choose, until the time comes for further instructions to be given."

As the students got up from their desks, Dane signaled to Aurora, Aaron, and Cal to join him at the front. The transportation vortex started up, swirling from the edges of the classroom inward, and the group at the front waited in silence, watching as it swept across the room.

As the rest of the students were being transported away, Aurora caught the eyes of Jasmine, who stood staring at her from the middle of the room, one of the final students to disappear into the vortex. A sudden white flash in front of her eyes caused Aurora to draw a sharp breath in as a vision took shape in front of her. She saw a woman with long dark hair, dressed in white Lightworker robes in surroundings Aurora recognized as the Eternal Library. The woman was standing in one of the vast rows of soul books, staring forward at one particular volume. Appearing nervous, she looked around her before reaching forward toward the shelves in front of her as one book glided out of its position on the shelf and into her hands. As the book opened, a glow from its pages illuminated the woman's face, and Aurora saw tears falling from her eyes as she looked at its contents.

"No," the woman sobbed, shaking her head. "I have to find them. He has to have a future." In that second, there was a blinding flash and a golden cage descended swiftly from above the dark-haired woman, imprisoning her inside it, and she screamed out before crumpling to the floor, unconscious.

"Aurora . . . Aurora," Dane said insistently, putting his hand on her shoulder and gently shaking it.

"Huh!" Aurora gasped, startled by his contact as the vision faded and she was once more in the surroundings of the virtual classroom.

"Are you okay?" Dane asked her, a concerned look on his face.

Aurora looked back at him and felt her crystal start to pulse in the pocket of her robe; the words of Ajnagoz rang through her mind: "The full picture only becomes totally clear when *all* the pieces are fitted together." In that moment, she knew she needed more information and began to explain the visions to her father.

Dane looked toward Yanus, raising his eyebrows in question and Yanus nodded.

"They should be aware of what happened; it may be more vital than we know," he said, and Dane turned back to Aurora, Aaron, and Cal.

"On the day Marta Broach was taken by the Darkness," Dane began, "Joe Marsh mentioned there had been an incident when he had spoken with her about Aurora's detention."

"Yes, I remember that," Aurora recalled. "He didn't say anything else about it, though."

"No, because it wasn't the right time, then," Dane continued. "The incident he referred to was what you saw in your vision just now, Aurora."

Dane took a deep breath before he continued.

"The woman you saw in your visions is called Dayana. She is a Lightworker, and she is Jasmine's birth mother. Jasmine's birth father was called Shamar, and he was her Protector on Earth. Dayana's sister died, leaving her only child orphaned, a four-year-old girl called Keesha. The child was taken in by Dayana and Shamar, who looked after her as their own. Jasmine was eight at the time. However, Keesha's proximity to Jasmine resulted in her being mistaken for a Child of the Light." Dane looked at Aurora before adding, "As Sienna was." Hearing Sienna's name, Aurora felt the familiar tightening in her chest but released it, putting her attention back on her father's story.

"As with many of the stolen children, Keesha was taken by the Darkness while playing out in her garden. Shamar walked out and saw it happening. He tried to intervene and save Keesha, but he also disappeared at the same time she did. When Shamar was taken, the future pages within his soul book disappeared, as was the case with all the stolen children. Their futures were seemingly eradicated—they ceased to exist. In truth, we have to face the reality that we may never be able to rescue them." Aurora's heart sank at his words, but she forced her attention back to the story as her father continued.

"Dayana was not told about Shamar's soul book, and—"| Dane took a deep breath, letting out a sigh "—rightly or wrongly, we led her to believe rescue was possible in time. Joe Marsh is Shamar's brother, and he took over as Jasmine's Protector. Dayana was naturally devastated. The Gozzits, Yanus, and I helped her through her grief, and we believed that in time she had fully released it. But recently, it became apparent that the imprint of it was still affecting her, so Yanus and Namogoz began monitoring her more closely. We tried to talk to her, to convince her that any rescue had to be attempted at the right time, once you were all safely in Valhandra. But she became obsessed with thoughts of Shamar and, as you saw, she went to the Eternal Library and accessed his soul book."

"That's forbidden," Aaron said.

"Yes," Dane replied and shook his head sadly. "She broke one of the laws of the Universe by looking into the soul book of another. As a result, her future as a Lightworker was compromised. Once she had taken that action it could not be undone, there was only one thing for the High Council to do after that . . ."

"Was that what would have happened to Aaron if he hadn't chosen the Light?" Aurora asked without thinking, instantly regretting it when she realized Aaron may not know about that part of his story.

"Yes," Dane replied, "and don't worry, Aaron knows about it; he knows everything now."

Aurora turned to her brother, and he nodded to her in acknowledgement of Dane's words.

"Okay," she breathed out with relief, "so what about Jasmine?"

Dane went on to explain that Jasmine was as yet unaware what had happened to her mother, having been told that Dayana was away on a mission for the Gozzits. Yanus was concerned about the stability of Jasmine's soul, especially since Marta Broach turned to the Darkness; he had to ensure that she was kept from the truth for now. They could not risk losing another Lightworker before going into battle against the Darkness.

"But surely Jasmine's okay now her soul has received the new Consciousness?" Cal asked, looking from Dane to Yanus. At that point Yanus stepped forward, putting one hand on Dane's arm as he hastily interjected in the conversation.

"Jasmine's soul has had a more . . . troubled past than some," he explained slowly and looked at Cal and Aurora with purposeful consideration of his words, "and that has not been without its complications. But she has been prepared for this life, this mission, as you all have. She will be fine; I am certain of it."

Aurora and Cal looked at each other, and then Aurora at Dane, who didn't appear quite as convinced of that fact as Yanus was.

"So . . . we must proceed with the plans, one Lightworker down," Dane announced, "and for now it is imperative that Jasmine remain unaware of the truth about her parents."

Yanus turned to Aurora and Aaron, his expression more serious than they had ever seen it.

"It was vital that you completed your final lesson before we discussed the situation over Micah any further. Now I am going to ask you both to make a choice. It is no small thing which will be asked of you, and with it comes no small element of danger . . . to you both." He paused while Aurora and Aaron looked at each other and then to their father, whose expression confirmed the gravity of the conversation.

Yanus proceeded to explain what would be required of them.

"So," Yanus concluded, "what is your decision?"

Aurora felt a protective pull energetically from Cal as she looked to Aaron. The bond that the twins had shared from birth allowed them to know immediately what the other was thinking and the choice which they both would make. As they turned back to Yanus, it was Aaron who spoke.

"There is no choice," he said with absolute conviction. "We go."

As Yanus nodded in acknowledgement of their decision, Cal stepped forward.

"Wait. I can't let Aurora go in without me. I have to go too," he said determinedly.

Dane looked at Yanus, his raised eyes in question of Cal's statement.

"I don't sense he'll be a risk," Dane suggested. "I had the awareness to bring him here, that in some way his involvement is required."

After a moment's consideration, Yanus nodded, looking proudly at the three young Lightworkers standing in front of him.

"If ever I were to know that bringing you children here to Valhandra was the right choice . . . it is now. So be it. All three of you will go. There is no time to lose," Yanus announced, turning swiftly to Namogoz, his long white robes flowing behind him.

"Namogoz, transport us to the Eternal Library and have the Gozzits ready to put the shield in place around it once we are there. Dane, have Donna transported to Valhandra. I need all Lightworkers fully prepared to leave for Earth as soon as we have Micah out."

CHAPTER 38

The mood in the boardroom hung heavy from the effects of the dark smog spreading across the continents of Earth and the resulting depression sweeping though humanity. The huge screen on the wall at the front of the room displayed live video images of leaders and their teams from across the world and they, along with those around the table in the boardroom, frantically searched for ways to stop the virus that was spreading uncontrollably. The prime minister looked out of the panoramic window of the high-rise block, hope draining from her eyes as she surveyed the scene outside. Thick, gray smog hung over the city like a blanket in the sky, dripping its dark mist down through the air on to the ground below.

The chaos that had broken out when the smog first descended had given way to an eerie silence, the deserted city center now completely devoid of life. It was becoming difficult to see the ground, for the falling smog and black snake-like shadows seemed to be winding their way ominously through the streets. If she didn't know better, she would think that these shadows seemed to be alive, crawling along the ground as if they were searching, but searching for what—anybody who had not yet barricaded themselves into their homes? She shook the thought from her head, reprimanding herself for allowing the situation to play with her mind. These were simply shadows on the ground from the hovering smog, not some evil entities looking for prey. The country needed her to keep her sanity; she had to remain in control.

"I've never seen anything like it," the prime minister said bleakly to Ethan, her second in command, standing beside her. "How many have died so far, can we estimate?"

"It seems difficult to say yet, Prime Minister ma'am. The army are on their way out as we speak to assess the situation. We should have an online update from General Kerr any minute," Ethan replied, as they glimpsed the first deployment of tanks rumbling into view at the outskirts of the city.

"Protected?" asked the prime minister, more as a statement than a question.

"Yes, all with full hazmat suits as you instructed."

The prime minister nodded, putting her hand up to the window. "We need everyone to remain in their houses until we can determine a way forward . . . whatever that is."

Within seconds, the deputy prime minister's phone rang.

"Yes?" she answered hurriedly. "Of course, put him through," she replied, swiftly grabbing the visual display remote and pointing it toward the smaller screen on the front wall of the boardroom. The screen flickered into life to the image of General Kerr, the chief of staff and head of the army, a somber look on his face.

"General Kerr, thank you for your prompt response in deploying our troops," the prime minister said, silencing some general chatter around the table with a raised hand. "I need to know what arrangements are being made for the bodies of the deceased citizens. Wherever your mortuary sites are, they will need to be properly secured and guarded."

The general looked down to the table in front of him. "Well, ma'am," he began, hesitating as if trying to find words, "that's what I needed to speak with you about. The thing is . . ."

"What is the thing, General?" the prime minister insisted with an impatient edge in her voice.

"There are no bodies, they've all gone."

"What do you mean they've all gone?" the prime minister responded, confused.

"Disappeared, disintegrated . . . seemingly," General Kerr clarified. "All that is left is black dust on the ground where the bodies had been. I have a team of scientists carrying out tests on the dust, but so far, we can only guess that it is an extreme reaction of the virus on the body after death."

Silence fell around the room as the prime minister stared horrified at the general on the screen in front of her, then back out of the window to her side.

In the depths of Terhum, the Darkness looked on to the gray stone pit in the middle of the gloomy chamber, Marta Broach standing silently at its side. One by one the blackened, soulless bodies rose from the fiery center of the pit, levitated out of the flames and dropped to the ground with a sickening thud. A long wisp of black smoke snaked out from the throne at the front of the chamber, winding its way around the stone pit in the middle of the room, and as it reached its destination, it began to seep into the broken corpses. Slowly, the bodies began to stir, rising up from the ground, twisting and morphing into their new and terrifying form. Stretching up to their full height, evil yellow eyes staring out from beneath the hoods of their long robes, the newborn dark demons turned to face the front of the chamber, bowing to their master before slinking away into the shadows at the edges of the chamber. With each new recruit to its army, the power of the Darkness increased, while the virus continued to spread far and wide, draining the energy and life force of humanity . . .

The Darkness waited for the Light to make its move.

CHAPTER 39

As the group arrived in the foyer of the Eternal Library, the swirling mists of the transportation portal cleared swiftly around them.

Yanus headed immediately up the curved staircase. His long white robes flowed behind him as he reached the Temporal Gallery, raising his hand toward the golden shield surrounding it. The shield momentarily glowed brighter, and Yanus stepped through it, walking purposefully to a shelf of huge leather-bound books in the far corner of the Gallery.

Aurora gazed around her, in awe of the surroundings even more so than during their first visit.

"The shield is in place around the Library," Dane announced, and suddenly an image of Jasmine flashed into Aurora's mind. Startled, she immediately pushed it away, putting her attention firmly on Yanus, who was now coming back down the staircase toward them holding one of the glowing compendiums in his hands. As he reached them, he nodded toward the Dark Chamber.

"Come," he directed them all to follow him and headed over to the large golden door to the far left side of the Library.

With her eyes fixed on the black lettering of the sign above the door, Aurora felt an anxious flutter in her chest at the thought of what lay beyond it. She looked sideways at Aaron, who was standing a little too straight, and she knew that he was feeling the apprehension too. As they stopped outside the golden door, Cal put his hand on her arm.

"Are you still sure about this?" he asked quietly.

"Yes, of course," she said with as much conviction as she could manage, though even she heard the slight shake in her voice. Looking up at Cal, she communicated with him telepathically instead, trusting her inner voice more.

"I'm nervous, but I have to do this," she told him, and he nodded.

"I know," he replied, "and I'll be there with you every step of the way."

Yanus waved his hand to the side of the door, and a podium appeared. Placing the book on the podium, he opened it, the bright golden light from within its pages illuminating a huge arc in the space above it.

"Micah's soul book," Yanus explained. "It will help us to reach him in Terhum. The Chamber will use the memories held in Aurora's soul; it will then be able to chart a path to the areas she transferred to within the realm. This has only ever been attempted once before—" Yanus broke off as he and Dane looked at each other.

"Did it work then?" Cal asked, and Yanus looked quickly away from him back into the pages of the book.

"There was a . . . small amount of success," Yanus said hesitatingly. "We were unable to complete the mission." He turned back to Aurora, Aaron, and Cal and looked at all of them in turn.

"If anything goes wrong, or looks to be going that way, we will abandon the mission and pull you all out immediately. Attempting to reach Micah is a vital part of our current journey, but I will not sacrifice multiple souls for one."

Dane nodded his agreement with Yanus, adding, "No matter who that soul is. If the true Micah is in there, he would understand. I know that without doubt."

Yanus summoned the Gozzits and virtual images of all seven appeared instantly around the edges of the vast dome above them. Against the backdrop of the living root system of the Rainbow Forest, the myriad of colors sparkled and combined like a cosmic kaleidoscope across the Library.

"Namogoz," Yanus directed, "tether all three to the Light."

Namogoz nodded and looked up. The white lotus flower at the top of his canopy began to open, and as it flowered, a beam of white light emanated from its center, splitting into three separate beams that moved swiftly through the air toward Aurora, Aaron, and Cal, wrapping around their middles and tying in a knot to the front of their bodies, casting the familiar golden shield of protection around them. All three of them looked up at Namogoz, holding them to the Light as he smiled down at them, and they felt safe.

Dane opened the golden door to the Dark Chamber, and Aurora held her breath as they looked inside. A vast chasm of empty space stretched out before them, its cold blackness seeming to both pull them in and push them away at the same time.

"Aurora, please stand here in front of the book," Yanus directed, putting his hand on her shoulder as she stepped forward.

The light from the book expanded, wrapping around Aurora's body, and a portal appeared above the book. Aurora recognized the cold gray stone room, the hideously malformed rats scuttling around the edges of the damp walls. The image panned around like a video camera, as if she were simply reliving the memory. The stone bed came into view against the wall, the robed figure sitting with his head in hands in the middle of it exactly as she had seen him. Dane caught his breath at the sight of Micah, his eyes remaining rigidly fixed on the image above his daughter.

"Good," Yanus encouraged. "Now, Aurora, turn and direct the memory portal into the Dark Chamber." Aurora looked at him skeptically, and he answered her unspoken question. "Just be willing for the portal to go in there, imagine it, and it will happen."

Aurora did as she was told, and almost instantly the image of Micah in the room shot forward through the door of the Dark Chamber, which now appeared as if it were a door into the very room Micah sat in. As they all stood tentatively at the door to Terhum, the draw toward it felt even stronger.

"The power of the Darkness is strong, and it will try to pull you in. You will need to use all the powers you have been taught in order that you do not weaken to it," Yanus explained gravely. "Aaron, you will go in first, then Aurora, and lastly Cal."

"What do I say?" Aaron asked Yanus.

"You will know when you get there," Yanus replied.

"Okay," Aaron said dryly. "I hope you're right." He turned one more time to look at his father with an apprehensive half-smile, and then taking a deep breath he stepped inside, closely followed as instructed by Aurora and then Cal.

CHAPTER 40

Aurora's eyes quickly adjusted to the darkness of the room, and she felt the same lead-like heaviness in her body as when she had been here before. The same dank smell hung in the air around them with a stench that, although she had never witnessed it in her Earth life, she imagined might be the smell of death. Looking around her, she saw Cal immediately to her right side and Aaron standing in front and slightly to her left. The figure of Micah sat on the bed, elbows resting on each knee and his arms crossed between them. He was stooped so low, his forehead almost rested on his clasped hands. As they fully materialized into their new surroundings, the glow of the golden shield also appeared, shining out around them and illuminating the room.

Micah's head raised slightly, the hood of his black robes falling over most of his face, but Aurora could tell from the angle of his head that he was now looking farther across the floor of the room toward the light shining from them. Her heart pounded in her ears like a drumbeat. As he lifted his head more, she caught a glimpse of his face. The gray pallor she remembered from seeing him in the fields at home—and more recently in her visions—was still evident, but less than she remembered it, and she thought there was a slightly more normal tone to his skin. As he raised his head higher, his pure black eyes stared up at them blankly. Aurora caught her breath, wondering what he would do. Did they need to leave now?

"Dad," she heard her mind call out telepathically, almost just as a test he was there.

"We're here, Aurora," she heard his voice respond. "Don't worry, we are watching and will pull you out if we need to." Realizing she had been holding her breath, she slowly let it out, relaxing slightly in the knowledge that her father and Yanus were close by if needed.

Aaron held out his arm toward Micah, the arm with his bracelet on it. Looking directly at Micah, he spoke in a quiet but calm and perfectly steady voice.

"It's me," he said. "Micah . . . it's me, Aaron."

Almost immediately, the blackness in Micah's eyes began to dissipate, like clouds clearing from the sky. The rigidity of his face seemed to release as his eyes cleared and he stared at the bracelet on the arm Aaron held out to him.

"Aaron," came the deep, monotone voice. Pushing back the sleeve of his robe on his left arm, Micah uncovered his own bracelet, lifting his eyes slowly from Aaron's arm to his face as he did so. "You came," he said in a low whisper.

"Yes," Aaron replied, slowly moving a step closer to Micah, and Aurora put her hand to her chest with relief, feeling able to breathe again.

"We've come from Valhandra . . . to get you out of here," Aaron continued, more as a question than a statement, and with a tone of uncertainty in his voice he added, "if you want?"

Micah looked toward the others standing behind Aaron.

"This is my sister Aurora and our friend Cal," he explained as Cal nodded and Aurora smiled awkwardly, raising one of her hands, which were clasped tightly to her front, slightly.

"Sister . . . Dane's daughter?" Micah said slowly, and Aaron nodded.

Aurora was certain she saw a glimmer of tears in Micah's eyes as he looked at her. Suddenly, he grimaced and lowered his head, his upper body swaying forward slightly as he braced his hands down on the bed on either side of him, to stop himself from falling.

"I'm weak," Micah admitted. "I no longer have the ability to raise my own energy. I have had to depend on the Darkness for it, and now, well, that is denied me as part of my punishment."

"So what will happen when your energy runs out?" Aurora asked, and the look on Micah's face told her the answer.

Sitting on the bed, the shoulders of his giant frame hunched forward, there was a strange sort of frailty about him, which made Aurora feel sad.

"What about our energy? Can we give you some to help?" she asked, and Micah looked up at her.

"You would do that for me?" he asked, looking toward all three of them with a mix of confusion and hope in his voice.

"Yes," Aurora replied simply and with certainty, looking to Aaron and Cal, who nodded their agreement.

"Of course," Aaron added.

Micah looked at all three of them in turn, as if he wanted to speak but couldn't find the words. Instead, he finally held out his arms to them with a simple, "Thank you."

Moving closer to Micah, Aaron and Cal took one of his hands each, putting their free hands under his forearm. Aurora stood beside Cal, one hand further up the arm Cal was holding and one on Micah's shoulder, and all three began to flow their energy into him. Streams of energy began to run into his body, which reacted instantly, dragging the white light in faster and more intensely than any of them had ever experienced. The amount of energy coursing through her was making Aurora feel slightly light-headed, and she braced her leg against the stone bed she stood by to steady herself.

Suddenly, a black wisp of smoke appeared from below Micah, winding up around the lower half of his body and pushing at their arms, at the points where the energy flow was entering his body.

"What's happening?" Aurora asked, with panic rising in her voice, her energy field dimming slightly as she felt the pressure from the dark mist, as if it were trying to push them away from Micah.

"The dark energy is sensing the light energy. Keep going," Micah said and looked up at Aaron, his voice a mix of desperation and determination. He threw back his head, his face contorted in pain and his eyes wide open, as their color began flickering between inky black and clear blue. They could feel his body tensing against the dark cloud gathering below him, the internal battle raging inside him. "It's the dark energy in me fighting back. Just . . . keep . . . going," he insisted through clenched teeth.

Aurora met Cal's eyes and then Aaron's as they struggled to hold back the dark mists that pushed upward harder and harder.

"It's getting stronger," she communicated to them. "I don't know how much longer we can hold it back." Connecting back to Valhandra, she called out in her mind, "Dad, help!"

Suddenly, they felt an intense burst of energy into their own fields and heard Dane's voice in their minds.

"I'm with you. So is Yanus and the Gozzits. Just keep flowing," he said, and instantly the energy around all three of them flared, filling the whole room with light.

As their combined strength pushed back at the dark mists below them, its resistance finally gave way as if a pressure valve released. As it did so, the mists shot back down into the floor and disappeared, the three of them breathing out heavily with relief as Micah relaxed and the tension released from his body.

"Are you okay?" Aurora asked, putting her hand on his shoulder with slight apprehension as to whether it had worked.

His breathing steadied, and Micah slowly raised his head to look up at her. As he did so, she saw that his eyes had returned once more to a clear blue, and she gasped at the transformation, seeing the Micah he must have been before the Darkness set in.

"Thank you, all of you," Micah said and slowly began to stand up from the stone bed, his huge frame dwarfing even Cal's broad build. "I was—" but before he could say anything else there was a low rumble, which seemed to come from the walls and the floor in the room. Micah paused to listen, then spoke. "The Darkness is sensing the shift," he warned. "You have to get out of here."

"We're taking you with us," Aurora said to him. "That's what we came for. You can come back with us to Valhandra."

"I wish it were that easy," Micah sighed. "My soul has been solidified for too many years to survive back on Valhandra. You have given me the greatest gift I could have asked for with your energy . . . you've allowed me to feel the Light once more."

"But what will happen to you?" Aaron interjected. "We can't leave you here."

"The Darkness has replaced me. It will never allow me to leave this place, alive or . . ." Micah paused. "My fate is sealed now; nothing can change that. The energy you have given me won't last long. The Darkness will overpower it once more, and when that happens it will not allow there to be a second time. Rightly or wrongly, I made a choice many years ago, and now that choice will play out. Nothing can keep me from that fate.

But, before that happens," he said, pausing. "I can . . . I want to . . . put right at least some of the wrongs I've done. That is why I contacted you, Aaron, because for that I will need your help." Micah put one hand on Aaron's shoulder and looked at him, smiling but with sadness in his face.

"You look so much like your dad," he said, shaking his head, and Aaron blinked to clear the tears that involuntarily rose in his eyes.

"We'll do whatever we can," Aaron said with more determination in his voice than Aurora had ever heard. He turned to her and Cal, who both nodded in agreement.

Cal added, "We're all in. What do you need us to do?"

CHAPTER 41

"I'm not sure about this," Dane said in a worried voice to Yanus. "It's too risky. Something doesn't feel right. I think we should pull them out. We can try to pull Micah out too—it might work."

Yanus placed one hand on Dane's arm in a reassuring gesture. "Let's just see what Micah suggests," he said slowly, his eyes fixed on the scene within the portal window.

"You are tethered to Valhandra, and I am assuming to Namogoz?" Micah asked, and Aaron nodded. "Between us and with the strength you can summon from the Gozzits through the cords, we can break the chains barricading the cell door. Down the corridor is the throne room of the Darkness, and right now it is empty. The children stolen from Earth are imprisoned in a portal, a separate realm, which is hidden within the throne of the Darkness."

Aurora held her breath. *Sienna,* she thought, and listened as Micah continued.

"I know the key curse which can release them from their prison," he said, "so you can transport them back to Valhandra and safely home to their families." Micah's eyes rested on the golden cords tied around their waists and his gaze followed them back to the wall of the stone cell, where they disappeared.

"I assume Yanus and the Gozzits are watching," he asked, looking back to Aaron.

"Yes," Aaron replied, and with his mind on the plan he continued without thinking, "and—"

"Yes, they are," Aurora cut in quickly, shaking her head to Aaron as a warning for him not to say their father's name, and clamping his mouth shut, Aaron understood.

"Okay," Micah replied, narrowing his eyes slightly but continuing, "so they will know what I need them to do and when?" He looked at Aurora questioningly, and in her mind, she heard the voice of Yanus giving his agreement to the request, which she passed on to Micah.

"There won't be much time, so we will have to move fast. The Darkness will not detect you with the shield around you, but once the prison portal is opened, it will sense that immediately," Micah explained. "I can hold the Darkness back to buy you time, but not for long. Once it is done, you must get the children back here and through the portal to Valhandra. "And . . ." he continued with absolute insistence, "you *must* go without me. Do *not* look back."

"But—" Aurora began.

"*Promise* me," Micah cut in adamantly. "There is no other way. You must believe me on that. I want you to remember me like this, knowing that there was still some of the Light in me."

Aurora looked up at Micah, suddenly intensely curious at the total contradiction that had been lying inside him all this time. How was it possible for one person, one being, to be so evil but to have such caring locked up inside them all that time? Out of the blue, she felt a tight ache in her heart for what he had missed of life, what he had allowed himself to become, his immense potential within the Light destroyed because of the pain his own parents had caused with their rejection of him. It was that which the Darkness was preying on, the vulnerabilities in humanity caused by the actions of others and suffered by the victims only because of how much they truly cared. She found herself wishing in that moment that they had more time to get to know the real Micah, but she put that thought aside for later, because for now there was work to do.

CHAPTER 42

Standing by the huge door to the stone cell, they all rested their hands against the cold wood, waiting for the agreed-upon signal from Micah.

Aurora could feel her crystal pulsing in her robe pocket and was surprised at how calm she felt in the circumstances.

"Ready?" Micah asked, and all three nodded.

"Now," he instructed.

A bolt of energy came hurtling down their cords from the Gozzits beyond the portal, and they braced themselves against the door as the energy bolt slammed into it. Outside the door, the padlock holding the chains exploded, breaking them at their central point, the ends falling to each side of the door as it released and swung open.

"Follow me," Micah directed as he headed out of the door, his black robes flowing behind him.

Aurora, Cal, and Aaron followed into the damp stone corridor and toward another heavy wooden door that was already slightly ajar. Micah pushed it open and they ran in, stopping with him in front of a huge black throne.

"Jesus," Cal breathed, looking around him at the circular chamber—the stone pit in the middle, which was still smoking slightly at its center, black stone pillars around the sides of the room, stretching up into arches that framed the mass of demonic faces carved into the ceiling.

The air in the chamber felt as suffocating as Aurora remembered it from her visions, and she involuntarily coughed, gagging as she breathed in afterward, the stench in the chamber feeling like poison in her lungs.

Micah crouched down in front of the throne, the edges of which were carved into a mass of thick, twisted thorn branches. Resting one hand against each of the arms, he stared into the mass of thorns across the base of the huge structure.

"Okay," he said, "they're still in there."

Aurora moved over to stand behind him as he began muttering the key curse, her body buzzing with adrenaline, alternating anticipation and anxiety. Suddenly, there was a white flash in front of her eyes, and she found herself looking at a vision of the Eternal Library. Dane and Yanus stood near the door of the Dark Chamber, an anxious look on Dane's face as they watched the scene in the throne room through the portal window. Realizing that the vision was in real time, Aurora watched as the view panned round to one of the long aisles in the Hall of Records. About halfway down it, she saw the blurred image of a figure, pressed up against one of the bookcases as if they were hiding, and holding one of the huge soul books to the side of them. Aurora strained to see the figure more clearly, still aware of Micah's voice in the distance muttering the key curse. As her vision zoomed further in, the figure became clearer and she breathed out sharply with shock.

"Jasmine!"

"What?" Cal said, stepping closer to Aurora and putting his hand on her forearm.

Aurora looked at him. "Jasmine is in the Eternal Library," she said, panic rising inside her. "Dad," she called in her mind, trying frantically to connect to him.

Dane received the message from Aurora instantly, turning swiftly to Yanus. "Jasmine is in here," he said, already running toward the Hall of Records as he called back. "Aurora has just seen it in a vision." Seeing Jasmine try to run as she spotted him, Dane instantly transported, appearing in front of her and grabbing her by the arm.

"What the hell are you doing in here?" he said angrily to her, holding onto her arm as she struggled to pull away from him and dropped the book she was holding as she did so.

As the book fell to the floor, Dane saw that it was Dayana's soul record, and his heart sank.

"Jasmine, what have you done?" he breathed out, picking up the book and transporting with her back to Yanus outside the Dark Chamber.

Yanus turned from the portal window as they appeared next to him, his hands pressed together and a grave look on his face. Dane passed the soul book to him, and as Yanus saw it, his face fell.

"Jasmine, do you know how much danger you have put us all in?"

"You lied to me. You all lied to me!" Jasmine spat out angrily, still trying to pull her arm away from Dane's grip.

"We had no choice," Yanus told her calmly.

"You preach about choice," she sneered, "but you take it away, like you did with my mother."

"Choice comes with responsibility," Yanus said. "It is not simply a free commodity to do as one wishes, especially for us as Lightworkers. Every one of our choices must be for the good of all, not only ourselves."

"I know there's more," Jasmine went on, "and I'll find out." As her anger rose, a deep rumble sounded from within the portal.

"What was that?" Dane said, looking worriedly toward the portal window, and as his concentration broke, Jasmine wrenched her arm free and ran toward the main door of the Library.

"Namogoz . . . the cage!" shouted Yanus, thrusting his arm out toward Jasmine as she ran and throwing a bolt of light into the space above her.

There was a blinding flash, and she stopped, looking upward, terrified. In an instant, a golden cage appeared above her and descended swiftly, crashing to the ground around her. Jasmine swung around, and frantically grabbing the bars of the cage, she looked back at Yanus.

"I'll make you pay, Yanus, I swear!" she yelled as a faint wisp of black mist appeared from her mouth and she put her hand to her throat, her face contorting as if she were in pain. There was a second flash above her, and she screamed before crumpling to the floor, unconscious.

In the depths of Terhum, Marta Broach sensed a change. There was a flash as a portal opened in the air above her and a small blue spark of light fell out of it. Holding out her bony hand, Marta watched the spark float down toward her and land in her hand, snuffing out as it touched her cold gray skin like a flame starved of oxygen. She stared at the small black stone left lying in her palm, a satisfied smile playing at the corners of her mouth as she closed her scrawny fingers over it. The first dead light in her daughter's soul was hers.

CHAPTER 43

Micah completed the key curse and stood back from the throne, putting his arms out to guide the others back too.

"It's happening," he said, breathing heavily, his eyes fixed on the base of the huge throne.

The carved thorns began to shift and unravel, and as they did so, a black bubble began to ease its way out from between the branches. The bubble expanded, growing bigger and bigger as it escaped from the base of the throne. The four onlookers moved farther back as it drifted out into the room, now taking up half of the chamber as it floated in the air in front of them. Micah walked quickly over to it, putting his hands out onto its surface and muttering more incoherent words. The surface of the bubble began to dissolve slowly, and Aurora held her breath in anticipation as the prison portal opened. She clasped her hands over her mouth at the sight of what was inside.

In its fiery pit, the Darkness stirred. Sensing what was happening, it let out a furious roar that echoed through all of Terhum. Summoning Marta Broach, it swiftly began snaking its way across the dark realm toward the throne room.

Hearing the roar from the Darkness, Micah turned to the others. "Hurry, there's not much time," he said insistently.

The front of the bubble had fully opened now to reveal a vast cave full of children of all ages, at least a hundred of them, Aurora guessed, horrified. They began to step out of the prison portal, dazed and confused, clinging desperately to Aurora's hand as she helped some of them out.

Cal and Aaron had immediately begun to guide the released children to the door of the throne room, ushering them through as fast as they could down the corridor and back to the stone cell, to get them back through the portal window to Valhandra.

Among the crowd of children stepped out a tall dark-skinned man. He was carrying one of the younger children with one arm, and Aurora watched the bleakness in his eyes brighten with hope as he saw her on the outside. As he stepped out, Aurora saw that on his other side he held the hand of another small child, and as the child came into view Aurora ran forward.

"Sienna!" she cried out, dropping to her knees and hugging the little girl, who was as confused and exhausted as all the others and looked at her blankly, clearly not immediately recognizing her.

"Thank you, thank God," the older man said, his voice breaking with emotion and tears of relief in his eyes.

Aurora stood up and looked at him, instantly knowing who he was. "Shamar?" she asked, and he nodded.

As Aurora ushered the last of the children out of the throne room, she put her thumb up to Cal standing outside the stone cell at the other end of the corridor to signal they were all out. Cal nodded to her and turned to pass the message to Aaron, who stood at the portal window helping the children through to the safety of Valhandra.

A sudden explosion from the front of the throne room followed, and a twisting whirlwind of black mist spiraled up out of the seat of the throne. Hovering in the air, the black cloud began to settle and transform. Long, willowy limbs appeared from its sides, and as the head began to take shape, two eyes opened within it, staring around the room and focusing in on Micah. At the same time the Darkness arrived, a second figure appeared at the side of the throne. As it raised its head, the empty black eyes of Marta Broach looked out, surveying the activity in the room.

"So, Micah," the deep voice echoed around the circular chamber, "your betrayal is complete."

"Aurora!" Cal yelled from the end of the corridor, hearing the commotion in the throne room, and the eyes of the Darkness swung around in the direction of the voice.

It thrust one of its long limbs out toward the huge wooden door to the room, and the door swung shut. As it slammed against its frame, a thick gray metal chain appeared in the air and swiftly crashed into the wall either side of the door. The chain embedded itself in the stone, and the golden cord around Aurora's waist snapped at the point where it disappeared behind the door. Floating to the ground within the chamber, it dissolved into dust.

"No," Aurora breathed, suddenly terrified as she realized that the cord tethering her to Valhandra was gone, along with the golden shield around her. She was trapped.

"Ah," the Darkness breathed, moving its shadowy head toward Aurora, "that's better. I can see you now. So . . . this is one of the Light's little soldiers." It let out a low, menacing laugh as Micah moved sideways toward Aurora, gesturing to her to stand behind him.

"Aaron, Cal, what's happening?" Dane yelled, as one of the three cords from Namogoz disappeared. "We can't see beyond the cell!"

"The Darkness is there," Aaron said, the panic evident in his voice. "It's barricaded the throne room door with Aurora and Micah inside. Dad, Aurora's cord has snapped!"

"I'm coming to help!" Dane shouted.

"No, it's too dangerous," Yanus said, grabbing Dane's arm.

"I don't care, Yanus. Aurora's in trouble. I'm going in," Dane said determinedly, and shaking his arm free, he ran through the portal window into the Dark World.

On the other side of the portal window, Dane quickly got his bearings as his eyes adjusted to the dark. He rushed out of the door of the cell and down to the end of the corridor where Cal and Aaron were pushing their shoulders against the heavy wooden door.

"It's impossible to shift," Cal said frantically to Dane as he joined them, and they all tried unsuccessfully to force the door.

"We have to do it another way," Dane said, and he put both hands against the door.

"Micah!" Dane shouted through the door, and from inside the throne room, Micah stared toward the door, a shocked look on his face.

"Dane," he breathed, looking at Aurora. "But I thought . . ."

"Dad!" Aurora yelled frantically toward the door. "Hurry!"

"So," drawled the Darkness, turning its head toward the door, "reinforcements! Well then, Marta, let's give them the show they came for."

Marta Broach stepped forward toward Micah, and he moved directly between her and Aurora, shielding Aurora behind him with his arms. The Darkness extended one long limb toward Micah, and a bolt of black smoke shot out, connecting with Micah's chest and throwing him backward down onto the ground, leaving Aurora standing alone in the middle of the Dark Chamber as the terrifying cloaked figure of her former teacher approached. Seeing movement out of the corner of her eye, Aurora looked around to see the edges of the room filling with dark willowy shapes, slowly edging forward out of the shadows toward her.

"Let's see what she can tell us, then," the Darkness said menacingly, and Marta Broach grabbed Aurora's arm roughly, dragging her forward and thrusting her in front of the head of the Darkness.

Aurora's body felt weak, drained by the Dark energy, and she closed her eyes, turning her head toward the ground, away from the demonic yellow eyes, which felt like they were boring into her soul. The Darkness reached one long black finger toward Aurora's forehead, and she felt its freezing cold pressure pushing against the center point between her eyes.

She felt suddenly dizzy as images from Valhandra began to flood through her mind, escaping from the point on her forehead where the Darkness was pulling her thoughts out to a projected image in front of it.

"Dane!" Micah called out, raising himself up on to all fours. "Do something! They've got Aurora, and I'm not strong enough to hold them back!"

"Micah," Dane communicated telepathically from behind the door. "I need you to connect with me, have you got enough Light energy to do that?"

"Yes," Micah sent back and connected with his friend, both pushing back the flood of emotions at the reunion between them. "What now?"

"I'm going to try to break through, but I need you to stay connected with me from inside when the Light energy from Valhandra hits the door."

"You've got it," Micah sent back, looking worriedly toward Aurora. "Hurry, Dane! The Darkness is draining her mind."

"Okay," Dane said, communicating back to Yanus. "I need the full power of the Gozzits down the cords, Yanus, when I give the signal."

Yanus agreed and Dane, Aaron, and Cal braced their hands against the wooden door in readiness.

"Now!" Dane yelled out.

A surge of light filled the Eternal Library before disappearing through the portal window and into the Dark Chamber, running swiftly through the cords toward where Aaron, Cal, and Dane stood braced against the throne room door. As the surge of light hurtled toward them, Micah lowered his head where he knelt on the floor inside the throne room. A golden glow appeared around his body, illuminating the gloom surrounding him and shining out toward the door. The dark demons recoiled from the light, shrinking back into the shadows, and the Darkness looked up sharply from Aurora, the projections from her mind disappearing as it lowered its arm.

At the second the energy collided with the door, both from outside the throne room and from Micah inside, the chain across it exploded into the air, the heavy wooden door swung open, and Dane, Aaron, and Cal ran in amid a burst of bright light that filled the whole room. Marta Broach let go of Aurora to shield her eyes from the light, and as Aurora collapsed to the floor, Dane threw his hand out toward Marta, a bolt of energy shooting out from his palm and throwing her backward into the shadows. The Darkness pulled away, rearing up and recoiling from the light as it roared with pain and rage, spinning into a whirlwind of black mists as it shot back down into the base of the throne.

"Get Aurora and get back to the portal!" Dane yelled, and Cal ran toward her, helping her up and then heading back out of the door as Dane and Aaron went to Micah's side.

Dane held out his hand to his friend, and Micah took it, pulling himself up to standing as their eyes met once more, their energy fields merging instantly. With the glow of the light pulsing around them, they embraced.

"It's good to have you back," Dane said as they pulled apart, his voice breaking with emotion.

"It's good to be back," Micah replied, putting one hand out onto Aaron's shoulder, still clasping Dane's hand with the other. "You have some pretty amazing kids."

Before Dane could reply, the light noticeably dimmed around them.

"The light won't last long down here," Micah warned, looking toward the throne. "As soon as it fades, the Darkness will return."

"You're right," Dane replied. "We need to get back to the portal . . . now." They ran out of the throne room and back down the corridor to the stone cell, where Cal and Aurora were waiting.

"Quickly," Dane urged them, nodding his head toward the open portal window. "There isn't much time."

As he spoke, the last of the light emanating from the corridor flickered low before disappearing completely, followed by a deep rumble from the throne room, which vibrated through the floor in the cell.

"Now," Micah said urgently.

As Cal and Aurora disappeared through the portal window, Aaron paused behind them. He looked back, suddenly feeling a heavy ache in his chest as Micah's eyes met his.

"Don't look back," Micah said smiling.

Aaron nodded, and turning to the portal, he stepped through, disappearing into the black shimmering space between the worlds of Light and Darkness.

Propelled through the void in seconds, he barely had time to catch his breath before he was being helped out on the other side by Yanus, to join Cal and Aurora, back in the safety of the Eternal Library.

In Terhum, the rumbling from the direction of the throne room became louder, getting rapidly closer to the cell.

"Quick," Dane said to Micah, and the instant that he spoke, the Darkness came hurtling down the corridor in a whirlwind of black smoke.

Micah slammed the door of the cell shut against it, turning to Dane and following him into the shimmering void, as black wisps began to seep around the edges of the door and into the cell.

As Dane reached the other side of the void between the worlds, he looked back to Micah, just as two long black fingers entered the portal from the side of the Dark Realm. Micah turned and put his hand out, creating a golden shield to block the portal entrance from Terhum, and the two shadowy fingers retreated. Dane reached his hand out to Micah.

"Micah," he said, his voice echoing across the void, "reach out and take my hand."

"No," Micah said. "There's not enough time. The second I let go the Darkness will enter the portal . . . and Valhandra. Tell Yanus to close the portal. I can hold it shut this side until he does."

"No," Dane said still reaching out to him. "You'll be trapped within the void, you won't survive. Micah, we've come this far. I won't give up now. We need you here . . . I need you here," he pleaded.

Micah closed his eyes briefly, forcing more energy into the shield from his hand as it dimmed slightly.

"The Light energy the children gave me is running out," he said, breathing heavily as the dark mists gathered behind the shield. "Once it's gone, I can't hold the Darkness back anymore. This is the only way to stop it entering Valhandra."

"I can't lose you again," Dane said, his voice breaking as he desperately reached his hand out toward Micah.

"I've spent too long in the shadow of the Darkness to be able to live in the Light again," Micah said, shaking his head. "I can be more for you all from the spirit plane. There I can move on from the mistakes I've made this lifetime. You rescued me from that hell after everything I've done, and I can never fully repay you for that. But I can do this one final thing for you all. You have to let me do this. Please, Dane . . . let me go."

Closing his eyes at the truth of Micah's words, Dane breathed out heavily and dropped his arm in resignation before he turned and stepped out of the portal back into the Eternal Library. Giving his agreement for Yanus to close the portal, he looked back one final time at Micah within it, catching his breath as he saw that Micah's black robes had gone and he was now dressed in his white Lightworker robes once more.

"And Dane . . ." Micah said smiling, "tell Yanus he was right about the children."

With tears in his eyes, Dane nodded, smiling back as the portal spun shut.

In the space of nothingness between the realms, Micah's eyes closed, and his body began to disintegrate. As his soul slowly released from its physical body back to the spirit plane, Yanus sensed its journey. Closing Micah's soul book on the podium beside him, he turned to the others.

"Micah sacrificed himself for the Light, for all of us," he declared. "He will be remembered as a true Lightworker."

CHAPTER 44

Dane and Yanus made their way up to the Temporal Gallery and through the golden shield surrounding it. Aurora, Cal, and Aaron stood at the bottom of the curved staircase, watching as Yanus went directly to the Great Book on the podium and opened it. Within seconds he closed the book, turning back with Dane and heading back down to the foyer of the Library. He pointed his hand up in the direction of the domed ceiling as they descended the stairs toward them. As he did so, a projection of the earth appeared in the space below the glass dome; spinning slowly, its countries and seas were almost totally obscured by the black clouds that were inching further still across the surface of the planet.

"The time has come," Yanus announced as he approached Aurora, Cal, and Aaron. "The future chapters in the Great Book are now blank," he continued as he turned and stared up at the projection of the earth. "The outcome could go either way. The future is up to us now."

"The Darkness is moving toward Earth with Marta and the new recruits to its army," Namogoz informed Yanus, his voice echoing through the Library, "and the black cloud cover is affecting the stability of time and space; we must gather the Lightworkers for translocation to Earth without delay."

"And the rescued children?" Yanus questioned.

"Safely back at Dama-Garda," Namogoz replied. "Shamar and Donna will remain with them until you return."

"We're three Lightworkers down," said Dane in a concerned voice. "Can we do it?"

"We have to do it," Yanus replied somberly.

"Dad, look!" Aaron shouted out suddenly.

As Dane and Yanus turned, he held his arm out to them, and Dane caught his breath as Aaron's bracelet was moving of its own account around his wrist, just as it had done back in the classroom when Micah had first made contact. Suddenly, it snapped open and flew away from his arm, hovering in the air between them. As they all watched and waited, the gray infinity charm in the middle of the bracelet began to vibrate, then to spin, slowly at first, then faster and faster before it exploded in a bright ball of light in the air, causing the five onlookers to take a step back. As the light faded, they saw that the bracelet had changed, and in the place of the figure eight charm was a small piece of clear crystal, attached in the center of the gray chain.

Dane took hold of the bracelet, staring at it as it lay in his palm.

"Micah's crystal," Dane said and looked up at Yanus as the light shining from the crystal reflected upward. "He's sent it for us."

"He's still with us, Dad," Aurora said as she put her arm around her father's waist and he hugged her back.

"Yes, he is," Dane said, smiling as he held the bracelet out toward Aaron. "You keep it safe, Aaron . . . until we need it," he added and attached the bracelet back around Aaron's wrist.

Yanus gave the signal to Namogoz with a nod of his head, and a vortex swirled up around them, spinning them into rainbow mists before quickly clearing to the surroundings of the great hall at Dama-Garda, where the rest of the Lightworkers and students waited. Dane and Yanus made their way up the stairs at the front of the hall while Aurora, Cal, and Aaron moved back to stand among the other students. Donna stood near the top of the staircase, and after welcoming Dane and Yanus, a brief conversation between them followed before Yanus turned to the hall and raised his arms for silence.

"The translocation vortex will now take us all to Earth," he announced. Then he added gravely, "The situation there is worse than we anticipated; the Darkness is moving quickly across the planet. When it has covered the surface of the planet, it will begin to infiltrate the core. If the Darkness fills the earth's core, all will be lost, the planet will solidify and die, humanity will perish." As Yanus and the room around them disappeared into swirling rainbow mists, his voice continued to echo through their minds.

"Many humans have already lost their souls to the Darkness, and we must focus on saving those who are left. Remain together at all costs; we must trust in the Circle of Light to guide our way."

CHAPTER 45

As the rainbow mists cleared, the Lightworkers found themselves standing in the middle of a large, empty, multi-laned road in a deserted city. A cold and stifling gloom filled the air, and Aurora looked around as her senses settled, trying to get her bearings. Cal and Aaron were standing on each side of her, and around them the rest of the Lightworkers stood still and silent, waiting for directions from Yanus and Dane, who had arrived first and were standing out to the front of the huge group.

It felt odd being back, Aurora thought. Not just because she had never seen any city on Earth so empty and desolate, but because of an instant realization that this place, this planet, was no longer her home. It seemed as if she had been away for years, though this new detachment strangely didn't raise feelings of loss or sadness. Rather, she had a deep sense of protectiveness, along with a very different and more intense awareness of her surroundings, which she never recalled having before. The dim glow of the streetlights illuminated the thick black smog that hung above the city and seemed to drip down through the air like oil through water. The white traffic lanes on the road sat on either side of Aurora's peripheral vision as she looked ahead of her, converging in the distance and disappearing between tall buildings at the outer edges of the city.

She became aware of a low rumbling noise in the distance, and her hearing sharpened to the sound of voices, though she couldn't quite make out what they were saying. Her eyesight and hearing zoomed in wherever she focused; if she looked closely, she could even see the molecules in the air around her—expanding, contracting, moving in concentric circles. A heavy sense of fear lay across the city. Even the molecules she was watching in the air around her seemed to pull away from the Darkness infiltrating their space. Aurora wasn't scared, which briefly surprised her. In truth, her mind and body had never been this calm, and she knew she was ready for whatever lay ahead. Looking first to Aaron and then to Cal, she felt the strength of the bond they shared together. As she focused on that feeling she also began to see it with her eyes, like bright white frequency waves dancing around them. Suddenly the waves began to expand, out and around the other Lightworkers standing with them. Aurora felt the immense power of the group as a whole. Not just the three of them anymore, like the last time they were here on Earth. Now they were a part of something far bigger, the army of the Light. Taking a deep breath and pushing her shoulders back, Aurora knew she was ready.

As the rumbling in the distance grew louder and closer, Aurora caught a movement out of the corner of her eye. Looking over to her right, she saw a willowy black shape pull swiftly back behind the stone pillars that lined the shops at the side of the road. As her vision focused closer in, she took a sharp breath as dozens of piercing yellow eyes appeared within the shadows.

"Form a circle facing outward," Dane commanded, looking quickly from the Lightworkers back to the eyes, which had multiplied in seconds from dozens to hundreds within the dark shop doorways.

The group quickly did as Dane instructed and moved into place as he and Yanus positioned themselves between the group and the menacing creatures staring out from the shadows.

"Demons," Dane said looking around him. "The Darkness must be close."

As he spoke, black wisps of smoke began to seep out of a drain in the middle of the road not far from the group, curling upward like long fingers out of the holes in the metal drain cover. Suddenly, as the distant rumbling drew even closer, a convoy of military tanks appeared at the far end of the main road into the city. Trundling forward, they made their way toward the Lightworkers, and as they did so, the demons shrank back into the shadows, the dark wisps retreating swiftly back down through the grate into the tunnels below the city.

Immediately as the tanks came to a stop in front of them, three soldiers climbed out of the leading vehicle. Dressed in full gray hazmat suits and holding guns pointed toward the Lightworkers, they headed toward Yanus and Dane.

"Everybody has been ordered to remain inside their houses," the middle soldier instructed aggressively as he stopped a few meters from them, his voice muffled by the helmet of his suit. Glancing around at the Lightworkers behind them, Dane watched as the look in his eyes changed from authoritative to perplexed.

"Why are you all dressed like that?" he demanded suspiciously. "Are you some sort of club or cult?"

Yanus smiled at him and said calmly, "We are here to help."

"Well, that's our job, mate," the soldier replied sarcastically, "and I guarantee that without masks and suits out here, you won't be helping for long. So I just need to find out what we're going to do with you . . . lot." He looked Yanus up and down and, shaking his head, turned and walked back toward the tank while the remaining two soldiers remained, guns raised and pointed toward the Lightworkers.

Aware of occasional, very slight movements in the shadows, Aurora watched silently from the main group as the lead soldier arrived at the tank and pulled a radio handset from inside, turning to look back at them as he raised it to his mouth to speak. Her hearing sharpened instantly as she tuned into his conversation, which she knew every other Lightworker would be doing too.

"Yeah, boss," the voice said, "these clowns are just standing out in the middle of the main road in a circle wearing white robes. It's like a coven of witches. There's two out front, I assume they're the leaders," he paused, listening before continuing.

"That's the weird thing, boss. No masks or suits, and they seem fine; not even a cough out of any of them. Reckon they'll just drop dead any second and . . . well, job done."

Aurora tuned into a more distant voice at that point, speaking in reply: "Okay, Blackman, stay as you are. I'd better just check with the guvnor what the current status is."

"You're the boss," the soldier replied, "but we really need to get these idiots out of the way."

"Bit harsh," Aaron whispered sarcastically to Aurora and raised one eyebrow as she looked at him and giggled.

"Time is getting short," Yanus said quietly to Dane after hearing the exchange over by the tank.

"'We really need to get these idiots out of the way.'" Dane stifled a laugh in response before looking to the ground as the two soldiers in front of them thrust their weapons out a bit further as a warning. Yanus stepped forward toward the soldiers, just as Blackman was heading back to the group and the soldier picked up his pace as he saw the approach.

"Stay where you are!" Blackman barked. "No sudden moves, or my men will shoot!"

Yanus raised his hands in simulated surrender at the words and looked directly at Blackman.

"There is no threat from us," Yanus assured him calmly, "but I would like to ask you . . . respectfully, soldier . . . to allow us to deal with this. Please connect with the prime minister for further guidance."

As Yanus spoke, Aurora watched him manipulating Blackman's energy. Threads of white light were flowing through Blackman, from behind him and out the front of him, through Yanus and then through all the other Lightworkers, before the threads of light flew round in a circle and back to Blackman once more. Aurora was mesmerized at the sight.

Blackman looked at Yanus, noticeably startled at the request, his mouth opening and shutting several times before eventually he spoke.

"What?" he snapped back to Yanus with disbelief. "What the—You're . . . how . . ."

Suddenly Blackman appeared to run out of words. He looked at Yanus blankly for a few seconds as the energy flowing through him intensified. Suddenly, his tense stance seemed to relax, and in a calmer voice he said, "Wait one moment. I'm going to check with the prime minister on this situation. Lower your weapons, soldiers."

The two other soldiers raised their eyes at each other but did as they were instructed and lowered their weapons. Yanus smiled to them both, and Aurora watched as he did the same with their energies as he had done with Blackman's.

On Valhandra, Namogoz received the instructions Yanus communicated to him and connected telepathically with the prime minister.

"Olivia. This is Namogoz."

The intensity of the boardroom suddenly faded around the prime minister, and startled, she looked around the room trying to figure out where the voice was coming from. Nobody was speaking directly to her; she was still standing at the window between the devastation outside and General Kerr on the screen, who was addressing the members present in person and online on military responses.

"Ma'am . . . ma'am," the surly, commanding voice cut through Olivia's mind, and she shook her head in an effort to bring herself back to reality.

"Yes, General Kerr. My apologies, please go on."

"Ma'am. They're saying they're here to help. They want us to back off. I don't trust them." General Kerr waited for a response, and Olivia, for the first time in her elected office, didn't have an answer for him. Something was nagging in the back of her mind, pulling at a vague recollection she couldn't quite reach yet.

"General Kerr, Ministers," she announced to the room, summoning every bit of authority and poise she was able to, "please give me a few minutes to consider our next move." She turned and immediately walked out of the room, head held as high as she could, as her mind swam dizzily with a rush of distant memories.

Outside the room, the prime minister leaned heavily against the wall of the corridor, clasping her hands to her face as the reality around her faded to a memory from many years before. Suddenly, she was a young girl again, tucked up in her bed, her night light glowing dimly and her teddy bear tight in her arms, eyes wide at the bedtime story her mother was telling her.

"... Then a rainbow appeared, as if out of a dream
And fell from the skies on the forest of green.
The rainbow of colors gave life to seven trees
Bringing new hope with the rustle of leaves.
So there starts our story; one terrible storm
From a mystical rainbow, the Gozzits were born ..."

Olivia's childhood dreams of the Rainbow Forest and the Gozzits once more came to life in her mind. Distant memories long forgotten flooded to the surface as the words of her mother continued in the vision.

"So Namogoz and all the other Gozzits saved humankind from its certain destruction ... and the Darkness was banished from the world forever."

"Olivia, this is Namogoz," the voice repeated in her mind. "I need you to hear me."

The prime minister shook her head and clasped her hands more tightly to her face, her heart pounding in her ears. This couldn't be happening; she must be losing her mind. It must be the pressure. This was all too much. Talking trees and magical rainbows didn't really exist ... did they?

A lump rose in her throat and tears pricked at her eyes as she remembered looking upward after her mum had closed the bedroom door, the solid ceiling dissolving in her young mind to the stars and night sky, the words she had whispered to a faraway land before she contentedly settled down to sleep: "Night-night, Gozzits."

The haunting voice of Namogoz echoed in her mind once more, and this time, she replied.

"What?" she said out loud, her voice breaking. "Go on, I'm listening."

"Olivia," Namogoz continued. "The Darkness is moving in. If we do not stop it, it will destroy humanity and the world. The group your soldiers guard are our Lightworkers. They are here to save the earth and to bring in a new age of freedom. Please, stand your troops down and allow them to complete their task."

Instinctively, Olivia took a deep breath and held it, like she remembered doing when she was young. Her mind stilled, and she felt the same tingly giddiness she used to get, allowing it briefly to flow from her head down through her body before she let go of the breath. As her awareness returned once more to the surroundings of the corridor, the cold wall she was leaning against, she knew what she had to do. Wiping her forefingers briefly under her eyes, she pulled her shoulders back, raised her chin and headed back into the boardroom.

"Stand your troops down, General Kerr," she announced.

"But, ma'am—" he interjected, a look of disbelief on his face.

"Stand them down, General," she reiterated purposefully. "Allow the group to do as they wish."

The video link to the military headquarters went blank, and Olivia looked out of the panoramic window to the gray gloom outside. The thick black smog had dropped lower since she last looked and now almost drew level with the floor above them, like an ominous black ceiling over the outside world. She watched the scene down in the center of the city, as the soldiers retreated to their tanks and the vehicles rolled slowly away from the circle of Lightworkers.

"Don't let me down, Namogoz," Olivia whispered.

CHAPTER 46

As soon as the tanks left, the tendrils of black smoke immediately began to appear once more from the grates along the edges of the road. They rose out of the ground, twisting ominously upward like a cage of gnarled branches through the air.

"Lightworkers," Yanus announced as he and Dane quickly took their places within the circle, his robe flowing behind him as he walked, "prepare for battle."

As he spoke, willowy black shapes began to emerge from the shadows, and as they drew closer, their forms became clearer. Ominous yellow eyes stared out from underneath the black hoods of their long robes, and the drawn, lifeless skin of the faces was just visible around them. Creeping forward, they swiftly gathered around the Lightworkers, hundreds of them closing in and creating an impenetrable barricade around the circle.

"Energy bolts, now!" Dane yelled, and every Lightworker thrust out their hands in front of them. Bolts of golden light shot out toward the dark demons, who let out a collective screech of pain as the bolts hit them, driving them backward.

"Keep going," Dane communicated telepathically, his voice cutting through the noise around them. As the demons closest to them were forced back, others behind moved in swarms over the top of them, their thin, bony hands clawing at the air as they crawled forward toward the Lightworkers. Aurora felt the energy rushing down through her arms, as along with everyone else she threw out bolts from one hand and then the next toward the demons in front of her.

"Expand your energy fields," Dane instructed them all, and instantly a ring of bright white light appeared around the circle, shining upward and illuminating the dense black smog above them. The hordes of dark demons shrunk back, shielding their eyes from the light.

"You cannot beat me now," the deep voice of the Darkness echoed around them, as the black cage-like tendrils of smoke rising around the group began to curve over in a dome above them, enclosing them within it. Immediately the light shining from them dimmed as the heavy lead-like energy of the Darkness forced it back toward them.

"Give in . . . surrender and join me, or I will destroy you," sneered the Darkness.

"We will never join you," the voice of Yanus echoed back.

Trapped inside the black dome, the hordes of demons moving in around them, Aurora felt panic surge through her body before hearing her father's words through her mind.

"Keep the connection, Lightworkers. Stay strong." She breathed out, expanding her energy once more against the darkness threatening to engulf them, pushing out against it using every bit of strength she could find.

From the boardroom, the prime minister looked out at the scene below them with horror, as the cage of blackness engulfed the circle of Lightworkers. As the dome closed at its top central point, an eerie silence fell across the city on the outside.

"What now?" Ethan asked her, and Olivia took a deep breath before replying.

"We wait," she said, nodding her head and not realizing how tightly her fingers gripped at the surface of the window in front of her.

"It's all we can do."

As the Darkness moved further through the outer layers of the earth's surface, the life force of the planet began to wane more and more. An unstoppable force, the black mist crawled menacingly through the dense terrain toward the core of the planet, leaving solidified black rock behind it as it advanced. Within the vast expanses of time and space, the movement of the earth began to slow. As its lifeforce was suffocated by the Darkness surging through it, it creaked and groaned in pain, and the Light felt its suffering as intensely as if it were its own.

Inside the dome, the Lightworkers continued throwing energy bolts at the Dark Army, as an ominous voice echoed through the dome they were trapped within.

"You can't win this," the Darkness said, mocking Yanus and Dane with a cold certainty. "Give up now and accept your fate."

"Never," Yanus replied defiantly as he moved to the center of the circle and raised his arms in the air.

"Elementals," he declared, "rise!"

From the earth's core, the Elementals heard his command and awoke. Soaring upward through the dense inner layers of the planet, they were forced to stop as they butted against the dark rock encapsulating the outer layers of the earth's surface. Looking frantically from side to side, they communicated the situation back to Yanus telepathically, and sensing their panic, he instructed Namogoz to assist.

Namogoz gathered the energy of all the Gozzits before opening the lotus flower at the top of his canopy.

"In the power of the Light, open the Rainbow Bridge," he instructed, and as he spoke, a beam of silver light shot from the center of his lotus flower. Soaring out into the solar system, the beam of light expanded into a shining mix of all the colors of the rainbow. Focusing in on Earth, the beam juddered briefly before swiftly picking up speed and catapulting forward toward its target.

"Elementals, prepare for impact," Namogoz instructed as the beam of colored light entered the earth's atmosphere.

The four Elementals drew back as the bolt of light collided with the surface of the earth above them. Within seconds, a channel appeared, breaking through the solidified crust of the earth and freeing a path from its center. The Elementals instantly took their opportunity, soaring upward through their escape route and out into the freedom of the air. Their eyes narrowed as they materialized out of the earth's surface, looking around and focusing in on the Dark dome from which they had been summoned. All four flew through the air toward their target like bullets, their movement slowing as they neared their destination and arrived at the surface of the dome. Twisting back and forth, they negotiated its shell, trying to find an opening. Rearing back and forth, they hurtled down against the dome but only ricocheted away, making no impact on it. Eventually, Yanus spoke to them once more, a note of concern in his voice as he watched the Darkness within the dome moving closer and closer in around the Lightworkers.

"Remain at the surface," he instructed. "Resist the Darkness and wait for further directions from me."

The Elementals circled the surface of the dome impatiently, periodically hitting against it but still unable to penetrate it. The smog fell further down toward the surface of the dome, trapping the Elementals within the constricting space around it.

Inside the dome, Dane was worried.

"Yanus, we can't hold it," he warned, as the golden glow from their collective energy was pushed further and further inward back toward them by the Dark Army. "The missing Lightworkers are creating too much of a weakness in the Circle."

Yanus looked around at the three faded areas of the Circle where Micah, Dayana, and Jasmine should have been.

"I know," he replied.

"Namogoz," Yanus said urgently, connecting back to Valhandra, "we need more help. What can we do?"

Unable to penetrate the dark dome, Namogoz implored the Light to seek the wisdom of the Universe.

"The Lightworkers will prevail," said the Light defiantly.

"They need your help," replied Namogoz.

"This *will* work," the Light replied. "It cannot fail."

"It *can* fail," Namogoz insisted with unwavering finality. "And *they* can fail. It is *you* who is unwilling to fail," he continued.

"Look *now* at what you are creating with your refusal to change track. Resisting the truth, fighting only with the desire to win will not generate the peaceful future you have worked for. Don't make the same mistake you made before. Ask the Universe for help and do it *now*, otherwise all you have created . . . with us . . . with the Lightworkers . . . will be lost forever."

The Light looked on at the scene in front of it. It saw its Lightworkers trapped within the dome, struggling to hold back the Dark Army, and it fought against its own need to be right. Suddenly, it saw a vision of the certain fate that would follow if it continued on this course. It saw in its mind's eye a future—the Lightworkers defeated, destroyed. Everything it had created and worked for all these years gone, just as Namogoz had warned. The Darkness would reign for all eternity . . . and for what? Because once more, the Light would not acknowledge that resistance and fight only created loss? The Light realized that, once again, it was perpetuating its battle with the Darkness, for the sake of the fight itself, for the sake of winning that fight, and it remembered the words of the Universe all those years ago: "If you destroy the Darkness, you will also destroy yourself. You must learn to accept the existence of the Darkness, to understand it and then to navigate a path beyond it."

Finally, the Light understood. It surrendered its fight and turned once more to the wisdom of the Universe.

"Universe, what can I do to end this, to stop this destruction?" it asked, looking in desperation at the scene below it on Earth.

"You have done well," the Universe commended, its voice echoing through time and space, "and you have succeeded in your task. You created the key to the future with your Lightworkers . . . and now, you are finally willing to move past your need to fight against the Darkness, to create a new future for humanity, along with them."

"So, what now?" the Light asked, relieved.

"This . . . now . . . is your choice-point," the Universe declared. "Look to the crystals, they will lead the way."

The Light did as the Universe asked. As it looked into the vast reaches of time and space, the crystal annulus of light appeared before it . . . and the Light knew what it needed to do.

"Namogoz," the Light commanded, "tell the Lightworkers to stop fighting and hold out their crystals in front of them."

Namogoz smiled and did as he was instructed. At the command from Yanus, the Lightworkers dropped their arms and held out their crystals in front of them. Golden bolts of energy shot instantly out from each crystal toward a point in the center of the Circle of Light. As the bolts of energy joined together, the crystal on Aaron's bracelet began to vibrate, and he instinctively held out that arm too. Micah's crystal lit up, and a stream of energy shot out from it to join the others in the center of the circle. In the faded space next to Aaron, the air began to flicker, and a translucent image of Micah appeared within it. Dane looked on and smiled in the knowledge that his friend was there with them.

The Darkness above the Lightworkers began to descend, like a blanket falling over them, and they felt the cold, dank breath of the dark demons on their necks as it closed in around them. Aurora looked down, steeling herself for what might come next. She felt Cal take her hand, and they looked sideways at each other as the blanket of darkness met the tops of their heads, sending a shiver through Aurora's body. Dane looked toward Yanus in silent question of whether this was the end, but Yanus shook his head, looking back toward the center of the circle. As he did so, the point where the threads of energy from each crystal met began to shudder. Feeling the change in energy, the Lightworkers stared toward the center of the circle as it vibrated faster and faster, rising up and down and creating waves of movement along the golden threads, before suddenly bursting into a ball of blinding light. The light traveled swiftly from the center of the circle back along the threads of golden energy and disappeared into each individual crystal.

Each Lightworker held their breath, cloaked in the falling Darkness, and the few seconds that followed felt like hours, before the crystals themselves began to shudder in the same way the center of the circle had done. Suddenly, every crystal exploded with light, engulfing the Lightworkers and everything around them, blasting back the blanket of darkness that threatened to suffocate them. As the world around Aurora dissolved, she found herself now suddenly floating in space, the stars and planets of the solar system replacing the darkness around her. As the bright light cleared, she saw that every other Lightworker was with her, still standing in their circle and holding out their crystals in front of them. A voice boomed out from nowhere, echoing through the air around them.

"Let go of your crystals, Lightworkers, and open your souls," it instructed.

Aurora dropped her hand away from her crystal and it remained there, hovering in front of her. As every other Lightworker did the same, an intense feeling of peace fell over them, and Aurora watched in a trance as her crystal began to move toward her. Closer and closer, it glided through the air until it reached the point of her solar plexus, where it stopped, hovering in space as the same voice came again through the air around her.

"Do not be afraid," it said. "I am the Universe, and the crystals you have been entrusted with have connected you with me. You have all earned your place within the Universe, and I invite you now to join me, to become one with me for all eternity . . . the choice is yours to make."

Aurora looked toward her crystal.

Yes or no? she thought, and instantly she knew the answer was "yes." She felt a deep sense of belonging to the crystal hovering in front of her, and as she looked left and right around the circle to every other Lightworker around her, reality around her faded away and she closed her eyes to the certainty of her choice.

The Light looked on as each of the crystals entered the body of its Lightworker. As each crystal merged with the soul of its owner, the Light felt its own energy increase, its strength intensifying. As the new reality was born, the Light saw the power of the Darkness weaken and its grip on the world finally begin to release.

The bright light settled and the Lightworkers found themselves once more back inside the dome of Darkness. Yanus immediately gave the signal, nodding as he raised his arms up in front of him. Each and every Lightworker followed his lead, and between them they harnessed the full power of the Universe, exploding it out around them in a blast of intense white light. The explosion of light collided with the Dark Army, thrusting them forcefully back against the sides of the dome, their yellow eyes closing as each one of them slowly disintegrated and disappeared. On the other side of the dome, the Elementals sensed the change and drew back, ramming again and again against its outer surface as it slowly began to give way until finally it dissolved into dust, along with the Dark Army inside it. The dark mists withdrew, retreating and collecting to the side of where the dome had stood until all that was left was one willowy demonic form in the middle of the deserted road, in black robes and with Marta Broach standing beside it.

The Lightworkers turned to face the Darkness, and Dane and Yanus walked purposefully out to the front of the group as the Elementals gathered either side of them. With its army destroyed, the ominous yellow eyes of the Darkness were just visible from under the hood of the insignificant figure to which it had been reduced. In front of Dane and Yanus, an intense golden light appeared out of nowhere, illuminating the city as the clouds parted and cleared to blue sky above them. After a few seconds, the bright light reduced to reveal a human but ethereal-looking form. Dressed all in white, it was at least twice the height of a normal human being, and huge golden wings extended out from its back.

"It's the Light," whispered Aaron to Cal and Aurora as they all looked on with awe.

"So," the menacing voice of the Darkness drawled to the Light, "finally you face me. And now you are going to destroy me."

A pause followed, before the Light answered with calm certainty. "No. I will not destroy you."

As the last remnants of the dark smog hanging over the city cleared, the Darkness shrank smaller still in the silence between them, before finally it spoke once more.

"You're a fool," it sneered. "But so be it. You have won this time, but you know if you do not destroy me, this is not the end."

"I know," the Light replied and smiled in that knowing.

The Lightworkers looked on as the Darkness and Marta Broach slowly dissolved into dust, which slinked sideways across the cold concrete of the road, down through the grates at its outer edges, and disappeared back into the fires of Terhum.

Yanus looked toward the government building, and his vision zoomed in to the prime minister standing at the window of the boardroom, looking down at them.

"Our work here is done . . . for now," Yanus communicated to her, and she nodded, smiling.

"Thank you . . . all of you," she replied.

The Light turned and smiled, first to the prime minister and then to its Lightworkers, before it expanded swiftly into a huge ball of bright light. The Elementals swept elegantly upward into the sky and disappeared, and as the bright light dimmed and faded away, peace and calm fell across the Earth.

Yanus instructed Namogoz that they were ready, and Namogoz prepared to bring them home. The white lotus flower at the top of his canopy began to open and a rainbow appeared from its center, soaring through time and space toward Earth. As it connected with the gray concrete road, rainbow-colored sparks of light flew out from every direction, illuminating the city around it. The prime minister and her colleagues watched in wonder from the boardroom as the Lightworkers walked across the rainbow bridge and headed home to Valhandra.

CHAPTER 47

When the Lightworkers returned to Valhandra, they had a sense of a very different future. This was bigger than even their first arrival here had been for them. This was not just a new chapter, this was the beginning of a new world, a new way for humanity to live . . . and they were responsible for bringing that future into existence. How, they didn't yet know. What they did know was that they had made a start. What followed would show itself in time; their job was to listen to the whispers of the Universe, and that they knew they could do.

The return of the stolen children to Earth was negotiated carefully. Governments around the world united to assist Namogoz and the High Council of Valhandra to make the arrangements. The parents would be told that following information received by the authorities: raids had been carried out on a worldwide network of criminals who had kidnapped the children years before and held them in underground dungeons. This, it was deemed, would be more readily accepted by humanity to avoid any questions or repercussions. Any uprising or rebellion would create a mass of negative energy the Darkness could prey on. As soon as the children arrived back within the physical realm, they would immediately develop to the human age they would have been on Earth, having previously been frozen in time within Terhum at the age they were when they were captured. As the process of returning the children to Earth commenced, the relief of the families at their return sent waves of joy out into the Universe, increasing the Light's energy as it looked on and smiled.

Aurora asked that she be allowed to go along when Sienna was taken home, and after a short discussion between the High Council, it was agreed.

Just before Sienna was due to return to Earth, she and Aurora were wandering through the beautiful gardens around Dama-Garda, chatting and laughing.

"Are you excited to see Mum, Dad, and Hazel?" Aurora asked her as they sniffed at the new flowers blooming around the gardens.

"I guess," Sienna replied, distracted, "but I want you to come too, Rory."

Aurora's heart ached, and she crouched down beside Sienna, taking her hands.

"I'll always be with you Si-Si," Aurora said gently and pressed her hand to Sienna's chest. "But you will need to feel me in here, in your heart, instead of seeing me in the future. Do you understand that?"

"Yes," Sienna replied with a deep sigh, "but I'll miss going to the playpark with you."

"Oh, me too! It was so much fun, wasn't it?" Aurora said, trying not to let the emotion get the better of her. "But I'll still be there. All you need to do is think about me and I'll be right there . . . I promise."

CHAPTER 48

The vortex cleared to the front yard of Hazel's house, and Aurora turned to look at Sienna beside her. Her breath caught in her throat as she watched the little girl change before her eyes, her hair growing longer down her back as she grew taller, almost past Aurora's shoulders. The features on her face matured, and her eyes sparkled as she turned to Aurora and smiled. Aurora looked over to Yanus, knowing that it was time to say goodbye to Sienna.

"Aurora," Yanus said, placing one hand on her shoulder. "Wait here out of sight. Leave this part to me. It will all be fine, I promise." He nodded to her, smiling, and Aurora stepped back behind the trees at the end of the driveway. As Yanus turned, his white robes transformed into regular human clothing and he took Sienna's arm, guiding her toward the front door.

Hazel and Sienna's mum, Nina, answered the door, and Aurora watched inconspicuously, holding her breath as Yanus spoke with Nina and Sienna rushed into her mother's arms in an emotional embrace. Eventually, Sienna and Nina disappeared back inside the house, and Yanus turned back to Aurora.

"Well, that's that then," he smiled gently.

Aurora smiled back, though feeling strangely unsettled, as if there were more to be done, and she stood looking blankly at the front of the house. Suddenly the door opened again, and Hazel appeared on the porch, looking toward the end of the front driveway where Aurora and Yanus stood.

"I will return to Valhandra," Yanus said to Aurora. "You follow when you're ready," he added, patting her arm reassuringly before he disappeared back through the transportation vortex.

Aurora turned nervously to Hazel, who was now making her way up the front path toward her.

"Thank you," Hazel said hesitantly, "for bringing her back." She paused, looking to the floor and appearing to search for the right words. "She doesn't seem to remember, to know . . . anything about what happened to her?"

Aurora remembered her father's explanation that Namogoz had erased the years of imprisonment from the soul books of each of the stolen children, erasing all physical memory of the Darkness from their minds.

"Some things are better not questioned," Aurora replied, looking Hazel directly in the eyes.

Hazel nodded. "I understand," she said. Taking a step closer to Aurora, she put her hands out and Aurora took them.

"I always knew you were different, Rory, in a special way . . . you know? When I realized how different, I got scared. I'm sorry."

"There's nothing to be sorry for," Aurora said, smiling through the tears shining in her eyes. "I thought you might have forgotten about me."

Hazel shook her head as she held Aurora's hands tighter. "We've been friends for as long as I can remember," she said, her voice breaking with emotion. "How could I forget about you?"

They stood looking at each other in silence. The strength of connection and friendship between them was stronger than ever, and this time, as Hazel felt the rush of warm energy run through her arms from Aurora's hands, she smiled and let it in.

"You know," Aurora began, then hesitated before continuing, "I'm not going to . . . be around . . . anymore."

A tear escaped from Hazel's eye and rolled down her cheek, but at the same time she smiled. "I know," she said, nodding.

"But I'll always be . . ." Aurora said and pushed their clasped hands to Hazel's heart, smiling through the tears streaming down her face.

"I know that too," Hazel managed to say, her voice choked by her own tears.

Sienna came running back out as Aurora stepped back from Hazel, light shining around her body as the transportation portal began to spin open behind her.

"You're all sparkly, Rory," Sienna smiled happily. "It's so pretty."

"Thanks Si-Si." Aurora smiled and gave Sienna a hug. "I have to go back now. I need you to look after your sister for me."

"I will," Sienna said, and she stepped back into the arms of her sister.

"We'll look after each other, won't we?" Hazel said, pulling her sister tightly to her, though her eyes never left Aurora. As the portal behind Aurora spun fully open, Cal and Aaron appeared on the other side. Hazel smiled warmly at them both, and Aurora turned, taking Cal's extended hands as he helped her back through the open vortex. Aurora's eyes met Hazel's one last time, and they smiled at each other as the portal between the worlds spun shut and disappeared.

CHAPTER 49

In the wake of the Lightworkers' return to Valhandra, there was a space of time that Yanus directed was required for resettlement and consolidation of all that had happened. It was not so much boring, Aurora decided, but unusually quiet, and she found herself pacing the gardens of Dama-Garda feeling, for want of a better word, restless in some way.

She stopped to admire some new flowers, remembering with a nostalgic smile her time with Sienna in those same gardens, when she heard a commotion of voices, and Cal and Aaron rounded the corner toward her in a hum of excited chatter.

"Rora," Cal said, "come quick. Yanus has called a big meeting in the Great Hall. He wants us all there right now."

"Coming," she replied. Anticipation sparked inside her as she headed toward him, and she wondered if this was what she had been feeling restless about.

Cal offered out his hand and she took it, smiling as he pulled her after him and she felt the familiar buzz of excitement through her from his touch.

Things had been fairly uneventful between them since they got back, though they spent most of their time together still—with Aaron too, of course. Probably, she thought, that also just needed some time to settle and develop. After all, there was no rush—they had forever!

As the Lightworkers crowded into the Great Hall, the Valhandran sun streamed in through the windows along the upper gallery of the room. Yanus, Dane, and Donna stood at the top of the wide staircase at the front, and as the door to the Great Hall closed, Yanus raised his hands for silence.

"Lightworkers," he announced, "the High Council have been in talks for some time about a particular change for all of us here on Valhandra." He paused as he looked around the room, a wide smile developing on his face, before he continued. "And I am pleased to tell you that arrangements are underway for all the Protector parents to be transmigrated to Valhandra to live here with all of us!"

A cheer broke out as shock and excitement at the news flew around everyone in the room. Yanus, Dane, and Donna looked on smiling at the joy erupting around the Great Hall. Aurora, Cal, and Aaron flung their arms around each other in a hug, and as they pulled apart, Cal put his arm around Aurora's shoulder, pulling her against him. She happily rested her head on his shoulder, smiling as Aaron groaned out loud.

"Oh, all right, you two. Leave out the mushy stuff," he droned, rolling his eyes to the ceiling and shoving his tongue out in mock disgust. However, as Aurora and Cal both knew, he wouldn't have it any other way!

Yanus went on to explain that the Gozzits and the High Council believed that the Protectors should be both rewarded for the successful completion of their vital task on Earth and afforded a future with their loved ones here on Valhandra. They too would receive the new Consciousness into their souls, so increasing the collective strength of the Lightworkers and contributing to the future work required back on Earth to integrate humanity into the New World.

Yanus waved his arm toward the huge doors of the Great Hall, and at once the surroundings dissolved around them.

They found themselves outside of Dama-Garda, looking toward the Rainbow Forest, where Yanus now stood at the edge of the hill with his arms outstretched in front of him. He looked back toward Namogoz just as the petals of his lotus flower bloomed open and a beam of light shot upward from the middle of it. Soaring up into the sky, the beam of light cast a bright golden glow across the fields between the Forest and Dama-Garda, where the Lightworkers stood watching.

Suddenly, the vast open space between them became a swirling mass as portal after portal spun open, birthing a new civilization into the ancient lands of Valhandra: a city full of every different type and style of home. Wood cabins with quaint wrap-around verandas appeared next to sprawling suburban-style houses, and tall, multi-story townhouses stood alongside single-level bungalows. Aurora immediately recognized Mack and Cal's barn as it appeared far over to the right of Dama-Garda, along with its outbuildings and stables. And as another portal swirled open next to it, the familiar and comforting sight of Aaron and Aurora's Victorian-style home appeared from the mists within it. As the portal around it gradually receded and the house came fully into view, the heavy, old oak front door slowly opened, and there, standing in the shade of the porch, was Aspen.

A choked sob escaped Aurora's throat, tears of happiness welling in her eyes as she began to run toward her mother, closely followed by Aaron. When she reached her, Aurora flung her arms around Aspen, almost knocking her backward, as Aspen—half laughing, half crying—hugged her tightly and Aurora buried her head in her mum's shoulder.

As he reached the house, Aaron was welcomed into their embrace. He was soon joined by Dane, who tenderly wrapped his arms around his family, and the four of them stood together in silence, with no words needed, just grateful to finally be together once more.

From the edge of the Rainbow Forest, Yanus looked on, deep in thought, his robes flowing in the slight breeze around him and Namogoz standing behind him. A contented smile tugged at the corners of his mouth, and he nodded slowly as he surveyed the new landscape of Valhandra.

"The New World is rising," he said, gazing out at the sea of reunions before him.

"Yes," Namogoz answered, the beam of light from his lotus flower casting a shimmering glow over the Forest like diamonds floating through the air. "But . . . even with the Darkness banished from the souls of humanity, we still have much to do, and there will be many challenges to face."

"Of course," Yanus replied, taking a deep breath as he looked to the clear blue sky above him. "After all, this is only the start of the journey . . ."

ACKNOWLEDGMENTS

I had a dream when I was young of what I wanted to be when I was older, and that dream was to be a published author. I lost sight of that as the years went on, but I'm forever grateful to many people who helped me to finally realise it, and I want to thank all of those here:

Thank you first and foremost to my dear late Mum and my sister Mandy, who many years ago had a vision of a group of trees that came to life . . . and named them the Gozzits. I wrote the poem "The Legend of the Gozzits" about those trees, and though it took many more years for that poem to develop into this story, I am so proud to say that I finally did it.

Next to my dad, who has taught me in his words and actions to keep going and never give up, no matter what life throws at you. You've always been my biggest support, Dad, and my rock in the times I've needed it most. And thank you for always making me take my vitamins (even if sometimes I did throw them away over the garden fence!)

I have been lucky enough to have very special Godparents, Val and Jack, who really were second parents to me. I credit my dear, late Uncle Jack with much of my obsessive attention to detail . . . for all the hours I spent making sure I NEVER smudged outside the lines when I was colouring, in order to impress him! And I know my dad has never quite forgiven me for favouring Liverpool FC over Everton, just because my Uncle Jack supported Liverpool!

To Paul, who always believed in me and encouraged me that I could do whatever I set my mind to. I don't often say it, but you were right!

I am grateful to Mr. Day, my middle school English teacher, who always encouraged me that my creative writing was better than my lack of confidence told me it was. He told me I had it in me to make a name for myself in literature. It was a long time before I had the confidence to believe his words and to take that leap, but I've made a start. I like to think that he would have marked this book in the same bold, colourful script he would embellish our homework books with: "WOW! POW! YOU DID IT!"

I am lucky to have many lovely friends who I am so grateful for. I would like to give a special mention though to a few who have been constants by my side over many (many!) years, and who have always encouraged me to be the best version of myself I can be: To Mandy, Sharon, Amanda, Annie and Chris . . . thank you for being there for me, through the joy and the tears, the tough times and the fun times (what goes on tour stays on tour!). I love you all and couldn't have done this thing called life half as well without you.

To Indrani . . . for always believing in me. I am so very thankful that I met you in the lift in Vienna all those years ago, and I hope you know how special you are to me.

And to Amber . . . for your constant support over the challenges of the past few years, and for having faith in me when I didn't! Despite having known each other for a relatively short time, if there is such a thing as true kindred spirits, you are mine.

My huge thanks go to the team at DartFrog publishers. Gordon McClellan, who shared my dream for this book from the start. Suanne Laqueur, who has helped and guided me through this new and often overwhelming process. My very talented (and patient) cover designer, Mark Hobbs. My social media coach, Amanda O'Connor, who has pushed me WAY out of my comfort zone—but if we are never challenged, nothing ever changes. And my amazing editors, Caitlin and Andrew St. John. I'm so grateful to all of you for giving me this chance, for your hard work over the months, for your patience with me, and for your vision for this book.

I would also like to express my thanks and admiration for some of the amazing young people who have been part of my life and family. Over the years you have all given me your own special and unique inspiration for the Children of the Light:

Becky and Jamie, John, Eleanor, Jack, Astraeus, Chloe-Derin, Nathan and Izzy, Imogen, Holly and many more. You are the future, and if I can give you any advice for that future it is to be YOU, always. A light exists in all of you, and in each of you that light is different. Shine your own unique light out into the world with pride and purpose. In the words of Gandhi, "Be the change that you wish to see in the world," and even if your light is too much for some people, never dim it for anyone or anything.

Going back to those dreams we often forget, push down or disregard because we don't think we are or will ever be good enough. I set myself a task while writing these acknowledgements, to attempt to summarise what I've learnt from life so far, and this is what I have come up with:

Have faith in yourself. Change the things you can change, and don't beat your head against those you can't. Instead, learn from them and move on with tenacity, strength and greater awareness. Above all, never give up on your dreams. It might be the hardest thing you ever have to do, but in the words of Harvey Mackay:

"Nobody said that it would be easy . . . They just promised it would be worth it."

ABOUT THE AUTHOR

Tracy Earle grew up in the south of England and spent her younger years lost in imaginary worlds, writing endless stories. She looked to inspirations such as Jo March (*Little Women*), *Anne of Green Gables*, Beatrix Potter and the Brontë sisters.

In later years, Tracy took well-meaning advice to get her head out of the clouds, and swapped creative writing for a 26-year career in the UK police force. During this time, her writing challenges consisted of operation orders and prosecution files. This, along with raising a family, meant the Children of the Light spent many years existing only in Tracy's imagination.

The day came, however, when the Children of the Light and the Gozzits began fighting more fiercely to be freed from Tracy's mind.

Eventually, they won that fight . . . and now they are finally entering this world and yours!

www.ingramcontent.com/pod-product-compliance
Lightning Source LLC
Chambersburg PA
CBHW021800190726
48290CB00005B/1332